TAME THE WILD

LYNN ELDRIDGE

WOLFPACK
PUBLISHING
— EST 2012 —

Tame the Wild

Print Edition

© Copyright 2021 (As Revised) Lynn Eldridge

Wolfpack Publishing

5130 S. Fort Apache Rd. 215-380

Las Vegas, NV 89148

wolfpackpublishing.com

Paperback ISBN 978-1-63977-400-5

TAME THE WILD

To My Family and Friends,
Happiness is a choice.

It is not in the stars to hold our destiny but in ourselves.
—*William Shakespeare*

CHAPTER 1

San Francisco, California
New Year's Eve 1905

"Yes, here's my invitation," Genny said politely, handing it to the concierge of the Palace Hotel.

He can purse his lips 'til the cows came home, she thought smiling slightly. Perhaps he has the idea that his job is guardian of the Palace's patrons. She had realized years ago she had no right to expect better treatment and grudges were a waste of time.

Maintaining the charade of not knowing who she was, the concierge acknowledged her name on Seth Comstock's guest list with a reluctant nod. Eyes darting back and forth he then dismissed her with a flip of his wrist, as one might shoo a fly, in the general direction of three sets of closed double doors.

Before she had to ask which ones, two grinning bell-boys rushed toward her. The redhead, with freckles dotting his cheeks and a nametag that read Patrick, reached her first. Giving him Comstock's name, she made note of the large and lavishly decorated area of plush sofas and chairs, tables and towering palm trees. After taking her white shawl, Patrick slowly opened the double doors revealing a sunken ballroom filled with over a hundred guests.

"Oh no," she said under her breath as the bellboy closed the doors behind her.

Genny stood paralyzed on the marble step of a dance floor where violins and cellos played amidst black tuxedos and expensive gowns.

"SHALL I announce the scavenger hunt before the next number, Mr. Comstock?" the leader of the stringed ensemble asked the host. "It's ten o'clock."

"Indeed. I thought the New Year would arrive before she did." Seth Comstock didn't bother to hide the irritation in his voice. The woman had not had the courtesy to RSVP, leaving him to fret and fuss for nearly a month as to whether or not she would attend his soirée.

"Ladies and gentlemen." The conductor raised both hands, one holding a baton, to address the crowd. "The time has come for what we have all been waiting for. You will begin the next waltz with your current partner. Each time the music stops, you will switch partners with the couple nearest you. When you least expect it, the music will end for the final time, and you will be in the arms of your teammate for the scavenger hunt."

"WHO'S THE LATE ARRIVAL?" Luke asked the brassy blonde in his arms.

"I'm certain I don't know," the woman replied, subtly tightening her grip on him.

BETWEEN THE ANXIETY churning in her stomach and the thrum of excited voices washing over her, Genny could hardly hear herself think. She knew what a scavenger hunt was, but she'd had to consult her dictionary for the definition of soirée. French, it meant an intimate evening gathering with conversation or music. Not a ball. Maybe this was a small party to a rich and ritzy crowd. But what madness had made her assume she could blend in with them? Maybe it's not too late to escape, she thought, a second before someone grabbed her elbow.

"May I have this dance?" asked a rotund, bald fellow.

"Umm...you may," Genny said, only because she had suddenly noticed her host.

Genny had given Seth Comstock the benefit of the doubt having only his photograph in the *San Francisco Chronicle* to go by. Not to be unkind but seeing him in person caused her to pray that he had a warm and winning personality. In the newspaper his hair appeared blond not gray. Tonight, a sallow complexion indicated he might not be entirely healthy, and his tuxedo hung on a skin and bones frame well under six feet. She smiled her best smile toward him. A feeling of dread came over her when the smile he returned didn't reach his complacent, pale brown eyes.

The music began again, and her bald partner clutched her to his sweat-damp tuxedo. Genny tromped his toes but maybe it was due to being crushed against his potbelly and not the fact she didn't know how to dance. Much less waltz.

"Perhaps if you loosen your grip," Genny suggested for an apology.

"No need. You're as light as a feather."

"Luke, let's not switch partners when the music stops," the clinging blonde said.

"That would be cheating, and I don't cheat," Luke replied as he waltzed his way across the dance floor toward a woman so exquisite, she had turned dozens of heads with her fashionably late entrance. From one end of the ballroom to the other, men stared at her as women tried to reclaim the attention of their partners. That would prove difficult because the lady with shining black curls, twirled under a little white hat, had smiled. One smile, so heart stopping it had seized Luke and was holding him captive. No doubt every man present wished she'd smile his way and become his partner. They continued to steal glances at her, many maneuvering closer. As she danced, her snug aquamarine gown hugged a perfectly rounded fanny and swept the floor with a small train. Damn, who was this siren's song?

"WHO ARE all of these people, Seth?"

"For the umpteenth time, Selma, they were on Harriett Peak's social register of people who will attend most any event where someone else is footing the bill," Seth Comstock reminded his twin sister.

WHEN THE MUSIC STOPPED, Genny eased out of her partner's arms only to be instantly snatched up by the next, then the next and the next. Her current partner was swarthy, short and even though he didn't have a potbelly she stomped his feet. She was acutely aware that if her plan was to succeed, she needed some lessons and not just for dancing.

At that moment, the host was out of reach. But even if he weren't, she had no idea how to elegantly maneuver herself into Seth Comstock's arms the next time the music stopped. Maybe if she were closer. With that thought, she took a less than graceful step in his direction.

Tonight's opportune invitation had come as a complete surprise. Since the post office only delivered to rural addresses once a month, she'd had little time to prepare, much less respond. Without Patty's knowledge, she'd frantically fashioned her gown out of the only three matching tablecloths in the house. Though she'd used every scrap of fabric, there wasn't enough for sleeves, and the neckline was much lower than she'd intended on this dress she'd sewn in only two days.

Unexpectedly her partner moved right. But Seth Comstock was at her left. The course of her life depended on meeting him and with extreme good fortune being his teammate for the scavenger hunt.

"Pardon me," her partner said. "But the man is supposed to lead."

"Don't count on me to follow," Genny replied, edging toward Comstock.

With the waltzing shifting people this way and that, Seth Comstock turned to speak to someone, but she couldn't see who. What she could see were her chances of teaming up with him fading as a well-known newspaper reporter wiggled her fingers at the host over the shoulder of her dance partner.

"YOU HAVE that social register because you told Harriett Peak you're somebody you're not," Selma said. "What happens when she figures out you lied to her?"

"She's not clever enough to figure it out. Harriett writes *Peak's People* which is nothing but a gossip column, sister dear," Seth said. "Stop worrying."

"The *San Francisco Chronicle* is quite the reputable newspaper and Harriett is an award-winning journalist."

"Forget about Harriett Peak. But do not use your tired excuse of being five years past half a century old to forget my purpose for all of this."

"Your precious purpose is burned into my memory, brother dear."

FROM THE LUXURIOUS comfort of high-stakes Mississippi riverboats to this unfamiliar Bay area, Luke had never laid eyes on a more magnificent woman than the ebony haired beauty he had decided to make his partner. When she had smiled at the host upon her arrival, Luke had literally felt his jaw drop. From the moment the ethereal creature, who reminded him of a mythical mermaid, floated into the ballroom he had gone on his own kind of hunt.

"Thank you for the dance," Luke said when the music stopped, releasing the buxom redhead who'd been clutching him.

Genny heard the deep voice, turned her head and attached the resonating drawl to a man who rivaled Adonis. In a crisp black tuxedo and starched white shirt, whose thick, chocolate-brown hair was combed straight back, he fell nothing short of a Greek god. She realized she was staring when he grinned at her, a savvy glint in eyes.

Suddenly aware the dancing had ceased, panic struck Genny. She tore her gaze away from the strikingly handsome man and looked back toward Seth Comstock. She pushed out of her partner's arms so fast she had to readjust her hatpin to keep from losing her crocheted hat. She'd worn the small cap to cover any mistakes she might have made in her Gibson girl chignon copied from the *Chronicle*.

"You can't dance, and you don't keep up your end of the conversation but looks like I'm the lucky man who's your partner for the scavenger hunt," the swarthy man said.

"No," Genny said, not only to her partner but to the situation. Surely the music would start again. Please. She was so close.

"You are now teamed up with your partner for the scavenger hunt. At the double doors, the concierge will provide you with the list of items to find," the leader of the quartet said as Seth Comstock did an about-face and worked his way through the crowd toward the stringed ensemble. "The first couple to return to the hotel with the most items, wins. You must be back by midnight when corks pop and champagne flows to celebrate the New—"

Interrupting the conductor, the corners of Comstock's almost lipless mouth turned down as he said something and waved a boney finger. Comstock's long face contorted further when Harriett Peak grabbed his wagging hand at the same moment someone grabbed her own. Genny tried to pull free, but the swarthy man held tight.

"What're the prizes?" the swarthy man called out, running his other hand over his oily hair.

"A mink stole for the lady and a case of bourbon for the gentleman," Seth Comstock blurted out, yanking free of Harriett Peak.

Genny, planning to leave, tugged at her hand, but the swarthy man jerked her closer, his unpleasant breath assailing her. Comstock began snapping his fingers at the conductor to hurry up and do...something. But what? Harriett's face reddened with anger or embarrassment, Genny wasn't sure which. Maybe both. Whatever the case, Harriett Peak was giving Seth Comstock a piece of her mind.

This night was a complete fiasco.

"My apologies, folks, I uh...I meant to say that after the music stops this *next* time you will be with your partner for the scavenger hunt," the conductor announced.

In stunned disbelief, Genny noticed Comstock coming her way as the music began.

"Time to switch partners, ya'll," the gorgeous man drawled.

"No." The swarthy man's grip tightened painfully. "She's my partner."

Genny gave the swarthy man a shove with one hand and pulled free. He stumbled backward as her new partner smoothly swept her into an embrace that was both powerful and gentle. With a chuckle her handsome partner turned, his shoulder brushing a redhead into the outstretched arms of the swarthy man. Comstock slowed his approach, and a frowning Harriett Peak was able to catch him again. Comstock's eyelashes fluttered and then his features faded into a resigned expression as Harriett waltzed him away.

Genny looked up at the man who had so skillfully dealt three couples a new hand.

"Day and night," she whispered, comparing the pasty and spindly Seth Comstock to the dark-haired rogue, whose muscles rippled under his tuxedo, completely overshadowed her intent to team up with the host.

"Am I the day or the night?" he asked.

CHAPTER 2

"I DON'T KNOW," GENNY SAID SOFTLY AND CLAMPED HER LIPS together to keep from telling this stranger that he was so attractive he could command the sun and the moon as he saw fit.

"I've never seen eyes like yours," he said. "What do you call that color?"

"Not violet or blue or purple," she replied. His eyes, the deep green of a flourishing forest, were the color of strength and energy and new life. "But I've read that my eyes are shades of dreams and imagination and new—" She shrugged. "There is no name for the color of my eyes."

"The way they tilt up at the corners," he began, his appraising expression flip flopping her heart, "makes me think of a cat's eyes. You have lilac cat eyes."

Cat eyes she knew, but lilac? Funny, she'd never thought of that because she loved the smell of lilac. Lilac. Yes, she liked it.

"What's your name?" she asked.

"Luke Harper."

"Luke?" she asked, surprise raising her brows. "Really?"

"Yes, why?"

Effortlessly waltzing her toward the ballroom's double doors she wondered if this man, who danced so well that she wasn't tripping, might find the scavenger hunt items before anyone else. Maybe she still had a chance.

"If your name is Luke, then you're the day."

"I'd rather be the night," Luke replied.

"But Lucas or Luke means the bringer of light."

"I didn't know that." Luke smiled.

"My grandfather gave me a book about names for my seventh birthday."

"What's your name?" he asked.

"Genevieve. It's French and means a woman of society, community or tribe." Raising her chin, she said, "I was named after my grandmother. My grandfather told me that Saint Genevieve was a Medieval patroness of France who defended Paris against Attila the Hun with her rational thinking, courage and power."

"Genevieve is a beautiful name," Luke said, enjoying the enchanting lilt in her voice.

"The name doesn't fit me because I'm not French, I'm not a part of San Francisco society and I'll never have ties to anything French." Then with a tilt of her head, she laughed softly and the touching vulnerability in her voice broadened Luke's grin. "But I like Genevieve better than Frances which was my mother's second choice. Did you know that San Francisco was named after Sir Francis Drake?" Luke shook his head. "Once upon a time, San Francisco used to go by the name Yerba Buena Cove."

"So you go by Genevieve even though it doesn't fit you?"

"My grandfather nicknamed me Genny which is also French, so it's spelled with a G. It means, oh nevermind, it's not nearly as important as Genevieve." She added, "Grandpa was my hero."

"Did he bring you into town?"

"He drowned in our fishing pond last month."

"That's too bad. Because he couldn't swim?"

"Because Moby-Dick lives in our pond."

"Which means you're not going to tell me."

Luke thought the name Genny was as sassy as she was. He couldn't believe his eyes when she had shoved her former partner. Though the musical ensemble played on, Luke was ready to escort his current partner out of the ballroom, with or without the list of scavenger hunt items. Holding onto her hand, Luke led Genny through the now open double doors.

"Don't forget your wrap," said the freckle-faced bellboy hurrying toward them.

"Thank you, Patrick." Luke generously tipped the courteous young man who thanked him, and as proper manners dictated, presented the shawl to Luke before backing away. "So, what does the name Patrick mean?"

"Noble, decent, gracious," Genny replied without hesitation.

Luke's fingers brushed petal soft skin as he placed the crocheted wrap around her slender shoulders. Her thin, sleeveless gown with the daring décolletage seemed a chilly choice for a winter's night. Thanking Luke, she closed the wrap across her full breasts hiding her alabaster cleavage. The concierge averted his gaze, but not before Luke caught him staring. Who could blame him? Genny was *the* prize of the night.

"Good luck, Mr. Harper." The concierge handed him a list. "Not that you'll need it, sir."

"Edward," Luke simply said.

Luke offered his arm and enjoyed the feel of Genny holding onto him as he escorted her across the palm tree-filled lobby. Aptly named the Palm Court, comfortable seating, along with mahogany tables placed in groups on thick red carpets, offered guests a virtual oasis to lounge.

"Edward, or the nickname Teddy, means rich and happy protector or guardian," Genny said when they reached the large, white pillars framing the hotel's main entrance on Market Street.

"Do you need a rich and happy protector?" Luke teased,

walking her into the starry night illuminated by a full moon.

Ignoring the question, Genny asked, "How did you come to be at tonight's ball?"

"I received an invitation because I'm staying at the hotel while I try to unload my ranch."

"Why aren't you living at your ranch until you sell it?"

"Most of the furniture was lost to gambling bets," he replied, pausing in front of the hotel. "Do you know a Teddy?"

"Teddy Roosevelt, our cowboy president," she said. "The president was here in the spring of nineteen and three. I read about his visit, and I really wanted to meet him."

"And did you?" he asked, walking her down Market Street.

"No, because of his guards. But I'd planned to ask Mr. Roosevelt if I could sign up to be one of his Rough Riders. Did you know that Rough Riders was a nickname for the first United States Volunteer Cavalry?"

That was not the answer Luke was expecting. Who was this young woman with the unorthodox behavior and impromptu history lessons?

"Yes, I did know that. But the Rough Riders disbanded in eighteen ninety-eight after the Spanish-American conflict resulted in Spain ceding Cuba to the United States. Not to mention that the Rough Riders were men."

"So I was told by one of the president's guards who never knew I was female." Her lilac eyes twinkled with mischief. "He said that even if the Rough Riders were still around, I was too young, too small and too fragile to be one." Her arched brows drew together at that, and as the wind blew in off the Bay, she clutched her shawl more tightly. "Little did he know."

"I can't imagine the Secret Service couldn't see you're female," Luke said. Small boned with a graceful neck and delicate hands, he liked the way her gown clung to her taut and curvy figure. He was six foot three and guessed her to be about five foot five. "Why would you want to be a Rough Rider anyway?"

"Well, umm...I love horses." When he cocked a brow at that flimsy excuse, she quickly added, "Wouldn't it be amusing to reinvent oneself?"

"I find you amusing just the way you are," he replied, curious as to why she wanted to reinvent that which was perfect. "When I first met the president in nineteen and two, he had recently succeeded in convincing the United States to purchase the French assets to the Panamanian Canal Zone for forty million dollars."

They had reached the black, two-seater, doorless, leather-topped 1905 Cadillac Runabout parked under a streetlamp. As Luke helped her into the vehicle, she looked up at him with eyes full of awe.

"You actually met President Roosevelt?"

"Twice," he replied. It was all Luke could do not to pull her to him and kiss the glistening full lips that had parted in surprise. "After Roosevelt's Square Deal platform helped him win the nineteen and four election, I attended his inauguration this past March fourth."

"Are you important? Someone I should know?"

"I'll let you decide."

"Here's what I've decided." She tugged her elbow out of his grasp and held up a finger. "First of all, I think you invented all of that meeting President Roosevelt nonsense to impress me." When she folded her arms under her breasts, her shawl slipped down her shoulders rewarding him with an abundance of cleavage. Holding up two fingers, she said, "Secondly, my mother, Garnet, was run over by an automobile. I'll take the trolley."

"I'm sorry to hear about your mother," Luke said, handing her the scavenger hunt list. "But the trolleys aren't going to win any races, and I promise this won't be a *rough ride*. So just relax and tell me what's on that list."

"Streaks 'n sockdolagers," she huffed, standing on the left side of the vehicle.

"What?"

"That's what my grandpa said whenever he was mad at Garnet, which was most of the time." She grasped her skirts and, revealing red cowboy boots, settled onto the leather tufted seat. As if in warning she said, "A sockdolager is a wild punch."

"Boots? Well, hell." Taking his chances at getting socked, Luke swept back the sides of his jacket, jammed his hands onto his hips and laughed.

"Come on," she said, making a circular motion with her left hand. "Quit your gawking and start your walking."

He'd attended the ball out of boredom, never guessing he'd meet someone like the woman sitting in his automobile. Grinning, Luke rounded the front of the Runabout as she studied the list of items in the light of the streetlamp. He swung himself into the driver's seat, to the right of her, as easily as he did a saddle and rested a hand on the steering wheel.

"What's first, Genny?" he asked.

Her eyes narrowed at his familiarity, but his smile was so charming, she replied, "Seaweed, a knife, a silk stocking and—"

"Hold onto your hat," he said, driving away from the hotel. "You're probably wearing the stockings and I have the knife. Let's go get the seaweed."

"Blast that devil. Who is he?" Seth Comstock seethed, watching the Runabout vanish into the night. "You bungled your part by failing to distract Harriett Peak. This is all your fault, Selma."

"You're the one who told me to forget about Harriett," Selma said. "Genevieve was the belle of your ball. After seeing her in person, surely you realize you're in way over your head."

CHAPTER 3

"The water looks as dangerous as—" Genny began as Luke stopped near a pier.

"As what?" Luke asked.

"You."

A streetlamp revealed the intimidatingly built man sitting beside her. When he cocked a rakish brow, she tugged her boots off her stockingless feet and slid out of the Runabout. The ocean's salty-sea scent and the sound of lapping waves on this moonlit night could be romantic to some, but she would never make the mistakes Garnet had.

With every second ticking closer to midnight, she pulled up her skirt and pranced through the cool, damp sand toward the water. She'd prayed to find some seaweed washed up on the beach but no such luck. Moonlight hinted it was floating several feet out. Before she could talk herself out of it, she waded in ankle deep and holding her dress out of the cold water with one hand, she grabbed at some. The receding tide pulled it further away forcing her to venture out to her knees. The elusive seaweed, like so much that truly mattered in life, remained out of her reach. Desperate, she tried again, and her third miss was followed by a freezing wave slapping her hips.

"Now there's a sight I've never seen before," Luke called,

standing on the shore. "A woman in a hat, dress and shawl up to her cute little *fanny* in sharks." Genny screamed and splashed back toward the shore. "There goes her shawl," he said as it slid off her shoulders and into the water. "And her hat."

"No!" Genny shouted, as her hair tumbled down in front of her eyes.

Something suddenly pulled her right foot from underneath her and she hopped blindly out of the water. A split second before she expected to fall face down in the sand, sinewy strong arms swept her up against a rock-hard chest. She wound an arm around his neck and shoved her hair out of her face. Those treacherous waters could have meant death to her, and she shivered until she realized how safe she felt in the arms of this stranger.

"Got all your toes?" he asked.

"Something has them."

"Seaweed."

"You're the shark for scaring me."

"You're a mermaid who can't swim."

She kicked her foot, sending the precious seaweed flying back into the Bay.

"Put me down," she cried, wondering if her trembling fear had given away the fact she couldn't swim. Grandpa hadn't known, so neither did she. She started after the seaweed but was stopped short.

"Oh no, you don't. Once was risky enough."

Genny whirled to find his foot on the small train of her gown and gave her dress a tug. When cold air chilled her body, she realized she'd ripped out most of the hastily sewn stitches on the right side of her gown. Luke's expression was one of stunned amusement as he took in a generous side view of her body barely concealed by thin underpants plastered to her gooseflesh skin.

"I lost my shawl, my hat and my seaweed because of you. And now you've ruined my dress and cost me the chance to win the scavenger hunt." Molding her right arm to her side, she held the torn gown together as best she could. "I've had it with you, Harper, you…you…city slicker."

"You haven't had me at all, Genevieve, you little mischief maker," he said with a wicked grin. "But I am thoroughly enjoying your unexpected *side show*." He smothered a laugh.

"I thought you were a gentleman, but you're a wolf in sheep's clothing."

"And you're a sea nymph in cowboy boots."

Without warning, he grabbed her wrist and yanked her behind him.

"Need some help?" a man bellowed, ambling toward them from the street.

"Yeah, wanna share her?" the man with him hollered.

This wasn't at all how Genny had pictured the night turning out. She had imagined impressing Seth Comstock, though he hadn't her, and…and…well she hadn't figured out the next part, yet.

"Get outa here." Luke's voice was gruff as the men neared them.

"Nah, it's two against one," the second man said.

"Two against two," Genny said, moving to Luke's side.

The first man lurched to a stop and reached for Genny. Lightning fast, Luke slammed his fist into the intruder's face. The man's nose crunched, and blood spurted before he hit the ground unconscious. Baring grimy teeth, the second man threw a punch which Luke blocked then rammed his fist against the man's jaw. The man landed in a sorry heap on his backside. As Luke clicked open a menacing knife the man spit blood and teeth and held up his hands in surrender.

"I need to learn how to throw a sockdolager like that," Genny whispered.

"And how to waltz." Luke rubbed his fist as he headed for his automobile.

Darting a glance from the winner of the fight to the losers on the ground, Genny stood rooted to the spot.

"Quit your gawking and start your walking, sea nymph," he called over his shoulder.

"You've called me that twice as well as mermaid," Genny said. "You know my last name, don't you?"

"What is it?" Luke asked and without a backward glance motioned with his knife for her to come on.

Genny swiveled away from the defeated opponents and hurried to catch up. This wild man had turned the tables on her. She'd considered herself the one in charge, but now she was running after him. Reaching his vehicle, he took off his jacket and pocketed the knife before sliding onto the right-hand side of the bench seat. He held out his left hand to her but needing to keep her ripped dressed closed, Genny stepped onto the running board unassisted and landed with a plop beside him.

"I suggest you put this on," Luke said, offering her his jacket.

"Maybe you aren't a wolf in sheep's clothing after all."

"A wolf would have already had you and a sheep couldn't have stopped those men from sharing a little lamb."

A slashing brown brow cocked as a muscle worked in his square jaw. True. She would have been in big trouble without Luke. When he started the engine, she put on the coat which was warm from his body heat and smelled good, like him.

"I'm not a woman to be shared," she said as her thank you.

"Tell me where you live, and I'll take you home."

"Just take me back to the hotel. I walked there and I'll walk home."

Sitting next to Luke, Genny was both aware of and confused by the magnetism that drew her to chase after him instead of running from him. They rode in silence and reaching Market Street, Luke stopped under a three-lamp streetlight, half a block away from the Palace Hotel.

She figured he was relieved there was no closer place to park. Leaving the ball with her was one thing and not his fault. But the concierge had made that sly comment when they'd left, and Luke Harper wouldn't want to be seen returning with her. What else was new? She reached toward her cowboy boots, but he got to them first and held them away from her on the opposite side of the automobile. Now what? Stretching his other arm across the back of the leather seat he slid his hand under her hair and touched the nape of her neck. Tingles raced up and down her spine,

"*Home* is out in the country because if you lived in town, you wouldn't have worn cowboy boots tonight," Luke said.

Genny opened her mouth to protest, but he was so dead on accurate she pressed her lips together and folded her arms under her breasts. His gaze dipped to her cleavage and a grin formed on his lips as his eyes met hers.

"I won't slap you for staring, since you were my hero on the beach."

"What if I'm a bad guy and not your hero?"

CHAPTER 4

"Doesn't matter because I'll never see you again," Genny said. "Now please hand over my boots."

Luke's eyes smoldered as he slid his hand into the jacket and cupped her left shoulder. He pulled her closer, dropped her boots to the street and touched his other hand to her cheek. Genny's heart pounded at the thought of this man's mouth touching hers.

"I don't kiss on a first date," she said.

His grin was wicked. "Neither do I."

Luke shut his eyes, lowered his head and tasted her lips. Yeah, they were as dewy soft as they looked. He'd wanted to kiss her since she'd entered the ballroom and caused his blood to stir. She didn't resist, nor did she respond. He leaned back to find her lilac eyes wide open in what? Astonishment? Placing his fingers to her eyelids, he felt them close. He kissed her again and when her lips slowly began imitating his every move the thought of never turning this woman loose crossed his mind. Hell no. He was going home soon.

"How old are you, Genny?" he whispered after gently breaking off their kiss.

"I'll be twenty-one—" she whispered back, eyes still closed. With her next breath, she pulled away, opened her eyes and blurted out, "Streaks. That's none of your business. How old are you?"

"Twenty-nine," he said with a chuckle. "Now, don't sock me for asking again but where do you live?"

"On the dark side of moon, so I'll be moseying along if you'll give me my boots."

"You probably do live on the moon because you're a lunatic."

Luke swung out of the Runabout, grabbed her boots and handed them to her. She pulled them on as he walked around to her side of the automobile. As Genny swiveled in the seat, her skirt slipped between her legs, baring most of the right one. Quickly, she tossed her skirt into place. Shaking his head and grinning, Luke touched his hands to her waist. Where her bodice was ripped, his palm and fingers molded to bare flesh. Looking into her eyes it took every ounce of willpower he possessed not to move his hand higher. When she elbowed his arm, he gave himself a mental shake and lifted her out of the vehicle.

"It's cold out here, let's go," he said.

"I'm going." She took off his jacket and handed it to him. "Goodbye, city slicker."

"I didn't mean by yourself, in your semi-naked state, mischief maker."

A confused expression flashed in her eyes and vanished just as quickly. "I'll survive. I always do," Genny said and brushed past him. "Just you watch."

Watch he did as he sauntered along behind her. Arm plastered to her side and clutching her skirt she walked up Market Street. He liked the way her wavy black hair bounced across her slender back, almost to her waist, which drew his gaze to the saucy sway of her hips.

When three men emerged from the darkness of Annie Street, between the Palace Hotel and a nearly completed structure Luke had heard referred to as the Monadnock Building, he wondered if there'd be more trouble.

The cat calls started immediately. No surprise there.

Genny was sensational with or without a ripped gown putting her legs on display. The men were staging a line across the sidewalk to block her path.

"Hurry up, wolf," Genny called, turning and motioning to Luke. "And cock that loaded gun we found at the pier."

This would be the last damn time he didn't have his own loaded gun with him, Luke thought. But he'd not anticipated needing it at a gala held in a ballroom of the Palace Hotel.

The would-be troublemakers instantly broke their line and crossed to the other side of Market Street. Walking toward her Luke smiled, thinking that maybe she didn't want him in another fight because of her. How many women would have been brave enough to stand beside him at the beach? None he'd ever met.

"Good job, little lamb," Luke said, reaching her. "You called their bluff."

Other participants in the scavenger hunt were returning to the hotel in horse drawn buggies and automobiles. One excited couple called out to everyone that they had found all ten items and hoped to claim the prizes.

"I got you back safe and sound." Genny stopped short of entering the hotel but kept her eyes on the pillared entrance.

"You got me back?" he asked and laughed. "Who are you looking for?"

"The host, but I'm sure Seth Comstock thinks I'm spending the night with you. So that's that for now."

"So spend the night with me, Genny."

"Which means a half hour mattress dance," she said nonchalantly, avoiding eye contact.

Impressed by this one-of-a-kind wildflower he had plucked out of a patch of ordinary blooms, Luke wasn't ready to let her go. "I want more than half an hour with you," he admitted.

"That will never happen."

"Whatever happens, I ruined your dress. I feel responsible for you tonight."

"You go in ahead of me and back to the ball. I'll wait overnight in the big room where people who can't afford the Palace stay."

"The Palm Court lobby? What? No," he said as she nodded. Not about to leave her as prey for more predators, Luke gently took hold of her chin making her meet his eyes. "You're coming with me. I'll get you a room."

When a blustery wind blew in off the Bay, they both shivered and Genny's torn skirt fluttered away from her legs. Without another word, Luke helped her into his tuxedo jacket and buttoned it. Satisfied, she wasn't showing any of the skin he'd seen and touched, he slipped her arm through his. As he did so, they both noticed the three men who'd blocked the sidewalk, loitering directly across the street.

"The Palace is truly that," Genny said, as they entered the hotel. Craning her neck back she seemed to notice, for the first time, the spectacular view of the six stories of white columned balconies above the Palm Court. Candelabra-like electric lamps mounted on the decorative railings illuminated the floors with a welcoming glow. "What's way up there on the seventh floor under the domed skylighted ceiling?"

"I don't know, but we can find out."

Just inside the expansive lobby, the concierge greeted Luke with the same expression of lust he'd had when Luke left with Genny. More than one bellboy nodded enviously as he and Genny made their way further into the hotel unaccosted by anyone including the host.

Genny glanced toward the parlor where couples from the ball were gathering for midnight champagne and prizes. Luke's gut tightened as he wondered why she was looking for Comstock. He had a bad feeling about the odd duck whose behavior toward the conductor and a dance partner had been obnoxious.

"I'm sorry if I cost you a case of bourbon," Genny said softly, looking up at him.

"I couldn't care less. Sorry if I cost you a mink stole."

"I couldn't have brought myself to wear it."

"Let's get your room and go see the seventh floor."

Leaving the parlor they were told there were no rooms available. New Year's Eve had booked the hotel to over-flowing. When Genny glanced over her shoulder again at the lobby, Luke took her hand and led the way to a floor-to-ceiling marble wall. He pushed the round button in the center of a shiny brass plate next to an elaborate, black wrought iron gate.

"So if the mink doesn't interest you, is it Comstock?" Luke asked. "Are you friends?"

"I've never met him," she said, answering part of his question and changed the subject. "San Francisco is farther north and gets colder than visitors realize. Although you have a ranch, you're not from around here like I am, are you?"

"Nope."

"Where are you from, Luke?"

"Where do you live, Genny?"

"Nope," she said. "I think you have a southern drawl." She tilted her head. "Right?"

"I think you should take a leap of faith," Luke replied.

"Oh, no," Genny said, shaking her head. "I'm not getting in that…what do they call it, a lifting room?"

He chuckled. "Rising room."

"I don't know why such a dangerous thing is allowed in this hotel."

"Cocktail Boothby told me earlier today that William Ralston, the banker and entrepreneur who built this five-million-dollar hotel, insisted on having four of these hydraulic elevators installed for the convenience of guests," Luke told her as the rising room came to a stop. "There are electric call buttons and private bathrooms in all seven hundred and fifty-five rooms."

"With running water?" Her eyes widened as he nodded. "Who is Cocktail Boothby?"

"William Boothby, a hotel bartender who's famous for the cocktails he invents." Luke opened the gate-like door. "This is the fastest and easiest way up to the seventh floor. But always take the stairs in case of fire."

"I'll pretend there's a fire and take the stair—" Genny suddenly stepped into the rising room and whispered, "This better not be a rough ride."

Luke stood his ground because Comstock had come into view. Noticing Luke as well, the man halted in the distance and stared. Certain that Comstock couldn't see into the redwood paneled rising room Luke had the distinct impression the host of the ball was trying his damndest to figure out if Genny was with him. Standing alone outside the hydraulic lift, Luke scowled at Comstock, thinking a scarecrow made of straw had more of an expression than this one of skin and bones.

What Comstock did have was a tell. At a poker table the fluttering eyelids would be a dead giveaway of the cards he held, probably bad.

A pretty hand reached out from the rising room and grasped the front of Luke's white shirt. With a smug grin at Comstock, Luke let himself be pulled into the elevator.

"I SWEAR HE HAS HER," Seth said in a monotone and chewed his thumbnail.

"I only saw him," Selma replied.

"That figures. Every woman at my soirée was swooning over him."

"Did you find out his name?"

"Yes, yes. Of course, I did, you idiot."

"You're so hateful." Selma sighed and walked away.

. . .

LUKE OPENED the wrought iron gate and they stepped onto the nearly empty seventh floor called the Conservatory Room. The name was a bit misleading as it consisted of wide open, spacious, carpeted corridors protectively surrounded by the decorative white railing. From this towering height, one could circle and view the lower six balconies and Palm Court from all four sides.

When Genny turned and smiled at Luke, his heart skipped a beat. He wondered if she had any idea how many men at the ball had had their eye on her, or how lucky it made him feel to be the man to leave with her.

Trailing her fingertips along the railing, Genny walked slowly past lush tropical plants as she studied the artfully arranged statuary. Luke, too, enjoyed the view thinking that none of the elegant feminine figures, painstakingly chiseled out of stone, could match Genny's natural flawless beauty.

As they came almost full circle back to the rising room, the candelabra-like lamps flickered and dimmed. Genny's seductive mystery intensified when she disappeared around a corner and into the shadows. Luke caught up with her and Genny turned to him just as the Conservatory Room went completely black.

Brilliant fireworks burst high in the midnight sky. Somewhere a clock chimed twelve as every color of the rainbow sparkled above and twinkled down through the domed ceiling of glass.

"Magical," Genny whispered. "With a bird's eye view thanks to you."

"The seventh floor was your idea," Luke replied. "Happy New Year."

Under the rocketing explosions and a shimmering moon, Luke took her into his arms and lowering his head he gently touched his mouth to hers. When his lips parted, so did hers as she shyly kissed him back. Tame as this kiss was, Luke found it more exciting than any other New Year's Eve kiss he'd had. Ever. But then he'd never met a woman as wildly thrilling as this one. He wanted her like he'd wanted no other woman.

The hydraulic elevator suddenly brought a group of people to the Conservatory Room, breaking into the magic. As they spilled onto the floor in awe of the fireworks, Luke took Genny's hand.

"Let's go to my room," he whispered in her ear.

CHAPTER 5

GENNY TREMBLED AS SHE STEPPED INSIDE LUKE'S ROOM decorated with flocked wallpaper and thick carpets. Her lips were still red hot from Luke's New Year's Eve kiss. Wrapped in his arms with his warm mouth on hers had heated her entire body from head to toe. So, if she wasn't cold, why was she shivering? Why had she let this stranger kiss her? Most importantly, what was he expecting from her in this bedroom?

In Palace Hotel style, his room was large and plush boasting several overstuffed chairs, a Victorian sofa, a round marble-topped table, and a night table between twin beds. Luke quietly closed the door and clicked a lock into place.

"Don't get any ideas," Genny blurted out nervously, with a nod toward the beds.

"I have an idea you're going to get yourself into trouble with Comstock," Luke replied, walking toward the marble table where a silver bucket of ice set chilling a bottle of champagne. "If you don't know him, how did you get invited to his party?"

"I'm not really sure how I came to be invited," she admitted, holding her skirt in place as she followed him. "But I need to meet him."

"Why?" Luke asked, as they faced each other.

"Because Harriett Peak, who writes a who's who column for the *San Francisco Chronicle*, says he's the newest, most eligible bachelor in town."

"What?" Luke's green eyes widened and then narrowed. "He's old enough to be your father. Hell, he's old enough to be mine."

"But since he's new here he doesn't know things."

"What things?"

Would she ever learn to be quiet? When she shrugged and said no more, Luke picked up the bottle of champagne, popped the cork and after partially filling two slender champagne glasses, held one out to her.

"I don't drink," she said, surprising herself when she took the glass. She'd also told him she didn't kiss on the first date. Although she'd never been on a date, she certainly hadn't anticipated kissing any man twice in an automobile and again at midnight. What spell was this man casting over her?

"Try your first glass with me and we'll toast your first kiss," Luke said knowingly as he held his glass toward hers.

"How did you know that was my first kiss?" she asked, bringing her glass almost to his. "Am I a bad kisser?"

"You have potential," he replied with a grin and clinked his glass to hers. "Here's to lessons in dancing, fighting, kissing, and drinking."

"Lessons. Yes, lessons." Waving her arms wide, Genny sloshed some champagne onto the floor. Glad that she hadn't spilled any on his tuxedo she put her glass on the table, took off his jacket and handed it to him. "I can't learn everything from books. I need actual lessons. Especially in the art of seduction."

"Well, hell yeah." Handing Genny her glass, Luke drank his champagne in a single swallow and said, "It's customary to drink after saying what you're drinking to and clinking the glasses."

"Oh, of course." She tossed back her champagne exactly

as he had done. But it caused her to cough until her face turned red, partly from humiliation.

Smothering a grin, Luke gently patted her back. "Are you all right?" he asked, taking her glass and placing it on the table with his.

Nodding yes, she choked out, "I'll pay you for the lessons."

"I'll seduce you for free," he said, unbuttoning his shirt.

"I want you to teach me how to seduce you."

"You already have," he replied, tugging his shirt out of his tuxedo trousers.

"Then you'll have to work on resisting me," she said earnestly.

"Oh, I could resist you," he assured her with a sexy wink. "But I don't want to."

"Not even if we work out a square deal for both of us, like President Roosevelt's?"

Refilling their glasses, he handed Genny hers and said, "Sip it this time."

She took a sip, followed by a small cough. "Can we please toast to making a square deal?"

"Not yet." He took a swallow of champagne. "I agree with the president's belief in an equal opportunity for everyone on equal terms. But tell me how Roosevelt's—"

"I need an equal opportunity."

"To do what?" he asked, but her answer was lifting her left shoulder. "Tell me how Roosevelt's Square Deal relates to me resisting you."

"Because of the fact that you *could*." Warming up to her topic, she explained, "Only if you resist me, can I practice the art of seduction until I get it right." When his brow furrowed, she hurried on before losing her nerve, "You know how to drive a newfangled automobile, and something tells me you know how to swim. I'll bet you've even been to a real live opera, haven't you?" When he nodded, she clasped her glass of champagne to her heart so fast, it splashed the bodice of her dress. Better her gown than his tuxedo. "I've always wanted to go to the opera. But they're only for society folks, the who's whos."

"Says who?" He threw back his champagne and set his glass on the table.

"Me."

"Let's see if I've got this right." He pulled his shirt back and put his hands to his hips. Genny stared at his bare chest and forgot how to breathe. Moving her gaze down his flat stomach made her dizzy. Maybe it was just the champagne. "I'm supposed to teach you to seduce me and all I have to do is resist you and then you're going to pay me."

Taking a deep breath and trying to blink away the dizziness she said, "Exactly." Forcing her gaze up his masculine body to his eyes, she asked, "Will you give me the lessons?"

"I'm not staying in San Francisco much longer. But if I were, what's the catch?"

"There is no catch."

"The hell there isn't, and I think I know what it is." He folded his arms across his broad chest. "But I want to hear it from you. Why do you need all of these lessons, Genny?"

Raising her chin and squaring her shoulders, she looked him in the eye. "To give me an equal opportunity, like the society ladies, to seduce Seth Comstock."

"Then you'd better learn how to fight."

"With you?"

"Comstock," Luke grumbled. "Because he's a bad guy."

Genny started to protest, but Luke held up his hand. He shrugged out of his white shirt and handed it to her. Realizing her nipples were clearly beaded against her damp dress she wondered if giving her the shirt was Luke's proof that he could resist her. But would he teach her?

Frowning, Luke swung a hand toward the private bath. Placing her champagne glass on the table, Genny had to steady it with both hands. When Luke tilted his head, she twirled away from him toward the lavatory. Ooh, that was too fast of a move, and she really had to concentrate on walking straight. Those beds behind her with their plump pillows and fancy spreads were beckoning her to come back and slip under the covers. At least for an hour or two.

Lessons or no lessons, she had gotten herself into one fine mess tonight. So far, Comstock couldn't possibly know where she was. She'd keep it that way by not leaving Luke Harper's room just yet. Not to mention that the run-ins with the men at the beach as well as those three in front of the hotel had convinced her that she might not make it home at night in one piece.

Bumping against the door of the bathroom she glanced over her shoulder to see if Luke had noticed. Staring out a huge bay window, he rubbed his temple as if in deep thought, or maybe she'd given him a headache. Shutting herself in the room with a wash basin, a claw foot tub along with a water flush bowl and seat, she took a moment to appreciate the modern luxuries.

Then perching on the side of the tub, she scolded herself. She'd been plain old lucky to make it from the country to the city unscathed. She berated herself for not allowing Vern to bring her and pick her up instead of sneaking away from her ranch after dark. How foolish she'd been to hope that such an eligible bachelor as Seth Comstock would not only seek her out but offer to get her a room as Luke had done.

Luke Harper. Adonis. Where in the South had he come from? Was he going back there when he left San Francisco? What did she care? He didn't fit into her plan unless he gave her those lessons. He was the perfect man to do so for the reasons she'd cited and because he'd soon be gone, leaving her to pursue Comstock unencumbered. The perfect man? Luke?

I'm not staying in San Francisco much longer. A sharp pang unexpectedly hit Genny.

Giving herself a mental shake, she changed out of her dress and into Luke's shirt. How nice it would be if she could change all that was wrong with her as easily. His shirt was way too big for her and Luke, himself, was way too much man for her. Too much man for her that is, if she were hoping to catch him. Not a problem since she only planned to learn from him. Comstock was the man she had to catch.

But it was to Luke her thoughts kept returning. He was sophisticated and savvy like a who's who. Luke was as powerful and potentially deadly as the wolf she'd accused him of being. Through the door she heard him rustling bedcovers. Did that mean he planned to start the lessons with seduction? Wouldn't that lesson come later? Much later? After a drinking lesson?

"Are you sleeping in the bathtub, Genny?"

"I might," she snapped, startled out of her revery of questions and confusion.

"I'm coming in there in two shakes of *lamb's* tail."

Genny whipped open the door and ran smack-dab into him. He caught hold of her upper arms before she landed on her backside in the middle of the bathroom.

"Don't look at me," she cried. "I'm in a semi-naked state."

"Hell, you've been semi-naked since we were at the beach."

The skin along her ribcage, which no one had ever touched except for Luke, suddenly felt on fire again. Towering over her, masculinity exuded from this muscular rogue making her acutely aware of her femininity in a way she had never experienced.

"Let go of me and close your eyes until I'm in bed, Harper."

"Sure I will, Genevieve," he said and released her.

Both beds had the bedcovers folded down causing her another unfamiliar and undeniable pang at the image of crawling into bed alone instead of with Luke. No. She had absolutely no intention of sleeping with Luke Harper and with that thought she hurried away from him.

"There's another sight for sore eyes," Luke said from somewhere behind her. "A scared lamb wearing only my shirt and her cowboy boots."

"I'm wearing my panties, too." Genny skidded across the wet spot where she'd spilled her champagne, spiraled her arms for balance and kicked off her boots. "I told you not to look." Doing a hop and a skip, she jumped into the closer bed and yanked the covers over her head. When Luke's hearty laughter filled the room she said, "Another lesson I need; not blurting out so much information."

"You didn't need to blurt it out. I saw your panties."

"You did not."

"They're the same color as your dress."

From under the covers, she heard him close the bathroom door. Genny suspected there was no amount of lessons that could fix her. She closed her eyes and sighed. But when his footsteps sounded a moment later, she knew she had to face him. She was an adult, not a child. Once he was in his bed, she pulled the covers down to her shoulders.

Luke was staring at the ceiling, hands stacked under his head. Shirtless, he'd dropped his trousers across the end of his bed. The sheet was pulled low across his stomach. Genny swallowed hard. He was only four feet away. Perusing all of him she could see, her pulse raced, and her breathing grew shallow.

His skin had a sun bronzed tone to it. The South was warm. Maybe he liked to work or relax without a shirt. She pictured running her fingers over the muscles in his broad chest and down his washboard stomach. What would it feel like to trace the dark hair lightly swirling his indented navel and narrowed to a thin line before vanishing under the sheet?

"I'm not giving you lessons to help you seduce Comstock," he said quietly.

"Yes." She bolted upright in her bed. "The lessons were *your* idea." Folding her hands as if in prayer under her chin, she said, "Please, I need him to look at me the way —like—"

"Like I do?" Luke asked, turning his head, eyes locking onto hers.

"Yes, because he didn't." She smiled her very best smile.

"Don't smile at me like that." Luke rolled to his side, facing away from her. Muscles rippled across his shoulders and down his back to his tapered waist. "But I'll give you a ride home whenever you decide to tell me where you live."

SEAGULLS SCREECHED and Luke awoke to sunlight streaming in through the bay window. Last night, in the bed next to his had been a woman so captivating that when he'd finally drifted off to sleep, he had dreamed of her. Her lilac cat eyes mesmerized, and he'd be forever haunted. In his dream, she closed those eyes when he kissed her and kissed him back. Her ivory cleavage was as sexy as her skin was soft, and he wanted to touch more of her. But there would be no next time if she was gone. Just get it over with and look.

"Dammit," he muttered and sat up on the side of his bed.

Across her empty bed she'd left her torn gown and a note. Rubbing his eyes, he picked up the note and read that he could hold her gown hostage for borrowing his shirt and tuxedo. She would wash his shirt, iron the suit and bring it back to the hotel as soon as she could. But would she, he wondered.

To hell with it. He wasn't going to wait around; he was heading home. He would contact his lawyer, put the ranch up for sale and buy a train ticket today. He stood, went to the wardrobe and pulled out a shirt and pants.

The image of Genny seducing Comstock turned Luke's stomach. Maybe he just needed a good breakfast. He'd go downstairs and order one in the American Dining Room. In the hotel office he'd ask for a list of the guests at the ball.

If he could find out her last name, he might be able to figure out where she lived. Why did he care? Well, he had to retrieve that tuxedo because it was rented.

Luke shaved and as he dressed, he remembered Edward, the concierge, making a remark about not needing luck on the scavenger hunt. Maybe Edward knew *things* about Genny. Luke headed downstairs and nearing the office ran into a bellboy.

"Morning, Patrick," Luke called to the freckle-faced young man. "Do you know where I can find Edward?"

"No, sir," Patrick replied. "Edward is no longer with the Palace Hotel."

"Why not?" Luke asked and was told that Edward had been relieved of his duties after one too many impolite interactions with and inappropriate remarks to the guests. "Do you remember the woman I was with last night?"

"Yes, sir, Mr. Harper," the young man said, instantly brightening and nodding. "I will always remember her. She's so beautiful."

"Would you happen to know her last name?" Luke asked.

"No, but we could look at the guest list. It was handed to me when that brawl broke out because of the scavenger hunt, about half past midnight."

"What brawl?" Luke asked.

Patrick explained that there was no mink coat or case of bourbon to be won by the couple who had returned with all the scavenger hunt items. The couple was furious and the manager on duty consoled them with a free night's stay during the following week. Patrick along with another bellboy had forcefully escorted a belligerent Comstock off the hotel's premises.

"That's the last any of us, and Miss Peak who was here to write about the ball for the *San Francisco Chronicle,* saw of him, Mr. Harper," Patrick said.

Luke knew there was something off about Seth Comstock. Patrick retrieved the list and Luke perused the guests. Three names were possibilities: Gen, which could stand for general, the second one was simply the letter G and lastly there was a Jenny. In alphabetical order, the first one's surname was Jones, the second one was Morgan, and the third possibility was Waters. When he'd called Genny a sea nymph and a mermaid, she had accused him of knowing her last name.

"Where's the *San Francisco Chronicle* building, Patrick?" Luke asked.

"Just down the street, corner of Third and Kearny. But it's likely closed since it's New Year's Day."

Luke thought a moment. "Where's the nearest library?"

"Larkin Street. But it won't be open today, either."

"Well, hell, the train station's probably closed, too."

CHAPTER 6

"IT'S BEEN THREE WEEKS SINCE I SAW HIM FIGHT AT THE beach. I know I already told you about it, but I can't forget the way he threw a sockdolager," Genny said, sitting on a patch of winter ryegrass. "I can still hear him telling those men to leave and when they didn't, he knocked one unconscious and left the other one spitting teeth. When I was with him I felt...safe."

Late afternoon sunlight streamed through the evergreens and the branches of maple, elm and oak trees. Clusters of flowers on the acacia trees were blooming bright yellow as they always did in midwinter. Before long, the bushes she and Grandpa had planted would bud with lavender flowers and scent the air with sweet lilac. Just south of the two-bedroom farmhouse, set back from the road and hidden by foliage, was the pond. Pretty good size, there were fish in it along with a bullfrog named Moby-Dick.

"A year ago, you made me promise to escape the ranch and be the person I wanted to be." What she hadn't wanted was to leave her grandfather who said he was too old and slow to go with her. Then things had changed so suddenly and drastically Genny barely recalled thoughts of moving away, writing, fashion, and most of all having a family someday. "I fear my destiny is to stay a nobody fish in a disgraceful pond. But I haven't forgotten my promise to learn to swim." From where she sat, she couldn't see the pond but nodded in that direction. "I miss you, Grandpa. I'll be back later. But right now, I have to go to the ranch to help Patty and Vern serve Sunday supper."

Genny brought two fingers to her lips then touched them to the wooden cross bearing the name Samuel Morgan 1835-1905. She grasped the cowboy hat hanging on a cord around her neck and pulled it low on her head.

Near the dirt road she heard an automobile in the distance. Her mother had been killed in the blind curve of this road just north of the little farmhouse. These days more and more people came to the ranch in automobiles instead of horses and buggies. Grandpa had warned Garnet that bend was dangerous because of all the newfangled contraptions. Garnet hadn't listened. But Genny had and always crossed further down on a straight stretch of road near the pond.

Since almost everyone turned into the ranch, located at the worst part of that treacherous curve, Genny didn't pay much attention as she moseyed across the road. But the approaching automobile hadn't slowed nor made the turn into the opening of the split rail fence around her ranch. In fact, it was kicking up dust, spewing rocks into the air and barreling straight for her.

"I APPRECIATE you taking such good care of this place," Luke said to Ying Wu as they stood beside the Runabout in the front yard of the large, two-story log home. On the porch were a couple of sturdy rockers and lanterns. The interior had three lamps, an overstuffed chair with a matching ottoman, and a kitchen table. A roll top desk was the only furniture left in what probably had been a first-floor office. Luke had briefly met the young man named, Ying, at the ranch the day before he'd met Genny.

"Mr. Cavender said he'd be gone for a month when he hired me two months ago," Ying said. Ying's parents and grandparents had been born in San Francisco, but a couple of years prior had succumbed to the Black Death, known as the Bubonic plague. Unlike many Chinese men, Ying didn't wear the traditional long braid known as a queue or the round black Mandarin hat, which was a staple in Chinatown. He considered himself Chinese American, wore a cowboy hat and spoke fluent English. "I've been here every day because I couldn't let ten American Quarter horses and a Border collie starve. Some nights I slept on a cot in the barn, and other nights I'd walk back to town."

Luke had won the ten-thousand-acre horse ranch in a high stakes poker game aboard his Mississippi riverboat. After Cavender had lost all his money to Luke, he had begged for one last chance to win some of it back. Against Luke's advice, the man put up the deed to his ranch. And lost it.

"I drove out here today to tell you that I've put the ranch up for sale with the attorney I hired named Joe Sanchez," Luke said. When Ying's face fell, he added, "Ying, you've done a fine job tending the horses, and they deserve a stable that doesn't leak." Ying nodded. "So, I've decided to invest some money into the property." He'd also decided he couldn't leave San Francisco without finding Genny. He'd been brooding over her Square Deal proposal and at the very least wanted to know that she'd made it home safely. "Besides the roof on the stable, a bunch of fence posts either need repaired or replaced."

"I would be happy to help you with all of that," Ying said eagerly.

"Good. I moved out of the hotel this morning. We can keep each other company while we work on the ranch. When I leave, I'll pay you to stay on until it sells, if you're interested."

"Yes, sir, I'd live on this ranch forever if I could," Ying said. "I'll stay on as long as you need me, Mr. Harper."

"Just call me Luke."

A few weeks ago, Luke hadn't wanted to leave *Femme Fatale*, the largest of his riverboats and his home away from home. He'd known it would be an exhausting train trip from the sunny, warm climate of Biloxi, Mississippi to a questionable ranch just outside of foggy and much colder-than-he-liked, San Francisco. He'd boarded Southern Pacific's *Sunset Limited* train in New Orleans and traveled to Los Angeles where he'd transferred to the *Coast Line* train which had brought him north to San Francisco. Maybe he was dragging his feet on leaving town because he just dreaded that long trip back.

"Luke, what do you do in Biloxi?" Ying asked as he petted the tricolor collie's head on the white fur between a brown ear and a black one.

"Among other things, I manage three riverboats that cruise the Mississippi Sound."

What Luke didn't say was that he owned the three huge, steam powered paddleboats. Nor did he add that his custom built French provencial mansion, on the beachfront of the Mississippi Sound, was as big as his riverboats. His older sister, Mattie, liked to tease him by hinting that the interior of his brand-new house needed a woman's touch. Though exhilarating, neither his Rolls Royce Silver Ghost nor the black and green Cadillac Runabout parked in the circular drive of his estate would ever replace the thrill of riding the family's American Quarter horses along the Gulf Coast beach where he'd grown up.

The Harper family represented old Mississippi money started with a sugarcane plantation back in 1800. Blue bloods for generations, the Harpers not only owned the most popular seafood restaurants in Biloxi, they owned the shrimp, oyster and fishing boats that supplied them. The best of the best hotels was the majestic Harper House Resort, by far the most palatial lodging to be had in all of Mississippi. Located on the top floor of the hotel was the

Harpers' business headquarters, where Luke, older brother, Robert, and support staff had offices.

Away from the hustle and bustle, and semi-retired now, John Harper, the well known and respected patriarch of the family, ran the sugarcane operation. When Luke's beloved mother, Phoebe Harper, was not beside her husband in the plantation's eight-bedroom home, where Luke and his two siblings had been raised, she could be found volunteering with local charities.

Robert and his family lived on a sprawling cattle ranch. Their Quarter horses were for riding and working the ranch which supplied the filets, steaks and prime rib served in the elegant dining rooms of Harper House Resort as well as the family's other eating establishments.

The famous, the wealthy and the influential from around the world flocked to what had become a favorite vacation spot to those who could afford it along the Gulf of Mexico. The reservation lists confirmed the constantly increasing interest of those wanting to experience the excitement on one or all of Luke's magnificent riverboats.

"What are the riverboats used for?" Ying asked, wide-eyed.

"*Femme Fatale*, the largest one, is a floating casino that cruises the Sound," Luke replied regarding the riverboat which raked in millions of dollars every year. "*Plan B* is the fastest of the three and it's a favorite of tourists, some of whom come to see Beauvoir, where Jefferson Davis, the president of the Confederacy lived after the South lost the Civil War. Investors board *Plan B* for sightseeing the countryside and the mansions for sale along the Sound and Back Bay which together surround the peninsula of Biloxi. *Moonstone* serves noon dinners with entertainment for all ages, and every evening there are moonlight suppers with music for dancing. Night or day, *Moonstone* always sails past the cast iron Biloxi Lighthouse."

Luke means the bringer of light. Genny's favorite might have been *Moonstone*.

"The Cat's Eye Ranch, just north at that sharp curve in the road, is known for gambling, entertainment and offers its own manner of sightseeing."

"Cat's Eye?" Luke hadn't been able to get Genny's lilac cat eyes out of his mind. At the Larkin Street library, he'd ruled out the surname Jones even though it meant gracious or favored and Waters which was simply a variation of Walter. His research predicted Genny's last name was Morgan.

Ying said quietly, "I know someone from Chinatown who works at the Cat's Eye." A sudden frown said he was troubled by this. "If she goes from working on her feet to her back, it will be my fault."

"What do you mean?" Luke asked. When Ying shrugged, eyes downcast, Luke figured it out and wondered if it would hurt or help the sale of his new ranch. "So the ranch I passed on my way here is a bordello."

"Yes." Ying nodded. "Until recently it was run by a madam called Garnet."

A memory of Genny saying her grandfather was usually mad at her mother, named Garnet, suddenly knifed Luke's gut.

"Do you know what Garnet's last name is?"

"Morgan."

Hell.

When he'd told the beautiful woman that home was in the country, she hadn't denied it. Could she be on the ranch next to his? If so, was she a prostitute? Maybe the name Garnet Morgan was a coincidence.

"Why does Garnet Morgan no longer run the ranch?" Luke asked.

Don't let Ying say that she was run over by an automobile...as Genny had said.

"She was hit and killed by an automobile. Her daughter inherited the Cat's Eye."

There it was. Dammit to hell.

Luke had pictured taking Genny to bed the moment he

saw her. If she had inherited a brothel, bedding her should be no problem. But why would she need those lessons if she was the madam of a whorehouse?

Her smile was as heart stopping as her fanny was sexy. She had made him laugh while stirring his blood. She had also brought out a protective side in him that he'd never known he had. The thought of the young woman entertaining countless men on her back, painfully twisted that knife in Luke's gut.

Who the hell cared? Genny was interested in Seth Comstock and Luke had plenty of women waiting for him to come home. So why was he hoping against all impossible odds that the answer to his next question was no?

"Garnet's daughter's name is Genevieve," Luke said. It wasn't really a question after all.

"Yes." Ying's expression brightened. "Do you know Genny?"

"We've met."

"Genny started a tradition of serving Sunday supper to the girls who work there, even though all but two of them don't appreciate her for it. They may each invite one special guest," Ying said. "I have a standing invitation from my friend, Tricky, who I can tell you is outspoken for a Chinese girl. But then, she's had to be strong to survive the bloodshed."

"There's a lot about San Francisco that I don't know, Ying," Luke said, glancing out across the pasture where his newly acquired horses grazed on winter grasses. Although these horses were a sturdy breed, they needed to be fattened up on oats and hay. "Where's the bloodshed?"

"Chinatown," Ying said. "And three blocks of Pacific Street known as the Barbary Coast. There's an ongoing war between the gangs in Chinatown and the shanghaiing gangs that rule the Barbary Coast. Recently, Tricky spoke up on behalf of her brother, Huan Li, and her life was threatened."

"I see." Luke had heard both concern and admiration

for Tricky in Ying's voice. Thinking of Genny, who was constantly on his mind, he said, "Well, I like outspoken and strong."

"Want to meet her?" Ying asked with an ear-to-ear grin.

"IF ONLY YOU could have met him, Tricky. Luke Harper was the most handsome man I've ever laid eyes on," Genny confided to her new friend in the alcove separating the kitchen from the dining room.

Tricky's given name was Tung-Mei Li. Her older brother, Huan Li, couldn't properly pronounce her name when she was born, and his version had stuck. Genny had met Ying after he had chased a collie through the wooded shortcut between her ranch and the Cavender ranch.

Genny knew well that Huan Li was a feared man in Chinatown. The unchallenged leader of Chinatown's most brutal gangs, known as the Five Fingers of the Monkey's Fist, Huan owned and operated several businesses. Whenever profits were jeopardized, or an innocent man, woman or child in Chinatown was harmed, Huan Li unleashed destruction and death and never looked back. Vigilante violence along the Barbary Coast had its place and the police were otherwise conveniently occupied whenever the Monkey's Fist struck.

Genny had learned this from Ying after a night involving several gang-related fatalities on Pacific Street. Ying had also told her about Tricky and the threats. It had been Genny's idea to walk into town and talk to Huan Li. Ying had later admitted, after suggesting to Huan that Tricky could come to the country, he was afraid they might be the last words he ever spoke. Huan had scowled at Ying, listened to Genny's job offer and then rolled his eyes at a smiling Tricky. Huan had nodded at Genny and Tricky was sent to the country. One stipulation Huan had made was that Tricky would live with Genny and not at the Cat's Eye Ranch. Genny had offered up Grandpa's empty room and was thrilled to have a roommate. It was a bonus that Tricky already knew how to deal cards.

"And what else do you like about Luke Harper?" Tricky asked.

"Luke was not only as handsome as Adonis, you know the Greek god I read to you about, but he was funny. He was brave and pleasant just like the meaning of his last name."

They entered the dining room then where Vern had just placed baskets of biscuits and butter on the tables. Genny set bowls of Patty's delicious vegetable soup in front of Sapphire and her guest as Tricky did the same for Emerald and her guest. Patty's husband, Vern, served Ruby and chatted with her guest, a lawyer named Joe Sanchez.

Tricky motioned Genny back into the kitchen where Patty was waiting with more bowls, full of her canned green beans, corn, tomatoes, peas, and carrots. These bowls went to two more guests along with two cousins who were brand new to the house. Having heard about the ranch, the impoverished cousins had knocked on the back door and asked for work. Genny had discouraged them. But when they thanked her and said they'd try the Barbary Coast next, she took them in. Going by Turquoise and Topaz, their real names were Grace and Ruth meaning kind and friend. The young women were both to Genny as she was to them. This evening they were dining with their first and favorite customers, Mike and Jimmy.

"I want you to forget Seth Comstock and concentrate on Luke Harper," Tricky said.

"I couldn't concentrate on Luke even if I wanted to, which I don't." Genny knew part of that statement wasn't exactly true. "I mean I can't waste time getting sidetracked."

Interrupting them and with a nod toward the dining room Patty handed them plates of apple pie. Genny took a couple of steps before Tricky blocked her in a nook between the kitchen and the front part of the rambling farmhouse.

"I have never seen you smile all the way to your pretty eyes. But you just did when describing Luke," Tricky said.

"Doesn't matter." And yet, it did. Since New Year's Eve, Luke hadn't been far from Genny's thoughts.

"We must find him," Tricky said, undaunted.

"We can't." Genny swallowed an unfamiliar catch in her voice. "When I went to the Palace Hotel to return his clothes, I was told he's gone."

"You fell hard for this Luke Harper." When Genny didn't deny it, Tricky said, "Don't worry, Huan can find anybody."

"No." Genny shook her head. "As I was leaving the hotel I ran into the leader of the quartet. He said that the man who had set his sights on me was actually thrown out of the hotel because he couldn't pay his bill. That fits with Harper saying he was trying to unload a ranch after gambling away the furniture. Luke is dirt poor like me."

"And Comstock is filthy rich," Tricky said with a frown.

"You almost ran that boy down, Seth," Selma complained as they reached the city.

"I heard you the first time," he sneered. "Your constant nagging distracted me on the way to the properties I intend to have."

"Nagging? I was begging you to slow down. I nearly fell out of this contraption. What if that boy can identify us?"

"That boy is a nobody," Seth said, and screeched to a stop. "Get out."

"Nob Hill is still too far away for me to walk."

"I said get out."

"Or what?" Selma asked.

"Surely you know the answer to that."

"Turn there, at the opening in the split rail fence," Ying said and pointed.

Luke was unaccustomed to the apprehension churning in his stomach as to what and whom he'd find at the Cat's Eye Ranch. He turned the automobile onto the dirt path. Set back in a clump of apple trees a big, white farmhouse slowly came into view. Horses, some pulling buggies, were tethered to hitching posts and parked near a wide, front porch was a single automobile.

When Luke brought the Runabout to a stop, he did so away from the porch and faced the vehicle toward the main road. He didn't know how long he'd be staying or how mad he'd be when he left this place.

A couple of women, one with skin blacker than coal and one so pale she appeared ghostly, sat in a porch swing. Luke noted their faces were rough and their expressions hardened, making them appear older than perhaps they actually were.

"Onyx is the one with dark skin and the Chinese woman with her is Opal," Ying said quietly. "They're never uh…closed even though it's Sunday."

A full moon shone in the early evening sky and Luke recalled Genny saying she lived on the dark side. He wanted to hear what else Genny had to say about where she lived.

"Ying, are you here to see me tonight?" Opal called out.

"I'm here to see Tricky as always."

"Who's that with you?" Onyx asked.

"A friend," Ying said, climbing out of the automobile.

Luke stayed put. A second Chinese woman, this one young and pretty with an innocent air about her, pushed open the screen door. Dressed in a white shirt and dark trousers, she stepped onto the front porch and with a smile waved at Ying.

"Welcome, Ying," she called with a slight forward tilt of her head. "It's almost seven. You're too late for supper."

"We didn't come for supper," Ying replied and turned toward the Runabout. "Tricky, I want you to meet my new boss."

Manners dictated Luke needed to get out of the automobile to meet Tricky. He did so as Tricky walked down the porch steps and met up with them in the yard.

"Luke Harper, this is my friend, Tricky Li," Ying said, as Tricky's mouth fell open.

"Genny," Tricky barely whispered, in the direction of the screen door. Dark brown eyes wide, hands cupping around her mouth, she then shouted, "Genny, Luke Harper is here."

Luke and Ying looked at each other, neither having anticipated this reaction from Tricky.

"She's done for the night," said a man as he came around the side of the house, carting two scarecrows, one under each arm.

"I'm not done for the night, Luke," Opal called from the porch swing.

Ignoring Opal, Luke greeted Tricky while wondering exactly what Genny was done doing. When Onyx and Opal shouted his name at the same time, Luke gritted his teeth.

"Vern, as you may have just heard, this is Luke Harper," Tricky said to the man carrying the figures made out of straw.

"Vernon Tucker. Everybody calls me Vern," he replied, seeming to look Luke over he shifted the scarecrows around and shook hands. "Pleased to meet a friend of Tricky and Ying's."

"Likewise," Luke said, not sure that he meant it as he wondered about Vern's connection to Genny.

"Mr. Harper is the man Genny met at the Palace Hotel," Tricky said to Vern.

"Don't look like him one dern bit." Vern frowned and said, "That man in that newspaper photograph was a skinny feller pert near old as me."

"Yes, but that was Seth Comstock," Tricky clarified. "This is Luke."

"Why didn't you give her a ride home?" Vern asked.

"Who are you to Genny?" Luke asked in return.

"Since Genny was a baby, I've been tending bar, doing chores, and helping my wife, Patty, with the canning and cooking. We're adding to the garden this year on accounta Genny would rather make more money in the dining room and less upstairs. So we need two straw men to keep the crows off the vegetables." Vern shot a glance toward the road. "I know it was them soaplock Skidmore brothers over yonder who stole last year's straw man."

Luke knew soaplock meant hoodlum as well as being a haircut that was short in the back, long in the front and parted down the middle to fall below the ears on the sides. Somehow, he had a feeling both definitions applied to the Skidmores.

"Vern also keeps the peace around here," Ying said.

"As best I can," Vern said to Luke. "I'm getting older, and the men keep getting younger. Meaner and rougher, too, some of 'em anyhow." His voice had trailed off and he shrugged.

Satisfied with Vern's answer, Luke gave one of his own, "I offered Genny a ride home, but she wouldn't say where she lived and snuck away from me."

"Sounds 'bout like her," Vern said and shook his head.

Luke had not asked Ying if Genny worked here, and he would not ask Vern. He wanted to hear that answer from Genny herself.

"Where is Genny?" Luke asked.

"Hey, handsome," came the voice of Opal or Onxy, Luke didn't know or care which. "You don't want Genny. Come on up here on the porch with us."

"Be still," Vern ordered the women who cackled.

"Genny must have started home before you and Ying arrived," Tricky surmised.

Luke nodded and offered to give Ying a ride. But with his eyes on Tricky, Ying said he'd stay and visit with her before taking the shortcut through the woods to Luke's ranch.

CHAPTER 7

THE GLARE FROM THE TWO GAS POWERED HEADLAMPS WAS blinding as the automobile headed straight for her. She'd had two warnings; Garnet's death and nearly being run over herself. Earlier, there'd been so much flying dirt and rock she hadn't been able to get a good look at the driver. But it appeared he was back, and she was ready. Clutching a fistful of winter wildflowers intended for Grandpa's grave in one hand, she grabbed up a rock with her other hand and loaded it into her slingshot. Aiming at the driver, she let the rock fly at the same second he swerved to miss her.

Something shattered. Streaks and sockdolagers!

"Hey, kid," a man shouted. "You broke a headlamp."

That unforgettable Southern drawl. With less glare shining in her eyes, she recognized the Runabout and the man driving it. But with her braids tucked into her cowboy hat, along with her checkered shirt and blue overalls she suspected he hadn't identified her…yet. She couldn't let him see her and maybe figure out she owned a brothel.

Genny raced toward her house.

"Get back here, kid. You're going to answer for what you did."

Genny ran ever so fast, but she was no match for the

automobile. Luke pulled into the grassy yard of her house and hopped out of his vehicle just as she jumped onto her small porch. The doorknob turned in her hand, but as usual the door stuck. Hearing Luke's footsteps right behind her, Genny hoped to take a flying leap off the side of the porch. But Luke grabbed the back of her overalls and hauled her up short.

"Let go of me."

Instead, he twirled her around to face him.

"Genny?"

"Yup." She smacked his arm with her flowers. "That's twice in one day you raced around the killing curve and tried to run me over, Harper."

"You stopped in the middle of road and shot a rock through your flowers, and this is the first time I've seen you in three weeks." Taking a step back, he looked her up and all the way down to her red cowboy boots. "What kind of get-up is that?"

"The same get-up that fooled President Roosevelt's Secret Service into thinking I was a boy." With a sharp nod of her head, she grabbed the doorknob and shoved against the door again to no avail. "Goodbye."

"Goodbye?" Luke raised a foot and kicked open the door. "Like hell it is."

Genny darted forward but he grabbed her overalls again with one hand and flattening his other hand to her door kept her from closing it on him.

"I said let go of me," she demanded, but he clapped his hand on her shoulder and guided her inside the small house.

He released her then and frowned. "I'm mad at you."

"Well, I don't care," she said, but curiosity instantly got the better of her. "Why are you mad at me?"

"Let me list three reasons," he replied and held up a finger. "First, I had to pay for a missing tuxedo I only rented for a night."

"Oh, hush up, Harper." She batted away his finger with

her flowers. "I didn't have your clothes ready because I've been so busy. Anyway, I was told you were gone when I tried to return your tuxedo today."

"Today?" He'd practically camped out day and night in the Palm Court waiting for her. Steeling himself, he asked, "What have you been so busy doing?"

Face flushed, she snapped, "Turning a long-forgotten basement into two nice rooms for two sweet cousins."

Holding up two fingers, he said, "The second reason; your vanishing act on New Year's Day."

"I told you I had walked to the hotel, and I'd walk home." Tossing her slingshot onto a nearby chair and switching her wildflowers from one hand to the other, Genny dug into her front pockets and then the back ones but couldn't find a single cent. When Luke cocked his head to one side, she said, "I still have your clothes. How much does a headlamp cost?"

Hands on his hips, he said, "The broken headlamp's the third reason I'm mad, but maybe you can work it off."

"How would I do that?"

"You tell me," he replied, his green eyes narrowing in appraisal.

Genny smacked his broad chest with the flowers. "You think I'm one of the Cat's Eye Ranch girls."

"Are you?"

"Well, I own the brothel," she blurted out. "No, according to my dictionary I own a disorderly house because we also have games of chance. Blackjack and poker keep the men busy while they wait their turn for a half hour mattress dance."

Luke stood just inside her front door and a breeze ruffled his dark brown hair. His hair had been combed straight back at the ball, but tonight it was windblown, and she pictured running her fingers through it. What? No.

Even as the handsome man frowned at her, she felt the new and exciting pull to him that she had the night they met. His broad shoulders and chest filled out his long-sleeved brown shirt. Dark blue denim pants were snug against his muscular thighs, and he wasn't wearing his shiny black shoes this evening.

"Do those cowboy boots mean you're a cowboy now?"

"Do those empty stems mean you're deflowered?"

Realizing she had knocked every last petal off the flowers, she tossed the stems next to her slingshot and asked him, "Are you a virgin?"

"What do you think?"

"No." When he neither confirmed or denied it, she raised her chin and said, "What would you think if I told you I was deflowered when I was twelve and have been mattress dancing ever since?"

Luke's jaw clenched. Genny's lilac eyes glittered just the way he remembered. The checkered shirt couldn't hide her full breasts, and his memory served him up with a picture of her ivory cleavage. The overalls clung to her hips, and he wanted to run his hands over her rounded fanny. How well he recalled the beautiful naked legs her torn gown had first revealed on the beach. Her words echoed in his ears.

Whatever you've heard, I'm not a woman to be shared.

"I'm holding your dress ransom for my tuxedo." With that, he turned his back on her. Crossing the porch he said, "We'll make an exchange when you're ready to come to my ranch and tell me exactly what you do at your disorderly house."

"I don't even know where your ranch is."

Walking away from her as he'd done on the beach, he replied over his shoulder, "It's the one south of yours."

"The Cavendar Ranch?"

"It's the Harper Ranch, now." After Luke got into his vehicle, he said, "Be prepared to settle up when you get there."

Stepping onto her porch, she said, "Don't hold your breath, Harper."

"You've got twenty-four hours before I come after you, Genevieve."

. . .

LUKE CLOSED HIS POCKETWATCH. The lanterns casting a warm, flickering glow on the front porch had showed him that she had ten more minutes. Sitting in one of the rocking chairs, he leaned the rocker back and crossed his booted feet atop the porch railing.

He and Ying had put in a good day's work. Ying had cleaned the horse stalls while Luke groomed all ten horses. The horses had exercised in the pasture and then the nameless collie, good at his job, had helped round them up. Eight of the horses were back in the stable for the night. Ying had politely declined needing a horse to go visit Tricky and reminded Luke that he was accustomed to walking. But he had closely watched Luke saddle one of the horses and after some pointers Ying was ready to ride.

Once Ying was gone, Luke had pumped water from the well and washed up. A second horse, the largest of the ten, was saddled and tethered to the hitching post just in case Genny didn't show. With daylight fading he couldn't safely drive his automobile since it was down to one headlamp. Thinking of Genny's beautiful cat eyes, Luke shut his.

A mermaid in an aquamarine gown danced so close he could almost touch her. Splashing in the ocean like a sea nymph she followed him along the sandy beach, and he kissed her before a real live scarecrow emerged from the shadows. Luke frowned until a siren wearing his white shirt scampered across his hotel room and dove into the bed next to his. That gorgeous woman vanished only to reappear as a farm boy.

"Are you asleep?"

Luke opened his eyes and there she was.

Perusing him from under the brim of her cowboy hat and standing beside the horse, his tuxedo lay draped over her right arm. Underneath her thin coat she wore form-fitting dark gray overalls and a snug red shirt with a scooped neck. On her feet the red cowboy boots were dusty.

"Cat got your tongue?" Genny asked.

"C'mere and find out," he said and sat forward, putting his feet to the wooden planks of the porch. He'd been irritable all day and now that she was here, he felt a grin tugging up the corner of his mouth. God, she was sexy.

"I can't stay," Genny said, not meeting his eyes.

"Sure, you can." He patted the seat of the rocking chair next to his. "Sit down."

"I'm returning your tuxedo which I've pressed twice now and the shirt which is washed and twice pressed as well. You paid for these clothes so you may as well keep them." She placed her bundle over the porch railing and paused at the porch step. "How much is the headlamp?"

"I don't know. Come up on the porch."

Instead, she petted the nose of the large, chocolate brown horse. "I love all of your horses, but this one and the black mare are my favorites."

"What's this one's name?"

"Mr. Cavender didn't name his animals."

"But you've named him. Right?"

"He's your horse." She lifted one shoulder. "But I call him E-ta-law. Etalon means stallion in French."

"Can you ride?"

"I've ridden the mare bareback a couple of times. She's still a little wild, so I call her Es-pree. In French, Esprit means spirit."

"You need a saddle next time." Visualizing the beautiful woman with black hair riding the beautiful black horse, he smiled. When the dog bounded toward them from the pasture, Luke asked, "And the dog's name?"

"Roscoe, meaning from the forest." When the collie sat down beside Genny, she petted his head. "One day he just wandered out of the woods between our ranches and visited me."

"Take a seat. We're going to discuss your ranch."

Staying in his chair, Luke held out his hand to her. Hesitating for only a moment, she squared her shoulders and extended her hand. The second her hand slipped into his, the same thought about never letting Genny go crossed Luke's mind. He tugged her onto the porch, and she sat in the rocking chair next to his. Roscoe followed her and curled up between the rockers.

Hell, this felt right.

"Let's discuss your place first," Genny said, folding her hands in her lap. "How'd you come to own this ranch that you're trying to unload?"

"Five-card stud onboard the *Femme Fatale*," he said and when she tilted her head he added, "She's the largest river-boat along the Mississippi Sound, named for her seductive charms. A femme fatale can spellbind a lover of her games into financial rewards or disastrous consequences. Depends on the player, but *Femme Fatale's* name is her own warning to beware." Luke studied Genny as she silently processed what he'd said. Was she still plotting to spellbind Comstock?

"Do you have any idea how to take care of American Quarter horses?" Genny asked.

"Yes."

"Well, sure you do, city slicker," she said with a smirk and a glance at his boots.

"Do you know how to take care of horses, mischief maker?"

"I know they like flat cake cookies." She smiled then and petted Roscoe.

"Did you bring some with you?"

"Not today, but on my sixth birthday I walked over here with a batch to make friends with the horses I'd heard about. Mr. Cavender was always at the Cat's Eye poker tables, so I never suspected there was a Mrs. Caven-der. But there was and she called me a—" Genny's eyes had widened in memory. "Never mind that part, she chased me off. I was afraid to come back to see the horses until a few years later after we heard she had left Mr. Cavender."

"What did she call you?"

"Oh, suffice to say her ranting and raving ended with scarlet harlot," Genny replied matter-of-factly. "When I told Grandpa about it, he cheered me up by taking me to the library where we discovered *Heidi*. Every birthday after that he bought me the book of my choice."

"Good for your grandpa and shame on Mrs. Cavender."

"I never held a grudge against Mrs. Cavender because," looking Luke in the eye Genny said with quiet conviction, "the Cat's Eye Ranch ruined the Cavenders. It ruins people. Grandpa predicted my ranch would be too infamous to sell and so far, he's right. If you don't unload your ranch and leave town, my ranch will ruin your life."

Her voice was so soft and sincere it touched Luke's very soul.

"Has the Cat's Eye Ranch ruined your life, Genny?"

"Sell your ranch and go back to…where are you from?"

"Biloxi, Mississippi in what was originally known as *French* Louisiana, Genevieve the French woman."

"I knew your accent was from the South." She smiled, but her eyes met his only briefly this time. "Leave as soon as you can, Luke. That's what I plan to do."

His heart suddenly skipped a beat.

"Where're you going?" Luke asked.

CHAPTER 8

"Nob Hill of course," she said and just like that her pensive, protective mood was gone.

Luke reached over and nabbed the hat off her head. Long braids tumbled out and when she swiped at her hat, he held it out of her reach. Ample breasts jiggling, her lilac eyes sparked, and her full lips pursed. No matter the tomboy get-up, Genny oozed sensual femininity from head to toe. She was the siren who beckoned him during the day and the mermaid who danced with him in his dreams every night.

How much romancing would it take to get her naked under him? He'd never had to romance a woman before, but he was open to such a wild adventure with her. And only with her. Only her? He rubbed his forehead. Yeah, maybe. What the hell...why?

Because the gorgeous sea nymph had splashed into his life and he couldn't forget her.

Truth be told he was sick and tired of waking up in the dark of night not remembering the name or face of the latest woman he'd escorted off his riverboat. Dammit... since when?

Since New Year's Eve. He bowed his head in confusion and dawning and noticed her red cowboy boots. Since the woman wearing those boots made him long for...some-thing...more.

With a slight frown, he said, "We'll exchange my tuxedo for your dress, but if want your hat you'll have to tell me about your ranch now."

"Well...let's see." With an askance glance at him and straightening her long braids over her breasts, Genny then tilted her head back and rolled her eyes skyward. "Hmm... Garnet, my mother, got pregnant by a married man. Sooo...he bought her a house in the country to keep her from spilling the beans to his city wife. Then umm...as revenge against him for not leaving his wife, Garnet turned the house into a dance hall, which quickly evolved into a brothel. I was born and the father I never knew was shot and killed by his jealous wife. After Garnet died, I inherited an infamous ranch on twenty acres of tainted land. How's that?"

"How much of it is true?" Luke asked.

"Let's say all of it is."

"Then fill in some blanks for me."

"Like what?"

"Like where was your grandfather when all this was happening?"

"In the little house, on his thirty acres of land with a pond, where you found me." Genny gazed away in that general direction. "Garnet picked out the Cat's Eye house because it was so close to Grandpa's house, and she figured she'd need help with a baby. Grandpa whose name was Samuel, meaning a prophet heard by God, predicted the ranch would be the ruination of Garnet. But as usual she didn't listen."

Genny kicked at a pebble on the porch.

"Then what?" Luke prodded.

"Grandpa never forgave her and never set foot on the Cat's Eye property. The incident I told you about with Mrs. Cavender was the last straw for Grandpa. He asked me to live with him, and my mother let me choose. I was thrilled and chose Grandpa, of course." Genny's voice took on a stoic tone. "My mother ordered me to call her Garnet from that day forward."

Luke didn't comment but couldn't imagine issuing such an order to one's child. "Vern says he's been there since you were a baby. I think he said his wife's name is Patty."

"Yes, Patty was the first girl to work for Garnet," Genny said and nodded. "Patty had been working in a Barbary Coast bordello and was kicked out for slapping an important customer who was brutally beating her. Garnet happened to be shopping for girls when she ran into Patty on Pacific Street. When Vern came along, he said Patty was a real jewel. Garnet liked that and Patty went by Jewel until Vern did something truly unheard of."

"What?"

"He married Patty and she never again worked on her back." Genny smiled at that. "Patty became the cook and housekeeper. Vern bought chickens, built a chicken coop and planted the vegetable gardens. Madam Garnet hired three more girls away from the Barbary Coast and named all of them after jewels. The notion of bedding a jewel instead of a prostitute caught on and the Cat's Eye Ranch flourished."

"So Garnet, Patty and Vern all contributed to a clever business idea," Luke said as Genny frowned in the direction of the ranch. "But I'm guessing your grandfather didn't like it."

"Grandpa felt Garnet had used the jewel idea to spite him. My grandmother died in childbirth, and they hadn't discussed names so he named my mother Garnet. It's the stone connected with January, her birth month. Grandpa said she was as pretty as a jewel. But Garnet decided he didn't care enough to think of a real name. I don't know, maybe she did use the jewel idea spitefully." Genny shrugged, seeming too embarrassed to make eye contact. "Grandpa said he looked at my eyes when I was born and came up with my middle name."

"What do you mean? What is it?"

"Moonstone." Genny hugged herself and looked at him then. "As in cat's eye moonstone."

Luke hadn't seen that coming. His paddle steamer *Moonstone*, was known far and wide as the riverboat for romance. He'd already figured it would be Genny's favorite and stared at her until she turned away. Genny's shoulders squared, and she rocked forward in her chair as if preparing to leave.

"I know I tend to blurt out too much information, so if you'll give me the dress I'll be moseying along now."

"The moonstone protects those who travel upon the water," Luke said. Genny's head snapped around, her eyes filled with surprise. "The moonstone is said to encourage our truest life's journey; floating deep into one's soul to retrieve what's missing." Genny's pink lips formed a small oh and Luke finished with, "And because cats can see in the dark, the cat's eye moonstone brings parts of the soul which were lost back into the *light*."

Genny rubbed the goosebumps on her upper arms. Luke knew as sure as he was sitting there she remembered telling him that his name meant the bringer of light. It occurred to him that Genny might be a bringer of light, too.

Genny whispered, "However do you know all of that, Luke?"

"Moonstone is mystery and we're both living on the dark side."

"I have to go." She bailed out of the rocker and nabbed her hat from him.

"Just hold on." Luke chuckled. Grabbing his clothes off the railing he noted the freshly washed scent of the shirt and neatness of the pressed tuxedo. He opened the door to the house and inclined his head. "Let's get your dress."

When Genny hesitated, Luke took her hand. Her thumping heart pounded even harder as the powerful man tugged her through the door of the log home into a spacious and nearly empty front room with a high ceiling. Ying had told Tricky that he slept on a cot in the barn. Since a pillow and blanket lay on top of a big, overstuffed chair and matching ottoman Genny figured that was Luke's bed. Roscoe followed them into the house.

"You were serious about the furniture being gambled away," she said.

"Cavender didn't know when to quit." Luke released Genny's hand.

"True," Genny said. She'd assumed Luke had gambled away the furniture, but whatever the case, Mr. Cavender had lost his wife and ranch over not knowing when to quit.

"Stay," Luke said as Roscoe came to stand beside Genny.

"Are you talking to me or Rosco?"

"Both."

Roscoe obediently sat and Genny crossed her arms under her breasts. When Luke's eyes dipped to the top of her overalls, she uncrossed her arms and waved him on. With a shake of his head, he left the room and returned with her gown. As soon as he handed it to her, she could see that it had been cleaned, pressed and was no longer ripped.

"How did you fix my dress?"

"Ying took it to a seamstress in Chinatown."

"I'm even further in your debt." Genny was astonished that he had gone to so much trouble and mumbled, "I still owe you for the headlamp."

"We'll call it even if you'll tell me what *you* do at the Cat's Eye Ranch."

"Since Grandpa and Garnet are dead, I've been working there."

Luke's eyes narrowed and a muscle worked in his jaw. "Doing what exactly?"

"Besides cleaning the basement...listen here," she pointed a finger at him, "I've answered enough of your questions. I have some of my own."

"I doubt I'll tell you a damn thing until you answer my

last question," he replied, crossing his muscular arms over his broad chest.

"Are you going to give me lessons in dancing, fighting, kissing, and drinking?"

"Depends. What do you do at the ranch?"

"Are you going to give me lessons in the art of seduction?"

"Depends, femme fatale. What do you do at the ranch?"

Deciding to use that jab to her advantage she licked her lips, smiled her best smile and whispered in what she hoped was a seductive voice, "Will you at least teach me to swim?"

"Depends."

"On what, Harper?"

"What you do at the ranch, Genevieve."

The green glint in his eyes was so wicked and his cocky grin so challenging that goosebumps sprinkled her skin again.

"A picture is worth a thousand words." And with that, Genny turned on her heel and walked out the door.

"WHY DON'T you just rob them and be done with it, Seth?"

"Why should I settle for the jewels alone when I can have two houses, the big one for me and the little one for you, as well as fifty thousand acres of land and water?"

"Are you absolutely sure those jewels and thousands of acres exist?" Selma asked.

Seth glared at his sister. "Cecil was my roommate and had no reason to lie."

"Cecil was a murderer you were locked up with in West Virginia."

Hearing the clip clop of a horse's hooves, Seth jumped back, jerking his sister into the trees and smacking his hand over her mouth. The former automobile he'd stolen had been confiscated by the police and the vehicle representing his latest theft was hidden down a side road a mile away. This furtive trip to the pond had been made on foot. Barely contained rage shook him to the core when he recognized Luke Harper riding past them on an expensive looking, large horse.

"I need to find out why he's still here," Seth said after Luke was out of view.

"You need to get rid of Luke Harper before he finds out who you really are."

"Selma, that kind of thinking is why I keep you around."

"HEY, LUKE," Joe Sanchez, his attorney, called from the porch of the Cat's Eye Ranch and paused to wait for him. "What took you so long to come over here to the Cat's Eye?"

A thousand mental pictures.

During the remainder of January and first couple of weeks of February, Luke had worked long hours on his ranch. He'd tried to talk himself into leaving every day, and then spent even longer nights tossing and turning in the comfortable new bed he'd had delivered. It occurred to him that maybe Genny had tried to talk herself into not risking running into him at the Palace Hotel and welcomed busying herself in her basement. Yet, she'd eventually ventured not only to the hotel but to his ranch.

He couldn't venture back home without knowing the truth about Genny. So, here he was. According to Ying, except for Sundays, the house opened for business every night at supper time. They closed when the last customer left, and the women slept most of the day. Luke dismounted Etalon and after tethering him to the hitching post walked up the porch steps.

"Hello, Joe." Luke shook his new friend's hand. "Good to see you again."

"You're just in time to play cards with a couple of buddies I'd like you to meet."

Luke nodded and forced a polite smile. Genny was

nowhere to be seen as they entered the big white house with the garnet-colored front door and matching shutters. He stepped into a roomy foyer with a long hall to the left of a straight staircase. Down the hall and through a wide archway, he glimpsed a parlor filled with men, card tables and a long bar across the back wall. To the right of the staircase, suppers were being served in a dining room by Vern and a woman who appeared to be in her mid-fifties. Plump, plain and laughing at something a customer said, she noticed Luke at the same time Vern did and they both smiled.

From all the sights and sounds, this disorderly house was in full swing.

A redhead, with a red dot on her forehead, slithered in between Luke and Joe. As she took Joe's arm, she boldly perused Luke. Though wearing a red version of a sari, one so skimpy it bared much of her breasts, stomach and buttocks, the redhead didn't look Hindu.

"Luke Harper, this is Ruby," Joe said, pulling money out of his pocket and handing it to Ruby before turning back to Luke. "Meet me in the parlor later where the games are played."

"I can offer you a better game upstairs, Luke," Ruby said, pointing a long red nail toward the ceiling as she brushed her hip against him while giving Joe a tug.

As Joe followed Ruby upstairs, Vern called to Luke, and he was introduced to Patty. She offered him supper and not taking no for an answer, Vern ushered him to a table in the dining room. Luke had no sooner sat down when a gypsy wearing an emerald scarf tied around her head, a see-through scarf for a top and several more for a revealing skirt, sidled up beside him.

"If you've got five dollars it's your lucky night, handsome."

CHAPTER 9

"It's Valentine's Day," Tricky whispered to Genny at the blackjack table. "Maybe tonight's the night."

"I doubt it and I don't blame him for not coming here. I warned him this ranch ruins people," Genny said softly. "I have to go back to my post and check the jewel box."

Her mind on Luke, Genny wove her way between card tables ignoring the numerous men vying for her attention. With customers still calling her name, she left the parlor games behind and made her way down the hallway. Her post was a chair in the foyer where she'd left a wooden box, its lid decorated with colored glass in the shapes of diamonds, hearts, clubs, and spades.

The steadfast rule of the house was to pay the five dollars up front. If the madam happened to be away from her post, the jewel of choice was on her honor to place her customer's money into the bejeweled box. The box was separated into a slot for each of the seven jewels. Nightly, the money was locked away in a hiding place under the stairs and weekly, the jewels were paid two dollars per customer while the house kept three. Though all the jewels were busy at the moment, only Sapphire's slot was empty. Again.

Sapphire, with blue eyes and a Boston accent, based her

outfits on those of 1776 tavern wenches. Probably bawdier than those in Paul Revere's time, Sapphire's costumes consisted of blouseless corsets, thigh high skirts split up the sides, and a tricorn hat. Taking advantage of the turmoil that ensued immediately following Garnet's death, Sapphire had moved out of her room upstairs, leaving four we'd-as-soon-cut-you-as-look-at-you jewels on the second floor.

Turquoise and Topaz, who Genny preferred to think of as Grace and Ruth, had asked to live in the basement. They'd swept and scrubbed, painted walls and carted furniture down from the attic right alongside Genny, turning the basement into livable space. With a door in the hallway leading downstairs to their rooms, they quietly kept themselves apart from the other jewels. Their modest attire; Grace in dresses of blues and greens and Ruth in light browns or yellows, caused Genny to suspect they were no more cut out for brothel life than she was.

Sapphire on the other hand thrived on it and had slyly set herself up in the madam's former main floor bedroom. Opposite Patty and Vern's room, it was easily the biggest and most accessible bedroom of all the jewels, thus had the most money-making potential.

The Cat's Eye Ranch provided room and board, along with Sundays off and the new special Sunday suppers. Genny didn't appreciate being cheated in return. She shut the jewel box lid. Enough was enough, Sapphire.

With a calming breath, she squared her shoulders. She was learning the ropes and was well aware that in addition to the men in the parlor, more customers were waiting their turn on the porch or lingering over food and drink in the dining room. She had also discovered that all the jewels at the house, except for Grace and Ruth, resented her for avoiding the ranch until she'd had to take over. Despite their feelings toward her, Genny felt responsible for everyone who lived and worked at her ranch.

But the life of a madam was not the life she intended to live.

Genny literally visualized running out the front door and not stopping until she reached Nob Hill. However, she knew no one on Nob Hill except for Seth Comstock. Well, she didn't exactly know him, nor which house was his. When she pictured actually speaking to the skinny man with sunken cheeks, boney fingers and thinning hair, she shivered. But not with the same goosebumps she'd had with Luke.

Luke Harper. All man and gorgeous from his thick brown hair to his forest green eyes to his strong square chin. She could almost feel his warm mouth on hers and his muscular arms closing around her as he kissed her. Masculinity exuded from Luke, awakening parts of her brain and body that she hadn't known were sleeping. Luke was a man who had everything a woman could want except...the money she needed to reinvent herself...on Nob Hill.

How was she ever going to become who she wanted to be without Luke Harper to teach her all that she didn't know?

"Evening," a man said, bumping into her and her thoughts on his way through the front door. "Which jewel are you?"

Genny cringed as she recognized the swarthy man she'd shoved at the ball.

"Haven't I seen you somewhere before?" he asked, squinting at her.

"Jonesy," Emerald called, waving a scarf on her way out of the dining room. "You can be my first tonight."

His eyes boring holes through Genny, Jonesy climbed the stairs with the jewel dressed like a gypsy. He must be a who's who to some degree since he'd been at the ball. But a real who's who would never marry a madam. She had already decided Seth Comstock hadn't known who she was when he invited her to the Palace Hotel. But that could change at any second.

There was no time to waste in getting him to the altar.

Further proof of that reasoning was the fact she hadn't heard from Luke now that he was fully aware of her connection to the ranch. Luke was a drifting gambler. He could have disappeared by now. But wouldn't Ying have let them know if Luke had left town? Even if Ying came and told them right now, that would still mean Luke was forever gone.

Sadness, like a heavy tarp of eternal darkness, suddenly dropped over Genny so hard her entire body sagged.

Stop it, she scolded herself. The lessons were her only interest in Luke. Yet, drifter or not, Luke had a savvy air of sophistication about him. He spoke like a who's who, a well mannered, well educated and well dressed one. Hoping to clear her head of all things concerning Luke Harper, Genny gave herself a purposeful head-to-toe shake.

"Shake naked and maybe you earn keep like we must," Opal said to Genny with a contemptuous tone, coming down the stairs with a regular who smiled at Genny.

"Her? Naked?" Onxy snickered. "Don't matter that the old geezer's gone, Miss High and Mighty ain't gonna shed them overalls for no man, Opal."

Genny frowned at them for referring to Grandpa so disrespectfully, but picking her battles, let that poke to her heart go. She'd spent the last year caring for her failing grandfather and prayed he hadn't taken his own life in the pond in hopes she'd move away from the Cat's Eye Ranch. Rolling up her shirtsleeves, she knew Grandpa was rolling in his grave at her taking on Garnet's role as madam. But whereas Garnet went to bed with any customer who had five dollars, Genny would never have to do that.

If…she could get to Nob Hill.

Was Luke still at his ranch or not? She missed him. No, she needed him. And maybe he needed her help, too. He might still be in San Francisco only because he couldn't afford to leave. Her Square Deal proposal would have put some money in his pocket. Should she go to his ranch and try to discuss her offer with him again? Would he use her money to leave?

Anxiety mounted and Genny thumbed the brim of her hat up, careful to keep it covering her braids. Had her hair been hanging down long and loose, as she preferred wearing it, the swarthy man might have recognized her. Grandpa said hiding her hair and dressing like a boy helped protect her, but she was so tired of it. The *San Francisco Chronicle* showed today's fashionable coiffure as ornate and upswept. The Gibson girl topknot she'd worn the night she met Luke was the closest she'd been able to come to that.

She was trapped in a house she didn't want, in a life she didn't want, in clothes she didn't want, and with a hairstyle she didn't want. Genny took a deep breath and as she blew out a frustrated sigh the top button popped off her old blue shirt.

Streaks. Could things get any worse? Well yes, they sure could she thought as Sapphire came out of her new room with her customer.

A really rough looking customer.

"Sir? Sapphire?" Genny moved to the center of the foyer as they neared. "Are you prepared to settle up?" she asked, using Luke's phrase.

"Uh...she owed me a half hour," the customer said gruffly.

"That's not the way we do things." Genny looked from him to Sapphire. "Is it, Sapphire?"

"Maybe you haven't noticed, but *things* are changing around here."

Genny said, "The house's cut is three dollars and one of you needs to pay it."

"Ain't gonna be me, madam harlot," the customer sneered as Sapphire blatantly shoved two dollars into her corset before turning away. When Genny stood her ground the man bellowed, "Get gone or get whupped."

Genny held out her hand for payment. Baring his teeth, the man reared his arm back and Genny fully expected to be jack-slapped out of his way. But in the next instant the man's expression changed and his arm lowered. Without a word, he dug into his pants pocket.

"Here ya go, ma'am," the customer said as he handed her three dollars.

Shocked, Genny stepped aside to let him leave and met with a hard body at her back. As her rescuer steadied her with a firm hand on her waist, she turned her head to find a muscular arm beside her shoulder. Gripped in his hand, finger on the trigger, was a menacing gun.

Vern and Patty, in the doorway of the dining room, Grace and Ruth, having just come from the basement, had all stopped in their tracks, with expressions ranging from wide eyes to dropped jaws. Peeking around the parlor archway Tricky gaped at the latest commotion playing out.

"Sorry for the trouble, sir." The customer politely tipped his hat and headed to the door.

Genny glanced over her shoulder and the steely glint in the eyes that met hers and the set of the jaw said the unruly customer was smart to have settled up without further protest.

"Luke?" Genny said in surprise.

"How the hell often does that happen?" Luke demanded.

"I don't know."

"Often, Luke," Vern replied. "Part of keeping the peace."

The bedroom door at the end of the hall slammed shut with a resounding bang. The customer who'd just walked out yelped as if he'd been shot and tromped a fast retreat down the porch steps.

Slipping his gun inside a black jacket, Luke strode down the hallway and knocked on Sapphire's door. Genny tensed, bracing herself for whatever Luke did next. Sapphire opened her door and smiled up at him.

"Does your room have a draft?" Luke asked.

"No, it does not," Sapphire purred, tracing a finger across her nearly bare breasts.

"Then there's no reason for your door to slam."

"Come inside and make American Revolution fireworks with me, gorgeous."

"I prefer New Year's Eve fireworks."

That said, Luke presented his back to her. When she smacked the door shut in return he swung around and kicked it open. Sapphire screamed in surprise.

"If you like working here, don't rebel," Luke growled. "If you don't like it, take your damn tea party to Boston."

Sapphire glanced past Luke to Genny and nodded. After Sapphire soundlessly shut her door, the other spectators scattered.

As Luke made his way back to her, Genny noted how his broad shoulders filled out his lightweight jacket. Underneath it he wore a black leather vest and long-sleeved white shirt. Dark jeans were snug against his tapered hips and muscular thighs, the hems of which covered most of his black cowboy boots.

"You could tame this place, Harper." Genny didn't want Luke's life ruined and instantly regretted her observation.

"No thanks," Luke replied, his eyes dipping to the missing button on her shirt. Frowning, he boldly took hold of her shirt and closed it over the cleavage that Genny belatedly remembered had been on display. "Close it down."

"If I close it down, what would happen to all the people who work here?"

"They'd find other tea parties in other harbors," he said, hands going to his hips.

"And what would I do?"

"Sail away with me."

A jolt the size of Jupiter jackslapped Genny.

When she swayed toward him, Luke wrapped his arms around her. Thrilling to the memory of Luke's spellbinding kisses her eyes closed and she tilted up her chin. No kiss came. She quickly opened her eyes to find Luke's left brow cocked.

"What about my kissing lessons?"

"We haven't negotiated my payment."

"Three dollars?" she asked, stepping back and holding up the money.

"I'm not for sale," Luke said. "Are you?"

"No, never."

The grin on Luke's lips slowly spread to his eyes. "The name Genny means three things." He paused before saying, "Fair and polite, I've witnessed." He chuckled when her brows rose in surprise.

"How'd you know?"

"You're not the only one who goes to the library." His smile faded and he asked, "And pure?"

Chin raising, she asked him as he had her that night at her house, "What do you think?"

"Yes." When she neither confirmed nor denied it, his eyes narrowed appraisingly. "And I think Morgan means sea dweller or born by the sea." She nodded, slightly over-whelmed by this man who then said, "By the way I'll decide the order of your fighting, swimming, dancing, kissing, and seduction lessons."

Genny pulled herself together and smiled her very best smile. "I'll decide."

"No, you won't and don't smile at me like that," he grumbled. "Let's go see if you play cards any better than you collect money."

"Who will take my place collecting money?"

"Vern," Luke called. Vern immediately came out of the dining room to the foyer. "Please make a sign stating the house fees and set it on the table with the box."

CHAPTER 10

"Hey, Luke." Joe leaned around the archway of the parlor long enough to say, "We're dealing you in."

Luke snared Genny's hand as Vern took off to make the sign.

"Nobody will pay up tonight, Harper."

"I'm betting they all do, Genevieve."

Luke felt eyes on him from every corner. Entering the parlor with Genny's hand in his drew more attention. So be it. Luke was not only a new face, but the confrontations had been eyewitnessed or overheard. He hoped his righting of wrongs left a lasting impression. Wasn't the first time he'd settled things down with his automatic Colt .45. Introduced in 1905, this military model gun was said to be the most powerful pistol ever invented. The threat of a single bullet between the eyes was enough to back off the most disgruntled loser at one of his riverboat gaming tables. Not surprisingly it also worked with the disgruntled in disorderly houses.

"Luke Harper," Joe said, standing at a table where two men were seated. "I'd like you to meet the Johnson brothers. Mike and Jimmy are firemen in San Francisco."

Luke let go of Genny as the brothers stood to shake his hand. He instinctively knew all three men were making note of his familiarity with Genny, but they were either too polite or too cautious to point it out. The men took their seats as Tricky called to Genny who excused herself.

"Come back later," Luke said. "You're gonna be good luck."

Genny blushed and walked to Tricky who was dealing blackjack to a group of men. Joe also dealt out cards and Luke looked over the top of his at Genny. The pink on her cheeks deepened as a grinning Tricky whispered to her. When Tricky inclined her head toward Luke, Genny smiled at him. Luke's blood heated and he forced his attention back to his cards.

Conversing with the men at his table, Luke learned that Mike was the older brother, thirty-two and had recently broken up with a fiancée. Jimmy with a mop of blond hair was twenty-seven and claimed to be a confirmed bachelor. Luke wondered about that as the brothers spoke quite fondly of a couple of cousins named Grace and Ruth.

Vern entered the parlor and took up his role as bartender. He and Genny were soon delivering whiskey, rum or beer to customers in the parlor, dining room and on the front porch. For the rest of the evening, it stayed calm and most of the men took breaks from gambling to visit a jewel.

Even though his mind was on Genny, Luke had been on a winning streak at the poker table. After he laid down a full house with kings high, he caught Genny's wrist as she passed by the table. She paused at his side.

"What's your line of work in Biloxi?" Mike asked.

"Riverboats and gambling." Luke chuckled when the brothers groaned as Joe nodded.

"Don't bring him any more luck, Genevieve," Jimmy said and rubbed his forehead.

Luke scooted his chair back and tugged Genny onto his knee. Mike raised a brow and Joe grinned. Jimmy complained good-naturedly that he was almost out of money. The house was beginning to clear out as Joe dealt one last hand of poker. Luke reached around Genny to arrange his cards. He liked the way she leaned against him as he held his cards in front of her. The way she nestled on his lap felt perfect. Joe, Mike and Jimmy discarded,

and each took a couple of cards. Luke shook his head that he didn't need any. No one folded and bets were made.

"If I were you," Genny began and reached to the cards in Luke's hand, "I'd arrange the cards as red queen, black queen, red queen, black queen, and then the ace of diamonds."

"I'm out," Joe laughed.

"Me, too," Mike chuckled around a yawn.

"I thought I had a good hand that time," Jimmy said and tossed his cards on the table.

"Was I not supposed to say that?" Genny asked Luke.

"You have to hold your cards close to your vest," Luke said, and brought his cards to the open button of her shirt. "And bluff when you need to."

"Damn, Luke," Joe said, taking it all in. "With the queen on your lap and those in your hand, you *are* lucky."

"We're calling this one a draw." Luke pushed all the money on the table toward the other men and patted Genny's thigh.

She hopped up as if he'd burned her leg. Joe and the Johnson brothers shook Luke's hand and said they hoped to see him back at the ranch again. Luke agreed with a nod.

"Walk me out and you can say hello to Etalon," he said to Genny,

At the front door they met up with Ruby who smiled at Luke and, despite Genny's presence, pointed a long red fingernail upstairs. A shake of Luke's head sent the woman to the second floor alone. At the blackjack table, Tricky had told Genny that she'd heard he'd turned Emerald down in the dining room. Genny had witnessed similar with Sapphire. Now Ruby.

Luke held open the screen door for Genny and on the porch he stretched. Even though they only had the moonlight she could see and almost feel the muscles rippling in this man's body. Along with the hair, the eyes, the grin, and the confidence, Luke was overwhelmingly attractive. And that deep Southern drawl, no wonder women wanted to get their hands on him.

"This is the most unusual night I've ever had at this house," Genny said without looking up at him and added shyly, "the best night."

"There's no holding cards close to the vest with you, is there?"

She smiled that smile.

"Grandpa said on Valentine's Day, years ago that I wear my heart on my sleeve."

"Why don't you and your heart come home with me?"

"Isn't it too late to start on my lessons tonight?" Genny asked, blushing.

"It's never too late, Valentine."

A nervous thrill raced through her at being called that for the first time. "Tricky is my new roommate." Genny shifted from her right foot to her left and chewed her lower lip. "She might draw the wrong conclusion." When Luke chuckled, she asked, "How about one morning this week?"

"Noon," he replied. "Any day."

"What's our first lesson?"

Luke walked down the steps, untethered and mounted Etalon.

"How to fight."

With that, he disappeared into the night.

"I'LL SEE you at the Cat's Eye before supper time, Tricky," Genny said, in the tiny kitchen of her house as she tucked the red and white checkered cloth over the food in the picnic basket.

"If you run into Ying, send him my way," Tricky called

out from her bedroom. "He can give me some lessons this afternoon."

"Shh," Genny said. "You are sworn to secrecy about my Luke lessons."

"I won't tell a soul." Tricky laughed. "It's been a week already. Quit stalling."

"The lessons are strictly business," Genny said, leaving the kitchen with the basket over her arm. "And I'm not stalling."

"You're stalling just like you did last month because you're nervous," Tricky said, poking her head out of her room. "Just go find Luke and don't hurry back."

A scratch sounded on the front door which no longer stuck since Luke had kicked it open. Genny turned the knob and golden sunshine of the unusually warm February day spilled into the room. Surprised to find Roscoe on the small porch she instantly glanced around for Luke but didn't see him anywhere.

"Hello, Roscoe, she said and petted his head. "What are you doing here, boy?" For an answer, the dog trotted halfway across the yard where he stopped and waited for her. "Are you here to round me up and herd me over to Luke's ranch?"

Meeting up with Roscoe, Genny remembered Luke saying moonstones protected those who traveled on water. She wondered how safe she would be with Luke Harper today. With a churning mixture of trepidation and anticipation, she headed south through the woods. Roscoe stayed close beside her, and reaching the pond, the collie stopped abruptly. Genny stopped, too. She thought she'd heard twigs snap. She looked up on the hillside and into the trees surrounding the water but didn't see anything. Roscoe's fur hackled and he growled. The bullfrog croaked and Genny smiled.

"It's just Moby-Dick," Genny said. The frog hopped into the pond and swam away. "If all goes well, maybe Harper will teach me to swim in this pond, Roscoe."

. . .

"THERE WENT YOUR CHANCE."

"You know I hate dogs, Selma," Seth said, chewing on his pinky fingernail.

"I know you're terrified of dogs."

"Shut up," Seth hissed. "I'll poison it."

"And drown her."

"Yes, yes. After I marry her."

AT THE GATE in the fence surrounding Luke's ranch Roscoe trotted slightly ahead of Genny, seeming to know where his master was and wanting to show him that he'd done his job. Though her anxiety mounted with each step, Genny followed the collie around the side of the log home. A hammock was strung between two large maple trees, but Luke wasn't in it. A little farther, she stopped and stared.

Pulling water up from the well, Luke's broad back was to her. His shirtless back. Deep wells on both their properties were fed by an underground stream which also kept her pond full. As Luke placed a wooden bucket on the ledge of the well, muscles rippled from his sun bronzed shoulders, down his back to the top of the snug denim pants. After scooping out a drink of water, he plowed his fingers through his thick hair.

Beyond a shadow of a doubt, Genny knew she had taken on more than she could handle with this experienced rogue. Figuring to sneak away before he could see her, she started backing up. But Roscoe barked and when Luke turned, he had only to raise a brow to halt her escape.

Genny quivered with the new sensations she felt only in Luke's presence. Muscles defined his chest and flexed in his arms. From her night with him at the Palace Hotel, she remembered well the dark hair swirling his indented navel and trailing down his flat stomach. Today it teased her to the open button at the top of his fly where it dipped into the pants riding low around his waist. Bringing her gaze back up his body her eyes met Luke's. His knowing grin was so cocky and sexy Genny pictured dropping the picnic basket and making a run for it because…

Because Luke Harper crossed all borders of tame and vanished into the wild.

"'Bout damn time."

"I was heading your way when Roscoe arrived."

"Uh-huh." He sounded unconvinced.

Genny's heart pounded as Luke tossed his shirt over his shoulder and swaggered toward her. His green gaze was so appraising she lowered her eyes and found herself back at the open button of his fly where she'd left off. She'd originally seen his britches, famous for their reinforcing rivets around the pockets, advertized in the *San Francisco Chronicle*. Following the path of the button fly led her to the mysterious masculine bulge in the crotch of his pants. Never had she been drawn to notice the copper rivets at the base of the button fly. And never had she seen denim pants worn so well by any man.

Until now. Until Luke. Quick, she told herself, say something remarkably clever to cover up that outrageous perusal.

"Did you know your pants are called Levi Jeans and were first made on Sacramento Street right here in San Francisco?"

"That's where I got 'em," he said. "What's in the basket?"

"Payment for today's lesson. Is food acceptable?"

"Sure is."

He dropped his shirt on a stack of firewood near the back door of the log house and swiped the basket from her. She made a grab for the basket, but he held it out of her reach as he was known to do.

Hands going to her hips, she said, "I fixed Grandpa's favorite meal; corncakes filled with minced beef called beef dodgers."

"Maybe you were on our way over here." He set the basket on the woodpile and peeked under the checkered cloth.

"I was," she assured him. "I brought a drink called flip that Vern makes with beer, rum and sugar. For dessert, I found Patty's recipe and baked flat cake cookies for the first time in years."

"Lesson or lunch first?"

"Lesson?"

"Roscoe, go lie down."

With Roscoe shooed safely out of the way, Luke took a step back and looked her over. When he nonchalantly buttoned the top button of his fly, Genny's cheeks flamed. Although he'd seemed relieved she wasn't a prostitute, did Luke suspect she had only the barest notion as to what was in his britches? Grace and Ruth deemed her innocence a virtue. Luke might laugh.

"Remember when I grabbed the back of your overalls the night you broke the headlamp?" Luke asked. "You need to wear britches, so no one else can grab you like that." She nodded and he unfastened one of her shoulder straps.

"I can do it," she said and as Luke dropped the strap, she unfastened the other one. Suggesting she tuck them into the bottom half of her overalls, she did so as he placed his hands on his hips. "What's wrong?"

"Someone could strangle you with the cord on your hat, so the cord needs to go. For today's lesson, take your hat off."

She tossed the hat on the woodpile with his shirt and her basket. She'd washed her hair this morning and had one long braid twined into a bun at the back of her head.

"How's that?"

"If we get to some of your other lessons your hair should be long and loose."

"What do you mean if?"

CHAPTER 11

"Let's see how you throw a punch," Luke said, ignoring her question. He raised his hands into the air, palms toward her with his fingers pressed together.

"I hope that *if* doesn't refer to my seduction lessons," she said, her fists propped on her hips. "There's no time to waste where Seth Comstock is concerned."

"Why haven't you picked up those ideas at your ranch?"

"What's done at my ranch is not the art of seduction. Now, is it?"

"No," Luke grumbled. "I'll teach you to fight him." He splayed his fingers and cupped them close together again. "But I already told you at the Palace Hotel he's a bad guy and I will not teach you how to seduce him."

"Streaks," Genny seethed and tossed the flat of her palm and fingers against Luke's open hand. Skin smacked skin. And a sharp pain stung her wrist. "Oww."

"What the hell was that?"

"A sockdolager punch."

"A baby swinging a sock doll lands a harder punch. Make a fist and keep your arm straight or you'll sprain your wrist. Try again."

Rubbing her right wrist, she said, "You don't know that Seth Comstock is a bad guy."

"I guarantee you he is," Luke replied, turning the backs of his hands toward her and motioning her to throw another punch. "And when the bad threatens to show itself, his eyelids flutter."

"But he's rich."

"You wouldn't know a rich man if you saw one."

"I certainly would," she snapped. Closing her eyes, she scrunched up her hand and tossed a second punch. Skin smacked skin. And her index finger bent sharply backward. "Ouch."

"Don't stick one knuckle out past the others," he said.

"I thought it would hurt more."

"Yeah, it'll hurt you. Knuckles flat. Eyes open."

"They were open."

"They weren't."

"Ooh." Doubling up her fist again, her third punch slapped her thumb into his palm. Skin smacked skin. And her wrist, finger and thumb all throbbed. "Oww." She shook her hand in the air and stomped the ground. "Owwch."

"Stop." He took hold of her right hand and positioned it. "Fist tight. Wrist straight. Knuckles flat. Eyes open." Genny put up both of her fists this time and Luke cocked a brow. With a sexy smirk he said, "Come get me, *babydoll.*"

"Just watch me."

"You bet I will."

Not taking sides, Roscoe's head turned left and right as Genny threw one-two punches at the handsome, half-naked man as fast as she could. Her bun loosened letting the long braid fall down her back, but she didn't let that faze her. Deflecting her blows with his large, strong hands, Luke offered pointers and encouragement. When she winced, he caught her forearms, tugged her forward and inspected her hands and wrists. Worn out, Roscoe lay down on a patch of rye grass and closed his eyes.

"Your right wrist looks a little swollen," Luke said. "Had enough?"

"No."

Genny shoved wisps of hair out of her face and realized her hair was no longer braided. Luke grabbed her hat and broke the cord. Towering over her, he ran his hands through her long hair. Fire heated her scalp, and her face came within inches of his bare chest as he tied her hair at the nape of her neck. Her heart was pounding and her stomach flip flopping as Luke stepped back. When he plowed his fingers through his own hair, she nearly swooned. His muscles flexed and as his flat stomach bowed inward the front of his jeans revealed more skin beneath his belly button. Genny took a calming breath and stepped from one foot to the other trying to strengthen her wobbly knees.

"I'll throw the punches this time," Luke said.

He'd much rather be giving this sexy, gorgeous woman the lessons in seduction. But it would be a cold day in hell before he did it for any man's sake but his own. Did Genny know how delicate she appeared with the curling black tendrils spilling over her arched brows and around her dainty ears? Never had he run his fingers through hair so silky soft or which fell so thick and luxuriously down a slender back to nearly touch a tiny waist. How good would those long locks feel brushing his naked chest if he taught her how to make love to him?

So damn good.

Genny's long sleeved, buttoned shirt strained across her full breasts and Luke wished every last button would pop off. He suspected it wouldn't take much for her looser-than-usual overalls, riding low on her hips, to slip down around her red boots.

"Try to block my punches," he said, bringing himself back to this lesson. "Ready?"

"Ready." Frowning with concentration, she held up two dainty hands in the air palms out.

Closing his fist, he tapped one feminine palm and then

her other one. To her credit she didn't back up or close her eyes.

"That's a sock doll punch, Harper," Genny taunted him, splayed her fingers and then cupped them close together again as he had done.

"Well," he drawled. "I'm a lover not a hitter when it comes to women."

"Come get me, *loverboy.*"

"I'd like to hear you say that to me in the bedroom."

"Thanks for the first lesson in seduction."

Luke countered that with a lightning fast, soft tap of his right fist to her shoulder instantly following it with his left fist pressing lightly against her taut tummy. Her lilac eyes flew wide open, and her pink lips parted in stunned surprise. Touching his right fist under her jaw, he closed her mouth. She backhanded his fist away and placed her hands on her hips.

"That's a wolf in sheep's clothing fighting, Harper," she said.

"You'd better fight just like that if a wolf's at your door, little lamb."

Fuming, she charged him fists swinging. Luke blocked her every wild blow as gently as possible while backing up to soften the impact to her hands, wrists and forearms. Genny's hair bounced free of the cord, her breasts jiggled, buttons popped, and the overalls slid down her hips. She stumbled backward, frantically clutching at her overalls and shoving hair out of her eyes. Luke caught her right wrist and kept her from falling.

"Oww," she wailed. "My sore wrist."

When he released her, Genny stumbled backwards, let go of her overalls and windmilled her arms in wide circles trying to regain her balance. Luke grabbed her elbow and was careful not to let her fall even when she cuffed the corner of his left eye.

"Ouch," he barked and yanked her against him.

Skin smacked skin. And sizzled.

"Had enough?" she asked, her lips touching his shoulder.

"No," Luke said, his voice husky.

"I didn't mean to hit your eye."

He knew that and savored her warm whisper on his skin and the naked cleavage molded to his bare chest. When she leaned back just enough to look at his face it exposed her breasts almost to her nipples. He brought his eyes up to meet hers and she grabbed her shirt with both hands.

"Would you be a gentleman and pull up my overalls?"

Luke cocked his head to one side and then the other in a valiant effort to slow the blood pumping fast and furiously. He stepped back and surveyed the situation. The buttons had granted his wish, but she'd closed the shirt over her breasts. However, the cutest belly button he'd ever seen peeked out at him. The bottom shirt button remained intact, letting her shirttails hide the vee between her pretty legs. Her overalls lay clumped around the tops of her cowboy boots. With a groan, he grasped the overalls and pulled them up to her waist.

"Well, that went against every damn grain in my body, lady."

"Thank you, sir."

Genny placed the straps over her shoulders which sufficiently covered her breasts. Sooner or later, Luke intended to see this beautiful temptress stark naked from head to toe.

Later. When Comstock was no longer a threat.

"Forget what I said about getting rid of the overalls at least until you get some bigger shirts."

"I just finished making a pink blouse like one I saw in the *San Francisco Chronicle*."

"Good, wear it." Before she could reply, he added, "Hungry?"

"Starved. You?"

Yeah. For her. He put on his shirt and buttoned it.

"We'll sit in the rocking chairs on the porch while we eat," he said and grabbed the basket.

"And have a drinking lesson?"

"Hell, I need a drink. I'm probably gonna have a black eye."

A COUPLE of hours had passed when Luke heard the noise and opened his eyes. Genny's head lay on his shoulder and her right arm, with cloth strips immobilizing her wrist, rested on his chest. He wondered what she'd say if she knew her right leg was wedged between his thighs. Easing out from under her, he swung himself out of the hammock and walked to the front of the house. Riding shotgun in one of four delivery wagons, Ying waved.

The first order of fresh hay and oats had revived the horses. With this order they'd thrive. During the second half of January, he and Ying had put a new roof on the stable. In February they'd started on the fenceposts. The lumber being delivered now would finish that job. Ying accompanied the men with the hay and oats to the stable. Luke helped the other two men unload and stack wooden rails and posts near the corral. He'd already paid for all the supplies but gave the delivery men a bonus. Surprised, they thanked Luke profusely and left. Ying came around the side of the house, holding the reins to the horse Luke had taught him how to saddle.

"Is that Genevieve asleep in the hammock out back?" Ying asked.

"Yup."

"On my way here, I saw Tricky crossing the road to the Cat's Eye. I'm heading back that way and she wants to know if Genny is planning to work tonight."

"I doubt it. Please ask Patty to pack up a couple of suppers and I'll come by to get them."

. . .

WHEN GENNY ROLLED, so did her stomach and the world spun most sickeningly. She had a headache something terrible and put her hands to her forehead and stomach. Why was she still rocking? Why was her bedroom so bright? She moaned in misery.

"Time to wake up."

Squinting through her fingers, Luke was looking down at her and it all came flooding back.

The lesson, the lunch and...the flip.

On the front porch against Luke's advice, she'd had two shots of flip right along with him. He had discouraged her as she poured herself a third shot after pouring his. When she poured herself a fourth, Luke had taken it from her and drank it before she could do so. And that's where her memory left off.

"How'd I get in this hammock?" she mumbled, closing her eyes against the setting sun.

"I offered to tuck you into my new bed but you said no, so I carried you here after you proved you can't do shots of beer and rum."

"I'm dying."

Luke laughed. "I thought that a couple of times when I was twenty. Roll out of that hammock or I'll leave you here to die."

"I can't roll anything, Harper."

Luke leaned over and scooped her out of the hammock. With a whimper, she rested her head on his shoulder and flattened her right hand against his chest. When she mumbled that she had to work at the ranch, he just chuckled.

"You can't even stand up," he said, carrying her around the side of the house.

"I have to give the key to the hiding place for the jewel box to Vern or Patty."

"I'll drop you off at your house and take the key to them. Since it'll be dark soon, it's lucky I have two head-lamps again." When she muttered something unintelligible, he smothered a laugh. "Roscoe, come on boy, we're going for a ride."

The dog bounded after them. Closing her eyes Genny didn't open them again until Luke sat her in the seat of his Runabout. Pressing her lips tightly together, she managed to keep her beef dodger and flat cake cookie down. Luke started the automobile and at the gate to his ranch he stopped before turning onto the road.

"I'll try not to make this a rough ride," Luke said.

Genny rolled her eyes and that was her undoing. She lurched precariously over the side of vehicle and Luke grabbed the back of her overalls just as she lost her lunch. Wiping her mouth with her sleeve, she wanted to dig a hole, crawl into it and hide from the man who'd just prevented her from breaking her neck in a putrid puddle. He gave her a gentle tug and she was able to sit in the seat with less nausea.

"Maybe next time you'll listen to me when I tell you not to do something," Luke said and pulled onto the road to the Cat's Eye Ranch.

"Maybe...oh hush up, Harper."

Luke drove on and Genny closed her eyes again. Near the pond, furtive movement in a cluster of saplings caught his attention. There was no breeze, but those trees had swayed. He stopped the vehicle and scanned the woods. Roscoe growled. The gas headlamps were focused straight ahead on the road and the approaching twilight made it impossible to see into the woods.

Biloxi was as familiar to Luke as the back of his hand. He knew people in all the high places and in the lowest of the low. If your grandfather trusted their grandfather, the high and low didn't much matter. Along his stretch of the Mississippi Sound, you conducted business, you might interact socially and at the very least you watched out for each other. Back home, he had his family and loyal friends everywhere.

Not so in the Bay area. And something didn't feel right.

"What's wrong, Luke?"

"Probably nothing," he said and headed down the road again. "Don't go to the pond alone."

"But I cross the road by the pond to avoid the killing curve where you almost ran over me twice in one day."

"Once," he said seriously, his gut warning him not to let his guard down. "I take it you didn't get a look at the other driver."

"No, I was too busy running because he didn't swerve to miss me like *you* did." As they neared her home, she asked, "When I feel better, will you give me driving lessons?"

"Swimming lessons are next."

"You just passed up my house."

"We'll double back."

At the Cat's Eye Ranch, Luke took the jewel box key and hopped out of the automobile. He rounded the side of the house as he'd seen Vern do. Passing a root cellar, he followed his nose to the screen door of the kitchen. Patty was ready for him with a basket of fried chicken, mashed potatoes with gravy and apple pie. Luke gave them the key and explained about Genny and the flip. Vern chuckled and shook his head. Patty asked about the reddish bruise at the corner of Luke's left eye. As he pulled out money for supper, he told them of the fighting lessons. Tears sprang to Patty's eyes just before she hugged him. Vern smiled and refused the money.

"I CAN'T HAVE supper with you, Curt," Genny said, sitting in Luke's Runabout.

"Why not?" Curt Skidmore asked.

"I'm not feeling well and a friend is taking me home."

Curt was blocking the opening to her side of the vehicle and had never once lived up to the meaning of his name which was courteous.

"We done heared your grandpappy and his shotgun's

gone," Curt said, pushing strands of over-the-ears, greasy red hair out of his squinty brown eyes. "How 'bout I be your friend?"

There was never a shotgun. It was a rumor circulated by Vern and Patty to protect her.

"No. I umm…have…uh…*boy*friend."

"Since when does a madam have a boyfriend?"

CHAPTER 12

"Since he owns the ranch next to mine." Maybe it was just her befuddled state, but Genny thought that seemed like a good rumor to circulate. "And please don't refer to me as a madam."

And yet as the owner of a brothel that's exactly what she was. The word madam burned in her throat, churned in her stomach and Genny fervently wished Curt would go away. Luckily, he couldn't afford to visit very often, and Opal, with her black hair, was his usual pick. Curt's younger brother, who liked Onyx, always accompanied him and sure enough there came Billy Skidmore riding through the entrance to the ranch.

"I can give it to you better'n old man Cavender." Curt snorted and puffed out his chest.

Roscoe lay curled on the floorboard around her feet. But when Curt grabbed Genny's left wrist, the dog stood and growled.

If only she felt better, she'd punch him. "Let go, Curt."

"I want from you what I get from Opal." He tightened his grip.

Roscoe barked and snapped, baring his teeth in a vicious snarl.

"She told you to let go," Luke said as he walked toward them. "Now I'm telling you."

Curt turned to face Luke and made a show of releasing Genny by holding his hand in the air. He backed up as Luke set the basket of food in Genny's lap.

"Looks like you ain't too sick to have supper with him." Curt frowned at Genny and took another step away from Luke and the barking dog.

"Roscoe," Luke said, which resulted in the dog immediately quieting beside Genny.

"I recollect now Cavender's done gone," Curt said and then glowered at Luke. "Yer the boyfriend, ain't ya?"

Genny was fairly certain she was going to die of humiliation before this day ended. She prayed Luke wouldn't deny being her boyfriend because Curt and Billy were the mean and rough sort. About the same age as Luke, that's all the men had in common. Curt was plain and pushy, while Billy was short and stocky.

"Who are you?" Luke asked.

"Curt Skidmore. Me and my brother, Billy, got a farm over yonder." He jerked his thumb at a second man, with similar greasy red hair, approaching them on a scrawny, bareback donkey. "We done give this whorehouse a lot of business."

"Who's he?" Billy Skidmore asked his brother regarding Luke.

"Luke Harper," Luke replied for himself. Not skipping a beat or offering to shake hands, he added, "The boyfriend."

"We knowed Genevieve first," Curt said to Luke.

Billy slid off the donkey so fast he nearly fell. Trying to make his clumsiness look like the donkey's fault, Billy hit the animal in the side with his fist. The donkey's head lowered, and he wandered toward the kitchen. Genny's loathing of Billy's abuse was mirrored on Luke's face.

Hoping to move the Skidmores along, Genny quickly said, "Opal and Onxy will be happy to see you."

"We don't give a shit 'bout them whores," Billy sneered through rotten teeth.

"Then leave and don't come back," Luke said.

Not knowing what to say to that, Billy's face turned red, and he clenched both fists.

Joe Sanchez driving a four-seater Ford Model F, with the Johnson brothers in tow, pulled to a stop alongside the Runabout.

"Howdy, Luke," Joe said with a smile that quickly faded as he sensed the discord.

The Johnson brothers bailed out of the vehicle and came up behind Luke.

"Hey, buddy," Jimmy said, clamping his hand on Luke's shoulder.

Scowling at Curt and Billy, Mike stopped on Luke's other side and asked, "Is there a problem, Luke?"

"Doesn't have to be," Luke said as Joe joined them making it four against two.

"Ya think you can just show up and steal the purdiest gal?" Curt lifted the corner of his lip, displaying missing and crooked teeth.

"Harper didn't just think it," Mike said and folded his arms over his chest.

Not bright enough to pick up on Mike's comment, Billy elbowed his brother and said, "Steal her out from *under* us? Huh, Curt?"

"She was never under either of you," Luke replied, his expression one of cool disdain.

"That's for damn sure," Joe said.

"Not yet," Curt said. "Huh, Billy?"

Billy stepped toward Luke in a move of intimidation. Luke, several inches taller and far more muscular, didn't budge. Tension built as Luke stared down both brothers. Billy flinched and shifted a side glance at Curt who grabbed his shoulder and pulled him back.

"Next time, Harper, when the odds are even," Curt said.

"Step foot on this ranch again and it'll be your *last* time," Luke replied.

The Skidmores, their small eyes narrowed, and haphazard teeth gritted, backed away from Luke and the others. Curt shoved aside a stringy strand of hair and gave the house a longing look before slinking away. Billy hollered for the donkey, but it was nowhere to be seen, so he caught up with his brother and they meandered toward the opening in the split rail fence.

"I know you didn't need our help with the Skidmores," Joe said as the brothers trudged onto the main road, "but I'm damn happy we were here to see you get rid of them."

"Vern would fuss at them when they caused trouble, but they never listened," Mike said. "He'll be relieved they're gone."

"They drank, they stank, and they cheated at cards," Jimmy said. "Good riddance."

That broke the tension, and everyone chuckled.

"It was a united front," Luke said to these men proving to be his friends.

"Speaking of cards, let's play some poker," Joe said.

"I'm busy tonight," Luke said and turned to Genny who gave him a weak smile. "How about tomorrow night?"

Joe and the Johnsons agreed. Vern came into view from the direction of the root cellar. Patting the donkey's head, Vern was feeding him carrots. Luke figured Vern knew the animal belonged to the *soaplock Skidmores over yonder* and waved to indicate everything was all right.

"Luke," Genny said softly.

"We're going," he replied.

Luke shook hands with Joe and the Johnsons then got into his automobile. As he and Genny left the ranch there was no sign of the Skidmores.

Genny told him, "If I'd felt better, I'd have punched—"

"You're either coming home with me or I'm sleeping at your house," Luke said so firmly that Genny didn't even try to argue.

"My house."

"YOU GENTS NEED A RIDE?" Seth Comstock asked.

The men ambling along the dusty road looked at each other as Seth slowed the stolen, two-seater vehicle to a stop.

"Our farm's just yonder," the taller of the red-haired men said, eyeing him warily.

"Oh, then you've probably heard of the Cat's Eye Ranch," Seth said conversationally.

"Yeah, but we done been kicked outa there by a fella named Harper," the shorter man muttered.

"Why did he kick you off the ranch?"

"Cuz Harper knowed me and my brother been givin' it to his woman better'n him," the taller man replied with a snort and puffed out chest.

"I hate that son of a bitch," the short man said.

"Well then, we have something in common," Seth said, as Selma nodded her agreement. "And who might you be?"

"I'm Curt and this here's Billy," the taller one said.

"Want to earn some money and get even with Luke Harper?"

"Yeah," the red-haired men said together.

Yes. Indeed. Seth relished the rush of coming into his own again.

"Hop on the back of my automobile, boys."

IN HER COZY LITTLE FARMHOUSE, Genny lit kerosene lamps and invited Luke to make himself at home while she changed clothes. He sat down at a small desk where the society section of the newspaper was folded to a page of circled items, one of which was a blouse. A hurricane lantern illuminated an ink well, pen and paper. On the top sheet of paper, in what he recognized as Genny's handwriting, was a well written description of the fashions and the folks wearing them at the Palace Hotel. Along the back of the desk, propped against the wall, about a dozen books were held between horseshoe bookends. Next to a well-worn Bible, there were two books written by a Swiss author, Johanna Spyri, originally published in 1880; *Heidi: Her Years of Wandering and Learning* and *Heidi: How She Used What She Learned*. A brief description spoke of a young girl left in her grandfather's care in the Swiss Alps. Herman Melville's *Moby-Dick* was another book on the desk and next to it was Emily Post's *Purple and Fine Linen*. He noticed the book about the origins of names and another one explaining the meanings of colors. Webster's Dictionary was there along with an English-to-French translation handbook and a book on the history of jewels. Luke picked up a thick book on Greek, Roman and Egyptian mythology and it fell open to a page with a folded down corner that described Adonis. Flipping through the book, he read about Diana, maiden goddess of the moon, the hunt and nature. Praised for her intelligence Diana protected mothers and children, earning a place of honor among women.

In a chapter on Egyptian mythology, Luke was stopped cold by a man's name.

"You're welcome to borrow any of my books," came Genny's warm voice. "That is if you like to read."

"I do, thanks." He liked her a whole lot more and placed the book back in its spot. Turning his head in Genny's direction, Luke's entire body immediately caught fire. She either didn't realize the sex appeal she exuded or thought he was made of steel. The scooped neck of her loose, cotton gown displayed a tantalizing glimpse of cleavage and the hem floated just above slender ankles and bare feet. Ebony hair tumbled like a cape around her body. All lilac eyes and pink lips, draped in gauzy white, this woman was as ethereal as the mythical creature Diana.

The moonstone, her hunt for a safe and secure life, her love of animals and woodlands.

Genny was also the spitfire siren he'd just spent the day fighting and drinking with.

The seduction, her plan to marry for money, her lack of love for the intended husband.

Was Genevieve Moonstone Morgan the virgin goddess of light and goodness or the femme fatale able to mesmerize and destroy?

Virgin? Luke would like nothing better than to find out tonight.

No. Hell, no. Not a gamble he was willing to take under the circumstances. He'd vowed not to teach her anything for Comstock's benefit. Only his own. He frowned with frustration.

"You look hungry. I set up two places for us at the kitchen table. Follow me."

She turned away and follow her, he did. He would not follow her to her bedroom. He'd sleep on the daybed he'd noticed in the front room. It would make for a long night. Maybe she had some more of that damn flip in the kitchen.

"LUKE?" Genny said, hearing a chair scrape across the kitchen's wooden floor. No, he'd brought her home two days ago. She'd been dreaming of him. Again.

"Good afternoon," Tricky said coming to her bedroom doorway. "Luke checked on you yesterday while you were still sick and asleep. So if he spent last night here," she began, raising a black brow, "he's gone now."

Genny sat up in bed and rubbed her eyes. "It's afternoon?"

"Yes." Tricky nodded. "It's nearly time for me to go to work. I'm waiting for Ying. He's giving me a ride to the Cat's Eye on one of those big beasts he says Luke calls American Quarter horses. So was he?"

"Was he what?"

"Here last night?"

"Well now, if you were here last night, you'd know the

answer to that," Genny said with a smile and a raised brow of her own. Getting up and going to the kitchen, they talked as Genny heated water for a bath. Then Tricky sat on the end of Genny's bed as Genny sank into the oblong bathtub behind a small dressing screen. "And just where were you last night, Tricky?"

"Having a roll in the hay with Ying. Do you know what that means?"

"I know you're in love with Ying," Genny said, since she wasn't too sure about the answer to Tricky's question.

"It means making love." Tricky added in her outspoken fashion, "Last night we made love for the first time in the barn. And yes, I'm in love with Ying."

"You did?" Genny's eyes were wide as she sat in her bath. "Has he said he loves you?"

"Yes, and yes," Tricky replied somewhat dreamily and then giggled. "Of course, he probably said it because he's afraid of Huan."

"Ying said it because love is written all over his face every time he looks at you."

"I hope so." With that, Tricky drifted back to her own room.

Visualizing Luke's handsome face, with images of his naked back, muscular chest and flat stomach floating through her mind, Genny finished her bath. As she dried off, she was reminded of all the bare skin on her body that Luke had seen and some he'd touched. Wrapping the towel around her head, she recalled how her scalp had heated when he'd threaded his fingers through her hair. After dressing, she grabbed up her towel and planning to hang it outside to dry, she walked through the house.

"Have you seen Luke today?" Genny asked as casually as possible.

"Only at a distance," Tricky said from her bedroom. "He and Ying were already out working on the fence when I left the barn this morning."

A knock sounded on the door and Tricky called out excitedly, "Ying's here."

Genny opened the door to another mild day. Standing in the sunshine was Ying as well as Roscoe. Genny draped her towel over the doorknob and stared at the surprises with them. Tricky joined them on the porch and shyly pecked Ying's cheek. His face reddened as he grinned and hugged her.

"Ying, what's all this about?" Genny asked and swung her arm wide.

"Luke sent the black mare for you and the gray one for Tricky," Ying replied in regard to two of the four mares among the ten horses at Luke's ranch. He held out a folded piece of paper. "He sent this note for you, Genevieve."

Tricky turned in a daze to the pretty horse that was a little smaller than the one Ying had ridden. Leading Tricky to the mare, he helped her into the saddle and gave her some instruction.

"Are you coming to the Cat's Eye later, Genevieve?" Tricky asked, petting the horse's mane.

"Yes," Genny replied, note in hand. "But I need to braid my hair. I'll see you there later."

"Read the note first," Ying reminded her and mounted his horse.

Roscoe stayed, but Ying and Tricky rode toward the Cat's Eye. Genny unfolded the piece of paper. In a man's bold handwriting the note said for her to ride Esprit to his ranch and bring along something she could learn to swim in.

"I'm going to conquer a fear today," she told the horse and dog. With a quick pat to Roscoe's head, she stepped back inside and called over her shoulder, "I'll be right out, and we'll go find Harper."

Leaving the front door ajar, Genny returned to her bedroom realizing she had nothing but her regular clothing to swim in. Pondering that dilemma, she was about to braid her hair when something slammed through a front window, shattering the glass. The horse whinnied and Roscoe barked. Genny ran into the front room and across the porch. To her immense relief, both Esprit and Roscoe were unharmed. Esprit had shied away from the house, but Roscoe was already herding the mare back toward the porch.

The sound of a fleeing vehicle provided the sole clue as to the perpetrator of the crime. Shaken to her very core Genny grabbed the reins to Esprit. So thankful to Luke for the saddle, she leapt into it and called to Roscoe. Nudging the mare, Genny headed across the front yard and onto the road. Looking north, toward the killing curve, all that remained were dust clouds of a dirty deed.

But a maniacal laugh floated to her ears.

Making a split decision as to pursuing the culprit or confiding in Luke, Genny rode like the wind.

CHAPTER 13

LUKE HEARD THE GALLOPING HOOVES AND ROSCOE'S BARK. Having just washed up and changing into clean clothes, Luke was in the first-floor office he'd turned into his bedroom. Jeans and boots on, he tossed open the tall window and leaned out over the sill. Black hair flying and black mane fluttering a beautiful woman on her spirited horse raced his way. Her expression said she was terrified.

"Genny," he yelled.

"Luke!" The fright sounded in her voice, too. She steered the mare straight for his window and reined her in, coming to a fast halt. "Help me."

Plucking her off the horse Luke pulled her through his window. She wrapped her arms around him so hard and fast, he took a step back and they landed sideways across his bed.

"Help you what, babydoll?" Luke asked, holding her trembling body on top of his.

Slender arms locked around his neck as her knees and calves molded to the outsides of his hips and thighs. Her breathing came in shallow gulps, her heart thumping wildly against his bare chest. Smelling of sweet lilac, she wore a soft blouse with buttons down the back and dark britches that clung tightly to her perfect fanny. Luke had

pictured himself between her legs a thousand times. And
now here they were in his big, comfortable bed. He wanted
to roll her over and spend the rest of the day making love
to her.

"Please come to my little house with me," Genny whispered in his ear.

"Is this your idea of trying to seduce me?" he teased and
ran his hands down her back. As she seemed to consider
this, he slid his hands over her rounded bottom and gently
squeezed.

"Stop that, Harper." She wiggled her fanny and tugged
her arms out from under him.

Luke sat up, keeping her on his lap. When he brushed
her slightly damp hair away from her face, her lilac eyes
silently scolded him for where his hands had been. Her
soft, long-sleeved blouse, the same deep pink as her full
lips, must be her new one. The rounded neckline teased
him with a glimpse of cleavage. But he was glad there were
no front buttons to pop off, exposing her breasts to other
men. When she started to move off his lap, he clamped his
hands down on her thighs.

"Sit still and tell me what's wrong."

Staying put, Genny quickly related exactly what had
happened after Ying and Tricky left her house. Luke didn't
say a word but eased her off his lap and shut the window.
He put on a denim shirt, and grabbing his holstered gun off
the bedpost, he slipped the holster around his shoulders. If
her bottom wasn't already hot enough from his touch, the
danger and power emanating from this masterful man
spread fire throughout her entire body. After shrugging
into a jacket, he picked up an envelope and some cash from
a roll top desk and slid both to an inside pocket. Then
taking Genny's hand, he trailed her behind him down the
hall toward the front room.

"Luke, talk to me," Genny said, trying to keep up with
his long strides. "What do you think about this? Where are
we going?"

"I think we're taking the shortcut through the woods to the Cat's Eye. Vern, Joe, the Johnson brothers, and Ying will be there. You'll stay with them while I double back to your house. I'll meet you at your ranch later."

"No, absolutely not." Genny tugged her hand free, stepped in front of him and yanked open the door. "I'm going with you."

"The hell you are," he said as she darted across the porch ahead of him.

As Luke shut the door, Genny bailed off the porch and disappeared around the side of the log home. She was in the process of mounting Esprit when Luke grabbed her off the horse and stood her to the ground.

Facing him and nerves frayed, she cried, "You might need me."

"I do need you," Luke said a little gruffly, taking the conversation in a different direction. "But I can wait until you want me instead of needing Comstock."

"Can you wait, loverboy?" she asked. "Because if you think I was trying to seduce you a few minutes ago, I haven't even begun."

"I told you the night we met I could resist you." But not forever.

"Streaks!" She slid her foot into the stirrup and mounted Esprit.

Luke grasped the mare's reins before Genny could and led the prancing horse and prickly rider to the hitching post where Etalon was tethered.

"Roscoe, go to the Cat's Eye," Luke said, and snapped his fingers toward the shortcut.

The dog vanished into the woods. Luke tossed the reins to Genny and as he anticipated, she nudged Esprit into a gallop.

"Try to keep up, Harper."

Racing across the front of Luke's property toward the road, Genny was in the lead. But she heard Luke gaining on her. The stallion, like his rider, was bigger, stronger and faster than she and her mare. Luke galloped up alongside her and then easily passed her by.

Genny had forgotten about being afraid as she reached the road. But then she was with Luke afterall. Though he had passed her, he never went so far ahead that he was out of sight. Genny wondered where a riverboat gambler had learned to ride so expertly. It was as if he were born to it. By the time she reached her little house, Luke was examining the broken window.

"Did you leave your front door open?" he asked, pointing to it.

"Umm…no…" she replied, dismounting. Noticing her towel over the doorknob, she said, "Yes, I guess I did."

Luke went into the house with Genny right behind him. Amidst the broken glass, there was a slab of raw meat tied around a big rock in the middle of her front room floor.

"Whatever is that?" she asked.

"Poisoned meat."

"I don't understand."

"I'm guessing it was supposed to land on the porch for Roscoe," Luke said, then grabbed the towel and used it to pick up the poisoned meat.

"Oh no, why?"

"Somebody wants Roscoe dead," Luke said.

"Who?" Genny asked.

"The Skidmores come to mind," Luke growled. "I'll dump the meat into that big barrel out back where I assume you and your grandfather burned trash."

Genny found some matches next to a lamp and gave them to him. As he took off around the side of the house, she closed the shutter over the broken window and pulled the front door shut. Then she joined Luke who had deposited the meat in the barrel and set it on fire. No wildlife would be poisoned. As he took her hand and backed away from the fumes, her thoughts flew from being pulled through his bedroom window, to him setting her body on fire, to his seduction challenge, to his horseman- ship, to his caring about animals.

If only he had money and stability like Seth Comstock.

She momentarily closed her eyes as if she could hide from the truth; she did want Luke. More than she fully understood and more than he could possibly imagine.

Luke wrapped an arm around her and gave her a hug. She smiled up at him. The look on his face said he was not about to overreact, but neither was he treating this inci- dent lightly. Saying they'd get back to the swimming lesson soon, they mounted their horses. This time he rode beside her all the way to her ranch.

"We passed the Skidmores on our way here," Joe said a little later.

Luke was glad the Cat's Eye wasn't open, yet. Only Joe, Mike, Jimmy, Vern, Patty, Ying, and Tricky were seated or standing around the supper table, listening to what had happened.

"But they were halfway between the city and their farm," Mike said.

"How could the Skidmores have covered the distance from my house to where you saw them so quickly?" Genny asked.

"I say we pay Curt and Billy Skidmore a visit and find out," Jimmy said.

"The lawyer in me says they have plausible deniability," Joe said, shaking his head.

Luke nodded. "If they were involved, someone tried to give them an alibi."

"Who'd be in cahoots with the Skidmores?" Vern asked.

"Someone with an automobile," Luke replied. As that idea took hold, others voiced their agreement. He looked at Genny and asked, "You heard an automobile, right?"

"Yes," she replied.

"Was it the same one that almost ran over you?" Luke asked.

Since no one but Luke knew about that incident, his question set off a round of discussion and some scolding of Genny from both Patty and Vern.

"The reason for her fighting lessons?" Patty asked Luke.

"Partly," Luke said, and looked back at Genny. "Was it the same vehicle?"

"All I saw was dust," she said.

"I can see the Skidmores trying to poison Roscoe," Joe said. "But frankly, they don't have the brains to cover their tracks much less a vehicle to haul them halfway to the city."

"I don't know about the vehicle," Mike began, "but they're definitely not playing with a full deck of cards."

At the mention of cards, Vern noticed the time and unlocked the front door. Several customers moseyed in and mixed with the jewels just drifting into the parlor or dining room. Patty returned to the kitchen and Tricky headed to her blackjack table. Ying said he was going to check on the horses at Luke's ranch and would be back for Tricky. Ruby found Joe as the Johnson brothers went in search of Ruth and Grace. Sapphire and Emerald spotted Luke but kept their distance.

"Luke, I know you're keeping your cards close to your vest," Genny said when they were alone at the supper table. "But please tell me who you think is behind this."

"Comstock." Luke's answer drained the blood from Genny's face.

"No. Why would he want to hurt Roscoe?"

Luke remembered thinking he'd seen someone in the woods near her pond. Roscoe had sensed it, too. And that's exactly why Comstock wanted Roscoe dead.

"I didn't like ol' Comstock's looks in *San Francisco Chronicle*," Patty said, setting two plates of flakey fish and buttered corn before Luke and Genny. "Eat."

"It wasn't Seth Comstock." Genny shook her head. "There's no reason or connection."

"My gut says whoever almost ran you over, tried to poison Roscoe," Luke said.

"I was dressed in my overalls and cowboy hat when I was almost run over south of Grandpa's house. Seth Comstock wouldn't have recognized me," Genny pointed out. "I admit he knows the location of my ranch because he sent that New Year's Eve invitation to me. But how would he know where Grandpa lived or that Roscoe and I might be there today?" She paused a moment and said, "It's just the Skidmores."

"It's Comstock."

Genny shrugged and said she didn't have an appetite. Luke began eating and when he made a motion with his fork, Genny ate, too, and her color returned. After they finished their suppers, Genny returned their dishes to the kitchen. As she took up her post at the front door, Vern called to Luke from the parlor saying his card table was ready and waiting.

"I can't imagine the Skidmores have any friends with an automobile," Joe said as he met up with Luke in the foyer. "I can't imagine they have friends at all for that matter."

The two men sat down across from each other at the table Luke had asked Vern to move into a far corner of the parlor. With his back to the wall, Luke had a clear view of the entire room and hallway. Vern had placed shots of whiskey and a deck of cards in the center of their table.

"Did they ever catch who ran over Genny's mother?" Luke asked and threw back a shot.

"No." Joe did the same with his whiskey. "There was a rumor she was seeing a man from town and that it ended badly. No clue who or if the gossip was even true."

They thanked Vern as he dropped off two more shots at their table. He continued delivering whiskey and beer to customers in the parlor and some out on the porch.

"Any clues at the scene of the accident?" Luke asked.

"Evidently gasoline and sparks from the crash caught Garnet on fire. Her body was barely recognizable when found. Gruesome," Joe replied. "I don't know what kind of person leaves another human being to burn up in a ditch or who would attempt to run Genevieve down, but whoever tried to poison Roscoe is after *you*, Luke," Joe said.

"Yeah, I know." Luke threw back the second shot and drummed his fingers on the table.

IT WAS the evening of March fifth when Genny spotted Etalon and Esprit tethered to the hitching post in front of the Cat's Eye porch. After the attempted poisoning of Roscoe, a cold snap had prevented her swimming lesson. But Luke was here now to see her safely home later and she all but skipped through the dining room into the foyer.

"Aren't you just the prettiest little lady in all of San Francisco?" a robust man in his mid-forties said to Genny as he bustled his way through the front door.

"She is indeed," the man who walked in behind him said, ogling her. "That's why she's out here in the country and not in one of those sleazy dance halls in the Barbary Coast."

"I've never seen hair so long and lovely," the first man said, taking hold of a loose lock.

Somehow knowing Luke was nearby every day, Genny had forgotten all about braiding her hair and hiding underneath her cowboy hat. Both of these strangers were dressed in crisp suits and had arrived via a fancy automobile. She tugged her hair out of the man's plump hand and in a grandiose gesture he swept one arm in front of his chest and bowed.

"My name is Reginald, but you may call me Reggie," he said and held out his hand.

"Pleased to meet you." Genny shook his soft hand and when she tried to pull free, he held tight. "The Cat's Eye Ranch offers supper, card games and seven jewels to choose from."

"I choose you. My little diamond..." Reginald scrutinized her homespun blouse, britches and cowboy boots while still holding onto her hand and finished, "...in the rough." Turning to the man with him, he then said, "This is my friend, George."

Ignoring Reginald's comments, the introduction of his friend afforded Genny the opportunity to withdraw her hand from him and extend it to George.

"Welcome, gentlemen," she said politely. "Please make yourself at home."

Genny wasted no time putting distance between her and the two men by hurrying down the hall. All evening she had collected money in the foyer and helped Vern serve drinks. But her thoughts revolved around Luke as usual. She wanted to hear his deep voice and feel his reassuring touch. At the archway of the parlor, there were at least a dozen men playing cards, most of whom were waiting for a turn upstairs. Intending to make her way to a far corner where Luke sat with Joe, she took a step but was stopped by a hand closing around her upper arm.

"If we were in Sacramento, you'd beg to make yourself at home with me," Reginald said, his smile revealing a gold eye tooth. Holding onto her, his eyes traveled from her face to her breasts and, purposely leaning backward, on down to her buttocks. He made a loud, animal-like howl of approval and asked, "How about it?"

Luke caught Genny's eye and cocked a rakish brow as Joe and others turned to look.

"No, thank you," Genny replied to Reginald as George surveyed Tricky's blackjack table and other poker games going on in the parlor.

"But I'm so rich," Reginald bellowed with a boastful laugh as if everyone knew that.

"Let's pick out a couple of these cowboys and show 'em how to play poker, Reggie," George said under his breath.

"Go ahead, George," Reginald said, pulling some gold coins out of his pants pocket. Clinking the coins up and down in his palm, he asked Genny, "How much?"

"I'm not for sale."

"Everybody's got a price." He grinned, showing off the gold in his mouth. "How about you going ninety miles northeast with me?"

"No."

"I'll go to Sacramento with you," a woman said. "You may call me Sapphire."

Reginald turned to the nearly naked tavern wench and she clutched his arm. When she made a play for the gold coins in his hand, he let go of Genny and shook his head at Sapphire.

"Not settling for a sapphire when a diamond is at hand," he said.

Genny had stepped away from Reginald the moment he released her. He tried to catch hold of her again just as George inadvertently cut him off by stepping further into the parlor. Genny sashayed past George and began maneuvering through the roomful of customers, tables and chairs. Reginald followed her as she headed straight for the man in the far corner.

"Hey," Reginald hollered.

CHAPTER 14

"Hey what?" Luke asked, a challenge ringing in his voice. He caught Genny's hand and tugged her onto one knee, instantly stopping Reginald in his pursuit.

"I was making Diamond here a deal, cowboy."

"Here's the deal, city slicker." Luke slid one arm around Genny's waist, his hand cupping her left hip, just before his other hand flattened to her right leg, fingers spreading on the inside of her thigh. "She's with me."

Genny's heart pounded as his touch created red hot tingles between her thighs. She trembled. *Sit still* she told herself. She tried. Never had any man touched her fanny, hip or the inside of her thigh. But Luke had done it all.

Flashing before her eyes; Luke spying her panties at the hotel, closing her shirt over her breasts in the foyer, pulling up her overalls in his backyard, and eating dinner in her kitchen when she wore only her chemisette. Piece by piece she was revealing herself to this man.

How long could she hold her cards close to her vest? How long before Luke saw her heart on her sleeve?

"Play him for her, Reggie," George suggested, coming to stand beside his friend.

"Got any money for five card stud, cowboy?" Reginald asked. "I might as well make a profit along the way."

"Got a deed to a horse ranch."

"No," Genny gasped, not wanting Luke risking anything because of her.

Reginald's smile put his gold tooth on display. Genny's one word had assured him Luke had a horse ranch to lose.

"How big's the ranch?" Reginald wanted to know.

"Big enough," Luke replied with an insolent tone.

"How many horses?" George asked Luke.

"Ten."

"I have horses." George pulled out one of the chairs and sat down. "I'll play."

"No," Reginald said, took off his jacket, folded it in half and placed it over the back of the other vacant chair at the table. "I'm playing for her." He nodded at Genny and took a seat.

"Got more than a handful of coins?" Luke asked Reginald and squeezed Genny's leg as if encouraging her to go along with him.

"Certainly." Reginald pulled out a thick roll of paper money and set it on the table.

"Count it," Luke said.

Reginald blustered at first but counted out maybe a third of the money. "One thousand." He leaned back in his chair and splayed a hand with a diamond ring on his pinky, inviting Luke to do similar.

Luke removed an envelope from his vest pocket, no doubt the deed, and placed it on the table. "One thousand will get you one American Quarter horse," Luke said.

"A thousand dollars a horse?" Reginald glanced at George who nodded.

"Take it or leave it," Luke said.

Genny's already ragged nerves were about to snap. But Luke seemed cool and collected. When she squirmed on his lap again, he slid his fingers into the waist of her britches at the small of her back and held her still. Suddenly the entire length of her spine heated and there was that red hot tingling between her legs again.

"What's your name, pretty lady?" Reginald asked Genny.

"Genevieve," she replied with clipped coldness.

"To make it clear when I win, I get the horse of my pick and Genevieve for the night in San Francisco," Reginald said.

"Hell no," Luke replied. "One horse, one half hour and Genevieve stays right here."

"An hour," Reginald bargained.

"An hour?" Luke cocked his head to one side and said to Genny, "You're getting the money if I win. So what do—"

"I'm not taking any money," Genny said and shook her head.

"Yes, you are," Luke replied. "So, what do you say, babydoll?"

"I say don't lose, loverboy."

Joe's brows shot up at her answer more than any other part of the conversation thus far. Not knowing exactly how or why, Genny was gambling that Luke would not let anything bad happen to her. Jimmy walked into the room and made his way to the table.

"It's a bet." Luke stuck out his hand and said, "Luke Harper."

"It's a bet." Reginald shook his hand. "Reginald Moore."

"I can deal." Joe looked from Luke to Reginald.

"Use an unopened deck," Reginald said and removed a cigar from an inside suit pocket.

Cards were Tricky's territory, and she hurriedly retrieved a sealed deck from the table where she'd been dealing blackjack. She placed them in the center of Luke's table and went to stand next to Ying who had just entered the parlor.

"I'll shuffle the cards," George said as he opened the deck.

Luke agreed George could shuffle and Reginald nodded, while lighting his cigar, that Joe could deal. Mike joined them and stood next to Jimmy. Genny fidgeted in

Luke's lap again and this time he whispered in her ear before releasing his hold on her. She moved off his lap and became aware for the first time that every man in the parlor, Sapphire, Emerald, and Ruby along with Grace, Ruth, Patty, Vern, Tricky, and Ying were watching.

A horse, a grand and a promise of an hour were on the table. When Genny reached Tricky and Ying at the other side of the room, George was shuffling the cards as Reginald puffed his cigar. The tension crackling the air paled in comparison to the anxiety wracking Genny.

"What did Luke whisper in your ear?" Tricky asked.

Genny wanted to disappear. But she couldn't leave Luke to face Reginald alone. What if the worst happened and Luke lost? How was he going to control what happened next?

Tricky nudged her and Genny answered the question, "Luke said if he loses, to run because there could be trouble."

Mike and Jimmy left the ring of people steadily closing in to watch the boldest bet ever made at the Cat's Eye Ranch. Genny wondered why the Johnson brothers were leaving Luke and Joe until they came to stand on either side of her. She realized they had gotten some kind of signal from Luke.

"Shuffle 'em good, George," Reginald said around the cigar in a corner of his mouth.

George shuffled the cards and spread them in a semi-circle on the table. He slid them back together and shuffled them again. With his fingertips at the edges of the cards, he then scooted them in front of Joe. Joe cut the deck, looked first at Luke and then at Reginald.

"Five card stud, gentlemen," Joe said. "We play first and third cards face up."

"One hand, winner takes all," Reginald said, rolling the cigar from one corner of his mouth to the other.

Joe dealt each man one card face up on the table. Genny's head felt so light, she was fairly certain she was going to faint. There was a hush over the house, the likes of which she had never experienced since taking over for Garnet.

"Luke's showing a ten of hearts," Mike said to Ruth as she and Grace quietly joined them. "That could be good."

"The other guy got a ten of diamonds," Jimmy said, craning his neck and draping an arm around Grace.

Joe dealt the next two cards face down and then the third cards to each player were face up.

"Luke got a jack of hearts and Moore got a jack of diamonds," Mike said.

Hushed murmurs rippled through the crowd of onlookers.

"Damn, who would have guessed that?" Jimmy asked.

"With stakes so high this takes nerves of steel," Mike said.

"Takes balls," Jimmy said bluntly.

Joe dealt each player their final two cards face down.

After a moment, Reginald discarded two and was dealt two more. Luke discarded one and received one. Reginald examined his cards and chomped his cigar. As Luke studied his cards Genny caught a tiny flinch at the corner of Luke's slightly bruised left eye. Her heart thudded against her ribcage. Was that nearly imperceptible blink due to his cards, a result of their fighting lesson or did it mean nothing at all?

"Want to raise the bet, cowboy?" Reginald asked. "Say another five hundred?"

"Can't bet half a horse, city slicker," Luke said.

"How do I know these horses exist?" Reginald asked.

"You passed a stallion and a mare at the hitching post," Luke said.

Reginald glanced at George who nodded that they were worth a thousand each.

"Two thousand dollars?" Reginald placed another grand on the table, pointed across the room at Genny with his cigar and directed his question to Luke, "Two hours?"

"Two horses," Luke said firmly, meeting the ante. "One hour."

"I'll take that big stallion and the black mare off your hands."

"We'll see," Luke said.

"If the bets are final, please reveal your other three cards, gentlemen," Joe said.

Flashing the diamond on his pinky finger, Reginald said, "All diamonds, my strong suit." With quite the flourish, he announced his cards as he snapped them face up one at a time, "Jack, ten, nine, eight, seven."

"Straight flush," George said and smiled. "Well done, my friend. Well done."

Genny's head and stomach rolled as if she'd had three shots of flip.

"Luke?" Joe asked.

Luke silently turned over his remaining three cards in one fell swoop revealing an ace, king, queen, jack, and ten of hearts.

"Royal damn flush. The unbeatable hand," Joe said in awed surprise. "You win, Luke."

Whooping and clapping and whistling bounced off the parlor walls. After Joe, Vern was the first to congratulate Luke and pounded him on the back. Patty hugged Tricky and Ying and all three cheered. Mike and Jimmy shouted to Luke from where they stood still guarding Genny. Ruth and Grace clapped, and the Johnson brothers hugged the sweet cousins.

Suddenly, Reginald made a grab for the money. Luke's knife sliced down between two pudgy fingers, the blade nailing the money and deed to the wooden table. Red-faced, Reginald's cigar dropped onto the table. The hum in the crowd turned from jubilant to menacing. Ready to back Luke up, as she had at the beach, Genny sailed across the room.

"Mr. Harper outplayed you, Reggie," George said, shaking his head.

Joe said, "Hands off his winnings, Mr. Moore."

Reginald let go of the money, picked up his cigar and stuck it in his mouth. "Two out of three?" he asked Luke.

"No," Luke replied.

Reginald stood and clenching the cigar between his teeth, said, "As Reggie Moore always says there's moooore where that came from."

Luke also stood and pocketed his knife. Scooping up the money and deed with his left hand he stuck out his right and said, "Thanks for the game, Mr. Moore."

"Reggie," he replied and shook Luke's hand. "Thank you, Mr. Harper."

"Luke," he said, sliding the deed into his jacket pocket just as Genny reached him.

"For the record, you had no intention of letting this pretty lady leave the parlor with me, did you?" Reginald asked.

"I told you she stayed right here," Luke reminded him. "Had you won and been reasonable, you could have talked to her for an hour while she sat on my lap." Reginald nodded with resignation and Luke said, "Have a drink on me, Reggie."

Folding the two thousand dollars, Luke intimately slid the money into Genny's front pants pocket. Genny instantly knew that Luke had put the money where Reggie would not dare make another grab for it. Instinct said that Luke had also just given every man at the Cat's Eye a message which would spread far and wide.

In one fell swoop; Genny was with Luke.

George stuck out his hand to Luke and asked, "You're not a cowboy, are you?"

"No," Luke replied and shook his hand.

"Riverboat gambler," Joe said with a grin and also shook hands with George.

"I've never been that far off the mark before. Nor have I seen Reggie up the ante like he did. A compliment to you, Genevieve," George said. "Bluffs well played, Luke."

Genny realized George not only meant Luke's Levi's and boots but the flinch at his eye.

"All part of the game," Luke replied.

"Well, ya missed out on Reggie, pretty lady," Reggie said to Genny, accepted a shot of whiskey from Vern, raised it in the air and bellowed, "Sapphire, honey? Where are you?"

Reggie and George didn't make it far before Sapphire, Emerald and Ruby surrounded them. Everyone else crowded around Luke, congratulating him, eyes wide and heads shaking as they smiled at Genny. She had two thousand dollars in her pocket, all because of Luke Harper. After downing his free shot, Reginald bought drinks for the house and let Sapphire lead him to her room. Luke stayed at his table with Joe and the Johnsons.

The remainder of the evening passed quickly and much more quietly than that of the first half. As customers left and new ones arrived, the story of the bet traveled with them.

Genny heard it all as she collected money at the front door. Would Seth Comstock hear about the bet as well? The richest and most eligible bachelor in town knew she'd left with Luke for the scavenger hunt. Did Comstock assume she was spoken for? Is that why she hadn't heard from him again? How was it that he'd invited her to that ball anyway? Did she still need Seth Comstock? Well, the money in her pocket would not buy a Nob Hill mansion. Oh, it could buy a small house somewhere in San Francisco. But with her reputation, no decent employer would give her a job. She'd have no income to keep the property up, no money with which to support herself. She'd be right back on this ranch, in this disorderly house as its madam.

In her heart of hearts, she was certain Luke needed the cash more than she did. His horses needed taken care of and repairs to his ranch weren't cheap. Might as well return the money to him and save them both financial trouble and disappointment.

"Hey, *pretty lady.*"

Swaggering down the hall like the winning stud he was, Luke's teasing grin was a disarming one. Genny's heart sang a song all its own about Luke Harper. This man was teaching her invaluable life skills with patience, kindness, humor, and at times firmness.

A customer named Andy, who seemed tough rather than rough, stopped Luke halfway down the hall. Wearing a holster around his waist loaded with bullets and two guns, he spoke to Luke as if talking business.

Luke had kept her safe tonight as he had since the night they met. Like a candle lit in the darkness the light slowly dawned on Genny that with Luke at her side, she'd forgotten about not measuring up to the who's whos in Harriett Peak's column.

Not only with words, but with his actions Luke had talked her into being friends. She liked him. Her grandfather would have liked Luke, too, and taken him fishing. Grandpa's advice usually came at the fishing pond, and she remembered him saying she must not only love, but like the man she decided to marry.

Marry? But she planned to marry for money, not love and friendship.

A fleeting image of Luke asking her to marry him flashed before her eyes. He would never propose to her of course, nor could she accept. But…but dear Lord…

She was in love with Luke Harper. Head over heels.

Beyond any shadow of any doubt, she loved and liked Luke so much that he had the potential to become her very best friend. For the rest of her life.

As Luke spoke to Andy, he motioned to Ying who joined them. Wondering what they were discussing, Genny picked up the jewel box. Since the incident where Luke had encouraged Sapphire's rough customer to settle up, there had been no more problems collecting money.

Money? The cash Luke had given her was from a lucky bet.

With Luke, she would always be a bordello madam. No,

her mind screamed. Worse still when Luke was gone, and he would get the itch to go, he would take her heart with him.

Ying grinned at Tricky as Luke shook hands with Andy and came toward Genny again. Her heart sang and broke as she smiled her best smile just for him.

"It's late," Luke said. "Let's go to my house."

Simultaneously nervous and excited at that prospect, Genny asked, "Why your house?"

"Ying needs to stay at your house. If that's all right, will you come home with me?"

Home? Luke was a gambler who had won his home next door.

Tonight was proof positive that he could lose it all tomorrow. When that happened, he'd have nothing to hold him here and once he was gone, he'd never look back.

All part of the game.

Genny heard Tricky squeal with delight just before tossing her arms around Ying. When Tricky looked her way, Genny smiled. Without thinking herself out of going home with Luke, she nodded yes. As she locked the jewel box away it occurred to her that there had to be scores of women locked away in Luke's life. He was too handsome and charming not to have had his share and more of fawning females throwing themselves at him. Holding the key, she wondered if any lady in particular held the key to Luke's heart.

She joined him at the front door as Vern and Patty congratulated him one last time on how expertly he'd pulled off the win. When Emerald, Ruby, Opal, and Onxy joined in, Genny impulsively took Luke's hand. He gave her a squeeze. The customers might know she was with Luke, but these women didn't care. They'd escort him upstairs the second he was willing to go. They would take care of Luke like the professionals they were. They would not be fumbling or nervous or make mistakes like a novice. Like her.

What? She wasn't planning to go to bed with Luke or any man because sex led to getting pregnant with an illegitimate baby and...worse. She was so confused. One thing was for certain; none of these jewels were going to steal Luke from her if she could help it. Steal Luke? She had no claim on Luke. For all she knew, there was a woman somewhere holding that key to his heart.

"Goodnight," Luke said to the others and gave her a tug.

He led the way out the house, across the porch and down the steps to the horses. Roscoe followed. The moon was full, and its light spilled across the house and woods. Luke made sure Genny was safely mounted on Esprit before he swung himself into Etalon's saddle.

"We'll take your shortcut to my ranch, Roscoe," Luke said and pointed.

The collie barked once as if to say he was on duty and headed toward Luke's ranch.

"Hey, Harper," Genny called as her horse trotted behind his through the moonlit forest. "Do you have two beds at your house?"

CHAPTER 15

"Nope," Luke said over his shoulder. "I'll roll up a quilt and put it down the middle of my bed. You'll need to stay on your side."

Luke chuckled to himself when he heard Genny's huff of surprised indignation.

"That big chair and ottoman in your front room will suit me perfectly well."

If she only knew how perfectly well she suited him, Luke thought.

Too bad she was out to catch a rich man. But she was and she'd been honest about it from the beginning. Then again, Reggie Moore had announced he was rich and Genny had turned her back on him. On the other hand, she was still defending Comstock. Dammit.

Luke strengthened his resolve to let her believe he was just a riverboat gambler who survived on luck. On *his* damn riverboat. But she'd pegged him as jumping ships and living from one game of cards to the next.

How much longer would this game hold out before she saw through his bluff? And what would Genny say if she found out that he was wealthy? That she needed him? Wanted him? Talk about a high stakes gamble.

Hell no. Not a bet he was willing to make. He could not,

would not go through life forever wondering if she'd married him for his money.

Married him?

One gander at Genny and John Harper, the patriarch of the family, would clap Luke on the back in congratulations of winning such a beautiful woman. Phoebe Harper, the nurturing, cookie-baking mother Genny had never had, would hug this adorable young woman to her heart. His brother and Chloe, Rob's wife, would be thrilled to have her in the family and their children would be calling her Aunt Genny the first day. Mattie's little girl, at six years old, would hardly remember a time when Genny had not been part of her life. Steven, Mattie's husband, a United States Senator, would make sure Genny met President Theodore Roosevelt.

Yes, his family would fall in love with Genevieve Moonstone Morgan.

Dammit to hell. He had fallen in love with Genny. And he wanted to marry her. Of course, she'd say no to a riverboat gambler. But as he had finished the work needed at his ranch, the wild adventure of romancing Genny was all he'd thought about.

"Cat got your tongue again?" Genny asked as their horses reached the hitching post along the log home's porch.

"You're gonna find out this time."

Still atop Etalon, Luke grasped a rein to Esprit. He tugged the mare closer and yanked Genny out of her saddle, settling her across his lap.

His left arm supporting her, he buried his hand in the thick black waves at the back of her head. Tucking his right hand under her thigh, when he stared into her lilac eyes, she hesitantly twined her arms around his neck. Shutting his eyes, he pressed his mouth to hers and parted her lips. When his tongue touched hers for the first time, she was all that existed on Earth to the dark side of the moon. Their tongues played deliciously in her warm mouth. He touched his tongue to her lips and when her tongue traced his lips in return, lightning shot through his body, heating his loins. She gently placed her hand to his cheek and his embrace tightened.

Roscoe barked and with a groan, Luke pulled back.

"Consider that your kissing lesson." Luke's voice was huskier than he'd expected.

In a breathless whisper, Genny said, "I'll think of a payment."

With a nod, Luke then called out to the man walking toward them, "Hey Andy."

"Want me to take your horses to the stable, boss?"

"Yes." Luke carefully let Genny slide out his arms to the ground and then he dismounted. "Genny, I hired Andy earlier tonight at your house. He'll work with Ying to help with the horses and keep the ranch running. Safely."

"I'm sure Ying will appreciate the help," Genny said, instantly wondering if that meant Luke already had the itch to move on.

"I'll set myself up in the barn as of tonight and use that cot Ying said is out there, if that's acceptable," Andy said.

"Yes. Thanks to Genny, Ying has other accommodations."

"Thank you, sir."

"See you tomorrow morning, Andy."

So that's why Ying needed to stay at her house. Andy respectfully tipped his hat at Genny, took the reins to the horses and disappeared in the direction of the stable. Luke led the way across the porch and opened the front door to his house. After Genny walked in ahead of him, he closed the door behind her, and moonlight streamed in through the windows. When he lit a lamp next to the chair and ottoman, she noticed the quilt and pillow were no longer there. Without a word, Luke crossed the room and strode down the hall.

"Where are you going?" Genny called after him.

"My bedroom. Come on."

"Umm…I'll be fine out here."

Luke left her standing in the middle of the room. Roscoe tilted his head and sat down beside the chair. What was she supposed to sleep in? A little late to have thought of that. She wished she had her chemisette. However, Luke hadn't commented on it that night in her kitchen, so he must not have liked it. Just as well.

Did he expect her to sleep in her blouse and britches? Thinking of her britches, she pulled the money out of her pocket. She glanced around for a discreet place to leave the cash for Luke. When the wind blew against the house, she shivered and hugged herself.

"Need a quilt?" Luke called from down the hall.

"Yes, please."

He appeared at the edge of the front room. Shockingly, he wore only a pair of drawers. The waist rode low, exposing his belly button. There was a masculine bulge in the crotch of his snug undergarment, and she quickly averted her gaze. His thighs were muscular, his calves well defined and his feet bare. She took a step toward him, caught herself and bowed her head.

Studying the floor, she held out her hand and he gave her the quilt. Clutching it to her bosom, she knew he must think her silly by saying she'd sleep in the chair. She searched for a reason that might sound not only mature but considerate.

"If you recall, you slept in the front room at my house."

"Because you didn't invite me to your bedroom," Luke replied. "Where are you planning to put that cash in your hand?"

"Oh, well…uh…I thought you could keep it safe for me."

When he held out his hand, she gave him the money and Luke handed her an order, "Don't sneak off like you did at the Palace Hotel." Standing so close to him when he was wearing so little, Genny could hardly think. "It's too dangerous out there. Deal?"

"Deal."

"See you in the morning."

The moment he turned away, Genny's head snapped up and she watched him walk down the hall, all broad shoulders, muscular back and slightly rounded masculine buttocks. A pang knifed her heart that she wasn't going with him. He whistled and Roscoe trotted after him. Alone in the front room, she sank into the chair and pulled off her boots. She really wanted to curl up in bed. With Luke. No. Alone. She wanted to curl up alone.

By the sound of his footsteps, rustling of bed covers and creaking noise in the bedroom, she figured Luke had just stretched out in bed. Picturing him half naked, she was startled by the sudden hot tingling between her legs. Ignoring that recurring craving which she didn't fully understand, she put out the lamp. She wrapped the quilt all the way around herself and with a sigh, rested her legs and feet on the ottoman.

Leaning her head back she closed her eyes. Luke sat at the card table. He'd just won two thousand dollars. Then the man who had lost made a grab for the money. Luke's knife came down between the man's long, spindly fingers. The loser yanked his hand back and seized Genny around the throat. He threw her into an automobile and the wind blew his thin, yellow hair around the sallow complexion of his gaunt face. His laugh was maniacal as he dragged her toward the pond. Two beefy, red-haired men helped the thin one weigh her down with rocks and throw her into the water. She couldn't see. She couldn't breathe. She couldn't move her arms. She tried to kick her feet, but her legs were restricted, too. She was drowning when only minutes before she had been safe with Luke.

"I can't swim." She cried, "Luke!"

"Genny, wake up," Luke said. "You're having a nightmare."

Genny opened her eyes. Where was she? Tangled up in the quilt, cradled in Luke's arms. Held to his chest in the front room of his house. So tightly swaddled she could only move her head, she buried a sob of relief in his naked shoulder.

"I'll sleep in your bed tonight if you'll give me that swimming lesson tomorrow."

"Cold or not, you'll learn to swim tomorrow."

When she nodded, Luke carried her down the hall. His bedroom was dimly lit by a flickering lamp on a bedside table. He placed her on what she assumed was his side of the bed, so tried to maneuver to the other side. But she was still too tightly twisted in the quilt to move. Luke grasped the edge of the quilt and rolled her out of it.

Luke caught his breath. He thought she would be fully dressed, and she was anything but. Having come to a stop on her tummy, a white lace camisole had ridden halfway up her slender back and white ruffles danced across her saucy fanny.

"Don't look, Harper," Genny said, staying on her stomach, but turning her head toward him. "You're looking."

"Yeah."

"Stop it. I fashioned these underclothes out of petticoats and pantalets that I outgrew, never expecting anyone would see them."

"I like 'em." He fought the temptation to plant a kiss on the right cheek of those ruffles.

"Roll up my quilt and put it down the middle of the bed. No. Wait. Cover me with it."

Genny's voice cracked with a nervous squeak and Luke couldn't help but grin. The feminine ruffles decorating her bottom were as sexy as hell.

"Harper. Stop your gawking. Cover me up and put out the lamp."

"Genevieve. Stop telling me what to do. You're in my house and my bed."

"Please?"

With a mild oath, Luke fixed her quilt down the center of the bed. Then he stretched out on his side of it and turned down the wick in the lamp. The light of the full moon streamed in the same big window he'd pulled her through earlier in the day. He grabbed his own quilt and reluctantly pulled it up to their waists.

In bed with this goddess of the moon was exactly where he knew he shouldn't be. Below the belt he wanted Genny like he'd never wanted any woman, anywhere at any time. But his brain reminded him that whatever he taught her could be used to win another man.

"You're places in my mind you shouldn't be," Genny said, still on her tummy.

"Well hell, you just read my thoughts," Luke said, surprised at her admission.

Genny rolled to her side, facing him. Luke rolled to his side as well and swung his arm around her. Molding his hand to her naked, lower back he pressed her closer to him. She didn't struggle or scoot away. The quilt flattened between them as her head came to rest beside his on his pillow. Taking hold of her arm, he placed it around his neck. When he grasped her camisole, she tensed. He tugged it into place and was rewarded with her fingers burying themselves in his hair at the back of his head. He was on dangerous ground, and he knew it. Hot blood quickly hardened him. He kissed her anyway.

Genny's lips were sweet and supple and parted when his did. Sliding his tongue into her mouth he imagined her legs parting for him. He brought his hand from her back to her ribcage and slowly up to the perfect breast he'd longed to touch. She sucked in a small breath and through the camisole's thin fabric her nipple beaded against his palm. As he caressed her breast there was a catch in her throat just before the softest of moans escaped her. Trailing his hand down her side he gave her waist a gentle squeeze before sliding his fingers under the quilt and over her curvy hip. His hand settled on her fanny and when his fingers played among the ruffles, she tightened her hug around his neck. Craving the gripping sensation of burying himself deep inside her, he hooked his thumb into the waist of her panties. It would be so good. So easy.

And so damn opposite of romancing her.

"Goodnight, lamb," he said and kissed her forehead.

After he rolled away from her, she whispered, "Goodnight, wolf."

AT DAWN a chilling image jerked Luke into consciousness. Opening his eyes, the image of Comstock getting his hands on Genny, replayed across Luke's mind with vivid clarity. Taking several deep breaths his trepidation slowly subsided and his heart rate returned to normal.

She lay snuggled in the crook of his arm, her leg intimately tucked between his with the quilt barrier at her back. Her lilac eyes were closed, her pink lips slightly parted and her cleavage generously exposed. The lace edge of her camisole exposed the outer rim of nipples hinting a rich shade of expensive bourbon. He knew they'd be just as intoxicating when his mouth closed over them. He groaned at that, and she stirred.

"Am I crowding you?" she mumbled groggily.

"No, and evidently, this is your favorite position because it's how you slept with me in the hammock."

"I'm sure I did no such thing," she said and rolled to her back.

"I'm sure you did."

During the night, Luke had found her cuddled against his back. He'd turned over, gathered her to his heart and dreamed of the two of them. But fantasy turned to nightmare when Comstock intruded and instead of resisting Genny's seduction, he'd welcomed it.

Luke was in love with this woman and last night, she'd allowed him to the point where only his iron will had stopped him. She wanted those lessons in seduction which she didn't need. What she needed was for him to teach her how far she could take a man before he'd take her.

"This is my favorite position," Luke said and rolled on top of her.

"Harper," she gulped and gazed into pools of green.

Genny was instantly engulfed in flames from her cheeks to her toes. So smoothly did Luke's hips settle between her thighs that she hadn't even realized her legs had spread for him. His head lowered and his mouth closed over hers, parting her lips as easily as he had her legs. Without prodding from him, her arms wrapped around his broad shoulders. Muscles rippled under her hands, arms and against her breasts. Something as hard as a fencepost pressed into her soft belly. Never having seen such in the flesh, she had only the vaguest idea about it. But then she'd never been the least bit interested until Luke waltzed into her life.

Sleep had eluded her after they'd said goodnight as she'd tried to figure out why he'd abruptly turned away from her. She'd listened to his even breathing and longed to hug herself to this man whom she loved with all her heart. Despite him saying she needed to stay on her side of the quilt, she'd found the nerve to crawl over it and slip her arm around his waist. He'd sighed in his sleep, pulled her closer until her breasts met with his back and then flattened her hand against his rock-hard stomach.

In the dawning light of day, it was clear why he'd turned his back on her. He'd given her the chance to seduce him, and she'd failed. Streaks. He'd seduced *and* resisted while she did neither. She was a fumbling amateur. No wonder he'd lost interest in her lessons.

Sexy and commanding, Luke was all man, and she craved each kiss and every caress he was giving her now. His lips left hers and sensuous nibbles rained down her neck to her collarbone. Leaving her camisole in place, his mouth closed over her left nipple, and she gasped. Pleasure oozed through her like liquid fire, and she arched her back wanting more. Luke suckled her right nipple through the thin fabric, and she moaned his name. Thrilling to this new excitement, she whimpered a protest when he raised his head.

"Goddess of the moon," Luke whispered, his eyes meeting hers.

Rolling to his back, he took her skimpily clad body with him. As her breasts molded to his bare chest, his long, thick hardness reminded her that he was nearly naked. He placed his hand to the back of her head, and she lowered her mouth to his. Stretched out on top of him, he spread his legs trapping her thighs enticingly between his. One magical move after another and she had become lost to everything in the world but Luke Harper. His strong hands slowly slid down her back leaving goosebumps in their wake. He caressed her ruffled fanny causing a riot of red-hot tingles to play in a most secret place between her legs.

Adonis, she silently mouthed against his lips, too shy to call him that out loud.

Under Luke's spell, Genny floated into another time and place. When he started tugging her ruffled panties down, she instinctively raised her hips for him. With her panties at the tops of her thighs, only his drawers were between her and his long, hard fencepost. Suddenly he stopped and with both hands he lightly smacked her naked bottom.

"Tell me no, little lamb."

Softly she moaned, "No, wolf."

"Hell," Luke growled, pulled her panties up and stacked his hands under his head.

"Don't resist me," she purred, nibbling his neck as he had hers. "Teach me."

"I've taught you way too much. Get outa my bed."

Not wanting to fumble anything else Genny swung herself off him. So fast did she accomplish this feat that she flew over the edge of the mattress and landed smack dab on the floor. Bringing his arms from behind his head, Luke leaned over the side of the bed. She glared up at him and when he held out his hand, she huffed and swatted it away.

He lay back in his bed and howled with laughter. Genny grinned and did her best to suppress a giggle. But what she'd just done struck her as so ridiculous and hilarious that a laugh escaped her which she tried her darnedest to make sound like another righteous huff.

"That might have been the funniest damn thing I've ever seen," he said between chuckles.

"Oh, hush up, Harper."

She dragged his quilt off the bed and began the day as she'd begun the previous night; swaddled in Luke's blanket. Managing to stand, she hopped around the end of his bed and waddled down the hall, giggling the whole way.

"I hear you laughing," he called after her.

"I'll see you in a couple hours when I wake up and pretend that was all a dream."

"Hey, sleepyhead," Luke said standing next to the ottoman where the beautiful woman lay curled up in the chair, the quilt loosely bunched around her waist. When one eye squinted open, he told her, "It's actually warmed up some. Good day to swim."

"How long have you been awake?" she asked, taking in the fact he was fully dressed.

"Long enough to do a half day's work." Taking hold of her hands he pulled her out of the chair. "Put your clothes on and we'll go to the pond."

"What's your hurry all of a sudden?"

Her nightmare and his. "Your grandfather would be the first to say it's dangerous for you to go another day without knowing how to swim."

"I thought maybe you were thinking about leaving San Francisco."

"I think about leaving every day." But not without her.

She grabbed her clothes and sashayed as only she could down the hall to his bedroom. His thoughts hadn't been far from the bedroom all morning. Despite checking in with

Ying and Andy and hiring two of Andy's lifelong friends, Luke kept thinking about what had happened in his bed. Never had he been lost to a woman's seduction. Until Genny. He was always, always in control. Until Genny. This goddess of the moon possessed mystical magic because he'd been mesmerized almost to the point of no return.

"By the way, Harper," she called from the bedroom, "thanks for the seduction lesson."

"That's not what it was, Genevieve."

"What was it then?" she asked, peeping around the doorway.

"A lesson on saying no." But not to him. Why didn't he just take his damn gun and actually shoot himself in the foot? "You failed, babydoll."

"I've said no to every man except for you, loverboy."

"Keep it that way," Luke replied seriously. "Hurry up, storm clouds are on the horizon."

CHAPTER 16

"You two have sorely disappointed me." Seth kicked a straw man as it lay scaring nothing amidst dirt clods behind the Skidmore's farmhouse, and then continued berating the brothers, "Don't bungle today's job like you did in not poisoning his dog or you'll regret it."

"How ya figure we'll regret it, old man?" Billy Skidmore asked. "What're ya gonna do?"

Chewing on a pinky nail, Seth said around his finger, "Not pay you."

"We cain't spend it at the whorehouse nohow on accounta Harper," Billy muttered.

"That dog's as good as dead." Curt nudged his brother. "What's today's job?"

"Today's job?" Billy shoved a greasy strand of hair out of his eyes. "I thought the next thing was gettin' Harper shanghaied."

"I don't have that arranged in the Barbary Coast, yet," Seth said, knowing he needed to pawn more items from the house near Nob Hill to keep the Skidmores taking risks. "Your job today is to follow Harper with an eye on how we can catch him with no one suspecting us." Selma motioned to Seth, and he joined her in the automobile. "What do you want now?"

"Just kill him," Selma said under her breath. "That's what you did to the other five."

"After I killed the first three, I was caught and locked away for decades," Seth hissed and scowled at his sister. "I've taken enough chances here in San Francisco, thank you very much."

"Yes, yes." Selma inclined her head at Curt and Billy. "When they drop Harper through a saloon trapdoor, he'll be out to sea, and you'll have removed all but the last obstacle."

Seth nodded, turned to the Skidmores and said, "Report back to me tonight. Come after dark to the back door so that none of Harriett Peak's nosey neighbors see you."

"SINCE YOU DIDN'T WADE into the Bay the night we met, I'll warn you that the water this far north is cold," Genny said to the handsome man as they stood beside the pond. "Especially in March."

"Down in Biloxi your swimming lesson would be in warmer waters of the Gulf," Luke said with an exaggerated drawl. "Year round."

They'd ridden the horses to the pond and on the way Genny said she had nothing special to swim in. Fine by Luke, because neither did he. Moby-Dick croaked at them, and Roscoe barked at the bullfrog. In this secluded area of the woods with its rising hill as a backdrop, Genny stripped off her dark britches. Standing next to Luke, she wore her pink blouse over the camisole she'd slept in along with her ruffled panties. With a grin, he grasped the long braid down her back and brought it forward over her right shoulder. Wrapping his arms around her, goosebumps popped out on Genny's skin as he began unfastening the buttons down her back.

"I've seen you in your underclothes," he said as he unbuttoned the last button. "You'll be able to swim easier without this shirt."

Flattening her hands to his chest, she straightened her arms and backed out of his grasp. Leaving him holding her blouse, she waded ruffle-deep into the pond and then turned to him.

"Come teach me how to swim in a San Francisco pond, Harper."

"What's my payment if I do?" Luke asked, placing her blouse on top of his vest, gun and shirt before tugging off his boots.

"A dance I discovered in one of my books. I taught it to myself and then to Tricky after she moved in." Waist high in the water, Genny drizzled water down her arms. "I'll do it for you."

"That oughta be interesting," Luke said, dropping his jeans on the ground and walking into the water wearing his drawers. "Hell, this *is* cold, let's go back to my warm bed," he shouted.

"I CAIN'T SEE 'EM. But did you hear what he just yelled?" Curt asked Billy as they crouched behind bushes on the hill overlooking the pond. "That son of a bitch took her to bed."

"That'll starch Comstock's shorts," Billy snickered. "A'course that ol' man ain't got no more chance with Genevieve than us."

"'Specially not with Harper in the picture," Curt said. "I don't know 'bout trying to shanghai him. Harper's big and he don't scare. And he's smart, Billy. I can tell."

"He's a man. He bleeds."

"TAKE a deep breath and you'll float," Luke said, his hands under Genny's shoulders and thighs to keep her on the water's surface.

"If you say so."

She'd floated past all conscious thought in Luke's bed.

The cold water had her nipples beaded now, but it was Luke's warm mouth that had beaded them earlier. How in the world had she let him do that? Let him? She'd silently begged him for more by arching her back against his lips. He'd told her to say no to any man but him. Where did that leave her seduction lesson?

"Take that deep breath," he coaxed.

Genny did so and slipped under the water. She grabbed at his arm and found one side of his drawers instead. She'd yanked them down several inches before he had her raised to the surface again. Still on her back, she swiped water out of her eyes as he cocked a rakish brow.

"Is that for pulling *your* drawers down this morning?" he teased.

"Wh-what?" She laughed. "No, sorry."

"Let's try it again."

Despite the water temperature, they persevered and in a few minutes, Luke was able to take his hands out from under her without her sinking. Elated, she floated away. He grabbed her hand and pulled her back to him. Then standing her shoulder high in the pond, he instructed her on how to tread water by cupping her hands, moving her arms and kicking her feet.

"It's called dogpaddling," he said and demonstrated. "Try it."

Genny floundered, Luke encouraged and soon she had the knack of that, too.

"I'm swimming."

"Almost," Luke said, dogpaddling away from her backward so as not to lose sight of her.

"I can't touch the bottom here," she gasped, dipped down and spit out a mouthful of water.

"I know," he said putting more distance between them. "Dogpaddle."

"Harper, come back here."

"Lean forward into the water, cup your hands and move your arms like oars on a boat."

"I can't." She gulped more water and panicking, began sinking.

Luke swam back to her and took her into his arms. She probably didn't realize it but her wet underclothes were so sheer, she might as well have been naked. Clinging to him, her teeth were chattering and his were about to.

"Release your death grip on me, take another deep breath and swim to me like a mermaid born by the water, Miss Morgan." He pried her arms from him and dogpaddled away from her backward again.

"I can't do it." She managed to keep herself afloat by dogpaddling but was not moving forward.

As seriously as possible he asked, "Are there sharks in San Francisco ponds?"

Genny leaned forward and using her hands and arms exactly like oars, she kicked her feet. Luke grinned and when she neared him, he held out his arms. This time she swam into his embrace and his lips met hers in a jubilant kiss as she wrapped her arms around his neck and her legs around his waist.

"Now *that* was swimming, sea nymph."

"Thank you, Luke," she said, shivering in his arms as tears glittered in her eyes. "Grandpa would be so happy."

"Hold on and I'll give you a ride."

Positioning her chest to his back while keeping her arms around his neck Luke swam letting her float safely against his body. Close to shore he let go of her and wading out of the pond first, grabbed the quilt they'd brought. He held it open, and she splashed forward a few steps until glancing down her body.

"Streaks." She threw an arm over her breasts and a hand to the vee between her legs and said, "Cover your eyes."

"Aww, just come on." Luke's grin was wicked as he shook the quilt invitingly.

A blush heating her cold cheeks, Genny dashed into the warm blanket which he draped around her shoulders. Thrilled that she could swim, and that Luke was the one who'd taught her, Genny wrapped her arms around his shoulders, intimately folding him into the blanket with her.

Luke's mouth came down on hers as his hands flattened to her back. The tingling started between her legs and sizzled up her center, making her forget being half frozen. When his lips parted, so did hers and his tongue slid past her teeth to play with hers. Holding the edges of the blanket in her hands she wrapped her arms around his neck. His hands slid under her arms, and he lifted her against him. When her feet left the ground, she wrapped her legs around him as she had in the water. As his strong fingers laced under her fanny, she molded her breasts to his chest and poured herself into kissing him. Sprinkles from the approaching storm began to fall and Roscoe barked. Luke gently broke off the kiss and put her feet back on solid ground.

"If I didn't want to see your dance, I'd say that was payment enough."

Every fiber in her being on fire, she whispered, "I owe you the dance."

He repositioned the quilt saying he'd keep the raindrops and chilling air off her as she dressed. Taking her arms out of camisole straps, she slipped on one of Luke's flannel shirts instead of her pink blouse. From under the warm shirt, she pulled the wet camisole down and off. He grinned at that maneuver and then scanned the woods. She tied the shirttails at her waist and then tugged her britches on over her damp panties.

It was his turn and he warned her that he was about to strip off his drawers. She held the blanket up between them and he chuckled as she closed her eyes. When he took the quilt from her and said his Levi's were on, Genny placed a hand over her closed eyes. Playfully spreading her fingers widely apart she peeked to see if he'd spoken the truth. He had and after putting on a flannel shirt, he picked up his gun. Luke frowned a second before Roscoe growled.

"What's wrong?" Genny asked.

"We're being watched," Luke said as Roscoe barked again.

Roscoe charged forward as Luke aimed his gun. He called Roscoe back and fired a warning shot at the top of the hill.

"HOLY SHIT." Billy whacked his forehead against the dirt as the bullet buzzed just over his and Curt's heads. "That sounded like a big damn gun."

"I told ya we shouldna tried to get no closer." Flattened to the ground, Curt hastily retraced his belly crawl through the brush, weeds and sticks.

"But we couldn't see if she was swimmin' naked with him."

"He near shot us without even seein' us, Billy. I'm gettin' outa here."

"We ain't figured out how to catch him," Billy said, also slithering backward as fast as he could. "Alls we got to report is that he took her to bed."

"I ain't tellin' Comstock nothin' 'bout today," Curt replied. "He'd somehow blame us for Harper beddin' Genevieve."

"Forget Comstock. You and me both want Genevieve. Let's go take her from Harper."

"He'd shoot us and dump our carcasses in that pond. After Harper's gone, we'll take her from Comstock."

"WHO'S WATCHING?" Genny asked, atop Esprit as Luke swung himself into Etalon's saddle.

"I don't know," Luke said, leading the way to the road. "But I'm gonna find out what the hell's going on around here."

"How?"

"By going into town," Luke replied.

"I'll go with you."

"You're going to the Cat's Eye and stay there until I come back for you."

The concern in Luke's voice kept Genny from arguing. At the Cat's Eye, Genny told Patty, Vern, and Tricky about the swimming lesson. Placing a hand over her heart, Patty smiled until Luke recounted hearing someone in the woods. Ying arrived just as Luke informed them that Andy and his two best friends were former Rough Riders. Andy would be helping Ying, and one of Andy's friends would be at the Cat's Eye Ranch by the end of the day to help keep the peace. The third man would pitch in where needed and keep an eye on Genny's little house. Genny started to protest the expense, but Vern shushed her and nodded at Luke.

With Genny's help Patty talked Luke into eating a noonday meal with them while the storm blew over. The rain soon stopped, so leaving Roscoe with orders to protect Genny, Luke and Ying headed toward the shortcut to exchange their horses for Luke's automobile.

"I'm afraid," Genny said to Tricky on the front porch as Luke and Ying disappeared.

"You're safe with us," Tricky said.

"But Luke's not safe," Genny petted Roscoe. "Someone's after him."

"Let's practice our dance to take your mind off your worries," Tricky replied and nudged her. "Did you really learn to swim today?"

"Yes." She smiled at the exhilarating memory. "Thanks to Harper."

"Thanks for your time, Chief Dinan," Luke said, and shook hands with Jeremiah Dinan, the top man in the San Francisco Police Department.

Luke walked out of the police station without the information he wanted. Chief Dinan had heard from the Palace Hotel about Seth Comstock not paying his bill and there

was a warrant out for his arrest. But no, Comstock didn't
have any prior police record as far as Dinan knew. Luke
would have bet his last dollar Comstock had a record.
When he'd asked about Garnet Morgan's death, Dinan said
the case remained open but with no leads, it had stalled.
Nor had there been any report of trouble from a couple of
farmers named Skidmore. Back to Comstock, the chief had
noted the location of Luke's ranch. Since Luke suspected
Comstock of the property damage and attempted poisoning, Chief Dinan promised to get word to him if they
caught Comstock.

Luke headed to the *San Francisco Chronicle* building
next. Harriett Peak was at least a Comstock acquaintance,
if not an ally. In any event, shortly after New Year's she had
taken Southern Pacific Railroad's *Coast Line* train to Los
Angeles for a news-gathering trip.

He doubled back to the Palace Hotel. Every gut instinct
told him the scarecrow-like stranger who had invited
Genny to the ball and who had stared daggers at Luke
when Genny pulled him into the rising room was behind
the poisoned meat through her window, the watching in
the woods and who knew what else?

At the Palace Luke made a reservation for the next
evening. He had considered making the reservation at a
Greek revival masterpiece called the Fairmont Hotel.
Finding out it was on the eastern edge of Nob Hill, he'd
decided against it. The St. Francis Hotel over on Powell
Street presented an obvious choice due to its name. But not
only was the St. Francis ranked third of the three finest
hotels in San Francisco, it was in the midst of a new wing's
construction. The Palace was by far the grandest of all and
the one hotel Luke could be relatively certain Comstock
would avoid. With a nod at the smiling bellboy, Patrick,
Luke left the Palace's office.

His final stop was Fisherman's Wharf where he made
another reservation. Pausing behind the wheel of the
Runabout, not far from the pier where he and Genny had

hunted for the seaweed, Luke surveyed his findings. The police had no information. Harriett Peak would not be back until the first day of spring. The Palace Hotel had no information. How was he going to unravel whatever the hell was going on?

In Biloxi, Luke knew all the police. In Washington, D.C., his brother-in-law was always up for a challenge. With that thought, Luke asked a passerby the location of the nearest Western Union. Reaching the telegraph office on Market Street, not only did he send out a couple of telegrams but was told by an operator that his timing was excellent. A telegram had just come across the wire for him which they'd planned to deliver to the Palace Hotel. Back in the Runabout, Luke headed to Chinatown and met up with Ying on the corner of Dupont and Washington Streets.

"Anything on Comstock?" Ying asked.

"Not a damn thing."

"Huan Li wants to meet you."

"Good."

CHAPTER 17

"Baths taken, costumes sewn, and we know the dance," Genny said to Tricky.

"Nervous or not, tonight I perform for Ying."

"I hope I have the courage to perform for Luke. It's his payment for teaching me to swim."

It had been a long, quiet afternoon and behind the closed pocket doors of the parlor, they'd practiced their dancing and finished their costumes. Roscoe had stayed close to Genny as if he'd understood Luke's order to protect her.

"I'm betting Luke will teach you to make love after you're done paying him for the swimming lesson."

"Tricky Li," Genny gasped and remembered how Luke had stopped himself, swatted her bottom, pulled up her panties, and ordered her out of his bed. "He's not interested in me."

"You're blind if that's what you see when you're with Luke," Tricky replied.

"Even if he were interested, I'm not going to make love with any man." Did she still mean that after being in bed with Luke? Not once had she second guessed that decision until she had met Luke.

"Why not?"

"It leads to an illegitimate baby."

"Not illegitimate if you're married."

"Married men are unfaithful to their wives every day and every night. My mother and this ranch are proof of that."

"Are you saying Luke is married?"

"I never thought to ask him." Genny shook her head as her self-loathing surfaced. "Proof that I am my mother's daughter."

"According to Patty and Vern, you take after your grandfather not Garnet. Just ask Luke if he has a wife."

"He's too good looking not to have a wife, a fiancée or a mistress and a dozen women chasing him. He's thinking of leaving soon to go back to them."

"You're in love with him," Tricky said softly. Genny shook her head no, but when tears sprang to her eyes, Tricky hugged her. "Let's see what Patty has for supper while we wait for Ying and Luke to come back to *us*."

As they left the parlor, the front door burst wide open with the likes of one Reginald Moore and his friend, George. Bustling down the stairs with a bag in hand, Emerald shrieked his name as Sapphire raced down the hallway causing Genny and Tricky to scurry out of her way. Also toting a bag, Sapphire threw herself into Reginald's arms ahead of Emerald. Ruby, right behind Emerald, gave Genny a brief sideways look before handing her bag to George.

"We're taking your three best jewels to Sacramento," Reginald announced.

"What?" Patty asked coming to a stop at the doorway of the dining room.

"Did you clear this with Genevieve?" Vern asked, drawing up alongside Patty.

"Didn't have to since they said they don't have contracts with the Cat's Eye," Reginald replied as he, George and the women they'd come for gathered near the front door. Addressing Genny as she and Tricky paused in the hallway near the parlor, he added, "Besides, I figure you got enough of my money from that bet your riverboat gambler won."

"Good for you," Genny said, ignoring Reginald but with a smile at the women.

Patty, Vern and Tricky stared at Genny no less surprised than the others who must have expected an argument from her. Two of the three women, hardened by life, turned and walked out the front door without a word. Sapphire stalked back down the hall to Genny.

"I wish you nothing but happiness," Genny said to her.

Under her breath, Sapphire hissed, "I wish I'd found Luke Harper before you did." Then turning to Reginald with a big smile, she said, "Let's be on our way home, Reggie."

"Go with the others, Sapphire honey. I'll be right with you," Reginald said and moved aside so that she could join George, Ruby and Emerald in the big automobile.

"Supper's ready when you are," Patty said with a smile of concern at Genny before heading back to the kitchen.

Vern stayed put at the entrance to the dining room as Genny and Tricky walked toward him. Excited female voices were heard outside as all three women squealed Luke's name. Reginald quickly intercepted Genny as Luke stepped onto the front porch.

"Like I once said, pretty lady, everybody's got a price," Reginald reminded her as he pressed a card against her palm. As Genny withdrew her hand, Reginald said, "Please contact me. I can easily pay whatever you ask."

Luke filled the doorway with a scowl and muscles. His hair was damp, and he'd changed his clothes. He must have bathed after their dip in the pond, too. The relief Genny felt at having Luke near was exceeded only by her attraction to him.

His green eyes narrowed, and his strong jaw clenched as he stepped into the foyer. Ying entered behind Luke with a nod at Vern and a smile at Tricky. Roscoe barked, bounding forward to greet Luke. Vern made eye contact with Luke as if to say he was glad to turn things over to him and bowed out. Tricky took Ying's hand and they quietly headed into the dining room.

Addressing Reginald Moore, Luke said, "Like I told you, she's with me."

"Hello again, Mr. Harper," Reginald said, nervously clearing his throat.

"What's going on, Genny?" Luke asked.

"Mr. Moore and his friend are taking three of the women," Genny glanced out the door just as Sapphire puckered her lips in a kiss aimed at Luke's back, "home with them."

"Well now," Reginald harrumphed. "We aren't taking them home exactly because our wives wouldn't like that."

"Streaks," Genny whispered, stunned. Luke wrapped an arm around her shoulders and tugged her against him. "Do they realize that, Mr. Moore?"

"Yes. They've been assured that as our mistresses, we will provide a house for them across town," Reginald replied matter-of-factly. "They will never have to work in another brothel."

"Have a safe journey," Luke said cooly, opening the front door wider.

"We shall indeed." Reginald took the hint to leave but stopped on the porch and turned to them. Taking an unlit cigar out of his jacket pocket he pointed it at Genny and asked Luke, "Mistress or wife?"

"The right wife is a man's mistress," Luke said without hesitation.

"I bet so." Sticking the cigar in the corner of his mouth he turned and tromping down the steps muttered, "Reggie Moore will never know."

Genny stared in shock at the automobile full of people whose lifestyles would revolve around adultery. And what about Luke's reply to Reginald? She was certainly not his mistress. So, did Luke have the right wife? Her stomach tied itself in a knot as her mind swirled with confusion, but she snapped out of her daze when Luke smacked the door shut.

"Supper," Patty called.

Luke had not missed the lust on Reginald Moore's face when he'd pointed to the woman Luke wanted to marry. Feeling protective toward Genny, who Moore would hide away in a house as much a brothel as the Cat's Eye, Luke gave her a squeeze. When she looked up at him there was a question brimming in her eyes.

"What?" he asked.

"Do you have a wife?"

"No."

Genny ripped up the card Moore had given her. Luke cocked a brow when she stuffed the pieces into the top of his front pants pocket and remembered shoving the money he'd won from Moore all the way into her front pocket. Loving her so much as well as feeling a stab of possessiveness, he placed his hands to her face and lowered his mouth to hers. Her cat eyes closed as her full lips parted. Imagining a lifetime of her sensual kisses, it was not until he had buried a hand in her long hair that he realized it wasn't braided. He savored the feel of her soft breasts against his chest as he flattened both hands to her back and held her close. When their lips parted, he brushed a lilac scented lock away from her porcelain cheek.

"Why is your hair down?" he asked.

"For the dance I'm doing this evening to pay you."

"Let's go home."

"Don't leave yet," Vern said and leaned around the corner of the dining room. "We have a lot of extra food now. You gotta come eat some of Patty's supper or I'll be in trouble."

They followed Vern into the dining room, but Luke wanted to get Genny out of this place. Customers would arrive soon which meant Onyx and Opal would come downstairs. He wanted out of this damn whorehouse, too. Genny called hello to Grace and Ruth who entered the dining room as she pulled out a chair at the long, family style table. Motioning Luke into the chair at the head of the table, he sat down and Genny went to get their suppers.

Drumming his fingers on the table, Luke mentally walked the scenario of taking Genny to Biloxi. But there would be no masking how wealthy he was. In San Francisco, he was a gambler. In Biloxi, she would be safe with him and surrounded by family who would love her. Friends in this room loved her, too, but his gut continued to warn him that she risked danger in San Francisco from Comstock and whoever was helping him.

In Biloxi, she'd say she loved him. Here in San Francisco, she'd mean it.

Genny set two plates of Patty's fried fish, peas from the garden and steaming macaroni on the table then took a seat on Luke's right. Joe and the Johnson brothers arrived just before Grace and Ruth entered the dining room. Having already eaten, Patty arrived with more steaming plates of supper and Vern served drinks, both joining the conversation as they saw fit. The talk went from three of the jewels leaving the ranch to the watchers at the pond.

After supper, Genny said, "I'm taking up my post in the foyer."

"You will not," Patty said coming out of the kitchen with a chocolate cake which she placed in front of Genny. "Tomorrow is your birthday."

"This is from Patty, Tricky, Ying, and me," Vern said, and handed Luke a box.

"You know what the packages are inside the box, Luke, so you can give them to her tomorrow when the time is right," Patty said.

"You weren't supposed to make a fuss or tell anyone, Patty," Genny said with a choke in her voice as she glanced from her to Vern.

"I don't always do what's expected. Do I, Vern?"

"No, ma'am or you wouldn'ta married me," Vern said and shook his head.

"Thank you," Genny said, getting up and hugging Patty, Vern, Tricky, and Ying, as the others at the table wished her a happy birthday.

While the cake was enjoyed, the talked turned serious again.

"I take it you didn't find out anything about Comstock from the police?" Joe asked.

"No," Luke replied. "Which makes me think the name Comstock is an alias."

"Yeah, an alias." Mike nodded as did others around the table.

"Too bad there were no leads," Jimmy said.

"There will be," Ying said enthusiastically from where he sat across the table with Tricky.

"What do you mean, Ying?" Joe asked.

Ying immediately looked to Luke for permission to answer. When Luke nodded, Ying replied, "We went to Chinatown."

"Huan." Tricky's eyes widened as she looked from Ying to Luke and then settling on Genny, she said, "Comstock will be found."

"On that note," Luke began, scooted his chair back and stood, "good night, ya'll."

Holding the box under one arm he took Genny's hand and as she called goodbye over her shoulder, he trailed her behind him to the front door. Roscoe followed them and when Vern called the dog, Luke directed him back to Vern.

"Are they not planning to see me tomorrow?" Genny asked, realizing that not only had Patty said for him to give her the birthday gift but they were leaving Roscoe.

"They might not see you for weeks," Luke said mysteriously. "Tonight, you owe me a dance."

CHAPTER 18

ALONE BEHIND THE CLOSED DOOR OF LUKE'S BEDROOM, Genny quivered with anxiety. A single lamp flickered on the bedside table. Even though Tricky had given Ying her virginity, she had admitted she'd still be nervous to debut her dance for him. Genny was beyond nervous. She had donned her costume but lacking the courage to proceed, she was frantically trying to think of a substitute payment.

For the umpteenth time, she checked the golden hair pins at both temples which held a red scarf that dipped at the back of her head and fluttered down her loose hair. Smoothing the red satin, elbow-length sleeves jingled golden beads trimming her low cut bodice. Sewn into the hem of the bodice, more golden beads dangled against her flesh. Naked skin showed from under her breasts to an inch below her belly button. Except for brothels and dancehalls, a bare midriff was unheard of. What would Luke think? Around her hips ten separate, red chiffon panels were fashioned into a skirt allowing for all the moves of her dance. The skirt also jingled with beads and red satin trim swished above her bare feet.

Pasted into her navel was a moonstone. Well, not a real moonstone of course because they were expensive. As a child she'd painted a flat pebble pale lavender. Never having figured out a way to wear her make-believe moon-stone until now, tonight it was her piece d'résistance.

"Are you going to do your dance?" Luke called from the front room.

"Yes." Genny steadied herself praying that he'd find this silly, maybe stupid, yes silly and stupid performance worthy payment for a serious lesson that could save one's life.

Before she could back out, she opened the bedroom door and tiptoed down the dimly lit hall. She stopped at the edge of the front room where two lamps bathed the handsome, definitely intimidating and always commanding man in a warm glow. Luke sat about ten feet from her in the big, overstuffed chair, his boots off and feet propped on the ottoman.

From the moment she stepped into view, Luke stared at her without a word, without blinking, without moving a muscle. Then his eyes roamed from the red scarf on her head, to the beads falling into the crease of her cleavage, to her decorated belly button, to the red chiffon skirt so sheer and revealing her red satin panties and bare legs were visible.

Surely his silence was a polite indication that he didn't approve of her costume, her *get-up* as he would call it. Therefore, he wasn't going to appreciate the dance, either. Her cheeks flamed as she berated her silly, stupid self. She would back down the hall and hightail it out his window.

Oh but then, the wildest grin spread his lips and his eyes narrowed with a wicked glint.

"Genevieve Moonstone Morgan," Luke breathed, wondering if the mythical maiden from the moon had actually materialized into reality. "You beautiful goddess, please dance for me."

With a nod and poised curtsy, Genny slowly raised her arms into an arc above her head. Delicate hands almost touching, a bell-like sound from small cymbals attached to her fingers and thumbs, chimed. Luke wondered if he could make it through her dance without touching her. He'd try. Without stripping her. No promises. The only guarantee he could make was that nothing on heaven or earth could have moved him from this spot.

The magnificent woman lifted her head and enchanting lilac eyes glimmered in the soft lamplight as the sweetest of smiles parted pink lips. When her half naked torso undulated ever so sensuously, he pictured tossing her over his shoulder and taking her straight to bed.

Chime. Her dance shifted drawing his attention to her generously exposed cleavage as her right arm lifted like a gently lapping wave. Her left arm raised and floated just as effortlessly. Like a siren at sea, she beckoned. One shoulder rose as the other one fell, and slowly she made her way toward him. Step by step she was almost near enough for him to touch.

Chime. She quickly spiraled out of reach. Facing away from him, she bent over backward so far that her long black hair brushed past her rounded bottom covered by the red panties. Snapping her body upright her split skirt shimmied as her hips shifted back and forth faster than what Luke thought was humanly possible. He couldn't have been more captivated if chained to the chair.

Chime. Twirling on toes and hair flying she tantalized, dancing closer then slipping away like an elusive dream. As if reaching for him, her arms stretched forward only to tease him before crossing over her breasts. Shirts swishing, her legs appeared like flowers in a summer breeze and her feet seemed to float above the wooden floor. All the while shiny beads jiggling against her ivory breasts entranced, her flat tummy with its bejeweled belly button rippled and her curvy hips swept him into an erotic world of pure carnal desire.

Luke plowed his fingers through his hair, took a deep breath and blew it out slowly. Blood rushing hot and hard into his loins, he kicked the ottoman out of his way. Sitting forward in the chair and hands flattening to his thighs, he spread his legs.

Chime. About six feet from him, Genny dropped to all fours. Head up, cat eyes holding him hostage, she prowled toward him as sleek as a panther. Luke ached to take this feline fantasy into his arms as she crawled ever further and inescapably into his heart and soul.

With a flick of her fingers to her temples the red scarf became a billowing cape. In a gesture of disarming surrender, she placed one hand between his feet, her other hand coming to rest on top of it. With her forehead to the back of her hand, the scarf fluttered down over her head and upper body like an oyster covering its prize pearl.

Luke didn't speak for several seconds.

"Genny, you...that dance...was not...of this world," he finally said in a husky whisper. "I've never seen anything like it." He gently touched the top of her head. "What do you call it?"

In one fluid movement she slowly sat up, perching on the backs of her legs.

"Belly dancing," she said softly.

"I couldn't have asked for a better payment for teaching you to swim. Promise you'll do it for me again and again."

"For Adonis, I promise." Blushing as red as her costume, she lowered her gaze to the floor.

"Adonis?" Luke remembered the turned down corner of the page in her Greek mythology book. "I don't think—"

"You," she began, smiling up at him as she sat at his feet, "must be a Greek god. No man so wildly and wickedly handsome could possibly be...of this world."

"You are a little *wildcat*."

"Only for you."

Luke smiled, got to his feet and helped her to stand. Wrapping his arms around her, she melted against his chest and when his mouth lowered to hers, she kissed him with abandon. Luke scooped her up and carried to her straight to his bedroom. There, he stood her next to his bed and she placed her finger cymbals on the night table. To his complete surprise, button by button she unfastened his shirt. He shrugged out of the shirt and flung it onto a chair. Taking hold of the hem of her red beaded top, he paused, and she gave him permission by raising her arms in a graceful arc above her head. Luke pulled it off, tossed it onto the chair with his shirt and stared.

Genny's breasts, when naked, were even more beautiful than the gauzy or wet fabrics had hinted. Luke took the weight of her breasts in his hands and his thumbs gently skimmed nipples that were indeed the perfect shade of expensive bourbon. She bowed her head and shivered as her nipples beaded. Why was she letting him undress her? Placing two fingers under her chin he tipped her head up and she met his gaze. This time it was his eyes that held a question.

She suggested, "Belated payment for my kissing lesson?"

"No."

Luke placed Genny's hands to his chest. Her tender exploration of his naked skin unleashed desires in him as extraordinary as the woman herself. She never took her eyes off him as he unbuckled his belt, unbuttoned his jeans and tugged them down. When a shy smile tugged up the corners of her lips, he stepped out of his Levi's. Wearing only his snug drawers, he slid his thumbs into her sheer red skirt and pulled it down. Stripped to her panties, he tossed her skirt onto the chair. Only their undergarments separated head-to-toe flesh-on-flesh.

"My moonstone," she began, plucking the lavender stone from her belly button, "to always protect you," she raised her eyes to his and finished softly, "on or off the water."

He held out his hand. "Now *that's* my payment for your kissing lesson."

Genny placed the stone in his palm and tenderly closed his fingers around it. Luke thought she might just care a little about him after all. Tossing back the covers she crawled into his bed on all fours. Flipping her hair over her shoulder, she reached for him, and he let her tug him into bed. Scooting the pebble under his pillow he pulled her supple body halfway beneath his yearning one and leaned over her. Winding one arm around his side, she placed her other hand to the back of his head as he'd often done to her. She had learned so much so fast. And he was teaching her in spite of himself.

When his lips met hers, he flattened a hand low on her tummy. As their tongues played, Luke slid his hand down between her thighs. A little gasp escaped her lips, but she didn't break their kiss. When he slipped a finger into her panties, he brushed petal soft skin.

"Luke," Genny breathed, entranced by the magic of this man. She'd already gone so much farther than she'd planned. But she couldn't, in truth didn't want to, stop herself. When his finger caressed her most secret place, she thought maybe he had the power she lacked. "Umm…is this where I should say no?"

"Is that a question or are you telling me no?" His whisper was as thick and rich as molasses as his finger dipped deliciously inside of her.

"You told me to keep saying no."

"To every man but me."

"Oh, yes," she murmured, craving this new excitement sliding further and further into her. Her heart pounded, her flesh heated and with Luke's discovery of her body she sensed a dewy dampness around his finger. "I'm afraid."

His voice was deep, masculine, intimate. "Because you're a virgin."

"How can you possibly know that?" she asked as he gently pressed against something inside her body. Her maidenhead? He could feel it? Genny was instantly reminded Luke was the one with the experience. Despite her statement about mattress dancing since she was only twelve, he knew better now. "If I let history repeat itself, I'm as doomed as Garnet."

Taking his hand from between her legs, Luke rolled to his back and pulled her on top of him. Long and hard, his manhood pressed against her tummy. Oh, how she wanted to see him, feel him, have him do things to her that she'd allow only him to do. Her head resting beside his on his pillow, she savored the feel of his hands on her fanny.

"Let me love you, Genny." Luke's legs parted so that hers settled between his muscular thighs. By spreading his legs instead of hers, she sensed he was giving her power. Kneading her bottom with strong hands, he said, "Love me back and I promise you history won't repeat itself."

"It will absolutely repeat itself if I get pregnant." How she wished that weren't so, but it was. "I've stewed and stewed on it and my decision is that I can never sleep with you or…"

"Comstock," Luke said. "My gut says he's never bedded a woman and never will."

"Really?" Genny asked. "That kind of marriage would work very well for me."

"Hell, I'd have that kind of marriage annulled." Luke lightly smacked her fanny. "If you aren't gonna love me, get outa my bed. Without falling on the floor."

Genny rose up on her elbows but didn't roll off him. Her breasts burned from the sizzle of Luke's naked skin against hers. Between her legs scorching flames raged that could only be quenched by the man who had set her ablaze.

"You asked me once if the Cat's Eye Ranch ruined my life. If I don't escape, I'll always be a nobody fish in a disgraceful pond."

"Your life will be ruined if you're trapped in a loveless, sexless marriage with that odd scarecrow," Luke growled, rolled her off him and sat up on the side of the bed.

"A loveless, sexless marriage on Nob Hill would be less shameful than being a mistress in Sacramento where I could be left with an illegitimate baby, never knowing which married man fathered it." Genny felt her emotions rising along with her fears.

"Settling for a life because it's the lesser of two evils makes no damn sense to me."

"It makes complete sense to someone who's been called a scarlet harlot since the woman who lived in this very house first screamed it," Genny said, sitting up as hot tears burned the backs of her eyes and stung her throat. "Worst of all; never becoming the person I want to be."

"Become that person," Luke barked. "Otherwise, you're choosing to be unhappy." Clasping his hands between his knees, he shook his head. "That's something I'll never understand."

"I've been unhappy my whole life and you know why you don't understand that?" Genny asked with a choke in her voice. When he didn't respond, she swallowed hard and told him, "Because green is the color of strength and energy and new life." He had endless strength and energy to make one new life after another, wherever the next hand of cards took him. "I see a lifetime of happiness in your green eyes."

Luke looked over his shoulder at her. "Lilac is the color of dreams, imagination and new— what, Genny?" She was surprised he remembered that conversation from the night of the ball. When she shrugged instead of speaking, he said, "Answer me."

"Hope," she whispered.

"I'd like to see new hope, dreams and imagination in your eyes when you look at me."

"I'm *hoping* that by forfeiting happiness I will avoid becoming that scarlet harlot."

"Selling your soul for a house on Nob Hill is the definition of harlot." He turned away from her then and said, "Stew on that."

Silence permeated Luke's cozy bedroom. Genny gazed at his broad shoulders, down the muscles in his back, to the drawers riding low around his waist. From the night they met, his words had been changing her dreams, and his lessons giving her hope. But happiness? That seemed out of reach. Gingerly, she extended her hand and placed it in the middle of his back.

"I'll sleep in the chair this time." Luke stood and left the bedroom.

Genny buried her face in her hands and let her pent-up tears flow. She wanted to love Luke and only Luke in every sense of the word for the rest of her life. But she didn't have the nerve to admit that since he didn't love her. Cold proof was his admission that every day he thought about leaving. His ranch could sell tomorrow. Her time with him was running out.

Sniffling, she swiped away her tears, sat up and squared her shoulders. If she couldn't become the person she wanted to be, at least she could be honest about her feelings.

Yes. She would tell him she loved him more than all the miles to the dark side of the moon and back. The fact he was a drifting gambler and poor? It no longer mattered.

No. He would leave her with a fatherless baby. So be it. She would always have part of the only man she would ever love. Pregnancy was a risk she would take.

Picturing Luke's baby cuddled in her arms enveloped Genny with a sense of peace and fulfillment. But her baby would be shunned as she'd been. And what if Comstock was the bad guy Luke said he was and came after her…and a baby? By then Luke would be long gone.

Maybe she could track Luke down in Mississippi and they could be a family. In Biloxi, where scores of other women were no doubt in love with him, too? Genny saw herself standing on the porch of a small house, holding a baby and facing Luke and his wife or a fiancée or a mistress. At that soul crushing image Genny crumbled, buried her face in the pillow and sobbed.

"C'mere." Luke lay down and tugged her into his strong

arms. "Please don't cry. Moonstones encourage our truest life's journey. Remember?"

Genny nodded. "The cat's eye moonstone brings parts of the soul which were lost back into the *light*," she choked out, her head resting on his shoulder, her hand over his heart and her leg slipping between his.

"Tomorrow is your birthday and we have plans in San Francisco."

"We do?"

"Yes," he replied with a kiss to her forehead.

"Harper, starting tomorrow I'm going to let my imagination run wild."

"Imagine being wildly happy, Genevieve."

CHAPTER 19

"Why are we going to Nob Hill?" Genny asked, sitting beside Luke in the Runabout.

They had just finished a delicious brunch in their luxurious suite at the Palace Hotel where Luke said they would be spending the next few weeks while sightseeing, dining, shopping, relaxing, and enjoying the city.

Just like all the rooms in the hotel, they had a huge bay window with a spectacular view. Sunlight had spilled across the solitary, large bed instead of twin beds like the room Luke had on New Year's Eve. Luke had caught her eyeing the bed and his cocky grin sent hot shivers from her fingertips to her toes, leaving her imagining little else but the night to come.

"Have you ever been up to Nob Hill?" Luke asked, behind the wheel of the automobile.

"Well..." Wearing a simple gray frock, made for her by Patty, Genny shrank into the cushioned seat of the Runabout. "No, I haven't."

Veering away from Market Street and the hotel, Luke asked, "How come you've never explored Nob Hill?"

"There's no use being so close to the most perfect place to live in all of San Francisco if it's so far out of your reach."

"Nob Hill is five hundred feet above sea level and overlooks the city," Luke replied as he drove the Runabout onto California Street. "I'd like to take in that view."

"I liked the view from the Palace Hotel," Genny said truthfully.

"Isn't curiosity about to kill the cat?"

"No." She wanted the gambling drifter and his red-hot passion not *a loveless, sexless marriage with that odd scarecrow.*

"Wouldn't you like to see the palaces of the Big Four railroad tycoons; Stanford, Hopkins, Crocker, and Huntington who built the Central Pacific Railroad?" Luke asked.

"If you would," she replied.

"I would. We can take a *lesson* about Nob Hill together. Here," he said, handing her a small booklet. "You can teach us from this information I ran across at the *San Francisco Chronicle* building. Harriett Peak wrote it." Luke smiled and headed up the famous hill.

"If the booklet is anything like her column, *Peak's People*, we'll learn as much or more about the inhabitants than the houses themselves," Genny said.

"I'm ready to hear all about Nob Hill's who's whos."

"Miss Peak says—" opening the booklet, Genny read, "during the robber baron glory days of the eighteen seventies, Nob Hill was called California Hill." She glanced over at Luke. "I didn't know that."

He shrugged. "Me neither."

"Nob comes from the word nabob, an Anglo-Indian term for an ostentatiously wealthy man," Genny said.

"Ostentatiously wealthy? As in vulgar and lacking in good taste?" Luke asked with a tease in his voice. "On your perfect hill?"

Genny rolled her eyes and pursed her lips. They rode up the hill's steep grade in silence and at the corner of Powell and California Streets, Luke slowed the vehicle so they could take in the panoramic vista. Pointing, Genny said Russian Hill was to the north and the mission district lay to the south. Due east, straight ahead; Chinatown, the financial district, the piers, and the breathtaking blue Bay.

Craning her neck around, Genny waved the booklet at an enormous square house. Luke brought the Runabout to a stop in front of it. If ever there was a cold, inhospitable structure meant to intimidate the whole world this place was it, Genny thought.

"Leland Stanford's neoclassical mansion," she read and stared for a moment before consulting Harriett Peak's booklet again. "It was built in eighteen seventy-four by Stanford, the president of the Central Pacific Railroad. Ten years later, Leland and Jane Stanford took their only child on a tour of Europe. Leland, Jr. caught typhoid fever and died in Florence, Italy two months before his sixteenth birthday. The Stanfords were heartbroken and a year later signed a grant founding Leland Stanford Junior University. Nine years passed and then Mr. Stanford died leaving his widow all alone." Pausing with sympathy, Genny peered at the house and this time it loomed with loneliness. "In January nineteen and five, strychnine was found in Mrs. Stanford's bottled water. She was so afraid and depressed over the obvious murder attempt, she moved out of this house which well known for staff jealousies and treachery. Vowing never to return, she sailed to Hawaii."

"Poison, like the meat meant to kill Roscoe," Luke said.

"Yes," Genny said softly. "The following month in Honolulu, Mrs. Stanford drank bicarbonate of soda to settle her upset stomach. It was laced with a fatal dose of strychnine administered by her personal secretary, the only person present at both strychnine occurrences. Having feared to her final breath that she was being poisoned, Jane Stanford's last words were, 'This is a horrible death to die'." Placing a hand on Luke's arm, Genny whispered in shock, "What a tragic story."

"Tragic." Luke made no other comment and drove toward the next house.

Over her shoulder, Genny grimaced at the house of despair and death until Luke nudged her. Facing forward again, she held the booklet out in front of her.

"The house right next door belongs to the second Central Pacific Railroad founder and principal investor, Mark Hopkins," Genny said, as Luke stopped the Runabout again. She gaped at the gloomy, gray monstrosity with its pointed spires and arches, towering turrets and finials. As massive as it was forbidding, the sinister air of this place sent a freezing chill up Genny's spine. "It looks haunted."

"It does."

"Mark and Mary Hopkins never had children of their own," Genny read. "Mr. Hopkins died before this forty room Gothic-style residence was finally finished in eighteen seventy-eight. Mrs. Hopkins was in charge of completing and decorating the estate and was sued numerous times by workmen because she failed to pay them."

"Always treat those who work for you right."

"Yes, and even then, they might not appreciate it." Genny sighed, thinking of Sapphire, Emerald and Ruby. "Harriett Peak writes that despite his massive fortune and poor health, Mr. Hopkins died without leaving a will. However unseemly it may have been, Mary Hopkins ran off with and married her interior decorator, named Searles, who was twenty-two years her junior. Mrs. Hopkins did have a will and took an adopted son, Timothy, out of it. Less than four years later when Mary died, legal battles raged between Searles and Timothy. Even though Searles admitted and testified under oath that he had married Mary for her money, as well as fondness, Timothy lost his appeals. It was rumored Searles had had a lover and that Timothy blackmailed him because eventually Searles settled several million dollars on the Hopkins' adopted son." Genny shook her head as she looked at the Nob Hill house. "How awful all the way around."

"Awful to marry for money and not love," Luke said and cocked a brow.

"Point made," Genny said as he drove forward on California Street.

"Who's next?" Luke asked and chuckled.

"Charles Crocker. The third house belonging to one of the Big Four has been described as a failed attempt at a Second Empire Italian-style villa. Even taller than the mansions of Stanford and Hopkins, Crocker's twelve thousand square-foot house is a showoff with its seventy-six foot tower and wrought-iron widow's walk from which Crocker could observe the less fortunate." Genny paused as she and Luke took in the scenery as it were. "In eighteen seventy-eight, Leland Stanford arranged for the California Street Line Cable Cars to provide new accessibility up the vertically challenging hill, making this the most elite and coveted area to live in San Francisco. Thus, Mr. Crocker attempted to buy up an entire block surrounded by Califonia, Jones, Taylor, and Sacramento Streets in order to build his grandiose house."

"Grandiose?"

"Grotesque," Genny replied. "Luke, you know it is grotesque. At the risk of sounding terribly unkind, the prize for the darkest and ugliest house so far is a three-way tie."

"Read on."

Finding the place in Harriett Peak's article where she'd left off, Genny read, "However, Mr. Crocker couldn't claim ownership of the entire block due to a German immigrant named Nicholas Yung who refused to sell out. Accustomed to getting his way, during the leveling of his lot, Charles Crocker supposedly ordered workers to aim dynamited debris toward Yung's home. But Yung didn't give in because he and his family loved the sunlight and ocean breezes afforded them on Nob Hill. So, Crocker built a forty-foot spite fence around three sides of Yung's house to block the light and breezes." Genny looked at Luke and said, "How vengeful."

"What happened?"

"Mr. Yung, an undertaker, built a ten-foot-long coffin and decorated the lid with a skull and crossbones. He placed it on his rooftop facing Crocker's mansion, so the railroad baron would have to see it every day. Yung did not sell his land to Crocker, but eventually gave up and moved his house to a lot on Broderick Street. Although the *San Francisco Chronicle* called the spite fence a memorial of malignity and malevolence and San Franciscans referred to the fence as 'Crocker's Crime' he let it stand as a symbol of his wealth and power."

"Proof that money can't buy everything. A lesson you taught Reginald Moore."

Genny smiled her appreciation and read, "After Mr. and Mrs. Yung were dead, their daughters sold the land to Crocker's heirs and the fence was finally torn down in nineteen and five." Genny placed the booklet in her lap and shook her head while frowning at the entire block of property. "What a shame Crocker was cruel to Mr. Yung and his family. Just like with Mrs. Cavender, you can't always pick your neighbors."

"And the fourth house?"

"There. The house that looks like marble." Genny indicated a gigantic rectangular place resembling a government building much more than it did a personal residence. "Harriett Peak says that this house is painted to look like marble but in reality, it's only wood. Collis P. Huntington, the fourth and final railroad tycoon of the Big Four, bought this place after the most notorious lawsuit of the Gay Nineties."

"Another lawsuit? Let's hear it."

"This Roman and Corinthian-style house was built in eighteen seventy-two by David Colton, the chief lawyer for the Central Pacific Railroad. Colton was not one of the Big Four and in fact the four tycoons called him 'four and half'.

Colton was thrown from a horse, suffered internal injuries and died when he was only forty-six. His widow, Ellen, sued the Big Four, claiming they cheated her out of company securities owned by Mr. Colton. In turn, they accused her late husband of embezzling from the Central Pacific Railroad. But Mrs. Colton provided six hundred letters from Collis P. Huntington to her late husband directing him in all manner of espionage against rival railroads including bribes to politicians in Sacramento and Washington." Stunned, Genny paused and looked at Luke in disbelief.

"What else?"

"Although Mrs. Colton won the lawsuit, she put her house up for sale and fled San Francisco. Huntington, described as scrupulously dishonest, bought the house thus owning a Nob Hill mansion like Stanford, Hopkins and Crocker. Huntington has come to be known as such a symbol of corruption and greed that he is referred to as California's most despicable villain."

"A bad guy," was Luke's comment. "Hmm."

"Don't 'hmm' me, Harper. You read Harriett Peak's article and you already knew all of this. The richest of the rich on Nob Hill appear to have been anything but happy."

"I know old family money is often more stable than nouveau riche money."

"Nouveau riche as in ostentatious? Vulgar and lacking in good taste?"

"I'll let you decide," Luke said now as he had on the night they'd met after she asked if he were someone important, a who's who, someone she should know.

Genny read the last lines in the booklet, "On May tenth, eighteen sixty-nine the heads of the Central Pacific and the Union Pacific Railroads met at Promontory Summit, Utah Territory. The Union Pacific's locomotive; Number One Nineteen and the Central Pacific's locomotive; Number Sixty, better known as Jupiter, were drawn face-to-face and the golden last spike was driven in by

Leland Stanford joining the rails of the First Transconti-
nental Railroad."

"Well, what do you think of our lesson on Nob Hill?"
Luke said.

"I think I've been jackslapped to Jupiter and run over by
a locomotive."

"Nah, I have your moonstone for protection in my
pocket."

"It's not a real moonstone, Luke," Genny said earnestly
and took his hand. She looked from Crocker's property
back to Luke. "What's real is that if Mr. Yung can move his
whole entire house to a happier location, I can surely move
little ol' me to a happier place."

"Now you're talking." Luke winked and squeezed her
hand. "Light and ocean breezes are not exclusive to California, you know."

I'm not staying in San Francisco much longer.

"I know." Genny felt the sharp pang to her heart she
always felt when Luke hinted of leaving. "I'll keep that in
mind as I start imagining what I can do instead of what I
can't."

Luke wrapped an arm around her and kissed her.
Feeling the power and protection of his embrace, Genny
wished he'd never let her go just before he released her. He
steered the Runabout past some much smaller houses as
they wound their way out of the famous neighborhood
overlooking the unique city by the Bay. Not too far from
where they'd been atop Nob Hill, was a quaint Victorian
house. Luke slowed the automobile.

"Speaking of villains, look at that yellow and white
house on the corner of California Street," Luke said.

"Streaks and sockdolagers! Are those red-haired men
the Skidmores?" Genny asked in shock. "What would Curt
and Billy be doing at that house?"

"Something linked with Joe and the Johnson brothers
saying those two were walking away from the city the day
your window was broken with the poisoned meat. If you

weren't with me, I'd go find out what the hell that something is."

"Then I'm glad I'm with you." Genny placed her hand on his knee as the two men disappeared around the corner of the house. "Let's go back to the Palace Hotel. Please, Luke."

"Leavenworth and California," Luke said, making note of the address before heading back to the hotel.

"MR. HARPER?"

Stepping out of the shadows near the entrance to the Palace Hotel, the Chinese man who had spoken was joined by a second man. They were both solidly built and appeared to be in their late twenties. Luke noticed that like Ying, these men did not have queues or wear Mandarin hats. What they did have were definite no-nonsense expressions.

"I'm Luke Harper," Luke replied as he and Genny stopped. "What can I do for you?"

"Mr. Harper, Miss Morgan, my name Wong," the taller man said politely, his English just slightly broken. "This Chen." Wong indicated the man with him. "Boss, Huan Li, send us. Need ride Chinatown?"

"We have a ride to Chinatown for supper, thank you," Luke replied.

"Need anything?" Wong asked.

"Do you have time to check out an address near Nob Hill?"

"Yes, sir," Wong said as Chen nodded.

Luke provided them with the address and a couple of details. The two men vanished as discreetly as they had appeared. After entering the hotel, Luke took Genny's arm and tucked it through his as they crossed the grand Palm Court.

"Are you working with Huan Li?" Genny asked.

"We're keeping each other informed. After all, the house

where his sister is living was damaged. Huan has his own enemies, but he knows I suspect Comstock in this case."

Genny nodded. "Did you tell Huan the police have no leads on Comstock?"

"Yes," Luke replied. "Huan says there are four hundred thousand people in San Francisco and the police have their hands full. Huan and I agree that the police aren't apt to look very hard for Comstock or whatever his name is since as far as they're concerned the only thing he's done is run out on his hotel bill."

"What?" Genny said and glanced in the direction of the ballroom. "He was the one who couldn't pay his bill? When I tried to return your tuxedo the orchestra leader told me the man who had set his sights on me was thrown out for not paying."

Luke tilted his head. "And you thought that man was me?"

"I did," Genny admitted. "You were the one who made sure he was my partner for the scavenger hunt, not Comstock."

They had reached the same fancy wrought-iron elevator where Comstock had watched Luke being pulled into it by Genny. Suddenly wondering if the scarecrow would be just odd enough to return to the hotel, Luke's skin crawled. He glanced around but didn't see Comstock anywhere. Genny remembered the rising room too, because she playfully took hold of his shirt and tugged him onto the elevator with her.

"I didn't know we were going to Chinatown for supper," she said.

"We are." Luke pushed the lever. "Ying and Tricky will meet us there."

"That sounds wonderful," Genny said. As they rose toward their sixth-floor suite, she chewed her lower lip hoping that her mended aquamarine gown was appropriate dinner attire.

Stepping off the elevator Luke escorted Genny to their

room, where a maid was placing towels beside Genny's scented bath. Luke excused himself and left her to bathe alone. The maid handed her a silk robe for after her bath, saying she had just placed freshly pressed clothes in one of the two wardrobes. Luke's suit, Genny guessed. On her way into the bathroom, Genny glanced at the bed, alternately craving and stressing the night to come.

CHAPTER 20

AN HOUR LATER, GENNY WAS ABOUT TO TUCK A WAYWARD curl behind her ear when she heard a key turning in the lock. Luke entered their suite, dressed in a dark brown suit, crisp white shirt and dark brown shoes polished to a shine. Probably because he was from Biloxi, he didn't wear a derby hat like most men in San Francisco. She was glad because she loved burying her fingers in his thick brown hair.

"You've had a bath, too," Genny said, observing his slick-backed hair.

"The hotel made arrangements for me, so you could have privacy," he said coming toward her. "What are you wearing besides that robe and pretty smile?"

"Harper," she gasped when he seized the closure to her robe. Though this man had seen her nearly naked several times, she felt shy. "Only my unmentionables."

"Better stay away from me, then," he said with a low chuckle. "I see they delivered the champagne. Want to make a toast?"

"Certainly," Genny said and when he popped he cork, she laughed and caught most of the bubbling champagne with their glasses. "Last time we were here we toasted our Square Deal of dancing, fighting, kissing, and drinking.

What shall we toast to next?"

"Making love," he said with a wicked grin. "I'll rise to the occasion. Will *you*, little lamb?"

Without skipping a beat, she said, "I can't *imagine* a better birthday gift from you, wolf."

Luke cocked a rakish brow and clinked his glass to hers. They each swallowed a couple of sips and when Genny said she should finish dressing, Luke swung his hand toward her wardrobe. But instead of finding her mended dress there, she discovered a new, freshly pressed lilac gown, far fancier than the gray dress. Genny stared in surprise as Luke told her the maid had hidden her mended gown in his wardrobe. Vern wanted her to know that Patty had worked on the two birthday dresses for weeks. Patty in turn had shared that Vern's part was contributing tips from serving drinks and taking her into town to buy the gray cotton and lilac satin fabrics.

"They went to far too much trouble," Genny said, shaking her head in wonder.

Dress in hand, she moved behind a dressing screen outside the first real bathroom where she'd taken her first real bathtub bath. After washing her hair, she'd soaked in the steaming scented water until it had cooled. In back of the screen, placed on a chair, were white stockings and white leather, ankle high boot-like shoes with an inch and a half heel. Knowing the expense of the shoes, she bit her tongue to keep from voicing concern over the money she was sure Luke couldn't afford to spend on her. Perching on the chair she donned her first pair of stockings and fastened the white buttons of the sleek, new shoes.

Next, she slid the soft lilac gown over her head and slipped her arms into long sleeves that trimmed her wrists in white lace. Matching white lace adorned a vee neckline and a white bolero-style bodice tied under her bosom, pushing her breasts together and displaying her cleavage. The satin skirt fluttered to the floor where rows of white lace ruffles decorated the hem and a small train. Luke called to her, and stepping into his view, she lifted the hem of her gown to show him the boots and stockings.

"Come here." Luke crooked a finger at the most magnificent woman he'd ever known. As sensual as she was graceful, she may as well have been floating to him in a dream instead of walking over the thick carpets. Reaching him, he handed her a colorfully wrapped package. "This is from Tricky and Ying."

Genny peeled away the paper to reveal a clutch-type purple pocketbook decorated with a jade rabbit. A card inside said that in Chinese mythology a jade rabbit lived on the moon.

"How perfect," Genny said. "I can't wait to thank everyone, starting with you."

Laying the purse aside, she stood on her tiptoes, took his face in her soft hands and kissed him. Closing his eyes, Luke savored the feel of her fingers caressing the back of his head as only she could do.

"Harriett Peak says designers are calling my new white shoes, 'the immaculate foot dressing for the most fashionable woman'. How ever did you know I liked them?"

"You had the shoes and this hairstyle you're wearing tonight circled in an issue of the *San Francisco Chronicle* I read at your house."

Genny touched her Gibson girl topknot and said, "You have a good memory."

"I remember the most fashionable woman at the ball wearing her hair like this the night we met," Luke said, tucking a silky ebony lock behind her ear.

Hardly finding her tablecloth gown the most fashionable, she simply said, "Thank you for the stockings and shoes."

"My pleasure."

When he reached into his jacket Genny glimpsed the menacing Colt .45 at the left side of his ribcage. She'd seen him pull that big gun out of its holster as smoothly as he was removing a small box from an inside pocket.

"Happy twenty-first birthday from me."

"Whatever this is, it's too much," she said, gingerly accepting the gift with both hands.

As Genny opened the box, Luke enjoyed how her eyes widened and her lips parted. On white velvet lay a flawless lilac moonstone from the finest jewelry store in San Francisco. Suspended on a yellow gold chain the large oval stone was encased in delicate yellow gold filigree.

"Luke..." Holding the jewelry box in one hand, she wrapped her other arm around his neck. Hugging him tightly she whispered, "Since I was a little girl, I wished for such a piece d'résistance but not wanting to get my hopes up, I stopped dreaming. Thank you so much."

"You're welcome. Time to start dreaming and hoping again," Luke reminded her as he stood her back and took the pendent out of the box. "A real moonstone to protect you on or off the water." Clasping the chain around her slender neck, the moonstone touched the crease of her sexy cleavage. "The lilac moonstone is for lovers, Genevieve."

"And it opens one's heart to love, Harper."

Dare she hope and dream she could open his heart to love? No. Luke Harper was a man too wild to be tamed. She tilted up her chin and his mouth came down on hers in a hungry kiss. When he let her go, she wondered how long it would be before he gave her a last kiss goodbye.

"I've never owned a piece of jewelry," she said, pushing aside her worries. "Grandpa was never without his pocket watch, and Garnet always wore a strand of pearls she said my father gave her. But those keepsakes were missing when their bodies were found."

"Now you have your own keepsake."

A keepsake to remember him by when he was gone?

Letting her imagination run wild, she bravely whispered, "Lilac moonstones represent eroticism and carnal desire."

"And fertility."

. . .

"The big gun," Huan Li said with a slight bow of admiration.

"The big fist," Luke replied with a nod of respect.

Tricky and Ying flanked Huan. Behind Huan were three members of the Monkey's

Fist. Genny knew from Ying that Huan was never without trusted, high ranking bodyguards. As Luke and Huan shook hands, Genny recalled glimpsing the tattoo on the back of Huan's right hand on the hands of Wong and Chen, earlier outside the hotel. The fierce face of a gorilla with razor sharp teeth was also tattooed on the right fists of the bodyguards with Huan this evening.

"I cannot compete with the Big Four," Huan said to Luke, obviously privy to some inside information. Unlike the citadels of the railroad barons, Huan's large, brown brick fortress was tastefully understated. Tricky had told Genny that Huan's living quarters took up the entire second floor. Here on the ground level was his eating establishment, simply called *Li's*. A private entrance in the back led to his headquarters which was as big as the restaurant. Including Genny with a smile, Huan continued, "Welcome to Li's."

"Huan, thank you for inviting us to be your guests this evening," Luke said and shook hands with the man who ruled Chinatown.

Like Ying, Huan considered himself Chinese American and his black hair was short. Clad in a dark gray, jacket-like shirt with a stand-up collar, he wore black britches and black shoes.

"I am honored, Luke," Huan replied in return. A nice-looking man with a medium build, at six feet he was taller than Ying. His coal black eyes were sharp as if they took in everyone and everything at once. "Very nice to see you again, Genevieve."

"It's good to see you, too, Huan," Genny said, her arm looped through Luke's.

"Is my little sister behaving herself in the country?" Huan asked Genny, as Tricky playfully huffed, putting her hands to her hips.

"Yes, she is," Genny replied with a smile of loyalty and discretion at Tricky. With a smile to Ying as well, she indicated her jade rabbit pocketbook and said, "Thank you, both."

"Follow me," Huan said.

Huan led the way through the busy restaurant to a concealed dining room. Luke, Genny, Ying, and Tricky followed Huan but his men made sure that no one else came close. Once inside the room a red velvet curtain was drawn providing privacy. Taking seats at a round table, Luke sat with Genny on his right and Huan on his left. Tricky was next to her brother and Ying sat between Tricky and Genny.

"Will Jia be coming down?" Tricky asked her brother.

"Jia is a relative of mine who arrived in San Francisco about a year ago," Ying said proudly and quickly glanced at Huan to see if he'd overstepped his bounds.

"Jia is not feeling well and sends her regrets," Huan replied, closing that conversation.

Dish after delicious dish of traditional Chinese foods began arriving at the table. Genny especially enjoyed the sweet and sour pork, chow mein, Kung pao chicken, and spring rolls.

Conversations were lively and included numerous topics. At times Huan spoke only to Luke who listened politely and in turn kept his replies quiet. It was obvious that Huan held Luke in the same high regard as Luke did the man who kept would-be rivals in Chinatown contained and Barbary Coast enemies terrified.

After dinner was finished and the table cleared, the curtain was held back by a bodyguard for a man who Huan introduced as his restaurant's baker.

"Mooncake for dessert," Huan said as the baker placed a delicate pastry in the center of the table, before bowing and backing away. "Mooncakes, like a full moon, symbolize prosperity and completeness."

"Mooncakes are very special in China and shared only with the closest of friends and at family gatherings," Tricky added, smiling at Genny and Luke.

"Happy birthday, Genevieve," Huan said with echoes from Ying and Tricky.

Made with lotus seed paste and salted duck eggs, the thin-crusted mooncake was round, cut into wedges, and served with tea. Huan recommended the men have baijiu which he explained was rice wine. When Tricky suggested she and Genny would have wine, too, Huan frowned.

"Baijiu is similar to vodka," Huan said to Luke. "Ours is thirty proof."

"That's even stronger than Vern's flip." With a grin, Luke cocked a brow at Genny.

The women decided on the traditional tea with their mooncake.

"Genevieve, your moonstone is beautiful, and it matches the color of your eyes," Tricky said as Ying nodded.

"Thank you. It's from Luke," Genny replied and smiled at Luke. "I love it."

. "Moonstones possess the gifts of prophecy and the path to wisdom," Huan said.

"Moonstones are encouraging and calming," Tricky added.

No sooner had they finished the mooncake than a stone-faced bodyguard abruptly appeared at one end of the privacy curtain and held it back. Wong entered but silently retreated to the far end of the room. Huan excused himself from the table and met with Wong.

"Luke, please join us," Huan said in a matter of seconds.

Luke did so and as the three men spoke, Tricky identi-fied Wong as Huan's most trusted right-hand man. Genny noted that Wong spoke as if directly reporting to Luke. When Wong departed, Luke returned to the table, his expression grim. Huan followed him and poured another round of baijiu. With a nod of agreement from Luke, this time Huan included the women by pouring a thin layer of baijiu into their empty teacups. Genny tensed at this, assuming the men thought they were going to need a drink. She saw her concern mirrored on Tricky's face before they both took a sip. Genny coughed as did Tricky. Huan placed his elbows on the table and made a steeple with his fingertips.

"Huan?" Tricky choked and cleared her throat. "What did Wong say?"

"Wong and Chen went to the house Luke requested they visit," Huan replied. "The neighbors told them the house belongs to Harriett Peak." He paused and deferred to Luke.

"The Skidmore brothers were long gone, but Wong and Chen discovered a woman's body and a dead cat in a shallow grave in the backyard," Luke said.

"What?" Genny gasped.

"Oh no," Tricky said with a gulp.

"Who was it?" Ying asked.

Luke nor Huan answered.

"Luke, was it Harriett Peak?" Genny asked.

"No, she took the *Coast Line* train to Los Angeles in January," Luke replied. "The neighbors, who gathered around the burial site, told Wong and Chen they thought the three men going in and out of her house were renters."

"Wong and Chen will return to gain more knowledge of the people who did this," Huan said stoically and nodded at Luke.

Luke continued, "The neighbors identified the dead woman as Harriett Peak's housekeeper. There was an empty gasoline can near the grave." As sure as he sat here, this was a nail in Comstock's coffin. "The housekeeper was burned over most of her body."

"Dear Lord, no." Genny clasped her hands in her lap and felt Luke's hand cover hers.

"Do they know anything about the housekeeper?" Ying asked.

"Chinese," Huan replied, his voice deathly calm. "Fan Zhou from Chinatown."

That news set off discussions in both Chinese and English around the table. Genny was able to determine that the dead woman had been a childhood friend of Tricky's. Tricky bowed her head and wept as Ying comforted her with an arm around her shoulders.

"Andy and his two Rough Rider friends do more than help Ying with the horses and keep the ranch running," Genny said to Luke with dawning. "Don't they?"

"They're hired guns, Genny," Luke replied.

"Hired by the big gun," Ying piped up with a nod at Luke. "You should see the guns, pistols, rifles, and ammunition that belong to Andy and his friends. It's what they call an arsenal."

"Huan, you have a room like that," Tricky said, swiping tears from her eyes.

"During China's Song dynasty, an immortal figure emerged called Sun Wukong meaning the Monkey King," Huan said. "Half monkey and half human, the Monkey King was intelligent, fierce and rebellious. He was his own authority and ruled with a heavy fist. The five fingers of his fist represent five leaders each in charge of a team of ten or more soldiers. Thus, the Monkey King lives on in those of us who wage a righteous war against those bringing their evil upon us."

Silence reigned as information was digested.

"Egyptian mythology has an evil god of war," Genny said softly. "This malevolent god creates catastrophes, storms and chaos. Jealous of his good brother, the evil one killed him and became his substitute." She looked into Luke's eyes and somehow knew that he was already aware of what she was about to say. "That bad guy's name is Seth."

Luke nodded. "Well hell, I think we finally turned a corner."

"In addition to Chinatown and the Barbary Coast, the Monkey's Fist will watch Nob Hill," Huan said. "If the scarecrow and his soaplocks have created this evil they will die."

On that, Luke and Huan shook hands.

CHAPTER 21

INSIDE THEIR PLUSH SUITE AT THE PALACE HOTEL, lamplight glowed softly on a bedside table. Luke locked the door and took Genny into his arms. She felt small, delicate and vulnerable. When she trembled, he closed his eyes and rested his jaw against her head. She was safe with him. But what would happen if Comstock or the Skidmores caught her when he wasn't with her? Would she be poisoned? Burned? Buried in a shallow grave? Luke stopped those thoughts.

"A new bottle of champagne on ice," he said, glimpsing it. "Let's have a glass in bed."

She looked up at him and whispered, "I'd like that."

Luke shed his jacket and gun as Genny walked behind the dressing screen. He poured two glasses of champagne and placed them on the bedside table. He took off his shirt and then sitting on the turned down bed, removed his shoes and socks. As Genny tossed her gown over the top of the dressing screen, he rested his back against the headboard.

Luke thought about the nightgown he hoped she'd wear tonight. After his bath he'd purchased the gown along with a couple of dresses for her in one of the hotel's shops. He'd requested that the gown be placed behind her dressing screen when the maid returned to turn down their bed. However, under the circumstances involving the murder, he didn't expect Genny to wear it. Maybe she wouldn't have worn it anyway. He'd picked the white gown because it was the prettiest, like the woman herself. Virginal, too, he mused now as he looked back on his choice.

Was he going to take her virginity tonight? He damn sure wanted to. But she had to offer it and he wanted her to love him with her heart, not just her body. Maybe he wanted too much.

"Would you like to see my birthday suit?" Genny asked, snapping him out of his reverie.

"Yes." Luke turned his head and, like he had the night of her belly dance, took in every detail when she stepped into view. Her *birthday suit* was her birthday gown. He longed to touch the full breasts beneath the delicate white lace and spread the shapely legs draped in sheerest white satin. "You look beautiful. C'mere." He patted the bed and blushing, she floated to him. "I'd like to see your real birthday suit, too."

"You know what, Harper?"

"What?" he asked, tugging her to sit beside him on the bed and handing her a glass of champagne.

"Never mind." She picked up her new pendant from where it dangled between her breasts and ran her thumb over the moonstone. "I'm too shy to say it."

"Drink up then because I want to hear it."

Picking up his glass, Luke sensed an unspoken agreement of not discussing the earlier events of the evening. They touched their glasses, and he was sure she, too, was remembering their earlier toast to making love. When they had finished their champagne, he took her glass along with his and set them on the table.

"Now what were you too shy to tell me?" Luke asked.

"I want to see your birthday suit, too."

That was all Luke needed to hear. Rolling off his side of the bed and standing near the headboard, he undid his britches and stepped out of them. Clad only in his drawers, he faced the virginal maiden sitting in a pool of white in the center of the bed. With a sweep of his hand indicating it was her turn, his heart began to pound when she scooted off his side of the bed as well and stood near the footboard.

Her eyes roamed his naked chest as she slowly pulled a white strap off her slender shoulder. Tugging down the other strap, her perusal moved to his stomach. She studied the dark hair that swirled around his navel and disappeared into the waist of his low riding drawers. All the while, little by little she was revealing her gorgeous breasts. When the top of her gown lay around her waist, she raised her head and her gaze collided with his.

Luke smiled as she raised her chin and took a deep breath. She swept a slightly shaking hand in front of her, inviting him to make the next move. He did so by dropping his drawers. Luke's blood had rushed into his loins, hardening him well before her bourbon-hued nipples had come into view. Knowing he was well equipped, he hoped she wouldn't be afraid.

"Oh my," Genny whispered, her eyes widening and her hands going to her cheeks, fingers spreading across her full lips. "My first naked man."

"Your only naked man."

"My only naked man," she breathed in agreement. "Streaks, Harper. I'm quite certain your…your…umm… dancing partner is not going to…fit into my dancing partner."

"As in mattress dance?" he drawled. She nodded and when her eyes met his again, he said, "Let's waltz, Genevieve." And with that, he swept his hand in her direction.

Genny slipped her thumbs into her gown bringing her belly button into view. Wanting to hold onto this sea siren forever, Luke knew he'd always keep the small stone she'd pasted in her indented navel. Lowering the gown over her hips, she reached the tantalizing edge of the dark vee between her legs. There, she stopped.

"C'mon, you can do it, babydoll."

"Come do it for me, loverboy."

"If you really want me, you'll do it."

Genny gave the gown a shove and it fluttered to the floor. Carnal desire? Yeah, it slammed into Luke with a force he'd never imagined much less experienced.

"My God," he said in a hoarse voice.

From her lilac cat eyes and ivory cheeks to her cute little nose, to her pink lips, Genny's was the most beautiful face on the earth. He'd kissed her graceful neck and full breasts and pictured doing that again along with tasting her flat tummy and belly button. He ached to pull her curvy hips to him and spread those soft folds between her slim legs. Her body was truly that of a goddess and yearning to savor it all, his mouth watered.

"Luke, come here," she whispered bashfully, under his bold scrutiny.

Raising his head, in two strides, he gently cupped his hands to her soft face. His lips touched hers and when she opened her mouth their tongues played. Genny's kiss was wildly responsive and as she rose on tiptoes between his feet, she flung her arms around his neck.

Birthday suit smacked birthday suit. And sizzled.

Genny was letting this man, who dreams were made of, know in every way she could that she wanted him. So in love with him, she held him to her heart and poured herself into their kiss.

Luke plucked a couple of pins out of her hair, and she shook it into long curls. Picking her up, he braced a knee on the side of the mattress and placed her on the bed. She smiled at the handsome man who leaned over her as she lay on her back. His lips lowered to hers and as he stretched out beside her, he gently caressed her breast. She caught her breath at his touch and did her best to breathe evenly. He kissed his way down her neck and then his mouth closed over her left nipple. As he tasted her right nipple, she buried her fingers in his thick brown hair.

Yes, Genny wanted every bit of this and all that he brought with it.

Luke's hand slid down her tummy and ever so smoothly covered her womanhood. She tensed despite herself but in the next moment, spread her legs a little. When his fingers parted the folds of her most secret place she shivered with a combination of nerves, desire and fear.

Luke whispered, "Trust me and relax."

Too anxious to speak, she nodded. He kissed her lips as his finger dipped inside her. Oh my, feeling him do this to her was deliciously exciting. There was that familiar tingle heightening now into swirling sensations of what exactly she didn't know. Eroticism? Daring to explore this wanton new world with Luke and only with Luke she spread her legs ever wider.

Taking her invitation, he rolled on top of her, his muscular thighs coming to rest between her legs. His flesh and blood fencepost pressed against her womanhood which had become slippery wet. Luke's masculine virility surrounded her, sweeping her into exhilarating unknown pleasures. Her body began opening to his and that which made Luke all man entered her. The pressure was immense and though she wasn't convinced he could make it all fit, this dance of love was older than time and she was captured by his magic until—

A sudden piercing stabbed her like a knife.

"Oww," she gasped and instantly stiffened her entire body. "No, Luke."

"Don't tell me no unless you mean it because I'll stop."

"It's really painful," she cried, shocked by the red-hot stinging inside her. When he began pulling out, she clamped her knees against his hips and choked out, "Don't you dare stop."

"Wrap your legs around me," he said soothingly.

Tears burning her eyes, Genny did so with his help. He

pushed again and the second jab of pain was even worse than the first. "Streaks and sockdolagers," she whimpered and hugged him so hard, she couldn't breathe.

"Genevieve, your virginity doesn't want me to take it and I don't like hurting you."

"Luke Harper, you'll hurt me more if you don't take it."

"Keep your legs around me."

Luke tugged her arms away from his neck and sat up. Resting on his haunches, he gazed down and hesitated. Where their bodies were joined, he saw a trace of her blood.

"If you really want me, you'll do it," she echoed his words.

Grasping her hips, he quickly pulled her to him and thrust forward. A lightening bolt of pain hit her as he broke through her maidenhead. But this time the pain faded as her body accommodated his inch by long, hard inch.

Luke's brow cocked and a sexy grin spread across his lips. Genny smiled and took a deep breath. She reached for him, and he sat her up on his thighs, impaling her to the hilt. As her fanny nestled in his lap, she wrapped her arms around his shoulders. A powerful new feeling of femininity and fulfillment surged through her from head to toe. Her lips near Luke's ear, she murmured what she was thinking.

"You've made me into the woman I thought I'd never be."

CHAPTER 22

"I'M NOT DONE WITH YOU," LUKE SAID, WISHING MORE fervently with each passing second that she would fall in love with him so he could make her his wife.

Laying her down in the bed he pulled almost out then slowly eased back in and began a rhythmic thrusting. She was incredibly tiny and as her body gripped the length of his manhood, she instinctively began arching her hips to and away from him. He took her hands in his and as his plunges intensified becoming faster and harder their fingers entwined. Hell, this felt too damn good to be true. He didn't know how much longer he could hold out.

"Luke, yes...mmm...oh yes!"

Her heart pounded against his chest and her orgasm squeezed him over and over. Her ecstasy was his as well. With a final thrust and groan of pleasure, his release thundered deep inside of her. Finishing within a woman was not his style. But this was not just any woman. This was Genevieve Moonstone Morgan; the love of his life. As he pulsed again and again it occurred to Luke that never before had heaven and earth moved like this.

But then never before had he made love to the goddess of the moon.

"You shattered me," Genny whispered, their bodies still one.

"Shattered?" He rose on his elbows. There were half-dried tears on her cheeks, and he gently wiped them away. When she nodded, he asked, "Your virginity?"

"And my soul. I've been so lost. But you shattered that last bit of darkness and yanked me all the way into the light with you."

Luke grinned, pulled out and rolled off her. He grabbed her and she laughed as he tugged her on top of him. He slid himself back into her velvety tight warmth and ran his hands down her back to her rounded bottom.

"So, you liked it?" he asked.

"Yes," she breathed in a moan.

"Me, too."

Keeping him trapped within her, she sat up straddling him. She smiled that smile of hers and then placing her hands to his face, her expression grew serious.

"I'm in love with you, Lucas bringer-of-light Harper."

There it was. Here in San Francisco. He hadn't seen it coming. Luke looked into her eyes, and she didn't blink. She let her words stand. Luke was suddenly aware of her love surrounding not only his body but filling his own yearning soul. He sensed familiarity in this moment as if her love had been there all along. She'd trusted him, given herself to him and tonight he'd had the best sex ever. Letting all that Genny had said about darkness and light sink in, Luke realized that tonight he had truly made love for the first time in his life.

"Luke, from the moment you took me into your arms on New Year's Eve, I knew I was in trouble of losing my heart to you," she said with a smile. "Since I wear my heart on my sleeve, maybe you already figured out that I love you. I thought I could talk myself out of it for all the wrong reasons that you already know about it." She lifted a shoulder and then continued, "But I wasn't able to, so I quit trying. I don't care that you're a drifting gambler or that you're poor like me. I love you."

Her voice cracked and for the first time, she looked away from him to the pale light from the moon and stars streaming in through the sheer curtains drawn over the large bay window. With each word and every breath, this beautiful young woman further imprisoned his heart as surely as she had his manhood. She swallowed hard before meeting his gaze again.

"You cross all borders of tame and you'll vanish into the wild," she whispered. "But as long as you're in San Francisco, I'd rather be your mistress in your log home than a harlot in a loveless and sexless marriage on Nob Hill." She shook her head and said, "But don't worry because I don't expect you to love me back. I know that's not in the stars for us, Harp—"

Luke put a finger to her lips. "I'm in love with you, too, Genevieve," he said hearing the depth of emotion in his own voice. "Our destiny is what we make it. You're the wildflower I picked who became my wildcat. I'll never vanish, and I hope you'll never be tame."

Genny's eyes widened, and her lips parted in surprise. Then a single tear spilled down her cheek. He was just being kind because she'd given herself to him and she loved him all the more for it. When she was nearly out of control from countless emotions, stabbing pain and swirling sensations, Luke had taken command; his muscles flexing, his words soothing, his body invading. Shattering. Placing her trust in him had opened her heart to admit her love.

Luke took hold of a long, loose curl and when he tugged, she flattened her breasts to his chest. Their lips met and Genny's all consuming love and desire for this man knew no bounds.

"Let's vanish into the wild together," Luke whispered.

And so they did.

. . .

SEAGULLS SCREECHED and Luke awoke to a beautiful woman asleep in his arms, her leg between his. He smiled and kissed the top of Genny's head just as a knock sounded on the door.

"Room service with breakfast," a voice said. "Delivered by your favorite bellboy, Patrick."

"WE DON'T HAVE a pot to piss in because of Luke Harper," Seth complained. His nails chewed to the quick and bleeding, he gnawed on a matchstick as he picked out some kind of weevil from his bowl of cold oatmeal. "All because those stupid as dirt Skidmores didn't bury that Chinese bitch deep enough."

Within the infamous confines of the Barbary Coast, there were joints called Dead Man's Alley, The Living Flea, Murder Point, Sign of the Red Rooster, Bull Run, and Ye Olde Whore Shop. Here on Pacific Street the Black-Eyed Susan was one of the shadiest bars among the slew of sleezy dance halls, variety show saloons and jazz clubs located in the red-light district.

"The Skidmores are a liability," Selma said.

Under his breath Seth muttered, "They wouldn't be if they hadn't let Harper spot them at our house. Damn Harper to hell. He and the Skidmores deserve what happens next."

"By the by, it's Harriett Peak's house," Selma replied. He absolutely hated it when she corrected him. "The police won't find anything else, and we can sneak back in, Seth."

"You're as stupid as they are, Selma." Seth felt the anger fluttering his eyelashes. "With those Chinese devils watching the house we can't go anywhere near it. Besides, spring has sprung. We'll have to take the Skidmores' farmhouse."

"Concentrate on taking Genevieve Morgan's houses," Selma said.

"I am concentrating on it."

"You've been dragging your feet for weeks, because you're intimidated by the belle of your ball."

"Stop piling on the agony, Selma."

Seth punctuated that by slapping the wobbly table which nearly toppled a chipped vase of black-eyed Susans. He had fallen a long way since that ball which he'd cajoled Harriett Peak, a lonely spinster, into helping him arrange. He'd met Harriett by accident while casing the Palace Hotel. It was her fault he'd spent so much of what little money he had left in trying to fool her into thinking he was rich. After wining and dining her, she'd written a glowing article about him and his plan to live on Nob Hill. When she'd mentioned she was taking Southern Pacific's *Coast Line* to Los Angeles and wouldn't return until the first day of spring, he knew he'd have a place to hide from the Palace Hotel manager after his New Year's Eve soirée. With the money she'd cost him it served Harriett right that he'd pawned everything of value in her house before those Chinese bastards discovered the grave. His decline was Genevieve Morgan's fault, too. Why did she have to fall under the protection of Luke Harper? This was Harper's fault most of all.

"And tangling with Luke Harper absolutely terrifies you," Selma said. "How are you going to get rid of him without the Skidmores to help you?"

Seth sneered, "I recall a certain night you were terrified, Selma."

"Always ignoring the question when you don't have the answer." Selma shook a finger at him and warned, "The melancholy is already upon you and the imbecile is lying in wait."

"Shut up, you money squandering bitch."

Burl, the beefy owner of the Black-Eyed Susan, wore his dirty shirtsleeves rolled up to his crusty elbows, exposing thick forearms covered in bawdy tattoos. He was serving up the bowls of oatmeal and weevils. When he stopped beside the table his foul odor descended like a fog.

"Why don't you do this bickering act on stage tonight, Comstock?" Burl snorted and laughed. "You'd probably make more money."

"No," Selma hissed, her shriveled face reflecting the shrew she'd always been.

"My twin sister says no thank you."

"An evil twin? Hell-fire!" Burl gaffawed. "I'll tout you as *The Doppelgangers.*"

"No, no." Barely able to contain his fury, Seth's eyelids fluttered. Trying to cover that telltale tic, he spit out the matchstick and flashed the bar owner a sudden ear-to-ear grin. "Let's just stick to the delivery around midnight, Burl."

Squinting a sideways look, Burl said, "Them two packages better be easy, Comstock."

"Yes, yes, easy. You'll have my payment ready?" The bar owner nodded and moved on, but Seth called after him, "It's a deal then and by the by, the oatmeal is delicious."

"Stop groveling and prove me wrong about Luke Harper, brother dear."

"I'll prove it today, sister dear." Seth rubbed the back of his neck and the grime there barely registered. "Harper is about to experience a black eye of sorts."

"RED IS MY FAVORITE COLOR," Genny said glancing down at another new dress, a ruby red one with small white polka dots that Luke had surprised her with that morning.

"Really?" he asked with a surprised smile.

"Yes, that's why I made my belly dance costume from red materials."

"I love you in every color."

After a scrumptious breakfast in bed and making delicious love, they'd bathed and dressed. Her wardrobe had more than quadrupled since arriving in the city. It was almost noon now as they crossed the lobby of the Palace Hotel.

"Give me a hint about where we're going today, Harper."

"A hint, lady in red? Awright, we're—"

"Mr. Harper," called a man wearing a Western Union badge. "Telegrams." Waving two envelopes he hurried toward them. "Sir, when I gave you that telegram the other day, you said I could leave any others here at the Palace Hotel for you."

"Yes," Luke said and accepted the delivery. "Thank you."

Noting the senders, Luke shoved the telegrams into his inside jacket pocket. He tipped the clerk who thanked him and hurried away in the direction of the manager's office with a handful of other telegrams. Luke walked Genny through the Palm Court, out the columned entrance and down Market Street toward the shiny black Runabout. He hadn't said a word about the telegrams, and she didn't want to pry, but anxiety began churning in her stomach. She slowed down as they reached his automobile, but he gave her a tug and they walked on past it.

"Here's your hint, I thought we'd take the trolley to Fisherman's Wharf," Luke said. "It's only a couple of miles from here."

"Believe it or not, I've never ridden the trolley."

"Another new experience," Luke said with a sexy wink.

At the trolley stop they boarded the cable car and took a seat. As the trolley left the hotel behind and clipped along toward the bay, a warm spring breeze blew through their hair.

"Genny," Luke said and swung his arm around her. "The day I came into town but didn't find out anything about Comstock at the police station, I sent out two telegrams. When I was at the Western Union office a telegram had just come in for me as well. I answered it that day."

"Oh," she said as Luke caught one of her stray curls blowing in the wind and tucked it behind her ear. Given his opening, she asked, "Did you receive replies to your telegrams?"

"No, the ones today aren't from the people I contacted."

"It's none of my business."

"Yes, it is," he said. "Because I think there's more to Comstock than meets the eye, I sent a telegram to my brother-in-law who lives in Washington, D.C. part of the year."

"You have a brother-in-law?"

"Yes," Luke said with a chuckle at her astonishment.

"I never thought of you as having any family," Genny admitted softly.

"I do." He glanced up to see where they were in relation to Fisherman's Wharf. "We're almost there."

"Will you please tell me about your family?" she asked.

"Absolutely. Once we've set sail."

CHAPTER 23

"I THINK THERE'S MORE TO YOU THAN MEETS THE EYE, TOO," Genny said, sitting in the sleek sailboat with Luke. Pointing here and there, he'd named the essential parts of the boat like the bow, mainsail, mast, boom, jib, hull, and keel. Steering with what he'd called a tiller and a rudder, Genny was impressed at how skillfully Luke sailed away from the pier and over the gently lapping waves into the Bay. Her heart beat faster as she recalled that the first time Luke had visited her house and invited her to sail away with him. "So where did you learn how to sail a boat, Harper?"

"My grandfather taught my brother and me when we were kids. But just like your grandparents, mine are gone now," Luke said, adjusting the sails and steering into the deeper blue waters. "Off the coast of the Mississippi Sound where I grew up there are three islands close enough to explore; the Horn, the Ship and the Cat which are roughly five miles apart from each other. My brother, Rob, is eight years older than I am and we used to sail out to the islands. Horn Island has sugar white beaches and a lot of 'gators. Cat Island got its name from French explorers who mistook the island raccoons for cats. Along with raccoons, Cat Island's mostly bayous and marshes. Our favorite was Ship Island." He chuckled and shook his head at the memories. "On the rare occasion when our mother got wind of our island hopping, she had a fit."

"I can imagine," Genny replied, the shoreline already looking very far away. Feeling as if she were sailing into uncharted territory, she put her fingers to her moonstone pendant. The day was sunny and warm, and she prayed there were no storms on the horizon. "Are you close with your brother? Is your mother alive?"

"My mother is alive, and Rob and I are very close. Good thing because he and I work together in the family businesses with our father." Luke readjusted the sails as they caught the heavier breeze of the ocean. "Rob is married to his childhood sweetheart, Chloe. They live on a horse and cattle ranch with their two children. Charles is twelve and learning to sail. Megan is nine and loves horses like you do."

"How wonderful," Genny breathed in stunned amazement. "Are your parents in Biloxi?"

"John and Phoebe Harper. Yes, they live in the house where Rob, our sister, Matilda, and I were raised. It's in the middle of a sugarcane plantation inherited from my father's parents. My great grandparents started it all and it's still quite the *going concern* as my father likes to say." Luke smiled and nodded at the picnic lunch he'd bought for them along the wharf. "Hungry?"

"Don't you dare stop." Genny tingled, remembering saying those very words to this sexy and mysterious man just before he'd shattered her body and soul. "Please, tell me more."

"Well, Matilda is thirty-three and goes by Mattie."

In rapt awe, she asked, "So you're the baby of the family?"

"Yeah, and they all like to remind me of it," Luke said good naturedly, muscles flexing as he expertly maneuvered the sailboat through the water. "Mattie is married to a United States Senator named Steven Winsted. His family is a well-to-do, politically connected family in Jackson, the capital of Mississippi. Steve is a good guy and in the telegram I sent him the possible name of a local bad guy."

Of course Genny knew who he meant. "Is Senator Winsted the one who invited you to President Roosevelt's second inauguration and introduced you to him?"

"So you were listening the night we met." He cocked a brow and nodded. "Yes, Steve is well liked in Mississippi and D.C. and if he runs again, I predict he'll easily win."

Not wanting to miss a word, Genny tucked the wayward curls blowing in the breeze, behind her ears and asked, "Do Mattie and the senator have children?"

"A six-year-old little girl, soon to turn seven, named Audrey." Luke paused and for a moment, Genny thought he appeared sad. He was no doubt missing his family whom he hadn't seen at least since December. Then he said, "Audrey is pretty like my sister. And she's sweet and funny like someone who's sailing with me today."

Genny smiled, but so overwhelmed by how little she had known about Luke, she didn't comment. When he asked a second time if she was hungry, she nodded that she was. Together they unwrapped freshly baked fish sandwiches with sides of steamed shrimp. The wind picked up a little and blew them further out to sea as they ate.

"That's a lot of information to digest all at once, isn't it?" Luke asked and popped a shrimp into his mouth.

"The more I learn about you, the less I feel I know you. I hope you'll forgive me for not asking if you had a family, Luke," Genny said. "I am truly ashamed of myself."

"You asked if I had a wife," he said helpfully.

Genny rolled her eyes. "Oh, hush up, Harper."

They both laughed which broke the bit of tension between them. They ate and sailed. Luke had bought lemonade with the picnic lunch. He explained he hadn't brought alcohol because his father had made his sons a deal. He'd cover for Rob and Luke as much as possible, with their mother, when they sailed out to one of the islands but only if they would give their word never to drink when sailing. He and Rob and had solemnly sworn on a Bible and had always honored that promise. Luke chuckled, saying the Gulf of Mexico gets more than a little choppy and that bull sharks, sharpnose and some hammerheads live in the waters of the Sound. Since Ship Island was about eleven miles off the coast, he and Rob were probably lucky to be alive.

It came as no surprise that Luke was wild even as a boy. "Why was Ship your favorite island?"

"The harbor made for easy docking and Fort Massachusetts is there. The fort wasn't used much after the Civil War and closed in nineteen and three," Luke said. "But best of all Ship Island has a wooden lighthouse built in eighteen eighty-six."

"The bringer of light would be fond of a lighthouse," Genny said, just as a cloud passed over the sun and darkened the sky. "Your brother and sister sound wonderful, and your mother and father seem like loving parents."

"Yes, they are." Luke was quiet before saying, "My father's the one who sent that first telegram. He wanted to know when I'm coming home."

Genny braced herself. Had she told this man she loved him and made love to him only to lose him so soon? "What did you tell your father?"

"Soon." Luke patted his pocket as if recalling he had two new telegrams and then pulled one out. "Let's see what Rob has to say."

Genny's stomach tied itself in a knot. As Luke skimmed his brother's telegram, she dropped the last couple bites of her lunch overboard. Stuffing the envelope back into his pocket, a frown crossed Luke's face coinciding with the winds picking up. As whitecaps began to chop at the water, Luke began a slow arc turning the sailboat in the direction of the wharf.

"Bad news?" Genny asked.

"Nah," Luke said offhandedly.

"Harper, tell me the truth."

The shore was still off in the distance, but with the sailboat safely headed in that direction, Luke took the second telegram out of his pocket. When he'd read it, he crumpled it in his hand.

"Is something wrong with Rob or someone else in your family?"

"Something's wrong, but not with the family," he growled.

"Luke, what is it? Maybe I can help."

"I'm going to tell you, Genny," Luke said. His eyes glinted with anger and there was irritation in his deep voice. "You can help me by trusting me now, just like you did the first time we made love, to get us through the painful part to the best part."

"You're scaring me." Genny wrapped her fingers around her moonstone.

"The telegram from Rob was to warn me that a woman I barely knew and was avoiding in Biloxi found out that I'm here in San Francisco."

"Who is she?" Genny wasn't sure if the choppy sea or the telegrams or a combination of the two were suddenly making her nauseous.

"Her name is Mara. She introduced herself to me in our Harper House Restaurant about six months ago."

"You own a restaurant?"

"We own four. Anyway, that particular restaurant, along with Harper House Grill, is located in the Harper House Resort."

"What is the Harper House Resort?"

"Our hotel that offers the two restaurants, indoor swimming pool, bowling alley, men's workout room, and mineral baths for ladies as well as lawn tennis, croquet, and horseback riding. The resort is located in the middle of Biloxi along the Mississippi Sound. Our two other restaurants are on opposite ends of town also on the oceanfront."

"Streaks," Genny whispered. A woman? Restaurants? A

resort? Folding her arms around her waist, she hugged herself. "Why were you avoiding her?"

"Because she wouldn't take no for an answer. She kept returning to the resort and asking for me. When she couldn't get past the maitre d'hotel, she tracked me down on *Plan B*, one of my riverboats."

"*One* of your riverboats?" Genny asked, her stomach rolling with the waves. And here she thought he drifted from one floating casino to the next.

"I own three riverboats. I mentioned *Femme Fatale* to you once."

"Yes, but you didn't mention you owned it." Genny felt cold and clammy.

"Well, I do." Luke shrugged that off and plowed his fingers through his hair. "I thought Mara was in the past, but evidently she's determined in her pursuit."

"Mara's pursuing you just like I did Seth Comstock."

"Genny, you are nothing like her," Luke said, his gaze riveting and a muscle working in his square jaw.

"No?"

"No. I've been right here for your entire so-called pursuit of Comstock. You never spoke a word to him because you never met him, and you have never laid eyes on him again. You didn't follow him, didn't send him letters and didn't continually show up in places where you knew he'd be. Correct?"

"You know that's correct."

"So you're nothing like Mara," he said firmly. "I barred her from all three riverboats and Harper House Resort. As far as I know, she never found my house which is also along the Mississippi Sound."

"You have a house?" Genny asked. As he nodded, she took a deep breath trying to keep from drowning in the tidal waves of information. She swallowed hard and asked, "Were you lovers?"

"Hell, I knew you were going to ask me that."

"Were you?" Genny's lunch was threatening to reappear. When he didn't answer she answered for him, "So, yes."

"No." He shook his head. "You and I are lovers." Luke's smile was a reassuring one and he reached for her hand, but she kept it tucked tightly around her waist. When she frowned he withdrew his hand. "With her it was just sex. Once," he said dismissively, but looking Genny in the eye. "Sex doesn't mean anything until you fall in love."

"There's a difference between having sex and making love?"

"Damn right. I found that out with you. I made love for the first time with you." The boat bumped hard across several waves, but Luke handled it. "When I won the ranch next to yours it was an opportunity to put distance between Biloxi and me."

"You mean between Mara and you."

"Yeah," he gritted through his teeth. "The second telegram I sent was to a childhood friend of mine who's a policeman in Biloxi. I asked him if he knew anything about her."

"How did she find out you're here?"

"Rob happened to meet up with her on the road to the sugarcane plantation and stopped her before she could get to the house. She admitted sneaking onto *Femme Fatal*, the night I won Cavender's ranch. Word spread that the ranch was somewhere outside of San Francisco, and she hoped my parents would tell her how to find me. They wouldn't have."

"What does she want?" Bile burned Genny's throat, but she forced it down. Luke handed her the second telegram and after uncrumpling it she read, "Darling, I will arrive in San Francisco, Wednesday on Southern Pacific's *Coast Line*. Please pick me up at the railroad station."

CHAPTER 24

A JOLT THE SIZE OF THE CENTRAL PACIFIC'S JUPITER locomotive jackslapped Genny.

She quickly pressed a hand to her mouth to prevent losing her lunch into the ocean but leaned over the side just in case. Luke grabbed her arm, keeping her safely seated instead of bobbing in the Bay and thankfully, she managed to keep her food down. Luke yanked the telegram out of her hand and flung it into the waves.

"Genny, I'll deal with her," Luke said, holding the love of his life to his heart.

But the wind kicked up again and he released her in order to sail the boat. There was no color in Genny's cheeks, her eyes glittered with unshed tears and her hands were gripped so tightly in her lap, her knuckles were white.

"The Big Four would be happy trains are bringing people together. End of story," she said.

Luke had never despised Mara Sinclair more than he did at this moment.

"I'll remind her that I *ended* that *one* time story *six* months ago." Luke reiterated the most important facts. "Hell, Rob said in his telegram that he told her not to come after me."

"I think the name Mara means nightmare."

"She's a recurring one, that's for damn sure," Luke growled.

"Where and how will you deal with her?"

Fisherman's Wharf was nearly upon them, and Luke was wondering the same thing as he guided the sailboat into the slip they'd left earlier. He jumped out of the boat and helped Genny onto the dock. The man who'd rented him the boat took over and Luke thanked him. Walking Genny to the trolley, Luke sensed she felt anything but being back on solid ground.

"I'll ask the hotel manager if I can send Patrick on an errand. He can purchase a return train ticket for her," he decided just before they boarded the trolley. Once they were seated, he swung his arm around Genny and pulled her close. He anticipated that she might scoot away, but she didn't. "The storm brewing in the Bay seems to have blown over. The sun is shining again."

"Because the moonstone protects those who travel upon the water." She placed her fingers to her pendant again and looked at him as the trolley clanged its way along Market Street.

"The moonstone floats deep into one's soul to retrieve what's missing," Luke whispered, thumbing away a tear at the corner of a lilac eye. "You're what was missing in my life."

"Mara can roam the darkness, I'll stay in the light with you."

Thank God, Luke thought and said, "I love you, Genny. I want you to go home with me and meet my family. Will you—"

"Fire!" a fellow passenger on the trolley shouted, jumped up and pointed in the direction of the Palace Hotel.

Luke smelled the smoke. Shrieking whistles blasted the air and commotion broke out on the cable car as four large horses raced past them pulling fireman aboard a steam pumping engine. Sure enough, black clouds licked the sky not far away. Another engine, from a different direction, charged toward the hotel with horns blowing.

"Surely the Palace Hotel isn't on fire," Genny said.

Luke stood up to get a better look as the trolley slowed to a stop about a block from the Palace. The cable car conductor suggested everyone depart as Market Street was too jammed with arriving steam engines, gathering people, horses, buggies, and stopped vehicles for the trolley to continue. Luke took Genny's hand, and alighting onto the street they made it close enough to the Palace Hotel to see what was burning. Three automobiles were going up in flames.

Luke's Cadillac was one of them.

"What the hell," Luke muttered. "I liked that little Runabout."

"Luke!" Mike Johnson yelled. In his fireman's uniform and protective hat, he was helping his brother, Jimmy, hook up a steam engine to a hydrant. "Is that your Runabout?"

"Yeah!" Luke shouted as he and Genny hurried in the direction of the Johnson brothers.

"Fire Chief Daughtery, folks," a fireman said, stepping in front of them. "You'll need to stand clear of the fire."

"My automobile is the one in the middle," Luke said.

"I'm sorry to hear that, sir. I believe it will be a total loss."

"Do you know what started the fire?" Luke asked.

"Too soon to tell," the chief replied and relinquished the job of holding people out of harm's way to the police.

Luke thought Genny looked pale again. Wanting her out of this smoky, congested chaos he took her hand, and they skirted the growing crowd of spectators.

"I think the Johnson brothers will tell me exactly what started the fire," Luke said after they entered the Palace. "I'll take you to our room and then I'm going back to talk to them."

"Luke, lunch didn't set well with me," Genny admitted

and stopped in the middle of the Palm Court. "But I can certainly make it to our room by myself."

"I know you can." Placing his hands to her upper arms, he kissed her forehead. "But I want to make sure you're safe."

They continued across the lobby to one of the rising rooms. On the way to their floor, Luke draped an arm around her and thought how delicate she felt especially under the precarious circumstances. He'd caused her physical pain the night they'd first made love and today the pain of Mara Sinclair. Wanting to protect, not hurt Genny he gently tightened his embrace. She wrapped an arm around his waist and hugged him back. He took that as a good sign.

"I'm sorry about your Runabout," she said as they left the elevator and walked down the classically decorated, hallway that overlooked the Palm Court and five lower balconies.

"I was just renting the Runabout while I was here." Luke unlocked the door and let her into their suite. "This afternoon has not turned out the way I'd planned. Why don't you rest and if you feel better later we can have supper in the American Dining Room downstairs."

"Yes, that sounds wonderful." As she placed her purse on a round, marble top table, she noticed two lovely new dresses and a sexy red negligee hanging over the front of the dressing screen. "Are those for me?" she asked in surprise, looking from the clothing to him.

"If you think they're for me, you've lost your mind."

Genny laughed. "You're spoiling me." Flirting with him, she said, "I'm betting that wild, red gown *is* for you as much as for me."

"I'm betting it reminded me of your belly dance. Lock the door and I'll be back as soon as I find out about that fire."

Luke hadn't been gone ten minutes, when someone knocked. As Genny walked across the room she noticed a chipped vase of wilting, black-eyed Susans on a table near the sofa.

Odd, that vase hadn't been there when they left the room earlier. In a sketchy scrawl, a note propped among the flaccid flowers read, 'From your admirer'. She saw in her mind's eye Luke's handwriting on the note he'd written telling her to bring something to his house to swim in. The writing on that note was bold like the man himself. Whoever this admirer was, it wasn't Luke.

With her hand on the knob, she hesitated in opening the door as a sinking thought hit her. Maybe the flowers weren't for her. The second knock on the door startled her. Maybe the black-eyed Susans were to Luke from Mara Sinclair.

"It's Patrick, Miss Morgan. With flowers from Mr. Harper."

Genny swung the door open and found Patrick holding a crystal vase. The flowers were so spectacular she could barely see their favorite bellboy peeking out from behind them.

"Please come in, Patrick," Genny said. "How beautiful."

"Beautiful flowers for a beautiful lady," Patrick said with a beaming smile.

He centered the vase of flowers on the marble top table. Two dozen, long stemmed white roses had been dyed the perfect shade of lilac and surrounded by ivory baby's breath. A single rose the exact color of her red nightgown, bloomed in the heart of the stunning arrangement.

Now these were flowers Luke Harper would send.

"Thank you," Genny said and pulled two dollars out of her purse as she'd often seen Luke do. Patrick thanked her profusely, left with a bow and Genny locked the door. This card was straight to the point, 'Genny, I love you. Luke'. She smelled the red rose and dared to hope.

. . .

"I HOPE YOU'RE HAPPY, SELMA," Seth sneered, after peeking around the corner at the end of the hallway. "If those black-eyed Susans weren't pitiful enough on their own, Harper's flowers made them look ten times worse."

"A thousand times," Selma spat. "Since when can you pick a lock?"

"For the umpteenth time, how do you think I escaped that hellhole in West Virginia?" he asked. "And where were you when I picked the lock at Harriett Peak's house?"

"My tired excuse of a memory says I was wishing I was anywhere except with you."

"I wish you were scattered ashes like the other two spendthrift Evilsizers. I'm meeting the Skidmores in Chinatown. Don't follow me."

"By Chinatown, you mean an underground opium den, brother dear."

"The Devil's Needle is the only place I can escape you, sister dear."

With a wave of her hand, Selma said, "Perhaps they won't recognize your ever-deteriorating self and kill you."

"See you in hell."

Seth took a step around the corner but hearing a door open, quickly slunk backward out of sight. Motioning Selma to be quiet, he listened to footsteps travel in the opposite direction. Then, craning his neck, he peeked into the hallway and couldn't believe his eyes.

CHAPTER 25

FEELING BETTER, GENNY HAD DECIDED TO FIND LUKE AND help him figure out what caught his Runabout on fire. Walking along the balcony banister, she saw no sign of him in the grand lobby. And just who did Mara Sinclair think she was? Why, if she was in the past, was she showing up in the present? Reaching the rising room, Genny pressed a white button on the polished brass plate. When the elevator arrived, she opened the wrought iron door and entered the small, redwood paneled room. Someone entered on her heels and closed the gate-like door.

As Genny whirled around, the smell of something similar to kerosene wafted toward her. Limited to his profile pulled low over a wrinkled forehead; a derby hat, stringing past a long earlobe; yellow hair and between thin lips; a matchstick. Sliding the matchstick into his pocket he reached toward the lever on the brass panel. The back of his hand appeared injured. A burn?

"Palm Court?" When he turned, she came face-to-face with the scarecrow. "Why, Miss Morgan, what a pleasant surprise. Seth Comstock here. We met at my New Year's Eve's soirée."

"No, we did not meet," Genny replied calmly as her mind raced. Little wonder no one had spotted Comstock.

A far cry from the tuxedoed, albeit odd and obnoxious host of a Palace Hotel ball, this individual was disheveled with a scraggly beard. Appearing destitute to the point of living on the street, it was the calculating desperation in his faded brown eyes that chilled her to the bone. It crossed Genny's mind that if not for the distraction of the fire, a Palace employee may have stopped Comstock to inquire as to his business of being there. "I've not been feeling well today. If you'll excuse me, I need to return to my room."

"I'm sorry," he replied.

Placing one hand to his ear as if having trouble hearing, Comstock moved the lever with his other hand. Genny wasn't sure if he was sorry she was ill or sorry that he couldn't hear her.

"I said—" she began, her stomach and the rising room dropping.

Cutting her off, Comstock asked, "Did you know there is an atrocious fire outside?" Blocking the brass lever, the narrow door and thus her view, he commenced to studying his hand. "I was returning to my suite here at the hotel after fishing off my favorite pier a mile no…no I'd say just over a half mile from here when I saw the fire," he said as if details made his story believable.

"Fishing? While staying at the Palace?" Genny asked dubiously.

"I was trying to help douse the flames until the firemen arrived. I was heading to my room to wash up and attend to the burn I suffered."

"But you entered the rising room on the sixth floor," she pointed out, certain that the hotel manager would never allow Comstock to stay again. "Why were you going back downstairs before washing up and attending to your burn?"

"The lobby you said?" Comstock asked, avoiding her questions while continuing to obscure her view and block the lever.

"No, but I'll exit there."

Only when they stopped did Genny realize they'd passed the lobby and were in the basement. The Palace Hotel basement, but nevertheless not the place to find herself alone with Seth Comstock. Other than a mop and bucket, the empty room clearly indicated there was no one to help her.

"Please step aside," Genny said.

When she motioned for him to move, Comstock snatched her hand as if she were offering it to him to hold. His insincere smile oozed malice, and a shiver crawled up her arm.

"Let go of my hand," Genny snapped and as his grip increased so did her fear.

"Oh, please don't be offended, Miss Morgan," he said. "I just wish to make the very most of this unexpected opportunity by inviting you to supper."

You have to hold your cards close to your vest and bluff when you need to.

"Oh, I see." Genny swallowed and as her blood ran cold warmth rang in her voice, "How very nice of you. Supper, this evening?"

"Wh—why yes," he stammered. "Would that be possible?"

"Anything is possible, Mr. Comstock," she replied and was able to withdraw her hand from his boney, dirty one.

"Please call me Seth. Shall I pick you up at your small house or the big one?" When she didn't answer he hurried on, "You're probably wondering how I know where you live. A concierge here at the Palace told me you were Garnet Morgan's daughter."

"The concierge who was fired?" Genny hadn't missed the mistake in his remark. "If you didn't know who I was before the ball, how did I come to be invited?"

"Uh...perhaps we can toast Madam Garnet at supper."

Genny noted the ignored questions along with the word madam. "Did the concierge also tell you someone ran over Garnet and that she burned to death in the middle of the road?"

"How dreadful, but I'm not surprised," Comstock replied. "That road to your ranch is quite the treacherous one. Even so I was willing to risk driving there to appraise the madam's jewels."

"I never said where Garnet was run down," Genny replied and could hear Luke telling her not to show her hand. "So, you're a jewelry appraiser?"

"Yes, yes." His head bobbling up and down, Comstock said, "I understand Garnet has quite the collection. Shall I call for you at your big house?"

Storms of destruction and death were swirling in the cauldron of chaos called Comstock. Luke's suspicions about this man were right on target and Genny had some of her own.

"I'll meet you in the American Dining Room here at the Palace, Mr. Comstock."

"Six o'clock tonight then and please be more punctual than you were the night of my soirée." He started to reach toward the lever but stopped. Leaving the brass panel in view, his lips pursed. "What about Harper? I—I mean Mr. Harper."

"He won't mind."

"No. No. I don't believe that because you were the belle of the ball." Comstock's small eyes narrowed to slits and his thin lips stretched into a sneer as he shifted from one foot to the other. "Harper kissed you on your forehead in the lobby today. That is the kiss of protection a man gives to the woman he loves. Luke Harper will never let another *admirer* have you."

When his eyelashes suddenly fluttered uncontrollably, Genny remembered Luke's warning that the bad guy was about to show himself. She made a frantic swipe toward the brass control panel, but he blocked her again and shoved open the wrought iron door.

You'd better fight just like that when a wolf's at your door, little lamb.

Genny balled up her right fist and keeping her wrist straight and eyes open, landed a solid blow to Comstock's spongy stomach. That exact same punch to Luke's rock-hard stomach hadn't fazed him.

However, pain and shock registered on Comstock's face as he gulped for air and staggered backward out of the rising room. Instantly, Genny yanked the gate shut and shoved the lever to the right. The rising room rose as the mop tripped Comstock. Holding the door tightly closed, she looked down through the wrought iron bars. Knocking over the bucket and slipping in soapy water, Comstock landed on his scrawny backside. Scrambling to stand but crashing to his hands and knees instead, he glowered up at Genny. Through the bars, endless evil no longer masked, twisted Comstock's sallow face with untold ugliness. And then he was gone.

But a familiar, maniacal laugh followed her up the elevator shaft.

WHEN LUKE ENTERED the hotel suite, an ethereal vision in red lace and gossamer met his eyes. Standing beside the lilac roses Genny plucked the red one and brought it to her nose.

"Genevieve Moonstone Morgan, you sexy goddess."

"Adonis, you have returned at last," she said and glided into his embrace. He kissed her lips, and hugging him she murmured in his ear, "Thank you for the spectacular flowers."

"You're welcome." He sniffed the rose when she held it close and said, "Let me see you." Gracefully backing out of his embrace, she appeared as cool as an ocean breeze and as hot as the fire outside. As always, Luke's heart melted. "These roses are to replace the wildflowers you smacked me with at your house."

She laughed. "The night I asked what you'd think if I told you I'd been deflowered?"

"Which I did, so this is the least I could do."

Luke grinned at the blush on Genny's face as he shed his jacket. She placed the red rose back in the heart of the lilac ones, then took his jacket and hung it in his wardrobe. Sitting down on a plush sofa he removed his shoes, never taking his eyes off her.

"Did you find out what caused the fire?" she asked.

"Arson. Mike and Jimmy happened to be the first firemen to arrive on the scene and they found a can of gasoline near my automobile. The fire spread to the other two vehicles, probably by accident. All three fires are out now."

"Thank goodness."

Luke sighed and nodded. "Huan saw the smoke and sent Wong and Chen to check in with me. Wong said the gasoline can beside Fan Zhou's grave was identical to the one near the Runabout."

"Comstock and the Skidmores set both fires."

"Yeah," Luke replied. "The Johnson brothers showed Fire Chief Daughtery the can of gasoline near the Runabout and reminded him about the one in Harriett Peak's backyard. A police sergeant joined us and I made sure he knew about the Skidmores trespassing on her property. Wong told me that when he returned to question Peak's neighbors, they also described two red-haired men. But what I saw of Comstock on New Year's Eve doesn't exactly fit with the neighbors' account of a disheveled third man. In any event, I gave Daughtery and the sergeant the names of the Skidmores and location of their farm."

"That third man is Comstock."

Luke rubbed his forehead. "Along with the Johnson brothers' input and the Palace Hotel manager out on the sidewalk reminding everyone how Comstock ran out on his bill, the sergeant took the gasoline can for evidence and said he'd report the new information to Police Chief Dinan."

"On New Year's Eve, we saw Comstock in disguise, Luke," Genny said softly, but firmly. "Harriett Peak's neighbors saw the monster under the mask."

"What do you know that I don't?" Luke cocked his head as a frown creased his brow.

"I don't want you to get mad when I tell you," Genny said, holding her hands in the air in a placating manner. "I want you to remain calm."

"So that's why you have on that sexy red gown. To soften some kind of blow?"

"And yet," Genny began as Luke stood, hands going to his hips and his head lowering, "I suddenly feel like a matador waving a red cape in front of a bull who's about to be really angry."

Luke's green eyes narrowed, his strong jaw clenched and in a stern voice he growled, "Just tell me."

Genny took a deep breath. As she told Luke what had happened, she did her best to gauge the changing expressions on his handsome face. From incredulous to worried, when he passed anger and reached outrage, he picked up the chipped vase of black-eyed Susans and hurled it across the room. It smashed against a wall as foul oaths erupted in their suite.

Grabbing Luke, Genny wrapped her arms around him. His muscular body was rigid with fury. She held him to her heart until he relaxed some and hugged her back.

"Dammit to hell, Genevieve," he said. "I told you to lock the door and stay in our room."

"Actually, you just said to lock the door." Genny leaned back and smiled up at him. "You didn't say to stay in our room."

"You knew damn well that's what I meant," Luke replied. "He could have killed you."

"When his eyelids fluttered, I hit him just like you taught me," she said with a reassuring smile. "Comstock doesn't take a sockdolager to the gut nearly as well as you do."

"Hell, he's crawled back under a rock by now."

"Yes, but maybe he and the Skidmores will be caught soon," Genny said.

"They'll have a better chance with the police than if Huan Li catches them," Luke said. "Huan has posted a thousand-dollar reward to the person or people who deliver the scarecrow and soaplocks to him."

"Streaks," Genny whispered and clasped her hands between her breasts.

"I gave Wong a thousand and asked him to have Huan double the reward."

"Luke, if Comstock truly is the mastermind and the Skidmores helped…"

"Huan will kill three killers," Luke said matter-of-factly as Genny bit her lower lip. "San Francisco is on edge of the American Frontier, Genny. The Wild West lingers here."

"I know," she said and nodded. "Is it wilder than Biloxi?"

He shrugged. "Mississippi has 'gators and bayous and riverboat gamblers."

She wanted so much to be a part of Luke's life there.

"Back to Comstock, Huan says all of Chinatown, even the people running the opium dens underneath Chinatown, want that reward." Luke paused and dragged his hand across his forehead. "But there are tong hideouts, where people are less cooperative."

"What are you talking about underneath Chinatown?"

Luke walked to the bay window. Genny followed him and saw the charred remains of the vehicles in front of the hotel.

"Beneath Chinatown there are underground tunnels and rooms that have been excavated over the years and some are as deep as fifty feet," Luke said, hands on his hips. "A customer picks out a cot, pays for the amount of opium wanted and smokes it down there until it's gone." He turned to her. "You didn't know about that?"

Her eyes were wide as she shook her head. "No."

Looking out the window again, Luke continued, "Huan told me he owns only the dens selling opium. But there are tongs, in what's known as the Devil's Needle area of Chinatown, selling opium and running brothels with slave girls from Nanking, Canton and Shanghai. Being stolen and sold into slavery is how the term shanghied came into use."

"I've never heard of the Devil's Needle. And what does tong mean?"

"Tongs are the rival Chinese gangs who cause trouble if not left alone but can be useful to the Monkey's Fist if Huan looks the other way. The women are sold like cattle never escaping the smell of opium or seeing the light of day. They're known as troglodytes meaning cave dwellers."

"How awful." Genny shivered. "Why doesn't Huan stop the tongs from doing that?"

"Why don't you stop it at your ranch?" Luke asked. When she cast her eyes down and didn't reply, he put a finger under her chin. "People choose their battles, don't they?"

"I will stop it at my ranch."

Luke winked his approval and closed the drapes as if closing that subject. Taking hold of her he gave her a playful tug forward. She laughed while twining her arms around his neck. His mouth covered hers in a wild kiss and she raised up on tiptoes, molding her breasts to his muscular chest, her body craving his.

Then twirling out of his arms, she gave him her best come hither look over her shoulder as she walked toward the bed. She was rewarded with a gleam in his eyes as he shed his pants. The tingles he caused between her legs sizzled throughout her entire body.

"Wanna work up an appetite for supper, babydoll?"

"You know I do, loverboy."

CHAPTER 26

It was after seven by the time they entered the Palace Hotel's spacious American Dining Room. Decorated in gold and white, with incandescent lighting adding ambiance and elegance, the resplendent restaurant could easily seat six hundred. Though bustling with patrons dining before the opera or theater as well as hotel guests and Bay area locals, the maître d' immediately escorted Luke and Genny to a quiet, corner table and provided them with menus.

When their waiter arrived, he asked what they would care to drink. Before arriving at the Palace with Luke, Genny would have had no idea. But between sightseeing and shopping, Luke had introduced her to Chardonnay when having fish. And tonight, since they'd decided on the chef's special for their main course, she figured they'd drink red wine. Luke indeed suggested Cabernet Sauvignon and when Genny agreed he ordered the finest bottle on the hotel's wine list. The waiter returned with it and offered Luke a sample, but Luke said it only mattered if the lady liked it. Genny tasted a sample and smiled. Luke nodded at the waiter who poured their wine and left the bottle. They toasted to turning a tumultuous day into afternoon delight and a glorious evening. Their appetizer of French onion soup was soon served and as she spooned the first mouthful, Genny realized she was not nearly as nervous about making mistakes while dining in such luxurious surroundings as she'd been two weeks prior on their arrival at the hotel.

Clearly in his element, Luke had chosen a seat that gave him a full view of the enormous dining room and as usual his gun was holstered near his heart. To ease his concern over keeping an eye out for Comstock, Genny sought to distract him by indicating a few of the latest styles being worn by both female and male diners. She noted that Harriett Peak claimed the most fashionable women made an annual pilgrimage to Paris and were bringing to America less frilly, slightly shorter dresses without the long, dust sweeping train. All Genny's new frocks, courtesy of Luke, fit that description exactly. The well-dressed man wore a double-breasted coat, striped pants, a wingtip collar white shirt, and a tie. Luke Harper to a tee.

Though his being poor hadn't mattered for quite a while and couldn't stop her from falling in love with him, in her heart of hearts Genny was happy she'd told Luke she loved him before she knew he was rich. Not for her sake, but his. When he was once again home in Biloxi, he'd never look back and doubt her.

Thinking he'd probably heard enough of the latest trends and eager to learn more about him, Genny inquired as to the Harpers' Biloxi businesses. In between sips of the delicious red wine, spoonfuls of Gruyere cheese, caramelized onion broth, and bites of French bread he answered her questions.

"Rob's company manages the restaurants, which includes the ones in our hotel, much like the Palace. His cattle ranch supplies the beef," Luke said with a cursory glance around the dining room. Their appetizer was cleared away and making eye contact with her again, he elaborated some saying, "Biloxi lies on a peninsula with the Gulf of Mexico to the south. Back Bay stretches for about ten miles along the north. My company runs the shrimp, oyster and fishing boats in and around these waters. I'll bet you didn't know that in nineteen and four Biloxi was named the seafood capital of the world."

"I'll bet that is very much to your credit," Genny said with a smile as he shrugged. "And your father manages the sugarcane plantation."

"Right and we all share in the profits."

Their filets, slightly pink in the middle and so tender they nearly melted in one's mouth, had arrived with sides of mashed potatoes and grilled asparagus, on the finest china along with silverware polished to a high gleam. As they ate, Luke said that sugarcane plantations were usually found in the Mississippi Delta, on the western side of the state. But the Harper ancestors had gotten lucky with some very fertile land along the Back Bay and their sugarcane plantation had flourished over the generations. He explained sugarcane was a member of the grass family and the single most cultivated crop in the world.

"How do you make a grass stalk into sugar?" she asked.

"With a sugar mill."

"Do you own a sugar mill?" Her brows raised as her eyes widened.

"We do," he said with a chuckle.

Genny shook her head and smiled. "Why am I not surprised?"

"You are a businesswoman with land and property. Have you decided how to deal with it?"

"What would you think if I said I'd like to offer a thousand dollars of the five card stud winnings you gave me to Vern and Patty? I could divide the other thousand in equal amounts among Grace, Ruth, Onxy, and Opal and send the ladies on their way."

"I'd say yes and recommend you give your ranch to Vern and Patty. Surely they've earned it over the years."

"Yes, I was thinking the same thing," Genny replied and nodded.

"What about your little house?"

"It doesn't cost me anything to live there," she said and couldn't imagine living there again without Luke just down the road. Sadness suddenly seized her heart. She couldn't imagine living *without* Luke, period. "A vegetable garden and fish from the pond won't let me starve."

"Forget your little house and come home with me to Biloxi." Luke waited and when she didn't answer, he said, "I told you on the trolley I wanted you to meet my family."

"What would your family think of you bringing home a madam?"

"Stop that," Luke said. "I'd be bringing home a beautiful woman, with morals so high that, against all odds, she was a virgin when I met her. A lady who is not only smart and well read, but so fashionable she should have her own who's who newspaper column."

"The night we met I asked if you were someone important." When he modestly shook his head, she said, "You and your family are real whos' whos. Trust me, they don't want to meet me."

A knife turned in Luke's gut as it occurred to him for the first time that his wealth might actually cause Genny to turn away from him. From those mesmerizing lilac cat eyes to the full breasts that made his mouth water, to the luxurious long hair tickling his chest when she was on top to the captivating vee between her legs that made him rock hard, she was the most important person in his life.

"You're the only who's who I've ever wanted, and I can't get enough of you," Luke said.

She blushed and lowered her eyes. "I can't get enough of you, either." Underneath the long white linen tablecloth, she rubbed the toe of a new shoe across the inside of his ankle.

Luke cocked a brow and grinned. "Did I tell you that along the Mississippi Sound, you would already know some of the neighbors?"

"More who's whos?"

"Mattie, Steven and Audrey live part of the year in an American Colonial style mans— house not far from mine."

"You were going to say mansion," Genny said knowingly and slowly moved her foot up the inside of his calf. "What kind of mansion do you have, Harper?"

"French provincial with a French Creole wraparound balcony, Genevieve the Frenchwoman who was never going to have ties to anyone or anything French."

"Because I planned to live in a loveless, sexless marriage on Nob Hill," she whispered across the table, her eyes widening, confirming she had seen the error of her ways.

"All in the past," Luke said. "Everybody has one."

Genny lowered her foot to the floor as their empty dishes were cleared. The waiter poured more wine and after cheesecake was served, she ran her foot up the inside of Luke's leg to his knee.

"You received black-eyed Susans from your past today," she remembered to tell him as she licked cheesecake off her fork.

"I didn't see any other flowers." Luke lifted his glass and took a swallow. He slid his other hand underneath the tablecloth and grasped the toe of her shoe but kept a straight face.

"Well, that's because," Genny began and raised a brow at having her foot captured, "you dashed those flowers," she sipped her wine and continued nonchalantly as if they weren't flirting under the table, "against the wall."

He cupped the heel of her foot and asked, "Is this your foot between my legs, young lady?"

"I'm sure I don't know what you're talking about, sir," she said, bringing her other foot up between his knees.

Luke grabbed that foot, too, and tugged causing her to slide down a little in her chair. Genny quickly glanced right and left but none of the other patrons seemed to notice.

"Are you tipsy, Miss Morgan?" Luke teased and tugged again.

"Certainly not, Mr. Harper," she said, and when her

giggle ended with a hiccup, her eyes flew open and she put her fingers to her lips.

"Do I need to carry you to our suite?" he asked, not letting go.

"May I remind you that we are in the Palace Hotel dining room?" she said quietly, while subtly trying to pull her feet out of his grasp.

"So you'd rather we were in bed?" he said a little louder and gave her a playful yank.

"Shh!" Genny gasped, laughed and hiccupped again.

"Are you coming home to Biloxi with me?" He tightened his grip to emphasize the answer he wanted. When she didn't immediately reply he jerked on her feet and her bottom slid to the very edge of her seat. "Say you will."

"I will." She was rewarded with the sexy smile only Luke could smile. "Now behave."

"Why should I?"

"Because when we get to our room, I'll model my birthday suit for you."

Releasing Genny's feet, Luke signaled their waiter and billed the meal to their room. He tipped their server who appeared in grateful awe of Luke's generosity.

"Why, thank you, Mr. Harper," the man said with a small bow.

Luke rose, walked to Genny and politely pulled out her chair as if nothing unusual had been going on beneath the table. Genny knew Luke was right about being tipsy the moment she stood. She looped her arm through his and he kept her from wobbling as they left the room.

Crossing the Palm Court, they arrived at their favorite rising room. Luke pushed the button, then leaned against the wall and pulled her to him. Stepping between his spread feet, Genny wrapped her arms around his neck and molded her breasts to his muscular chest. When his warm mouth came down on hers, she felt his hands slide down her back to her bottom.

"Harper," Genny gasped against his lips and wiggled her fanny. "Move your hands."

He did so by switching places with her. Putting her back to the wall he placed his hands on either side of her, trapping her as he leaned into her. Lowering his head, when he kissed her this time his tongue played with hers. Genny was already picturing crawling into bed with him.

This man was the Wild West and American Frontier put together. Boldly claiming her as his scavenger hunt partner, fighting those men at the pier, giving her the lessons she wanted, pulling his gun on the customer who didn't intend to pay, displaying nerves of steel at the gaming table, backing down the Skidmores, taking on Seth Comstock, to teaming up with Huan Li, Luke was as fearless as he was wild.

Would she ever tame the wild in Luke Harper? She hoped not.

Attracted by his every word and each grin, craving his sexy winks and masculine touch, Genny slipped her fingers into the waist of his trousers. He encouraged her with a low groan of approval, and she tugged him closer. Luke was her one and only love of a lifetime. She prayed nothing and no would ever take him from her.

"Luke, darling!"

CHAPTER 27

THE SHRILL VOICE STRUCK LIKE A NIGHTMARE.

Luke slowly swung his head around and Genny looked over his shoulder just before he lowered his arm from her side.

"Why are you here?" Luke asked coolly, turning to face the person.

A woman with light brown hair and eyes to match, appearing a few years older than Luke, stood before them. About Genny's height, the woman's medium-sized bosom was amply revealed by the low-cut neckline of a dress accentuating broad shoulders and a...protruding stomach. The woman's eyes cut to Genny and became slits as she raked her up and down.

"If you mean, why am I here today instead of tomorrow," the woman began, looking back to Luke and smiling, "I fibbed about the date, so I could surprise you. I knew I'd find you in San Francisco's finest hotel and here you are. I came to take you home with us to Biloxi, darling."

"Stop calling me that and you're not taking me anywhere." Luke moved slightly in front of Genny and crossed his arms over his chest.

"But I'm pregnant," she said and placed a hand to her abdomen.

228 | LYNN ELDRIDGE

"Not my problem."

She smiled coquettishly. "Oh, Luke. You know it's your child."

"Like hell it is," he growled, without skipping a beat. "You have a return ticket at the train station. I suggest you use it, Mara."

"But, Luke, the return train isn't due until day after tomorrow."

"Again, not my problem."

"Whoever this one is," Mara said with a flip of her hand at Genny, "ask her to run along so that we can talk."

"My name is Genevieve and I'm not running anywhere," Genny said, and though reeling from Mara's arrival and announcement, moved to Luke's side.

Luke gave Genny a quick smile and said to Mara, "We have nothing to talk about."

"I have no place to stay tonight," Mara mewled and placed a hand on Luke's arm. "I don't know a soul in San Francisco."

Luke's gaze dipped to Mara's abdomen and when he didn't immediately reply Genny wondered if he was considering securing Mara a room. At least for the child's sake.

"Mara," Harriett Peak called, hurrying their way and waving a room key. "I'm sorry that I can't offer you my house tonight, but I secured a room with two beds on the second floor."

No place and not a soul? Fibbing about her arrival date? Genny wondered what else Mara might be lying about and wished she'd take her hand off Luke.

"Oh, Harriett, how terribly fortunate." Mara's voice was flat. She rolled her eyes and folded her arms under her breasts, revealing even more bosom which Luke ignored.

"Hello, I'm Harriett Peak," the columnist said. Luke and Genny introduced themselves as well and shook hands with Harriett. "I write for the *San Francisco Chronicle*."

"We toured Nob Hill recently and your booklet was our guide," Luke said.

"Yes, and I've enjoyed your column for years," Genny added.

"Thank you. It's a pleasure to meet you both." Wearing a large hat the same blue as her traveling suit the attractive journalist, appearing to be in her mid-fifties, said, "Genevieve Morgan, I've heard your name somewhere."

"Harriett," Mara snapped, "Luke Harper is the man I told you about on the *Coast Line*."

"Are you sure?" Harriett asked, her sharp blue eyes a pretty accent to her silver hair. "Because this handsome man looks as if he already has a sweetheart." Smiling at Genny and then at Luke, she said, "An extraordinarily lovely one."

"That she is on both counts," Luke said to Harriett, continuing to ignore Mara.

"Well, speaking of the Nob Hill area," Harriett began, "perhaps you read in the *Chronicle* that some maniac broke into my house, killed my housekeeper and my cat and buried them in my backyard. I've decided to stay here at the Palace Hotel until I can sort the whole mess out."

"Miss Sinclair?" a bellboy called to Mara. "I'm afraid your trunk spilled open. We'd like for you to inspect it before we take it to your room."

"Such incompetence." Mara's shifting brown eyes tossed daggers at the bellboy and her lips pursed, before she managed to say, "Oh, very well. Excuse me."

When Mara was out of earshot, Luke said, "We know about your property, Miss Peak. I suspect a man named Seth Comstock is behind what happened."

"Please call me Harriett." Pausing for just a moment, her perfectly arched silver eyebrows shot up and she said, "Seth Comstock is where I heard Genevieve Morgan mentioned. In fact, I recall now that he seemed quite obsessed with meeting you, Genevieve." Harriett dug in her purse and brought out a small, leather book with an attached pencil.

"That sounds right," Luke grumbled.

Flipping the book open, Harriett consulted her notes. "Seth convinced me he'd inherited a silver fortune from a relative, Henry Comstock, of the Comstock Lode fame over in Virginia City, Nevada. He claimed a long family connection to William Sharon, who acquired the Palace Hotel from William Ralston, his finance partner. I did some research and found that 'Friends of the Comstock Lode' had indeed hosted a dinner for Mr. Ralston back in eighteen seventy-six. Seth seemed pleasant enough at first, so I vouched for him with the Palace Hotel manager." Harriett shook her head. "But after the embarrassment that man caused me the night of the ball and not paying his bill, I didn't care what his name was. I just wanted rid of him. I don't care for lying troublemakers."

"Neither do I," Luke said with an icy glare toward the front of the hotel lobby where Mara was stamping her foot and waving her finger at the concierge and the bellboy.

Tapping the pencil to her book, Harriett said, "I'd like to hear what you suspect about Seth Comstock's connection to my property, Mr. Harper."

"Call me Luke. Genevieve and I are headed to our room now, but I'd like to hear what else you know about him as well."

"I'm exhausted from traveling so I may not be up too early," Harriett said, and covered a small yawn with her book. "But would you be free sometime tomorrow?"

"How about brunch at eleven-thirty?" Luke suggested.

"Yes. That's perfect," Harriett said and smiled. "See you in the American Dining Room?"

"Genevieve and I will be there." Luke swung an arm around Genny.

"I'll be there, too," Mara interjected, hurrying toward them.

"No," Luke gritted through clenched teeth.

"You weren't invited, Mara," Harriett said bluntly. "Luke

and Genevieve and I have serious business to discuss tomorrow."

"Luke and I have serious business to discuss tonight," Mara placed her hand on her stomach and glared at Genny. "Alone."

"No," Luke said again, and opened the wrought iron door to the rising room.

Genny shivered. Warm and cozy in the light of Luke's love, the darkness of his disdain was cold and forbidding.

The bellboy joined them with luggage on a brass cart. Luke held the door open, and the bellboy waited for Harriett and Mara to enter. Genny took a step toward the rising room as well until Luke tightened his arm around her shoulders, holding her to him. Luke shut the gated door as Mara Sinclair, hand on her stomach, gave him one last beseeching silent appeal.

"Dammit to hell," Luke barked, when the elevator was gone. "I'm sorry about Mara Sinclair being here, Genny. Believe me, she is not pregnant with my child."

"I do believe you, Luke. And I'm sorry about Seth Comtock or whatever his real name is," Genny said. "What matters is that we're a united front."

"Yeah," Luke agreed with a scowl.

Genny nudged him and smiled her very best smile. When the rising room returned for them, Luke opened the door and Genny tugged him in after her. This time, it was she who winked. He finally smiled as they were swept straight up to their floor.

CHAPTER 28

"THERE. FROM MISS SINCLAIR." GENNY POINTED TOWARD the note and broken vase in the far corner of the room. "They were here when we returned from sailing."

"A bellboy could have made the delivery while we were gone."

"Maybe," Genny said, walking further into the room. "But when I hesitated in answering the knock on the door earlier, Patrick, who delivered your roses, didn't try to enter our room."

"They aren't from Mara. She'd have taken credit for them," Luke said, walking across the room. "Comstock broke in. Hell, I wish I hadn't touched that vase."

"What do you mean?" Genny asked, feeling unnerved as she stopped beside the round table where Luke's roses brightened the chaos. "Why does it matter who touched the vase?"

"Shortly before Steven and Mattie went back to Washington, D.C. the last time, Steven was telling me that the United States Department of Justice has formed the Bureau of Criminal Identification," Luke said, squatting down beside the broken vase and wilted flowers. "The Bureau provides a centralized reference collection of fingerprint cards."

"Are you thinking there might be such a fingerprint card on Comstock?"

"It's a long shot, because he's no more related to Henry Comstock than I am. But there is a soot-like fingerprint on the back of this note."

"I sniffed the black-eyed Susans. They smelled like kerosene."

"Gasoline," Luke replied, holding the note by a corner.

"YOU DIDN'T HAVE to burn and bury them, Seth," Selma said, scurrying after him. "Shanghaiing the Skidmores to a bunch of pirates was brilliant and we have some money."

"Shut up!" Seth said, shoving the cash into his pocket as he slithered through the foul smelling alley just after midnight. "Hurry up before they catch us, Selma."

"The pirates?"

"The Chinamen," Seth called over his shoulder, alternately skidding around garbage, sliding through sewage and stomping on rats. "Burl said I fit the description of the scarecrow."

"The scarecrow? Who's that?"

"I don't know but after those two Chinamen walked into the Black-Eyed Susan, Burl was petrified and tried to grab the money back he'd just paid me. If pressured, he'll tell those Chinese bastards he thinks I'm the scarecrow."

"Since when is everybody petrified of everybody?"

"Since those Chinamen had the Monkey King tattoo on their fists." Seth's stomach rolled from the deathly close call and puke filled his mouth. He spat it out in the already revolting alley and hissed, "We have to find a place to hide."

"I LISTEN BETTER IN BED." Luke yawned, lying in the big comfortable bed.

"Luke, you aren't listening to me at all," Genny said,

hands on her hips as she stood on his side of the bed, wearing only a pair of frilly pantalettes.

"Because your tipsy little self isn't in her birthday suit, yet," he said huskily. "C'mere." He grabbed her and she let him pull her into bed with him.

"I want you to leave San Francisco while you're still unharmed," Genny said seriously, as she straddled his hips and flattened her hands to his broad shoulders.

"Not before I know that damn scarecrow's story," Luke countered, hands on her thighs. "Dead or alive I want him caught before we leave. I sure as hell don't need him tracking us down in Biloxi. I've had a reminder of how it feels to be followed and I don't like it."

"Maybe Mara will be gone day after tomorrow," Genny said, as Luke brought her forward, molding her breasts to his chest and then sliding his fingers into the waist of her pantalettes. "I want you safe and back home with your family who loves you."

"We'll both go home, and my family will love you, too." Tugging down her pantalettes, his

sexy grin was hypnotizing as he said, "For tonight, love me like only you can."

Unable to resist him another second, Genny placed her head on his pillow and raised her hips so that he could make her as naked as he was. When he had her pantalettes past her knees she used her toes to flip them to the floor. Luke rolled her onto her back, leaned over her and slowly looked his fill.

"Now I can listen, babydoll," he whispered.

"Shatter me, loverboy."

WHEN THE SEAGULLS screeched the next morning, Genny reached for Luke. Finding his side of the bed empty she was instantly awake.

"Harper?"

"Mornin'."

Genny smiled, loving that drawl in his deep voice, and so happy to be the lucky woman waking up to it.

"'Bout time you opened those pretty cat eyes."

Luke walked toward the beautiful woman to whom he'd made love the previous night and again about an hour before sunrise. Naked, tossled hair and a satisfied smile on her full lips, Genny stretched like a cat and then reached for him. Pants already on and buttoning his shirt, he came to a stop on her side of the bed.

"Where are you going at the crack of dawn, city slicker?" She snared his hand and tugged him to sit down beside her.

"It's hardly the crack of dawn, mischief maker," he said with a chuckle. "I'm taking that note to Chief Dinan at the police department, then I'll be back to take you to brunch."

"I'm afraid of what else Harriett Peak has to say." Genny pulled the sheet over her breasts and sat up. "But at the same time, we need to hear it."

"I'm going to ask the chief to check the fingerprints on the note against any they may have collected at Harriett Peak's house."

"Can they do that?"

"Yes. A match would tie Comstock to Harriett's break-in, our break-in here and link him to the housekeeper's death. Maybe even to the arson involving the Runabout."

"Let me go with you." Genny wrapped her arms around his neck and hugged him tightly. "I'll hurry and dress."

"No reason for you to go. But please wait in the room for me this time."

Genny nodded her head against his. "I will."

"We'll hear what Harriett has to say and figure out our next move." He leaned her away from him and said, "In the meantime, I want the police working on that fingerprint."

"It is the very least the Palace Hotel can do for our favorite guest," the manager said sincerely with a sweep of his hand toward the brand-new black Runabout he had secured for Luke. "Your automobile was set on fire during the hotel's watch after all."

"That fire wasn't your fault, Mr. Jeffrey, but thank you for the replacement vehicle."

With a slight bow, Harrison Jeffrey shook Luke's hand as he said, "From Patrick to Cocktail Boothby to the maids, the shop ladies, the dining room staff, and employees from all over this hotel I've heard how unfailingly generous and kind you are, Mr. Harper. If I may be of any further service whatsoever, please do not hesitate to let me know."

Luke took the opportunity to advise him that Comstock had trapped Genny in the rising room. Aghast, the hotel manager apologized profusely and described Comstock as the bane of his existence. Promising to keep a vigilant watch for Comstock, the manager promised a delicious champagne supper on the house for Luke and Genny. Luke thanked him again and as he strode toward the automobile, heard his name called.

"Hello, Wong, Chen," Luke said in greeting. "Have you heard something?"

"Yes, sir," Wong replied. "From Fist leader, soldier."

Luke motioned them over to the Runabout. "What did they say?"

"Scarecrow shanghai soaplocks," Wong said. "Barbary Coast."

"How did your men know it was the scarecrow?" Luke asked.

"Black-Eyed Susan owner tell," Wong said.

"Not catch scarecrow," Chen added.

"Black-Eyed Susan," Luke repeated, thinking of the wilted flowers and knowing it was another damning nail in Comstock's coffin. "How did Comstock fool the Skidmores into getting shanghaied?"

"Underground den," Wong said. "Tong gang."

"Yeah, opium would do it." Luke rubbed his forehead.

"Tong punished," Chen said.

"Soaplocks drop trapdoor," Wong explained. "Four pirates take."

"I'd hoped to tie the Skidmores to Fan Zhou's murder," Luke said. "But slaves at sea on a pirate ship is as good a prison as any."

Wong and Chen both gave nods of appreciation.

Then Chen told him, "Fist take soaplocks."

That shed a different light on the Skidmores' fates. Luke figured the pirates never saw the Monkey's Fist coming and even if they had, the pirates were outnumbered at least ten to four.

"Where are the Skidmores now?" Luke asked, just to make sure.

"Bay," Wong replied stoically.

The blood bath that must have taken place between Huan's soldiers and slave ship pirates flashed across Luke's mind. He was relieved to hear that none of Huan's men were injured.

"The Monkey's Fist made the Skidmores pay with their lives for Fan Zhou's death," Luke said evenly. "As agreed."

"Yes, sir," Wong replied.

"Are the pirates alive to talk?"

"No, sir."

"HOUSEKEEPING."

"Just a moment," Genny answered. She had finished dressing and was expecting Luke any moment. Thus, the maid had good timing she thought crossing the room. She opened the door to find a woman whose face was pinched into an angry frown. "Luke isn't here, Mara."

"I watched him leave the hotel," Mara Sinclair said. "I'm here to talk to you."

"I have nothing to add to what Luke said to you last night."

"I want the father of my baby back." Mara glanced demurely at her stomach and then suddenly placing her right arm across her midsection, spat, "He's my fiancé, not yours."

"Fiancé?" Genny asked, jolted. She covered it up saying, "You are not engaged. Luke told me all about you."

"Told you...after he was caught last night?" Mara snapped.

"Before you arrived. Rob sent Luke a telegram warning him about you, and I personally read the telegram you sent to Luke."

"Oh, well, Rob is jealous because he's in love with me, too."

"No," Genny said, shaking her head. "Rob is happily married to Chloe."

"Who?" Mara asked, showing her ignorance. Waving that away she said, "Luke knew I was pregnant and planned to marry me. But we had a spat and he left town."

"None of that is true. He left Biloxi due to winning a bet." Genny would not take this woman's word over Luke's and moved to shut the door. But Mara flattened her left hand to the door and propped the side of her foot against it as well.

"Are you calling me a liar?" Mara's brown eyes bored into Genny and in a patronizing tone, she said, "Whatever you think you have with Luke, so have dozens of other women."

"Everyone has a past," Genny said calmly. "I don't see a ring on your finger, Mara."

As Mara's face turned red, she quickly slid her left hand under her right arm keeping her stomach covered. Her foot still against the door, her lips drew into a sneer as she said, "Luke always comes back to me. You'll soon be yesterday's trash."

"Yet, you're the one he bought train tickets for," Genny said.

"My tickets are to ensure I'll be home waiting for him after he throws you away."

Genny remembered her thoughts of Luke vanishing but

said, "You're embarrassing yourself with this awkward pursuit."

Mara's worsening grimace was quiet unflattering. "You're the one making it awkward. I want you out of his room and out of his life. Luke and I need to be alone so that he can remember how much we love each other."

"Did Luke say he loves you, Mara?" Genny raised her chin and waited. When Mara merely smirked, Genny asked, "Did he laugh with you as you danced? Ask you to sail away with him? Defend your honor? Protect you from harm? Give you lessons on how to kiss and fight? Did Luke invite you home to meet his family?"

"You bitch!" Mara shrilled.

Genny didn't see the slap coming. Placing a hand to her stinging cheek, what Genny did see were feathers poking through the material across Mara's stomach. With protecting Luke foremost in her mind, Genny punched Mara square in her left eye. Mara's head snapped to the side, and she stumbled over her skirts until she caught herself on the balcony railing. Teeth bared and pushing off the railing, Mara charged Genny who simply let the feather pillow birth itself.

"Stop!" Luke barked, striding down the hall.

CHAPTER 29

"Luke, help me," Mara wailed, whirling to face him. "She hit me."

"Damn right she did," Luke said. "Pregnant with a pillow, Mara?"

"I—I had to get your attention long enough to marry—"

"Save it," Luke growled.

Luke cupped his hand under Genny's chin, turned her head and frowned at the bright red handprint. Snatching up the pillow, Mara held it as if she might try to smother Genny with it.

"I warned you Luke taught me to fight, Mara."

"Thank you for exposing her lie." Luke kissed Genny's forehead. "Her black eye'll be worse than mine." He gently eased Genny safely into their room and turned to Mara. "I don't know what I haven't said to you that you need to hear to leave me alone. So listen to this, you just slapped the only woman I've ever wanted to marry."

"No," Mara gasped, eyes shooting spears of hatred at Genny. "What about us?"

"There is no *us*. Hell, I didn't even know your last name until I got your telegram," Luke said with an incredulous tone. "You don't know me, either. You love the Harper money."

"You're wrong. I love you," Mara insisted with a nose-running-turned-down-lips display of blubbering. "I know you love me, too!"

"I know you're delusional," Luke said seriously. "Stay away from us, Mara."

The nasty smile that slowly brought the downward corners of Mara's mouth upward was...malevolent. That's the word that came to Genny's mind. Malevolent. Then the nightmare that was Mara hurled the pillow over the balcony and swayed toward the rising room as if nothing untoward had happened. With a look of disgust, Luke entered their room.

And kicked the door shut.

"Doors are shutting on us in San Francisco, Selma. All because of Luke Harper," Seth said, nearing the railroad station. "As long as he's alive, Genevieve, her jewels, land, and houses are lost to us." Holding up his fingers he ticked off, "We can't live in Harriett's house, and we can't hide out in the Barbary Coast. We can't risk going to the Skidmores' farm, yet, since the Chinese are on to us which also means I can't even seek sweet oblivion in the underground dens. We have to leave town while we figure a way to kill Harper and take my woman back."

"We will kill Harper, but Genevieve was always *his* woman, Seth."

"Damn that woman," Luke growled as Genny sat at a dressing table, in front of an ornate looking glass, patting powder on the cheek which had been slapped. Picking up the moonstone pendant from the table, Luke's strong fingers brushed the nape of her neck as he clasped the gold chain. As his chin brushed the Gibson girl curls on top of her head, his eyes met hers in the mirror and he said, "Keep this moonstone on."

"I'd been about to put it on when she arrived. My cheek looks fine now." Genny turned away from the mirror and smiled up at him. One thing Mara had said which Genny had already assumed was that there were dozens of women who had fallen for and wanted Luke. As intimidating as that confirmation was, she took a calming breath and focused on his advice of being wildly happy. "I finished something for you this morning while you were gone."

"Let's have it," he said with a grin.

"Close your eyes." When he did so she stood and tucked a white handkerchief, she had painstakingly mono-grammed with LHR in crimson red, into his suit pocket. "You can look."

"How did you know my initials?"

"I figured your attorney would know and sure enough, Joe did." She straightened the handkerchief just a tad and then gave it a pat. "There you go, Lucas Richard Harper. I have six more at my house each embroidered in a different color. One for every day of the week."

"I've never had anything with my monogram on it. Thank you," he said, folding her into his arms and pressing her against the handkerchief covering his heart. "Did I mention that I'm proud of you for sticking up for yourself this morning and for believing in me?"

"We're a united front, right?" Genny felt her confidence strengthening.

"Always." Luke winked and said, "That reminds me, I have something for you, too. Sit back down, hold out your hands and close your eyes."

Genny did so and something came to rest in her cupped-together palms. Told she could look, she found Luke on one knee and a small burgundy box in the middle of her hands. Staring into the open box, Genny's jaw dropped as her eyes met Luke's.

"Will you marry me, Miss Morgan?"

"You were serious when you said—" Genny's voice cracked, and her heart pounded with her all-consuming love for the man kneeling before her. Swallowing first, she finished in a whisper, "You wanted to marry me?"

"Yes, Genevieve," Luke replied. "What did you think my intentions were when I asked you to come home with me and meet my family?"

"I thought you meant for a visit or to see your house or…or I don't know, Harper."

"Mattie says I need a woman's touch in my house," Luke said with a grin and a shrug. "Will you marry me and be that woman?"

"It would be my fondest dream come true," Genny said, her eyes stinging with tears. "But…"

"But what?"

"I think marriage is a mighty big leap of faith between someone who lives in a French provential mansion along the Mississippi Sound to someone who owns a disorderly house in the country."

"You agreed to go home to Biloxi with me last night. My dream is to have you there as my wife," Luke said, and thumbed away a tear that escaped down her unscathed cheek. "But I'll stay here if you won't go with me."

"No," she said adamantly and shook her head. "Your life and your family are in Mississippi."

"My life is where you are. I want to have a family with you."

"A family?" she whispered, her mind whirling with new hope.

"Yes." His smile was as endearing as it was sexy.

"Having a baby with a husband who I loved was always too much for me to imagine," she said her throat aching with longing as a tear ran down the cheek that had been slapped. "Then I met you and I thought if you vanished into the wild and left me with a baby, at least I'd have a part of you to love forever."

"Aww…Genny, I see your heart on your sleeve," Luke whispered. "Remember the other night when I said we make our own destiny?" As he held her trembling body close to his muscular one, she nodded. "You're mine and I'd like to be yours."

"Luke, you *are* my destiny."

"Good." Luke took hold of the ring and set the box aside. "Then I'll gamble that this engagement ring will fit. If it does, we'll go to Biloxi and get married. If it doesn't fit, we won't. Wanna take that bet, little lamb?"

"Yes, I do, wolf."

Genny squared her shoulders and held out her shaking left hand. Luke steadied her hand with his and chuckled as she crossed her fingers. He put the ring to the tip of her third finger and paused.

"The size was just a hunch," he said with a tease in his voice.

"Are you raising the ante?"

"Yeah," he said. "I want more than one baby."

"If this ring doesn't fit, we'll have two babies. If it does fit, we'll have three."

"What?" He laughed and then said seriously, "Three sounds good to me."

"You've got yourself a bet. Let's see how good your hunch was."

Luke easily slid the ring over her first knuckle and stopped at her second knuckle. He cocked a rakish brow, and she raised her brow in return. With just the right amount of pressure he slipped the ring over her knuckle.

A perfect fit.

"We both win," Luke said.

"We do." Genny threw her arms around him, and he stood lifting her to her feet and swinging her around in a circle. When he placed her feet back on the floor, Genny sniffled, and Luke grinned as they both looked at the sparkling ring on her finger. "Luke Harper, this is the most extraordinary and totally extravagant ring I have ever seen." Set in yellow gold filigree much like the yellow gold around her moonstone pendant, the gem glittered like no other stone could. "Is this a…a…" she gulped, "diamond?"

"Yes, two carats," he replied. "The jeweler told me that in the year fourteen seventy-seven, Archduke Maximilian of Austria presented his betrothed, Mary of Burgundy with the very first diamond engagement ring. The diamonds on her ring were flat slivers. But that was back in the Dark Ages."

"Lucas, bringer-of-light, thank you," Genny whispered meaningfully, smiling at him and then moving her fingers to catch rays of sunshine with the diamond and gold. "It's beautiful."

"So are you, Genevieve. I love you."

Genny placed her hands to his face and kissed him. Twining her arms around his neck, she tightened her embrace never ever wanting to let this man go. As they kissed, his hands slipped under her arms and her feet left the ground again. Yes, she was surely walking on air.

"I love you so much," she whispered in his ear. "I can't wait to marry you."

"Next time you do your belly dance for me," he began as he put her feet back on the floor, "I might be persuaded to tell you where I see us getting married."

"I'M SORRY, but as you can clearly see on the message he wrote, your train tickets on the *Coast Line* to Los Angeles and the *Sunset Limited* to New Orleans are one way and not to be refunded," the railroad clerk said politely, slipping the message and tickets underneath the narrow bars of the ticket window.

"You listen to me, I don't care what his message says I demand the cash for these tickets," Mara hissed at the middle-aged woman sitting behind the counter. She shoved the tickets back under the bars at the clerk and was bumped by the man in line behind her. She was in no mood for it and turning abruptly said, "Mister, you're crowding me. Stop it."

"Pardon me, milady," he said, simultaneously sliding

one hand into his pocket and one over his heart as he took a step back.

"I apologize for any inconvenience this causes you, ma'am," the ticket clerk said.

"Damn him to hell," Mara shrilled and banged her fist on the ledge of the ticket window. When the clerk once again slid the tickets under the bar to her, Mara noticed the specifics. Snatching up the tickets, she rapped them back and forth across the bars of the window and spat, "These seats are in coach rather than sleeping berths in first class."

"The bellboy from the hotel said you were to return to New Orleans in the same manner in which you traveled here. Our records showed that your tickets were seats in coach."

"He sent a damn bellboy?" she all but screamed. "Did this bellboy make arrangements for me to travel from New Orleans to Biloxi?"

"He did not. But if you live in Biloxi—"

"I don't. Shut up, so I can think." Mara opened her pocketbook to shove her new tickets into her money purse, with her original ticket stubs, and then began digging through the handbag. "My money purse is gone. I know I had it with me." In a panic, she dug into her pockets, glanced at the ground and back at the clerk in the ticket window. "Did you steal my money purse?"

"Ma'am, I never asked for money. The bellboy made quite sure your fare was paid in full."

"Oh, I'm quite sure the bellboy did," Mara spat in a singsong voice and was just as sure the clerk smirked at her. "Bitch!"

"You're holding up the line," the ticket lady said. "I'll have to ask you to move along."

"Move along where? Without my money I'll have to sleep on park benches. Damn Luke Harper to hell." Mara whirled on the man behind her. "Help me find my money."

"I'll be happy to help you," the man said and stepped out of line. "Did I hear you mention the name Luke Harper?"

"Yes," Mara snapped, repeating the cycle of searching her handbag, her pockets and then glowering at the ground as if it had gobbled up her money. "Are you a friend of his?"

"Quite the opposite I'm afraid. Mr. Harper's the reason I'm leaving San Francisco."

"Well, Mr. Harper gave me this black eye along with the train tickets." At that, Mara focused on the skinny man with yellow hair and teeth to match. Though somewhat disheveled, he vaguely reminded her of her absentminded third husband. "Did Luke tell you to leave, too?"

"No, but he stole my Genevieve. She and I were planning to marry until he came along."

"I have news for you, mister; Luke plans to marry her now."

"No!" he yelped as if she'd delivered a blow to his stomach as surely as Genevieve had. Then composing himself, he said, "I—I'm sure you don't have time to hear of my heartbreak."

"Actually, I do." She gestured to the ticket window and asked, "But weren't you in line to buy a ticket to…?"

"Los Angeles. No matter, that train runs on a regular basis. I have servants who take care of my house and grounds when I travel, so I can return at my leisure." He gave a flippant wave of his hand and then sighed. "I do however miss my fabulous soirées on my manicured lawns of my cliff overlooking my private beach along the Pacific."

"Mara Sinclair," she said and extended her hand to him. "Pleased to meet you."

"Seth Comstock of the Comstock Lode fame." Taking her hand, he lifted it to thin lips.

CHAPTER 30

"You may have provided the information we need to catch him," Luke said, and taking Harriett's hand he helped her out of the the Runabout parked in front of the *Chronicle* building at the corner of Third and Kearny.

During brunch, Luke had gathered more evidence against Comstock as he and Genny exchanged information with Harriett over eggs Benedict, bacon, toast, juice, and coffee. Harriett, a journalist accustomed to giving precise facts, got right to the point. Seth claimed he was in San Francisco to appraise some expensive jewels. He had a twin sister, but Harriett hadn't met her because Seth claimed they were currently at odds. When Harriett asked the first name of his sister, Seth became so upset that his eyelids almost fluttered off his skull. Genny told of witnessing that same reaction in the rising room. Offering her final piece to the puzzle, Harriett contributed what Luke had hoped most for: a last name. Seth, as if muttering to himself, had referred to his sister as the worst spendthrift of all the *Evilsizers*.

"Until today, I assumed Evilsizer was the sister's married name, but now I think it is Seth's true surname," Harriett said as she stood with Luke on the sidewalk.

"I'll head back to the police station with that information," Luke replied.

"Seth has to be the maniac who was living in my house." Harriett sighed and shook her head. "As to the Skidmores, I won't ask how you know they're no longer a threat. I'll just say thank you for telling me, off the record, that I have nothing more to fear from the two men who helped murder my good friend, Fan Zhou."

There was a choke in Harriett's voice as she spoke of her friend. Genny smiled at Luke for reassuring Harriett, while protecting Huan Li and his men. Harriett then reached across the seat and took Genny's hand.

"Genevieve, I wish I hadn't been the one to realize it was your mother who Seth was courting."

"He alluded to knowing Garnet when he trapped me in the rising room," Genny said, holding Harriett's hand a moment. "But Garnet and I weren't close, and she never told me the name of the man she'd been seeing here in the city."

"Until you mentioned your mother's name was Garnet, I didn't make the connection, either," Harriett said, as Genny let go of her hand.

"It explains how I came to be invited to that ball."

"If it makes you feel any better, Seth admitted Garnet broke it off when he proposed." Harriett stood back then. "He claimed to be quite upset to hear of her death."

"Yeah, right," Luke muttered. "Killing Garnet cleared his path to Genny."

"I agree, Luke," Harriett said.

"But why?" Genny asked.

"*Your* fiancée knows she's as beautiful as she is fashionable, doesn't she?" Harriett asked Luke with a smile.

"I tell her every single day," Luke replied and winked at Genny.

"Luke, she's a prize to be won," Harriett said, and turned to Genny. "Genevieve, take good care of your handsome husband-to-be. I'm still waiting for the right man to come along. But I guarantee you there's not another man like Luke on Earth."

"Or the moon," Genny said with a smile at Luke.

"Thanks again for allowing my photographer to take your engagement photograph for the *Chronicle*." Harriett placed her notebook to her heart and sighed. "Genevieve, you in your lovely navy-blue frock and matching shawl, and Luke in his double-breasted suit standing in front of the Palace Hotel, will be the most attractive couple to ever grace my society page column." With a glance at Genny's sleek, white boot-like shoes, she said, "Immaculate taste." Harriett turned then and waving a hand in the air called over her shoulder, "Ta-ta."

Genny called goodbye as Luke climbed back into the Runabout. Their next stop was the Hall of Justice on Kearny Street in front of Portsmouth Square. In the heart of Chinatown, San Francisco's impressive police headquarters was only about a half mile from the Palace Hotel. Luke had appreciated its proximity more than once.

"The Hall of Justice was built in nineteen hundred," Genny said as she and Luke paused in the automobile a moment to admire the massive brick and terra cotta structure. "When Garnet got wind that I wanted to see it, she ordered me not to go saying I might draw the authorities' attention to the ranch. So, I waited until the ranch was extra busy one Saturday night and ventured into town."

"That doesn't surprise me," Luke said and shook his head. "Even though you would have been only fifteen."

"Grandpa was able to come with me back then. Garnet never found out. The police officers were proud of their new building and happy to give us a tour," Genny said. "When Jeremiah Dinan was named Chief of Police a year ago on April fifth, I was here to see that, too. I'd offer to show you around inside, but you've already been here more times than I have."

"I never expected to be here at all when I came to San Francisco."

"I know," she replied and placed her hand on his muscular thigh. "If not for me, you would have already sold your ranch and be safely home—" her voice caught in her throat, but she finished, "in Biloxi by now."

"My ranch is sold. Half of the reason we're on an extended stay at the Palace is to allow the new owner time to start renovating."

"What? I'm so happy to hear that, Luke," Genny said. "When did it sell and to whom?"

"Recently. To Huan."

"Huan?" Genny was wide-eyed and jaw-dropped flabbergasted. "Why?"

"Besides that threat against Tricky's life, which he resolved, Huan has his reasons."

"I'm sure he does." Genny paused a moment and then asked, "What's the other half of the reason we've been staying in town?"

"Genny, the Palace Hotel is representative of the life I grew up knowing. You've spoken so much about our differences that I want you to feel at home when we get there." Tears of the deepest gratitude stung Genny's eyes and a single drop rolled down her cheek. Thumbing her tear away Luke said, "If I'd gone home weeks ago, you'd have faced a maniac alone."

"Yes." How she loved this sensitive, compassionate man.

"That maniac sought Garnet out because he believed the jewels were actual gemstones. Maybe he thinks your land amounts to more than fifty acres and no doubt he wants your houses, too. Garnet got wise to him, so he murdered her and moved on to you. That's the 'why' to answer your earlier question."

"Garnet's spite in using jewels as names was the final ruination Grandpa predicted would come to her because of the ranch," Genny said, swallowing hard and feeling anxious. Perhaps she'd suspected what Luke had said, but hearing him lay it all out, confirmed her worst fear. She realized her hand was cold when Luke's warm one covered hers. When he gave her a squeeze, she said with conviction, "He knows he'll have to kill you before he can kill me."

"Hey, Luke! Genevieve!"

Joe Sanchez had said something similar to Luke weeks prior and now he pulled his Ford alongside the Runabout. In the front seat beside Joe sat Ying and in the middle of the back seat, Tricky. Joe said he was looking for Luke to deliver the final paperwork on the sale of the ranch and he also had the deed to the property for Huan. Having come across Ying and Tricky, Joe had given them a ride into town.

Everyone piled out of the automobiles, the men shaking hands and the women hugging. Per Ying and Tricky, everything had been quiet out in the country. The Johnson brothers were on duty at the firehouse so hadn't visited Grace and Ruth for a few days. The Skidmores' donkey wouldn't leave the Cat's Eye Ranch, but Vern had been feeding him. The donkey had made friends with Roscoe who was fine as were Etalon and Esprit.

"Why do you have a different Runabout?" Joe asked Luke.

Luke answered his question with a brief overview of the fire, the gasoline, black-eyed Susans, and Genny told of her rising room confrontation.

"Remember when you said there was a rumor Garnet was seeing a man in town and that it ended badly?" Luke asked Joe who nodded. "Harriett Peak confirmed it was Comstock. I'm on my way to inform the police of his probable real last name. Then I'm headed to Western Union."

"I can go with you to talk to the police. I know a number of the detectives and officers," Joe said. "And from the look in your eye, you might need a lawyer before this is all over."

"Yeah, I might," Luke grumbled.

"Engaged?" Tricky squealed and hugged Genny. "Genevieve, tell me everything."

"It was by far and away the single most special surprise

door. "What's wrong?" he asked, his heart beginning to hammer in his chest. "Where's Genny?"

"Come with me, Luke, Joe," Huan replied, ushering them further into Li's.

"Ying and I were talking with friends and the next thing we knew Genevieve was gone," Tricky said, quickly coming up beside Huan with Ying at her back. Tricky's cheeks were stained with tear tracks. "It's my fault because I wanted to hear about the engagement."

"I told her to stay close to you and Ying," Luke said, and remembered Genny's response; *You be careful, too, Luke.* Dammit, she'd done that to him once before and wound up in the rising room with Evilsizer. Each thud of his heart resounded in his brain more loudly than the last. As Tricky cried, Luke asked Ying, "Where did you see her last?"

"Near a trolley stop," Ying said. "I'm so sorry, Luke. Please do not blame Tricky. The fault is mine. I know that as the man, I should have protected Genevieve."

At the blatant confirmation on Huan's face, Ying winced and hung his head.

"No, it's my fault," Luke growled and ran a hand through his hair. "My gut said not to let her out of my sight. How long has she been gone?"

"Almost three hours," Ying said, his voice and face strained.

"Luke, all five fingers of the Monkey's Fist received orders to do nothing else until they find her," Huan said with resolute composure. "You have five leaders and more than fifty soldiers who will lay down his life or take one to accomplish this mission. The Fist leaders will not return without Genevieve."

"I need to go look for her myself," Luke replied, struggling to remain calm.

"Luke, I'll go with you, but where would we start?" Joe asked.

"Dammit it to hell," Luke barked, silently berating himself. "I don't know."

"Neither do I and I know San Francisco," Joe said with a helpless glance at Huan.

"Let's have baijiu in my office and give my men a few more minutes," Huan said. "When they find her, they will bring her to my private entrance."

Huan placed a firm hand on Luke's shoulder and nodded to Wong who stood waiting in the shadows with Chen. Chen disappeared as Wong came forward. Wong signaled two guards, one who led the way down a hallway and one who brought up the rear with Wong. Tension crackled in the air as Huan escorted Luke and Joe into his office and past an ornate desk and chair to a polished wooden bar with brass stools. Behind the bar, Chen was already pouring baijiu. Luke, Huan and Joe threw back their shots of the strong liquor and Chen poured another round. Ying comforted Tricky as Luke clenched his jaw in fear.

Fear? Yes. This sickening apprehension was a powerful emotion the likes of which Luke had experienced only once before today. It had involved a child and ended tragically. He would give Huan's men a little more time not only because they excelled at their job, but he thought that if and when she could, this is where Genny would come.

Huan said conversationally, "Fan Zhou's parents left here shortly before you and Joe arrived, Luke. When Harriett Peak was notified of their daughter's death, Miss Peak wired six months' worth of Fan's wages to them and paid for our traditional seven-day funeral and a proper burial for Fan."

"That sounds like Harriett. She said Fan Zhou was her good friend," Luke replied and Huan nodded his approval with a tight smile.

"Luke, tell everyone what we found out at the Hall of Justice," Joe said encouragingly.

Frowning, Luke said, "The police have an in-depth record on a Seth Evilsizer and have been looking for him. The only photograph they have shows him with long, shaggy hair and a beard. We know that's how he looks again. But his photograph last December in the *Chronicle* was as he appeared at the New Year's Eve ball. That mask along with the alias of Seth Comstock has allowed him to go undetected by the police."

"And by the Monkey's Fist," Huan gritted through his teeth. "How do you know Comstock is an alias?"

"Harriett Peak told Genny and me that Seth *Comstock* referred to a twin sister as Selma Evilsizer," Luke said, watching the private side door entrance.

"The police confirmed Seth *Evilsizer* had a twin sister," Joe added helpfully.

"The police here know about fingerprinting as a way of identifying people and they collected fingerprints at Harriett Peak's house after Fan Zhou's death," Luke said to Huan. "I gave them a note with a fingerprint on it that was left for Genny in our hotel room."

"And these fingerprints match?" Huan asked.

"They do," Luke replied

"The scarecrow dies before he kills again," Huan said stoically.

"Hell yes," Luke said.

They downed their shots and Chen poured another round.

"I never heard that," Joe said. Fishing two hundred dollars out of his pocket he handed it to Huan. "In fact, considering what else the police said, please add this to the bounty on Evilsizer."

"According to the police," Luke gave a nod of thanks to Joe as Huan accepted the additional reward money, "when Evilsizer was about twenty-five back in West Virginia, he was found guilty of murdering his socialite parents by setting them on fire while they slept. No state prison existed there at the time, so they locked him up in the West Virginia Hospital for the Insane. He kept setting fire to anyone and everything, so they diagnosed him as a pyromaniac, and he wound up spending the next three decades drugged."

"Why did he murder his parents?" Tricky asked, hugging herself.

"They were rich, and he wanted it all," Luke answered.

"Why did the asylum let him out?" Ying asked, draping his arm around Tricky.

"They didn't. But the twin sister convinced a new doctor that her brother was harmless, and they stopped drugging him," Luke replied, ran a hand through his hair and stood away from the bar. "He escaped not long after a locksmith became his cellmate."

With a concerned glance at Luke, Joe took up the story, saying, "Selma Evilsizer never married, visited him regularly and waited thirty years for him to be released."

"How did he come to be in the Bay area?" Huan asked.

"Harriett said that someone who once lived here, probably Evilsizer's cellmate, told him about the so-called *jewels* at the Cat's Eye Ranch," Luke replied and rubbed his forehead. "He came to appraise them, as in get his hands on them, and the properties through marriage to Garnet Morgan and now to Genny."

"He *is* insane," Huan replied.

Joe nodded and said, "The police referred to Evilsizer as a psychopath."

"Before he fled West Virginia, he figured out that during the thirty years Selma waited on him, she had gone through the family fortune." Luke glanced at the door, hoping against hope Genny would walk through it. She didn't. "So, he set fire to the sister while she slept. Evilsizer was long gone by the time Selma's charred remains were found."

As Luke stared out the window, Joe said, "One day last year, the San Francisco police happened to recognize Evilsizer, in his usual unkempt state, attempting, unsuccessfully, to set fire to a dog he claimed bit him. Since he was an escaped inmate from an insane asylum in West Virginia, he was sent to Agnew's State Hospital for the Insane in Santa Clara. But he picked a lock or two and escaped."

"Santa Clara is less than fifty miles south of here," Huan said.

"He burned your Runabout, too," Joe said to Luke.

"And tried to poison Roscoe," Ying added.

Turning to her brother, Tricky asked, "Are the Skidmores dead, Huan?"

"Yes," Huan replied and made eye contact with Luke.

Luke silently acknowledged that with a look and said, "I suspect Evilsizer drowned Genny's grandfather after running over and setting fire to her mother."

"I wonder why her grandfather escaped a death of fire," Ying said, shaking his head.

"The drowning opportunity probably presented itself when Mr. Morgan went fishing," Luke guessed, remembering how he'd sensed being watched more than once in those woods.

"He was too wet to catch fire," Ying surmised.

Fiery deaths and Genny's disappearance were too much for Luke to stand still another minute and he said, "I've got to go look for her."

That decided, Luke stalked toward the private exit of the office. Huan nodded at the guard, and he opened the door for Luke. Outside, two more guards stepped aside to allow Luke and Huan followed by Wong, Chen, Joe, Ying, and Tricky into the sunshine.

CHAPTER 31

From a distance, Genny saw him.

Her first thought was how much she loved this man. Luke stood facing away from her, but as he turned just slightly his hands swept back the sides of his jacket and his fists clenched on his hips. Her second thought was that his body stance was as fierce and formidable as she'd ever seen him. Taller and more muscular than anyone in their group of friends and any of Huan's bodyguards, Luke Harper appeared ready to kill.

On the way here, she'd been closely flanked by two tough Chinese men, one of whom had informed her they were leaders of the Monkey's Fist. Glancing at their hands, each was inked with the tattoo of the Monkey King. For a tong gang member to have the sharp-fanged gorilla head tattoo meant removal of his hand. With complete confidence she had gone with them.

Having explained they were following the strictest of orders to find, protect and escort her to Chinatown, the leaders were initially accompanied by half a dozen members of the Monkey's Fist. She'd noticed they seemed to work in twos and four of the men had discreetly paired up and departed along the way. Now, with Luke and Huan in sight the two leaders escorting her dropped back a pace and walked with two soldiers just behind her.

"I'm sorry to have caused you trouble," Genny said, looking over her left shoulder and then her right. "Thank you all so much."

Turning back toward Luke, she couldn't wait to hug him. Her heart and mind raced ahead to how warm and happy he made her feel whenever a sexy grin tugged up the corner of his mouth and his arms closed around her. Despite his probable anger, she wanted Luke Harper in this moment as much as she did every waking moment.

Hastening her step, she imagined the intimate caresses of his strong hands on her naked skin. She craved the way his rock-hard body took control of her creating rolling raptures of ecstacy deep inside her. More mysterious than the moon and more smolderingly gorgeous than any mythical god known as Adonis, she picked up her skirts and ran.

"Luke!"

When Luke turned in her direction, his eyes closed, and his head bowed for just a moment. Then he walked away from the small crowd surrounding him and opened his arms. A moment later, she was locked in his steely safe embrace. Hearts pounded against each other as his lips came down on hers in a quick kiss.

"Where have you been?" His whisper, fairly near a growl, was music to her ears.

"I'll tell you everything." Rising on tiptoes, she wound her arms snugly around his neck and he hugged her more tightly before standing her back.

"I'll tell *you* something, dammit," Luke said. "You're in trouble."

"With you?" she flirted.

"Yes, with me. I'm madder than hell at you for *vanishing into the wild.*"

"Actually, I didn't agree to your condition of sticking close to Ying and Tricky."

"Dammit, Genevieve, I knew you were going to say

that," he barked. "If you ever pull this kind of stunt again, I'll tan your little bottom when I get my hands on you."

"You'd have to catch me first."

"You doubt that I could?"

Luke cocked a brow and Genny bit her lower lip as desire sizzled up her spine. He grabbed her hand and turned toward Huan and the others. The leaders of the Monkey's Fist appeared to be reporting to Huan outside his office. Tricky came running and gave Genny a big hug. Ying and Joe were close behind and they all began asking questions at once. Wong waved them in and politely announced that supper would soon be served in the private dining room.

"Sounds good to me," Luke said to Wong, then frowned just a little at Genny. "Huan will want to hear what you have to say as much as the rest of us, Genevieve."

A few minutes later, when seats were taken around the same table at which they had recently celebrated Genny's birthday, Chen poured baijiu for each of the men and a pretty Chinese woman appeared with small cups of rice wine for Genny and Tricky. When Joe gave the young woman an ear-to-ear grin, Genny nudged Tricky.

"This is our cousin, Suki Li," Tricky said and introduced the guests ending with Joe and taking an extra measure to say that he was a good friend and a lawyer in San Francisco.

A slight blush staining her pretty cheeks, Suki nodded at Joe with lowered lids. She left the room and when she returned with wonton soup and egg roll appetizers, Joe couldn't take his eyes off her. Glancing at a grinning Joe, the tiniest of shy smiles touched Suki's lips before she left the room a second time.

"Genevieve?" was all Luke had to say.

"Yes," Genny answered and snapping out of her reverie over Joe and Suki, realized everyone was staring at her. "Well, first of all, I'm so sorry for worrying you," she said, making eye contact around the table. "I was enjoying a little walkabout when a trolley stopped nearby." She felt her eyes widen as she saw it all again. "In the front seat of the trolley sat Seth Comstock and Mara Sinclair."

"What the hell?" Luke growled.

"Who's Mara Sinclair?" Joe asked, picking up an egg roll.

"The perfect conspirator," Luke said. "Are you sure, Genny?"

"So sure that I snuck on the back of the trolley." Genny grimaced at Tricky and Ying both of whom looked aghast. Their utensils, called duck spoons and filled with soup, had stopped halfway to their mouths. "I knew you wouldn't let me follow them if I told you."

"Yes, you are right about that," Ying said, placing his spoon back in his bowl.

"Where'd they go?" Tricky asked and took her sip of soup.

"They rode the trolleys, like tourists, all over town."

"Looking for a place to hide," Luke said to Huan who agreed.

"They even took a trolley close to Harriett's house." Genny glanced from Luke to Huan. "But two of your men were there, Huan."

"Searching for you," Huan said with a polite nod.

Scowling at Genny, Luke asked, "How did you stay hidden?"

Draping her navy-blue shawl over her hair, Genny slumped her shoulders and bowed her head. Stunned silence reigned as the beautiful woman disappeared into an inconspicuous figure.

"Your wild streak could have gotten you killed, Genevieve," Luke scolded her. When Genny lowered the shawl and patted his hand, he grumbled, "Go on."

"A couple of blocks away from the Palace Hotel, they finally left the trolley and started walking. Keeping my distance, I followed them." Genny ventured a glance at Luke, but he was scowling, and a muscle worked in his jaw, so she looked away and said, "Suddenly, they turned and ran down Annie Street between the hotel and the Monadnock Building."

"Please tell me you didn't follow them down that alley," Luke said.

Luke's his eyes narrowed with such a dangerous glint, Genny knew he was remembering the three men who had emerged from Annie Street on New Year's Eve and blocked her path.

"I was going to," she admitted and winced at Luke's darkening expression. "But I thought I'd been spotted when Seth screamed over his shoulder for someone to hurry up named Selma."

At the name Selma, conversation erupted around the table.

"Selma Evilsizer," Joe said matter-of-factly to Luke.

"Who's Selma Evilsizer?" Genny asked Luke.

"Seth *Evilsizer's* twin sister and the final nail in Seth *Comstock's* coffin."

"I only saw Mara with him."

"Because he murdered Selma two years ago," Luke replied.

As that sank in, Genny could only stare at Luke in disbelief while Seth's scream echoed in her head. She blinked as the meaning of Luke's statement clicked into place; Selma was long dead.

"Seth Evilsizer is crazy?" Genny asked, though it was more of a statement.

"He's spent most of his life locked up in insane asylums," Luke said.

As beef and pork dumplings, along with steamed rice, spinach noodles and crunchy vegetables were served, it was Genny's turn to be brought up to date on all that Luke and Joe had found out at the Hall of Justice. It was during this delicious entrée, that the conversation shifted back to the last place Genny had seen Seth and Mara.

"Where did you go after you decided not to follow them down the alley?" Luke asked.

Touching a napkin to her lips, Genny lowered it to her lap and said, "Like the night we met, I thought I should stay in the Palace Hotel's Palm Court where I'd be safe until I could figure out what to do next."

"Except that I didn't leave you alone in the Palm Court because I knew you'd take off," Luke cocked a scolding eyebrow, "and wouldn't be safe."

"Yes, well." Genny swallowed and said, "I asked our favorite bellboy if he could secure a ride for me to China-town. He said yes and while I was waiting there was a commotion on the second floor and the police arrived. The Monkey's Fist found me then, so I told Patrick I was leaving with them and here I am."

"Tricky, you will remain in Chinatown with me until we have Evilsizer," Huan said with such finality that neither Tricky nor Ying debated his decision.

Wong approached and as usual when he spoke to Huan it was in Chinese. Then he quietly stepped back into the hallway outside the dining room. Chen poured more baijiu for the men and supper dishes were cleared away. Joe grinned like a schoolboy when Suki returned with desserts of sesame cakes and custard tarts along with the traditional hot tea.

"My men searched many places for Genevieve," Huan began, mostly addressing Luke, "so we know that Evilsizer met the Sinclair woman at the railway station."

Huan slid a money purse across the table to Luke. Picking it up and looking inside, Luke found it held Mara's original train ticket stubs, but no money.

"Mara has return tickets and should leave tomorrow," Luke told Huan. "Evilsizer may try to board the train with her and run like hell."

"My men will be there to stop Evilsizer," Huan said, easing Luke's concern. "The Fist leaders posted two

266 | LYNN ELDRIDGE
266 | LYNN ELDRIDGE

soldiers at the Palace Hotel, and they also report the police being there," he added with a smile at Genny.

"Maybe my following them wasn't completely in vain," Genny said hopefully as she along with the others, enjoyed the mouthwatering desserts.

Narrowing his eyes at Genny, Luke turned to Huan and asked, "What did your men say caused the commotion at the hotel?"

"The lock on Harriett Peak's door was picked and her room invaded. Jewelry was stolen."

"Poor Harriett, she doesn't deserve any of this," Genny said, shaking her head.

"A hotel maid, the sister of a Fist soldier, saw a man fitting Evilsizer's latest description and a brown-haired woman running from Miss Peak's room. She alerted the hotel manager," Huan said. "But it was too late to catch them."

Luke's frown worsened. "Mara and Evilsizer were both in unique positions to know what Harriett had of value. Where would they most likely pawn something, Huan?"

"Barbary Coast. Dead Man's Alley," Huan said. "We are watching."

"Good. His time is running out," Luke growled.

Suki came for the empty dessert plates and Joe's gaze didn't leave her until she nodded farewell and disappeared from the dining room.

"If it is all right, Luke, I will give Genevieve her gift," Huan said.

"Yes," Luke said.

Huan handed the sheathed present to Genny and said, "It is a Chinese fighting weapon for a lady. Tricky has one as does Jia."

"I hope to meet Jia," Genny said and Huan nodded. Then revealing a knife with a white dragon carved into both sides of a pearl handle and a blade shaped like a leaf, Genny said, "It's beautiful. Thank you, Huan."

"The white dragon is a symbol of strength and brings

good luck to those who are worthy," Huan said, with a meaningful nod of his head at both Luke and Genny. "Come."

Scooting back their chairs and following Huan, he led the way down a hall, past his office, and around a corner. There he unlocked a heavy door to a warehouse-like room that could rival, if not surpass, any shop of weaponry. On countless shelves were knives, daggers and spears of every size. Swords and sabers, some single-edged and others double-edged, were mounted from floor to ceiling, side-by-side on two of the walls. Crossbows, arrows, and rifles filled two more walls also from ground to rafters. Inside several tall, glass cabinets and on shelves were pistols, revolvers and derringers arranged according to size and type. On a nearby table glimmered dozens of star-like weapons some with as few as three sharply curved points, some with as many as eight.

"An impressive arsenal," Joe remarked, studying it all in awe.

"Which you did not see," Huan said softly.

"Huan, my sight is as bad as my hearing," Joe agreed.

"By tomorrow the best will be gone."

The silent exchange between Luke and Huan told Genny that the Monkey King's finest and most valuable munitions were relocating to a ranch in the country.

An outline of a man was carved into the middle of a far wall and surrounded by a variety of axes. From inside his sleeve Huan deftly pulled a knife and threw it. The blade dug deep into the heart of the target. With a swing of his hand, Huan indicated Luke could take his pick of knives.

"A pocket-sized knife and a hat pin have come in handy," Luke said to Genny with a reluctant grin. Then choosing the wickedest of the knives he addressed Huan. "But this Bowie knife is what we're used to where I come from."

Huan said cryptically, "A recent gift from pirates. Now it's yours."

Luke threw it and the wide blade split the middle of the target's forehead. Huan nodded his approval. Then it was Genny's turn. She had carefully observed how the men had held and thrown their knives. She stepped up, tossed her knife and it clattered onto the stone floor.

"Streaks." Genny looked at Luke. "Can we have a knife throwing lesson?"

Whizzing through the air, with lightning speed, a star-like weapon landed directly in the target's crotch.

CHAPTER 32

"Ouch," Huan said, followed by the first chuckle Genny had ever heard him utter.

She and the others turned to find a beautiful and very pregnant woman standing behind them holding another star in her hand. Dressed in a floor-length, crisp lime green robe-like dress, she was petite and yet something in the tilt of her head and squared shoulders said she could hold her own. Her glittering black eyes locked with Huan's and his easy smile was both intimate and proud. With graceful poise she threw the second star sinking its lethal point, next to his knife, deep in the target's heart. Raising a black brow, her radiant smile was solely for Huan.

"The throwing star is called a shuriken," Huan said as the woman glided into his embrace. With both arms clasping around her, he tenderly kissed her cheek. Though protective of Tricky, this was a tender side to Huan that Genny had not witnessed. Keeping an arm around her shoulders, Huan placed a possessive hand on the woman's rounded belly and said, "The lady with deadly aim to the heart is Jia, my wife."

. . .

"WE'RE RIGHT BACK where we started earlier today," Mara hissed with a sideways glance at a plaque bearing the name Old St. Mary's Church. "I hate being on the run again."

"On the run again, my dear?" Seth asked, entering the sanctuary.

"I said I hate being alone again," she replied as they slipped into a shadowy back row pew. "I've been widowed three times."

"Were the husbands much older or in bad health?" Seth asked, noting only two or three others in the church." His stomach grumbling he said, "I wonder if they serve supper here?" When Mara ignored him, he remarked, "Surely you are too young to thrice be a widow."

Mara smiled at that and fingered the topknot on her head. "I'm only thirty-sev—one." She coughed after shaving off six years and hurried on, "My husbands were all... clumsy." Rolling her eyes, she waved her hand in a circle and tsked. "You know, falling down stairs, falling off a ladder, falling out a window. I'd hoped to leave those memories behind and start fresh in Biloxi."

"By marrying Luke Harper."

"Luke Harper is so magnificent he may never have fallen from his pedestal." Her mood quickly spiraled into teeth gnashing as she said, "Except that Luke's favorite word to me was no. No, thank you. No, don't come back. No, leave me the hell alone." Mara pounded her fist into her palm. "Then and now, it's always no! No! No! No!"

"Lower your voice," Seth snapped with a nervous glance around the church. "I never married because I devoted my life to caring for my twin sister. Then I heard about an opportunity to increase my family's fortune here in San Francisco. If that could still happen, maybe Selma would stay in that little house and leave me alone."

"I shouldn't have threatened to get even with Harriett Peak when she kicked me out," Mara said, mired in her own world and not caring that Seth was lost in his. "I'm sure that bitch gave my name and description to the hotel manager. So I can't retrieve my trunk now." Wringing her hands she went on, "Even if I wanted to leave tomorrow I can't risk returning to the railway station...or to New Orleans. The police are waiting for me everywhere."

"You were the one determined to find your money purse in Harriett's room, not I."

"You picked the lock."

"That was quite helpful of me, wasn't it?"

"No, because my money purse wasn't there," Mara fumed. "But you stole Harriett's jewelry and that will be blamed at least in part on me."

"Ahhh...yes. True," Seth agreed, tugging a drawstring bag out of his pocket. Pouring rings, earbobs, necklaces, and bracelets into his hand, he said, "My mother wore fine jewelry and I do enjoy collecting it."

"You owe me, Seth. You benefited from that little escapade at the Palace Hotel while I don't have so much as a penny in my pocket."

"How shall I repay you, milady?" he mumbled, focused on the jewelry in his hand.

"By helping me get even with Luke for choosing Genevieve over me." Mara smacked the underside of his hand which popped the jewelry into the air and scattered it across the floor.

"You jealous shrew!" Seth dropped to his knees and frantically scrambled around on the floor. Finding this trinket and that bauble, he stuffed them into the draw-string bag. "I don't care if you get even with Harper or not."

"I thought you wanted Genevieve back."

"Yes, yes," Seth said, eyelids fluttering as he sat down in the pew again. "My Genevieve represents the crown jewel."

"Engagement to Luke Harper means *your* Genevieve will also have the finest and biggest diamond ring that money can buy," Mara said.

"Diamond?" Seth's mouth dropped open at the very idea.

"Yes." Mara squinted as she took in his eye-batting,

stringy hair and shaggy beard. Indicating his worn coat, she said, "Something about you doesn't add up, Seth."

"I told you I lost my own trunk and a good deal of money when my vehicle recently burned in front of the Palace Hotel. Three automobiles were involved. My Runabout was not only the nicest but the middle one, so it suffered the most damage," Seth said with such a shifty-eyed expression that Mara strongly suspected he was lying.

"That may have happened to someone's vehicle, I'm just not convinced it was yours."

"Well, everybody saw it or read about it in the *Chronicle*," Seth insisted. "The hotel manager refused to compensate me and that's why we aren't speaking."

"Oh, whatever, Seth. Shave your head and beard and no one will recognize you." She noticed that calmed the frantic flapping of his eyelids. "So what other fine hotel are you going to secure for us tonight?"

"The Fairmont Hotel on Nob Hill and the St. Francis Hotel over on Powell Street are both out of the running since you are on the *run*." Seth's sarcastic laugh said he'd heard her correctly the first time. "Perhaps the less particular Valencia Street Hotel in the Mission District."

"HARD TO BELIEVE we left our ranches for the Palace Hotel five weeks ago," Genny said, taking a deep breath of country air as she rode beside Luke in the Runabout on the warm spring evening. "It's April eleventh already."

"The time has flown by since I met you on New Year's Eve."

Luke was glad to be halfway to their ranches and would be even happier when they were on a train to Biloxi. But Evilsizer had to be caught first. In the meantime, not only were the hired guns still in the country but Huan had a team of workers at the ranch he'd purchased from Luke. After Huan had toured Luke's ranch, they discussed the price. Luke had insisted his asking price was fair. Huan had argued the ten-thousand-acre horse ranch was worth a lot more. Luke reminded Huan he'd won it all in a card game and was pleased it was going to friends. Luke's one request involved Etalon, Esprit and the two horses he'd once chosen for Ying and Tricky to ride. Then he held out his hand and Huan shook it making the deal official.

Thus, Huan's men had been busy at the roomy, two-story home replacing thin window panes with thick glass and flimsy doors with sturdy ones. Inside the house, drafty wooden logs were being insulated with walls of smooth plaster to keep cold winter winds away from tender baby skin. The largest of the four bedrooms upstairs was across the front of the house with a bedroom on the north side and one on the south. The fourth bedroom along the back of the house would be Huan's office. Downstairs, the room Luke had slept in was now a dining room just off the brand-new kitchen, much like the one at *Li's*.

A second log house just a few acres away on the other side of the corral was already framed up for Tricky as was a stone building with security in mind, near the barn, that Huan would use as he saw fit. In order not to slow down the renovations and construction, Luke told Huan that he and Genny would stay in her little house until they left San Francisco.

Wiggling the fingertips of her left hand against her cheek, Genny broke into Luke thoughts with, "Sir, have you seen my chickens? They up and vanished into the wild."

"No, but I see that ring on your finger." Luke grabbed her hand and kissed it. "That ring means my fiancée promises not to up and vanish again without telling me."

"Is that what my diamond engagement ring means?"

"Yes," he said and cocked a scolding brow. "Doesn't it?"

"Yes," Genny said, so happy and so in love. "Along with many other promises I shall make to my fiancé."

"Such as?"

With a flirtatious smile she tilted her head and out of

the corner of her eye, she looked him up and down. "I promise to love you, to cherish, honor, and sometimes obey you."

"That sounds about right, little lamb," he said with a begrudging chuckle.

"What do you promise me, wolf?"

"To love and protect you, teach you to shoot a gun, throw a knife, and take you to bed."

"Harper," she laughed. "Those aren't vows."

"The hell they aren't."

"Look!" Genny said and pointed. "There's Vern's missing straw man."

At the road leading to the Skidmore farm, was a sign held by a scarecrow. Scrawled on the sign in big letters; *Onyx and Opal*. Under their names a large arrow indicated a left turn.

"Good," Luke said. "Two more out the door and bigger split for Grace and Ruth."

"Do you think Onyx and Opal know the Skidmore brothers are…gone?" Genny asked.

"They probably figured something had happened when they didn't collect their donkey while we were gone," he replied, never slowing down as they left the sign in the dust.

They stopped at the Cat's Eye Ranch just as Patty was taking her famous fried chicken off the stove. Of Patty, Vern and Roscoe it was hard to say who was most thrilled to see them. Patty confirmed that Onyx and Opal had relocated their business to the Skidmore farm. Stating the donkey was part of the farm they'd piled bag after bag of belongings onto the animal. But the donkey refused to budge and shook off the load on his back. The women cursed him as well as Vern and carted the bags away on their own backs. Vern loved the gentle, brown donkey that followed him everywhere and voiced being glad the animal had stayed.

"Don't know what to call him, though," Vern said in the kitchen.

"Bruno means brown," Genny said.

Vern smiled from ear-to-ear. "Bruno it is."

Grace and Ruth were the next to welcome them back and on the subject of names, Genny told Luke that Grace meant love and kindness and the meaning of Ruth was companion and friend. As the cousins, so aptly named, set the table for supper, Vern created his special flip. Genny quietly made a sign saying the Cat's Eye Ranch was out of business. Luke fixed the sign to the front door and locked it.

When the six of them were gathered around a dining room table laden with Patty's home cooking, Luke took Genny's left hand. As she wiggled her fingers Luke said that he'd proposed, she'd accepted, and they were moving to Biloxi. With tears of joy, the women hugged Genny and admired her diamond ring. Vern swallowed hard and swiped at his eyes. He shook Luke's hand and kissed Genny's cheek. Luke grinned at Genny, and Vern poured flip for everyone.

Then Genny laid out her plan, starting with Patty and Vern. They were getting her big house and the twenty acres of land along with a thousand dollars. Patty threw her arms around Genny and cried. Vern said no, they couldn't accept such extravagant gifts. Genny insisted.

Genny then turned to Ruth and Grace saying she would like for them to have her little house, its thirty acres of land and a thousand dollars. The pond rights would be shared with Vern and Patty. The cousins also protested such generous gifts. Again, Genny insisted. The ladies, overcome with gratitude, accepted promising they would always tend to Samuel Morgan's grave.

"Luke's the one making it all possible," Genny said softly and smiled at him.

"We're a united front." He winked at Genny and raised his glass. "To new beginnings."

Glasses clinked and deals sealed.

"C'MERE MY MOON GODDESS," Luke said later that evening in the cozy, candlelit front room of Genny's little house. Leaning forward in his chair, he took the hands of the woman who had just danced so sensuously for him. Pulling her up from the floor between his feet he tugged her onto his lap. "That belly dance is one of the sexiest things you do to me."

"Are you sure you weren't bored?"

"Bored stiff." With a low groan he moved her left hand to the hard bulge in his Levi's. "Why don't I slice a hole in the red panties of this costume, and you can straddle my lap?"

"Shall we use your knife or mine?" As she boldly straddled him, the smile that touched her lips was one that always melted him. Who was he kidding? All her smiles made him feel like the luckiest man alive. "But first things first, I danced for you and now it's your turn to tell me where you see the ceremony taking place that changes my name."

"You mean to Genevieve Moonstone Harper?"

"Yes," Genny's heart skipped a beat at hearing him say it for the first time. "I like the sound of that."

"Me, too." He moved a long black curl away from her face. "I think your favorite of my three riverboats would be the one known for romance. During candlelit suppers for two and dancing to a string quartet it sails slowly past the Biloxi Lighthouse every evening. I'd like to reserve it for our wedding and–"

"Yes, let's get married on your riverboat. Luke." Genny's lilac eyes lit up and she clasped her hands under her chin. "I love that idea."

Grinning, Luke cupped his hands to her hips and squeezed. "My mother, Mattie and Chloe will be thrilled to do whatever you ask of them for our wedding. My father, Rob and Steve will throw us one helluva reception."

"Do you think Mattie and Chloe would agree to be my bridemaids? Megan and Audrey could be flowergirls."

"Absolutely and Charles can be one of our ushers."

"Nothing could make me happier."

"Unless I told you the name of this riverboat is *Moonstone*."

CHAPTER 33

"Oh hush up, Harper," Genny said with a laugh in her voice. But when Luke nodded, her eyes grew wide and she whispered, "*Moonstone*? Really?"

"Really." Sliding his hands up her back, Luke pressed her to him for a kiss. Roscoe suddenly sat up and gave a little bark. "It's just Andy, reporting in."

Luke eased Genny off his lap. All personal belongings at Luke's ranch had been carefully packed and transported to Genny's house by Huan's crew. Tossing her the quilt she'd once used at his house to wrap herself like a mummy, Genny sat back down in the chair as Luke stepped outside to talk to Andy. The horses were fine and there had been no sign of trouble on the three properties. When Andy left to check on the Cat's Eye, Luke called to her.

"I want to talk more about our wedding," Genny said, waltzing onto the porch. In the romantic glow of the moonlight, Luke stood in front of the hitching post.

"More?" Luke teased his own personal belly dancer whose every sexy move was accentuated by her skimpy red costume. "That was already a lot of talk for a man about a wedding." He chuckled and then sobered. Holding a Colt Model 1903 Pocket Hammerless in his right hand, he walked to the porch steps. "I bought this pocket pistol for you from Andy. While nothing else bad may happen, I want you to be prepared."

Genny stood at the edge of the porch and when Luke came to a stop on the bottom step, she was only slightly shorter. He held the gun out for her to see and after taking a look, she wrapped her arms around him flattening her hands to his shoulder blades.

"Nothing else bad will happen," she murmured.

"In case it does, you're going to know how to handle a knife and a gun," he said as her hands trailed down his back and over his belt to his rear end. "Hey, pay attention."

"I'm busy handling you." Genny molded her breasts to his chest and kneaded the cheeks of his buttocks most provocatively. "Give me a lesson of a different kind."

"The only hell of our wedding vows will be the one where you don't obey me."

"But you promised to take me to bed."

Genny smiled as he did his best to frown. Giving in to a grin, his mouth closed over hers and she moaned against his lips. As he kissed her, Luke plucked her off the porch and put her feet to the ground. Breaking off the kiss, he clamped a hand on her left shoulder and turned her in the direction of the pond. Placing the weapon in her right hand and straightening her right arm, he then brought her left hand to the gun to help her steady it.

"There are no bullets in it tonight, but never put your finger on the trigger until you're ready to shoot," he said near her right ear, molding her back solidly against his chest. Then suggestively pressing his lower body against hers, he whispered, "Loaded, it's got a kick."

"I know and I want you," she flirted with a whine in her voice, attempting to turn to him.

Covering her right hand with his, he kept her facing forward by flattening his left hand to her half-naked belly and said, "Put your finger on the trigger and squeeze." Genny did so and the gun clicked. "Tomorrow we'll put the bullets in, belly dancer."

"Tonight, I'll put you in, cowboy."

"You ripped a hole in the scarecrow's gut with your white dragon knife," Luke praised Genny the next morning in regard to the straw man with a floppy hat and outstretched arms that he'd borrowed from Vern and Patty's garden. Roscoe had not let them out of his sight since they'd returned and sat at Luke's feet. Luke raised his chin in the direction of the scarecrow and handed the woman in overalls and undershirt, the weapon. "Rip a hole with your gun."

"I'll try." Genny raised her right arm and Luke stood behind her. Placing her left hand to the pearl handle as he'd taught her to do the previous night, she said, "It's heavy."

"It's twenty-four ounces of nickel-plated steel. It'll fit in your purse or pocket and the hammerless feature will let you smoothly slip it out. This pistol is a semi-automatic with eight bullets, so finger off the trigger after this first shot."

"Sounds scary."

"Should you ever find yourself face-to-face with Evilsizer again, let this gun give you courage against the man who murdered your grandfather and Garnet. Roscoe, go sit on the porch, boy." As Roscoe trotted off, Luke put his hands to Genny's waist to steady her and said, "Cowboy boots apart, finger on the trigger. Use the gun sight to aim."

Genny eyed the scarecrow and fired. The recoil was more than she counted on and would have knocked her flat if not for Luke.

"Streaks!" She dropped her hands to her sides in disappointment. "I missed."

"Finger off the trigger," Luke calmly reminded her. He straightened her right arm, made an adjustment to her left hand and stood back from her. "You've felt the kick so don't fall on your pretty bottom like you did when you fell out of my bed." He smothered a laugh at that fond memory as she huffed and then he sobered. "Aim and shoot."

She fired again and stumbled back a step, but to her credit didn't fall down. "I missed. Are there bullets in this gun?"

"You know there are."

"Maybe I could hit one of those tin cans you lined up on the board atop the trash barrel."

"Concentrate on hitting the scarecrow first," he said with a pat to her rounded fanny.

Genny took her stance, aimed, took a shot, and missed a third time. "Something is wrong with the bullets in this gun."

Luke took the pistol and his bullet, much like the Bowie knife, blew a hole in the middle of the scarecrow's fore-head. In rapid fire, he blasted all four cans off the board across the top of the trash barrel.

"What *can't* you do, Harper?"

"Teach you to shoot?"

Lilac eyes narrowed dangerously, and dainty fists clenched atop shapely hips. Luke grasped her elbow and shuffled her a few feet closer to the scarecrow. Once there he showed her how to reload the gun and carefully handed it back to her.

"If I hit the scarecrow, will you take me to the Grand Opera House?" she asked. When he didn't immediately answer she said, "I've never been and always wanted to go. At brunch last month, Harriett Peak said Enrico Caruso will be there singing Don José in *Carmen*."

"I remember." Luke turned her to face the target, but she swiveled back to him.

"The Grand Opera House is just South of the Slot."

"South of the Slot?" he asked.

"Yes," she said enthusiastically. "It's an area on Mission Street between Third and Fourth Streets south of Market Street that's an actual slot between the cable car tracks."

"Is your finger off the trigger of that loaded gun in your hand?"

"Now it is," she said, her cheeks reddening. "The Palace

Hotel also had information about the April seventeenth opera because Mr. Caruso will be staying there when he comes to town," Genny said, with a slight wave of the pistol, which Luke promptly took from her. "The opera was written by Bizet, a Frenchman and it's a love story of sorts. I read the book at the library."

"A gypsy seduces a soldier, and he kills her in a fit of jealous rage."

"Oh," Genny sighed. "You've seen it."

"No," Luke said. "But Mattie sounded just like you after Steven took her to see it in Paris where it was sold out every night."

"The Grand Opera House only holds three thousand people, so in a city and surrounding area of almost half a million people the tickets are probably all gone."

"Maybe not." Luke placed a finger under her chin and said, "But please focus on this lesson like you did when I taught you how to fight and swim. You shattered the head-lamp on my Runabout with your slingshot," he reminded her. "If you can do that, you can do this."

"I was actually trying to hit the driver not the head-lamp," she confessed with a grimace and raised shoulders. "Besides, I'd rather focus on you shattering *me*, loverboy."

"Spread your legs, babydoll," he drawled, cocking a brow at the woman who was as sultry and sensuous in overalls as she was in her belly dance outfit, "and plant your feet further apart this time." With a will of iron to make her lesson a priority, Luke gave the gun back to her and placing his hands on her shoulders, turned her toward the scarecrow. He stood back from her, hands on his hips. "Aim and shoot."

Genny pulled the trigger and missed. "Streaks and sockdolagers. I absolutely cannot do this, Harper. I quit."

"No, you don't." As he had the previous evening, Luke molded his chest solidly to her back. He placed his right hand over hers on the gun and slid his left hand inside her overalls and under her shirt. Flattening his palm and fingers to her naked tummy, he said, "Evilsizer's a psychopath so aim for that hole in the scarecrow's head."

Genny did as told and with Luke's help this time the scarecrow's hat flew into the air. "We did it," she squealed and grinned at him over her shoulder.

"Do it again." Keeping her in his arms, the next shot hit the scarecrow's right shoulder.

"Did you see that?" Genny asked with a triumphant smile.

"Yes." Loving her so much that he couldn't imagine life without her, Luke shut his eyes against that image and pressed his lips to her temple. "I'm going to let go of you this time, but I want you to focus on exactly how it feels right now while I'm still holding you. If you hit the scarecrow by yourself, we'll see about tickets to *Carmen*, South of the Slot."

"I'll pretend the gun sight is the eye of a needle I'm threading," she decided.

"What?"

"Evidently I need to teach you how to sew, Harper."

"Aim dead center, squeeze the trigger and always shoot to kill."

Genny closed her eyes to memorize the moment in Luke's arms and as she opened her eyes, he very gently released her. This time she severed the scarecrow's left arm. Whirling toward Luke she accidentally fired a wild shot.

"Finger off the damn trigger!" Luke barked.

"Shooting *is* like sewing," Genny exclaimed, following his command.

"The hell it is."

Luke pointed and Genny's eyes widened at seeing the bullet hole in the side of her house. Roscoe had jumped up and was staring at them. Luke told him everything was all right and the collie curled up on the porch again.

"But I also shot the scarecrow," Genny said with a nervous giggle and ear-to-ear grin.

"Good girl." His hand covering hers, as she held the gun at her side, he hugged her with his other arm. "Shoot at least one of the cans off the board and we'll spend the night of the opera at the Palace. Shoot two cans and I'll buy you a new dress."

Genny's eyes glistened, and her chin quivered as she gazed up at him. "What's your favorite color?"

"My favorite color is you."

Genny's throat ached with love as she closed her eyes and rested her head against the broad shoulder of the protective, patient man. "Whatever I did to win you, Luke Harper," she began, listening to the beat of his heart, "I hope I never lose my touch to keep doing it."

"Lilac," he said. "But Patty already made a lilac dress for you so pick another color."

Smiling into his eyes, she whispered, "Forest green."

Back to business, Luke said, "I'll give you eight shots to hit two cans. So reload the magazine like I showed you." When she had done so all on her own, he winked his approval and lined up the four cans. "Three cans and I might give you a driving lesson."

Concentrating like never before, Genny faced the trash barrel and spread her feet. Letting the memory of Luke's grip on her hand, pressure on her tummy and support at her back focus her aim through the needle-eye-gunsight, she squeezed the trigger eight times.

"I'll be damned, three cans," Luke said with a chuckle and grinned at her.

"You taught me to shoot."

"Once I found the right incentives."

Holding tight to her empty gun, Genny tossed her arms around Luke's neck. He lifted her off the ground and swung her around in a circle. Wrapping her legs around his waist, his hands flattened to her fanny and their lips met in a hungry, victory kiss. Pulling back, she grinned.

"Bed or driving lesson first, city slicker?"

"Bed and some breakfast first, mischief maker."

. . .

"YES, SELMA, I HEARD THE GUNSHOTS." Chewing this fingernail and that, Seth was once again lost in his own world as he drove the rickety buggy down the country road.

"I said I'm starving," Mara hissed louder this time, bumping along next to Seth.

Mara hated being ignored, hated being out of bed before noon and hated being stuck with Seth Comstock. Not only did the Valencia Street Hotel fall well beneath her standards, but Seth had awkwardly rebuffed every one of her sexual advances. Damn that bitch, Genevieve, for snaring the hearts of two millionaires. Making matters even worse, just last week in the *Chronicle* she'd spied an engagement photo of Luke and Genevieve in Harriett's *Peak's People* column. Spitting on the picture before shredding it, Mara swore to get even with both Luke and Genevieve.

"Onyx and Opal?" Seth read and reined the horse to the left.

"Who are Onyx and Opal and why are we going down this disgusting cow path off the main road?" Mara frantically waved away the dust being kicked up by the horse and buggy.

"I happened to know there's a vacant farmhouse down this cow path." Seth scratched his bald head. "Onyx and Opal can be valuable jewels and may be linked to the Cat's Eye Ranch."

"Oh, enough about her bordello." Mara's mouth shriveled up like a prune on the last word.

Seth took a matchstick from his pocket and mumbled, "The Cat's Eye Ranch, the little house, the pond, five thousand acres and a fortune in jewels are all within our reach, Selma."

"Seth, you're just plain stupid if you still think any of her property is within your reach," Mara snapped, bobbing her head and waving her index finger. "I can tell you right now that everyone who knows Luke Harper knows he's a master when it comes to business and property. He owns half of Biloxi and what he says goes along the Mississippi Sound. He'll sell everything here and take Genevieve home to *his* empire where she will live in the lap of luxury."

"Blast that devil to hell!" Seth suddenly shrieked, eyelids fluttering. "Selma and I have hated Luke Harper since the night of my soirée."

"Where in Hades is this sister of yours anyway? And why do you talk to her like she's right beside you when she's nowhere to be seen?"

"Never mind about Selma. The concern is the saddled horses at the hitching post." He jerked the buggy reins and barely avoided sliding into a ditch. "We'll turn around, take that sign down and come back when the riders of those horses are gone and get some answers."

"What makes you think anybody will tell you anything, Seth?"

"Because I'll light a fire under them."

CHAPTER 34

"This Cadillac Runabout Model K is a one cylinder, two speed transmission. That means it has two speeds forward; high and low," Luke said to Genny as they sat in the vehicle facing toward the road in front of her little house. "And of course, it has reverse."

"Is this automobile similar to the Runabout you have back home?" Genny asked, behind the steering wheel of the running automobile.

"Yes," Luke said, already figuring to buy the gorgeous siren a new red Cadillac Runabout with front and back seats when they got to Biloxi. In his mind's eye he saw her pulling into the circular drive of their mansion, her long black hair windswept from the Gulf Coast breeze, lilac cat eyes mirroring the love he felt for her, and that smile only she could smile curving up the corners of her full pink lips. Luke grinned at that happy vision of their future and said, "I also have a larger automobile made by Rolls Royce, called the Silver Ghost. I think you'll like it."

"Do you believe the automobile is here to stay?"

"Absolutely. This is just the beginning," Luke said. "I know you're nervous now that you're behind the wheel, but this is another important lesson." He pointed to a lever and asked, "What did I tell you that's for?"

"Changing gears."

"Correct. The vehicle engages in low gear and the lever is for moving into high gear or reverse." Pointing to the floor, Luke said, "The pedal to the right of the steering column is the brake and the other one is the gas." Next, he indicated where the engine was located under the seat. "This model has ten horsepower."

"What does horsepower mean?"

"It means the engine has the equivalent power of ten horses."

"Oh," Genny's eyes widened. "That's why it can go so fast. A buggy the size of this Runabout is usually pulled by just one horse."

"The Runabout only weighs about thirteen hundred pounds so with ten horses and a good road it can travel up to forty miles per hour." With a sidelong glance and cocked brow, Luke said, "But we're going to stay in low gear, Genevieve." Roscoe ran up to Luke's side of the vehicle and barked. "You might be taking your life in your hands again, pal."

"Ha! Ha!" Genny said. "Come on, Roscoe."

"When you release the brake we'll move forward," Luke said as he let Roscoe jump in and sit beside his feet. "Once we're going, don't stomp on the brake or you could throw all of us over the dash."

"What's the dash?"

"This." Luke reached forward and patted the knee-high dash. "In a buggy, horses dash up dust and mud from their hooves, so buggies have a dashboard to deflect most of the dirt," he explained and Genny nodded. "All right, smoothly let up on the brake pedal and then press down on the gas pedal."

She did as told, but it was anything but smooth and the vehicle lurched forward throwing their heads back. Genny tromped the brake pitching them toward the dash. Stomping both feet to the floor stalled the engine. Luke threw his head back and howled with laughter.

"Streaks!" Genny gasped, with a death grip on the steering wheel before narrowing her eyes at Luke. "What's so funny?"

"Nothing, but laughing is a helluva lot better than crying during one of your lessons." Still chuckling, he looked at her and said, "You stomped my feet on the dance floor like you just stomped the pedals. You've given me a black eye, nearly yanked my britches off in the pond, threw up over the side of my other Runabout, and I swear to God I thought you were gonna shoot Roscoe and me when I was teaching you how to use your gun."

"That does it, Harper." She smacked his knee and bailed out of the vehicle.

"Get back here," he called after her and laughed.

"No!" Genny fumed, hair bouncing long and loose, overalls snug over her rounded fanny and red cowboy boots clomping in the direction of the Cat's Eye Ranch.

"Vern and Patty will send you right back to me."

"Streaks!" She veered toward his former ranch.

"Huan's crew will send you back even faster."

"Sockdolagers!" Genny headed toward the pond.

"Moby-Dick will send you—" Luke couldn't even finish for chuckling.

"Dammit!" She whirled to face him, fists on her hips.

"What did you say?" Luke asked, brows shooting up. "Let's get her, Roscoe."

Roscoe bounded out of the Runabout ahead of Luke. Genny twirled and raced toward the pond but could hear Luke and Roscoe quickly gaining on her. Oh, but Luke Harper was wildly outrageous. Adonis, clad in a long-sleeved shirt, Levi's and boots he was all sinewy muscular man, exuding masculinity with each word and every swagger. What had he said about doubting he could catch her? That was her last thought before he grabbed her arm and tripped her into a thick patch of soft spring grass. He took the brunt of their fall landing on his back with her plopping down on top of him. Spreading his legs, he trapped her thighs between his and grinned up at her. Roscoe barked and took off to find the bullfrog.

"Don't smile at me like that, Harper." Bracing herself above him Genny did her best not to giggle. "I'm mad at you."

He grabbed her hands and tucked them around his neck. With her arms and legs ensnared, one of his hands slid over her fanny and his other one slipped under her hair at the nape of her neck. Bringing her head down, his eyes closed, and his mouth touched hers. She pursed her lips tightly against his.

"Aww…come on," he coaxed, opening his eyes. "Don't be mad at me."

"You made fun of me."

"What did I say that wasn't true?" When he chuckled again a giggle finally escaped her and trying to cover it, she squirmed against his lower body. "Stop that wiggling or I'll take you back to bed instead of teaching you to drive."

"Mmm…promise?"

"No, but I'll give you thirty seconds to up your ante," he challenged and cocked a rakish brow. "But I'll bet you end up in the Runabout."

"I'll take that bet."

Genny covered his mouth with hers and gave him her most scintillating kiss. In the distance, Moby-Dick croaked hello to Roscoe. Wantonly undulating her lower body against Luke's, she blew in his ear and nibbled his neck as she threaded her fingers through his hair. He kneaded her fanny and groaned as she kissed him, her tongue playing with his. As he rolled her over to her back, she pictured him making love to her right there in the grass. Instead, he got to his feet and grabbing her hands tugged her up and into his arms.

"I'll give you another head start and if you can make it to your house before I catch you, we'll stay in bed all day."

Genny took off running like her life depended on it. Luke shook his head in wonder.

"What did I do to deserve her?" he asked Roscoe as the collie trotted back to him. "Come on, boy." Man and dog sprinted after the beautiful woman. Sweeping her up in his arms near the Runabout, Luke plunked her behind the wheel of the vehicle. "Now, stay there and behave. You never know when you might have to drive one of our children to the doctor."

By the time Luke started the engine and slid into the left side of the vehicle, Genny was all business. Roscoe jumped in and assumed his spot beside Luke's feet.

"If we're going to have three children, you'd better teach me to drive," she said.

"Once again I found the right incentive."

"ACCORDING TO THE CHIEF DINAN, despite the fire destroying fingerprints on the Runabout, Evilsizer left his prints on the can of gasoline," Luke said the following afternoon as he and Genny met with Harriett Peak in her comfortable office at the *San Francisco Chronicle*.

"When we had brunch with you, we didn't yet know that the fingerprints on the note with the black-eyed Susans in our hotel room were a match to his," Genny said, sitting on a Victorian sofa next to Luke.

"The police chief told me Evilsizer's fingerprints were also found in my hotel room and at my house," Harriett said, sitting in a Queen Anne chair angled toward them.

"I received a telegram from my brother-in-law," Luke said. "Steve couldn't find fingerprints on Evilsizer back in D.C. We know now that's because he was locked up in the West Virginia asylum before fingerprinting was used to identify people. But a good friend of mine who's with the Biloxi Police Department found information on Mara Sinclair."

"Do tell," Harriett replied. "After the way she helped Evilsizer turn my hotel room upside down, I don't doubt that she has a criminal history. What did your friend find out?"

"She was the number one suspect in the death of her first husband in Pensacola, Florida, but there wasn't enough evidence to charge her with murder," Luke said. "However, she was tried and convicted of manslaughter in the death of her second husband in Mobile, Alabama and served time. Currently, there's a warrant for her arrest in connection with the death of her third husband in New Orleans."

"Just like the spider that kills her mate, Mara Sinclair is a black widow," Harriett said.

"They all suffered fatal falls," Genny said and shivered. The nightmare known as Mara could have trapped Luke in her web of murder, cruelly cheated him out of his life and Genny would never have known what love was. She placed her hand on Luke's knee and he patted her hand.

"Harriett, I feel responsible for the trouble the Sinclair woman caused you and for whatever she may have stolen," Luke said. "I'm here to repay you."

"Absolutely not, Luke." Harriett reared back in her chair and shook her head. "I'd never even heard of you when Mara befriended me on the train. When she and Evilsizer broke into my hotel room, I had my money with me, and my insurance company is covering my jewelry losses. Mara is not your fault, and you owe me nothing, but thank you," Harriett said firmly and turned to Genny. "And before you say Evilsizer is your fault, please don't. I should apologize to you for helping him arrange the ball that lured you into town. I feel so guilty about that." With a glance back at Luke, she said what they all knew, "If not for you, Luke, Genevieve might be dead."

A muscle worked in Luke's jaw, and he said, "I decided weeks ago that I'm not leaving San Francisco until he's caught or killed."

Genny squared her shoulders and shifted the subject

slightly as she said to Harriett, "The one thing Evilsizer inadvertently did was to make sure I met Luke."

"She sort of waltzed into my life that night," Luke said with a boyish grin.

"He means I stomped his feet." With a smile at Luke, Genny turned to Harriett. "Let's all look at it like that and never feel guilty again."

"Agreed," Harriett said with a sharp nod of her silver head. "My only regret is that the two of you are leaving San Francisco. Biloxi's gain is our loss," she said with a sigh and picked up an envelope. "But something Luke asked me about just came across my desk late yesterday. I was planning to have a courier deliver it to you today."

Harriett handed Luke the envelope with his and Genny's names printed on it. Without a word, he handed the envelope to Genny. When she peered inside the envelope, her jaw dropped. She stared at Luke, then at Harriett and back to Luke.

"Ten tickets to see Enrico Caruso sing *Carmen* on April seventeenth," Genny said, taking the tickets out of the envelope.

"Ten?" Luke asked with surprise and glanced at Harriett.

"You knew all along?" Genny asked Luke with a choke in her voice.

Looking back at Genny, he replied, "Harriett said she might receive a couple of tickets."

"Please consider the tickets a wedding present. An evening of celebration for you and your San Francisco friends before you leave," Harriett suggested with the warmest of smiles. "But if you'd rather, I also have tickets for *Babes in Toyland* at the Columbia Theater on Powell Street or you could see John Barrymore in *The Dictator*."

"*Carmen*, please," Genny said softly. "Harriett, thank you so much."

"Tickets are a benefit of my job as the society page editor," Harriett said. "All of the most fashionable people in the Bay area will choose *Carmen*. You have excellent taste, Genevieve."

"She does," Luke said and winked at Genny.

"Genevieve, have you ever considered writing a society column like mine?" Harriett asked.

Stunned, Genny said softly, "Actually, yes. It's a dream of mine."

"Well, please write one when you get to Biloxi because I don't think they have such a column," Harriett said. "The first time I saw you on New Year's Eve in that elegant aquamarine gown, and every time thereafter, I've noticed your exquisite style. And, my dear, you have an endearing way of engaging people with your poise and charm."

Luke said, "She sewed that dress in two days and it was a *side show* all its own." Thinking of her belly dance costume he added, "She made a red get-up that I like, too."

Now Harriett's jaw dropped. "Write the column, call it something like *Fashion with Genevieve*."

"I will," Genny said with determination.

"Since Evilsizer is still on the loose, I hope this isn't goodbye," Harriett said. "But if it proves to be farewell, I'll miss you." Tears glittered in her blue eyes. Pointing at the envelope of tickets, she said, "Front row, center. Best seats in the house. Have a fabulous time."

CHAPTER 35

"Come in, come in," Joe said with a smile at Genny, walking around his desk and extending his hand to Luke. "To what do I owe this unexpected pleasure?"

Walking past a large window filled with sunlight, Joe indicated for them to sit in the two wooden captain's chairs in front of his desk and then he returned to his wooden chair on rollers behind it. Genny told Joe of her property decisions and asked him to do the legal work of deeding the Cat's Eye Ranch to Patty and Vern and the little house and pond to Grace and Ruth with fishing rights for all.

"Consider it done," Joe said with a nod.

"Tell him the other reason we're here, Genny," Luke said.

"Harriett Peak gifted us with ten tickets to *Carmen* at the Grand Opera House, South of the Slot on April seventeenth. We wondered if you like to invite a date and join us," Genny said.

"Well, I'd be honored to go with you," Joe said with a big smile.

"Good," Luke said. "Genny and I will spend the night at the Palace Hotel, so we'd like you and your date to be our guests for supper. Along with Patty and Vern, we're inviting Huan and Jia, Tricky and Ying, Grace, Ruth, and the Johnson brothers to supper."

"That would be quite the extraordinary night. One for the record books," Joe said softly. "I wonder who would go with me."

With a quick grin at Luke, Genny said to Joe, "Suki Li?"

"Suki," Joe said, his face flushing. "She's so pretty. What if she has a male friend?"

"Tricky says she doesn't," Genny replied.

"Do you think I should ask her?"

"Yes," Genny said, suspecting that Suki was quite taken with Joe as well.

"Do you think Huan would give me permission to take her?" Joe asked Luke.

"Only way to find out is to ask him," Luke said and added, "before you ask Suki."

"I'm a little afraid of Huan," Joe admitted with a nervous laugh.

"No reason to be," Luke said. "Huan's on our side."

"Even if Huan agrees, Suki might say no," Joe said.

"It's noon. Time to eat. Let's go to Li's and you can find out," Luke suggested.

Twenty minutes later, Chen spotted them just inside Li's and they were escorted to Huan's private dining room. Tricky came out of the kitchen and took a seat next to Genny. Genny told her about giving away her properties and Tricky was so happy for everyone, her dark eyes glistened with joy.

"The Johnson brothers brought the cousins here last evening for supper," Tricky said. "They were excited because Mike won four tickets in a fire department raffle to *Babes in Toyland* on April seventeenth."

"Perfect. We'll have just enough tickets," Genny said softly to Luke and then told Tricky that Harriett had given them ten tickets to the opera and invited her and Ying to join them.

"I can't wait to tell Ying." Tricky clapped her hands under her chin and smiled.

"Is Huan here?" Joe asked and cleared his throat. "Is umm…Suki working today?"

"Yes, to both questions," Tricky replied as she and Genny exchanged knowing looks.

"Mr. Harper." Wong motioned to Luke, holding back the curtain to the dining room.

"Excuse me," Luke said and disappeared with Wong.

Suki quietly entered the room with a polite bow of greeting and stealing a covert glance at Joe, she poured rice wine for everyone. Between Suki and Joe, Genny couldn't say whose cheeks had more of a blush or who was more nervous. Joe made small talk with her, but heeded Luke's advice about getting Huan's permission and did not mention the opera. It was only a few minutes before Luke returned with Huan who politely asked if he might join them for the meal. The men sat down and Huan greeted Genny, then Joe.

"Are you going to the opera with us?" Genny asked Huan who nodded once.

"And Jia, too, if she is feeling well?" Tricky chimed in with a big grin.

"We shall see," Huan replied sternly.

"Is everything all right?" Genny asked Luke who had been quiet since they'd returned.

"Huan says that many trains have left for Los Angeles, but without Mara Sinclair on any of them."

"Oh, no," Genny said. "Despite Mara meeting up with Evilsizer, I was hoping she was long gone by now."

"You and me both," Luke replied. "Then again she probably knows the police are looking for her back East, which is another reason she came out West."

"Any sign of Evilsizer?" Joe asked.

"Yesterday," Luke said with an appreciative nod at Huan.

Huan placed his elbows on the table and making

steeples of his fingers said, "Always the chameleon, a bald man fitting the scarecrow's description stole an old buggy near the Valencia Street Hotel. He was with the black widow when they disappeared."

"They'll crawl out from under their rocks again," Luke said to Huan.

As Joe asked Luke a question, Genny noticed Tricky had captured Huan's ear. Huan glanced at Suki who was placing traditional Chinese dumplings on their table and then frowned slightly in Joe's direction. Tricky whispered a couple of additional words in Chinese and placed her hand on Huan's forearm. Indulgently, Huan patted Tricky's hand and then gave her a look that silenced her. Not giving up, Tricky gave her brother one last smile and Huan rolled his eyes.

"And what about the horses?" Joe asked Luke.

"Eight of them will stay here," Luke replied as Huan nodded. "Since I have room for Etalon and Esprit in the stable on my property back home, I will send them on ahead of us to Mississippi." Luke smiled at Genny. "Would you like that?"

"Yes, oh, my yes." Genny clasped her hands over her heart.

Entering the dining room, Ying, who had come into town on the horse Luke had taught him how to saddle and ride, was all smiles at seeing everyone. Tricky jumped up to greet him. With Ying working with Huan's crew at his new ranch, the Cat's Eye closed and Tricky living in Chinatown, Genny knew they didn't get to see each other as often as they once had. Genny had never known two people always so happy to be around others and genuinely thrilled for their good fortune as Tricky and Ying. Genny noticed Luke and Huan exchange a look that Genny instinctively sensed involved Tricky and Ying.

When Luke, Genny and Joe left Li's after the delicious midday meal, Joe and Suki had a date for the opera with Huan's blessing. Luke took Genny shopping, and she found a beautiful dress for the opera in the perfect shade of forest green. In turn, she purchased a forest green bowtie for Luke to wear with his tuxedo and a handkerchief with a green monogram would be in his jacket pocket.

Since the small bed at Genny's house was not nearly as comfortable as those at the Palace Hotel, they had decided to stay in town a night or two. At the Palace they made arrangements for April seventeenth and then their favorite bellboy, Patrick, escorted them to their luxurious suite.

Genny soon appeared in the doorway of their private bath, wearing one of Luke's unbuttoned shirts and a saucy smile. When she crooked her finger, Luke cocked his head at seeing the tub and then followed her into his first bubble bath. He lay back making room for her between his legs as she tenderly washed all parts of his hard body.

"You've made this bath so delightful, Harper," Genny flirted as he cupped her breasts.

CHAPTER 36

"THIS BUGGY IS DISGUSTINGLY DILAPIDATED, SETH," MARA whined. "Why didn't you steal an automobile?" she asked, bumping up and down over rocks and ruts in the dirt road. "Stop hitting the damn ditches before we wind up in one."

Closing in on the Skidmores' farmhouse near dusk, Seth muttered, "No horses at the hitching post. Taking down the sign was a good idea."

With a grip on the handrail along the seat, Mara said, "You're a horrible driver and I don't wish to walk back to town, especially at night."

"Yes, yes. She's getting on my nerves, too, Selma," Seth said. "I'll thank you not to question me or tell me how to drive, Mara. Your job is to hold tight to that kerosene can."

Only a few yards from the ramshackled house, a buggy wheel slid into what appeared to be a deep ditch of empty postholes and rotting fenceposts. Seth cursed the horse, grabbed the buggy whip and struck the mare on her back. The horse tried to pull them out of the trench-like hole, but Seth didn't think she was trying hard enough so repeatedly slapped the whip against the mare's hindquarters. Suffering the flailing, the horse's eyes bulged, and she made another useless lunge. When Seth stood up in order to strike her harder, the buggy leaned so precariously, the horse stumbled and fell to her side in the ditch. No amount of beating could right her.

"Get up, you worthless nag," Mara shrilled as she opened the can and sloshed kerosene onto the mare. The horse whinnied as the fuel oil burned her open wounds. "Oh, shut the hell up!"

"That stupid horse broke the wheel," Seth said and slithered out of the buggy.

"Who're you?" a black woman called from the doorway of the farmhouse.

"Visitors?" Seth said and waited for her reaction.

"Is today Sunday?" the woman asked.

"Yes, April fifteenth." Taking a matchstick out of his pocket, Seth walked toward her.

"We charge extry on Sundays, but we's always open." The woman stepped onto the porch and shouted into the house, "Opal, wake up. We got us some customers."

"By the by," Seth began, leaving Mara to crawl out of the toppled buggy on her own as he stepped onto the porch, "do you happen to have any connection to the Cat's Eye Ranch?"

"We did but they closed it down." The woman spat on the porch with contempt. "We's there the other day gettin' the last of what's ours."

"What's he asking about, Onyx?" Opal asked, a shadowy figure just inside the house.

Seth answered, "I wonder if you ladies know Genevieve Morgan or Luke Harper."

"We sure do," Onyx said. "We done overheard them two ol' fools, Patty and Vern, in the kitchen just agushin' 'bout 'em and all their fancy plans."

"What did they say about Luke Harper?" Mara asked, leaving the buggy and the struggling mare in the ditch.

"You have money?" Opal asked.

"Plenty of it, milady," Seth lied, chewing on the matchstick.

"Then we know all," Opal said.

"Yup. Ever'thing," Onyx agreed. "And if that there's kerosene in the can that woman's got, bring it with ya. We need some to start a fire in our potbelly stove."

"Well now, isn't this serendipitous?" Seth asked.

"THERE'S SMOKE ON THE HORIZON," Luke said, and pointed as they traveled the country road.

Genny sniffed the air. "I pray it's not one of our properties."

"Too far to the east, right now. But it could spread our way."

Following the smell and smoke, raised voices soon drifted their way as Luke turned down the path to the Skidmore farm. They saw the blazing fire and then the people. Mike was pumping water from a well as Jimmy, Grace and Ruth raced back and forth throwing buckets of water on the Skidmores' burning farmhouse. Patty was trying unsuccessfully to calm a terrified horse as it lay trapped on its side in a ditch. The ax in Vern's hands mostly just bounced against the wooden part of the harness pinning the helpless horse to an overturned buggy.

Luke shut off the Runabout and bailed out. With a shout to the brothers and cousins, he headed to help Vern and Patty with the horse. Genny jumped out after Luke and ran. He tore off his jacket and tossed it to Genny telling her to put it over the horse's head. Reaching Patty, Genny jumped into the ditch and covered the horse's eyes. When Luke grabbed the ax from an exhausted Vern, he and Patty then rushed toward the well as flames on the farm-house shot higher and higher into the evening sky.

A burning beam from the house suddenly slammed down on top of the old wooden buggy catching it on fire instantly. With a mighty blow, Luke chopped through the wood of the buggy harness closer to him. The unseeing horse struggled pitifully, surely feeling the scorching flames crackling mere inches from her.

"I smell kerosene," Luke yelled to Genny who was fearlessly determined to help save the ensnared, hopefully not crippled animal. "Grab those reins and be ready to pull."

"Be careful," Genny screamed. "You're going to get kicked or burned or both."

Luke brought down the ax in a heavy blow that splintered the other side of the harness still holding the horse in what was about to become a fiery grave. The force of the ax had unavoidably buried the half-broken wooden harness in the ground as flames licked their way ever closer to the horse. Patty and Vern came running with buckets and tossed water on the horse's hindquarters. Luke raised the ax, and the next blow freed the horse from the buggy.

"Pull the reins!" Luke shouted, knowing the worst case scenario was shooting the mare before letting her burn to death. "If the horse can't stand, everybody get away from the ditch."

Genny tugged hard and the horse thrashed, trying to regain her footing. The movements stirred the flames already perilously close to the mare's tail. Vern and Patty helped Genny by pulling on the harness. When Luke slapped the mare's behind, she finally managed to stand but was too petrified to move. Jumping over fire, Luke grabbed the horse's mane and swung himself onto her back. Digging his heels in her flanks he rode her out of the ditch a heartbeat before a second burning timber landed where the horse had lain. Grabbing his jacket off the mare's head, Luke reined her in and dismounted. A quick assessment assured him the horse would be fine. He turned the frightened animal over to Patty and Vern as Genny rushed into his arms.

"Thank goodness you got here in time to save this little mare," Patty said to Luke and Genny as Vern patted the horse's neck.

"The house is a goner," Vern called to the Johnson brothers. "Don'tcha think?"

"Yeah," Jimmy replied, tossing water on the flames before trading his bucket for a rake.

"And the well is nearly dry," Ruth told them taking Mike's place and pumping water into Grace's bucket.

"All we can do is let the house burn itself out and make sure none of the fires spread," Mike said, picking up a shovel and dragging his forearm across his forehead.

"I'll start with this one." Luke grabbed the ax again and chopped apart burning buggy boards and forgotten fence posts.

The house burned bright orange in the biggest bonfire Genny had ever seen. The inferno lit up the sky growing ever blacker around the moon and stars. Grabbing a bucket, she helped Grace make sparks hiss until the well water was mostly mud. The men worked just as hard raking out blazes, hacking away at boards and covering up flames with shovels of dirt. Acrid smoke burned the eyes, choked their throats and made it difficult to breathe.

"If San Francisco ever catches fire like this, we won't be able to stop it," Jimmy said.

"Why's that?" Luke asked, wiping sweat off his brow.

"Dennis Sullivan, the fire chief before Chief Daughtery, ran the department for twenty-six years. Sullivan knew the fire department and its shortcomings better than anybody," Mike said, shovel in hand. "Throughout his career, he fought to build a supplementary saltwater system and to reactivate our long neglected cisterns which run underneath the downtown city streets. But the supervisors never listened to him, and nothing was ever improved."

"Seven years ago, Lucky Baldwin's big hotel and theater on the corner of Market and Powell Streets caught fire and almost took the whole block with it," Jimmy said and coughed, continually raking the ground to suffocate flames and sparks.

"There are insurance companies and underwriters to answer to," Luke said, wielding the ax again. "What do they say?"

"Right." Mike rubbed his forehead and nodded. "The National Board of Fire Underwriters has declared San Franisco's thirty-six million gallon per day water system dangerously insufficient in case of a conflagration."

"Conflagration?" Ruth asked, her forehead marred with soot as she walked to Mike.

"A conflagration is a fire so large and destructive that it causes catastrophic, widespread damage," Mike replied, tossing another shovelful of dirt on the fire.

"Yeah," Jimmy agreed, raking out a line of errant embers near Grace. "In case of a firestorm like that, the city's current hydrant system is inadequate to deliver even the minimum amount of water needed to guarantee the safety of people and property."

"What about the safety of the city's firemen?" Ruth asked Mike.

"At least we know what we're up against," Mike replied with a shrug.

"I hope San Francisco never catches fire," Grace said softly and wiped her hand on her dress, blackened with soot, before placing it on Jimmy's dusty arm.

"If it does, San Francisco will cease to exist as we know it today," Jimmy said.

Setting her empty bucket down, Genny's head bowed, and Luke wrapped his arm around her slender shoulders. When she smiled up at him and slipped her arm around his waist, he swiped away a smudge on her nose.

By midnight when Patty and Vern finally left the farm, fawning over and sweet talking the little mare they had in tow, the flames had disintegrated the house. But thanks to the men trained to fight fires, those flames had not burst into an uncontrollable wildfire and raged across the countryside. To make sure nothing else ignited again, the brothers, cousins, Luke, and Genny stayed put all night. As dawn broke, bringing its pink light, Luke accompanied the Johnson brothers into the hot ashes of smoldering ruins.

"Hey, Mike, we got a body here by the potbelly stove,"

Jimmy said.

"Make that two," Luke said. "Along with a can of kerosene."

"YOU SHOULD HAVE FORCED them up on the roof and pushed them off so it would look like they fell to their deaths," Mara said at dawn, still furious after the tiring hike back to town.

"Why would those whores have been on the roof?" Seth asked, half asleep on the hard pew in Old St. Mary's. "No, no, that would have been suspicious. But a broken-down potbelly stove could easily catch that filthy farmhouse on fire while they slept. Vacant or not, Selma said that place was too hideous to hide out in."

"Oh, who cares?" Mara snapped. "The whores are dead and can't tattle to Luke about our visit." She sat up in her pew when Seth stood and stretched in the center aisle of the church. "I don't know if I believe you about that monkey gang being the reason we can't go back to the Valencia Street Hotel. Isn't that just an excuse because you're afraid to be alone with a woman?"

"The Monkey's Fist has me confused with somebody known as the scarecrow," Seth said, not making eye contact with her, but feeling the familiar fluttering. "Besides there's no money left for a hotel."

"Why can't you wire your bank for more money?"

Ignoring her questions, he replied, "We cannot return to Valencia Street and that's final."

"I found that place heinous anyway compared to the ritzy suite I glimpsed Luke had with Genevieve at the Palace."

Taking a match out of his pocket and twirling it between his thumb and finger, Seth paced up and down the aisle. Mara kept a wary eye on him. True, she was a murderer like Seth. But he was crazy.

"Yes, yes. I know, Selma, I know," Seth said sticking the

match between his thin lips. "Stop piling on the agony by reminding me the fabulous jewels Cecil told me about are worthless whores and not priceless gems. I am completely devastated by it, too."

"I'm sick to death of Selma," Mara muttered, rubbing her sore feet "Well, at least we heard about the opera."

Seth's jaw dropped and so did the match. "How can you even think about the opera?"

"Because knowing where Luke and Genevieve will be that night, means we can take our revenge. Think about the endless possibilities, Seth."

"I think my whole life is ruined because of Harper. Genevieve came to my soirée to meet me, not him," Seth sniveled. "Besides the jewels, I lost a big house for me and a little one for Selma."

"*Your* life is ruined?" Mara spat, swinging her arms wide. Her eyes narrowed and her mouth puckered as she pressed both index fingers to her chest. "*I* lost the grandest life a woman can imagine with the grandest man alive because of that bitch Genevieve."

"I'm the only one allowed to call my fiancée a bitch," Seth said and glared at her.

"Genevieve is not your fiancée," Mara snapped. "That photograph in the newspaper was of Genevieve and Luke, not of Genevieve and you."

"Shut up." Seth took another matchstick from his pocket and used it to point at her. "If I don't marry Genevieve, Selma and I can't inherit her land and houses."

"There is no damn Selma!" Mara shrieked at the top of her lungs.

"You and Selma both shut up." Seth struck the match and stared at the flickering flame. "We'll kidnap Genevieve the night of the opera. But before we kill the bitch, I'll make Harper pay a hundred-thousand-dollar ransom."

"A million and we'll split it fifty-fifty." Eyes going to the man nailed on the cross straight ahead, Mara said, "Burning Genevieve will crucify Luke."

CHAPTER 37

"FOUR TRUNKS OUGHT TO DO IT," LUKE SAID, ON MONDAY, April sixteenth.

From the front room of Genny's house he heard her in the bedroom mumbling something about misplacing her shoes just before taking her bath.

"Do you see them out there?" she called. "I want to wear them to the opera tomorrow evening."

"No, and I hope they aren't buried in either of these trunks," Luke said, surveying two, full-to-the-brim trunks near the front door. When she assured him they weren't and she was done with those trunks, he replied, "I'll close and lock 'em."

Dressed in a dark shirt with the long sleeves rolled up, blue jeans, cowboy boots, and leather chaps, he'd just returned from working with Huan and Ying in the corral of his former ranch. He'd demonstrated how to break in one of the American Quarter horses that had never been ridden. Vern was there as well and afterward, they'd toasted with shots of extra potent flip. Huan's eyebrows rose in appreciation of the homemade brew and the other three men nodded with a chuckle.

"Huan and Jia are settling in and Tricky was there," Luke said, locking a trunk.

"Were Jia and Tricky decorating the babies' rooms?"

"Yes. Jia sent her thanks for the rocking cradles."

"I told Jia and Huan it was a cradle from each of us," Genny answered.

Huan now had Jia in a safe haven to wait for what they suspected were twins on the way. Huan had recently confided to Luke that Ying had asked for permission to marry Tricky. Huan had granted it with stipulations of Ying always working hard and keeping Tricky happy and safe.

Honored and excited, Ying had since asked Luke where he'd purchased Genny's ring and allowed Luke to include Genny in on his secret intentions regarding Tricky. Although the diamond Ying bought was a fraction of the size of Genny's, Luke and Genny knew Tricky would be thrilled to receive it along with Ying's proposal. Huan's wedding present to Tricky and Ying, was the cozy new ranch house and twenty-five hundred acres of wide-open spaces.

The day he'd sold the ranch to Huan, Luke had arranged for Ying and Tricky to keep the two horses he had once chosen for them to ride. Those American Quarter horses, along with plenty of oats and hay, would now be his and Genny's wedding gift to the young couple. Huan's payment in full for everything else had long since been added to Luke's Mississippi bank account.

"While I was in town, I picked up a telegram from Rob," Luke said, making his way down the short hall to the door of Genny's bedroom. Hanging across the doorway and eclipsing his view of her was new clothing. "Etalon and Esprit arrived safely and are in my stable."

"I'm so thrilled they'll be in Mississippi with us."

"Not as thrilled as my family is that *you'll* be in Mississippi with us."

"I hope so," came her soft voice from the other side of the clothes barrier.

"I know so."

Parting the expensive boleros, capes and shawls, Luke saw new dresses of every color in and around the wardrobe as well as stockings and fancy lingerie draped across the bed. Genny, wearing only a thin white camisole and ruffled white panties, was bent over waist-deep in a trunk only partially filled with new pocketbooks, shoes, boots, and slippers. Leaning against the door, eyes on her fanny, Luke crossed his arms over his chest and whistled.

"I found them."

New shoes in hand, Genny straightened up so fast she bumped her head on the lid of the trunk and plopped down on a stack of blankets fresh from the clothesline. The damp topknot on her head came loose and long black hair cascaded down her slender back. Luke's brows shot up and he smothered a chuckle.

"My sexy goddess, have you been drinking flip?" Luke teased. "Baijiu? Whiskey?"

"No," Genny said and laughed. "I just got dizzy from bending over, that's all."

"Are you nearly naked because you can't find anything to wear?"

"No, but I'm saving my new things for Biloxi," she said, glancing around the room while sitting atop the blankets. "I don't know what to do with so many beautiful dresses and clothes."

"Pack 'em," Luke said, and held out his hand. Genny took hold and he tugged her to her feet. When she swooned against him and dropped her new shoes, he scooped her up in his arms. "Well, you're either tipsy or pregnant, little lamb."

Her arms twining around his neck, Genny stared at him and then whispered, "I'm definitely not tipsy, wolf."

"That leaves pregnant."

Genny kicked her bare feet. "Put me down."

When he did, she squared off with him at the end of the bed and smacked her fists on her hips. The bourbon-colored nipples of her full breasts clearly showed through the delicate camisole and the sheer panties drew his eyes to the alluring vee between her shapely legs.

"What's wrong?" he asked.

"If I'm pregnant, it's all your fault, Harper."

"Yeah. So?"

"So, I don't know how it happened."

"And yet, I've given you so many lessons."

"Ooh!" she fumed and tossed a wild punch in his direction.

"Hey," he chuckled, carefully catching her fist as she swayed. "Keep your wrist straight and your eyes open."

She yanked her hand from him. "I mean I don't know how it happened so fast."

"Only takes one time."

"So you have other children?"

"Hell, no," he barked, placing his hands on his hips.

"Liar!" She kicked his ankle, but his chaps and boots met with her bare toes. "Ouch!"

"Stop that." He placed a hand on her shoulder to steady her. "Settle down."

"How do you know you don't have any?" she asked and knocked his hand off her shoulder.

"Because."

When he lowered his head and cocked a brow, she turned away. Sashaying across the room, her hair bounced against her back and ruffles flounced across her saucy bottom. Twirling to face him, she doubled up her fists as if ready to throw a sockdolager.

"Explain that, Harper, and if I don't like your answer I'm going to tan your hide."

Knowing that was an empty threat, Genny nevertheless narrowed her eyes and stood her ground. Luke clenched his square jaw. Through his snug shirt, the muscles in his sinewy arms flexed as he crossed them over his broad chest. His belt buckle rode just above the leather chaps covering his legs down to the toes of his cowboy boots.

What the chaps exposed was the oh-so-sexy masculine bulge in the crotch of his blue jeans.

"Because Charles Goodyear invented the rubber vulcanization process and because my father gave me a lecture I'll never forget, I was always careful."

Genny was silent for a moment. "That's why you were so sure about Mara Sinclair?"

"Yes."

Though the possible pregnancy had Genny flustered almost beyond cohesive thought, she realized he had only let down his guard with her. She felt better but just for a moment.

"Streaks! Your parents will be shocked." Genny placed her fists to her cheeks at the anticipated humiliation. "Your whole family will know I didn't wait until marriage to…to…"

"We didn't wait," he corrected and sat down on the end of her bed. "C'mere, before you fall down again."

"You're a brave man," she said, hands still clenched into fists.

"I'd have to be to take you on." Luke reached forward and catching a wrist, brought her bare feet between his boots. His expression serious, he took hold of her chin. "I'm happy you might be pregnant, aren't you?"

"But we should have waited."

"I knew what to do and I didn't do it. Like you said, it's my fault."

"No, it's our fault," she said, calming down. "Running the bordello even for a short time, I figured they must be doing something to avoid…problems."

"But for us this isn't a problem." He smiled and she slowly nodded. "Anyway, Chloe blamed Rob and Mattie blamed Steve, so my parents won't be shocked."

Genny's eyes widened. "They were pregnant when they got married, too?"

"Yes," Luke said with a chuckle as he placed his right hand, fingers splaying, to her flat tummy. If you're not already pregnant, you soon will be." His eyes met hers and he said, "I love you so much, Genny."

"I love you so much, too." Genny's smile was shy as she covered his hand with both of hers. "You've made me the happiest woman from here to the dark side of the moon."

With a grin, Luke swept the lingerie and stockings on the bed out of his way. Hands going to her waist he lay back, tugging her on top of him. As she slid her arms under his neck, his hands flattened to her bottom making her tingle. When his eyes closed, she lowered her mouth to his. Luke's lips spread hers and his warm tongue slid past her teeth. So in love, she kissed him with unabashed abandonment.

He suddenly rolled over and she found herself underneath the powerful man. He eased off her and stood up at the end of the bed. Genny knew that glint in his green eyes and heat flooded her body blending love and lust into a wild and wanton craving. When he leaned over her and tugged on her camisole, she sat up and let him pull it over her head. She lay back down and inviting him to join her, scooted up in the bed.

Luke stretched out on top of her, and his mouth slashed across hers. She threaded her fingers through his thick brown hair savoring each kiss he rained down her neck and collarbone. When his warm mouth closed over her left nipple she purred with pleasure and arched her back. Her heart pounded against his lips as he trailed kisses between her breasts. His tongue played with her right breast, and she undulated under him wanting him inside her.

"Mmm," she moaned, spreading her legs.

Luke moved lower and his tongue dipped into her belly button. He kissed her tummy where his hand had been moments ago. When he eased off the bed and took hold of her panties, she sensed something different. Far from knowing all this man's moods and moves, she trustingly raised her hips. He pulled her old, homemade panties off and a rip sounded.

"Whoops." His grin was wicked as he momentarily raised his hands in surrender before stuffing the ruffles into the back pocket of his jeans. Standing at the end of the bed, fully clothed as she lay naked, Luke boldly looked her up and down. "All mine."

"Destiny," she whispered and not to be outdone, lowered her eyes to the area exposed by the chaps where a long, hard bulge clearly showed behind the fly of his jeans. "All mine."

"Destiny," he replied, unfastened his chaps and tossed them over one of her trunks.

But instead of removing the rest of his clothes, he knelt between her legs. With large, capable hands he scooped up the cheeks of her fanny and raised her hips off the bed. Before she had any clue as to what was about to happen his mouth touched her most secret spot.

Velvet met velvet. And sizzled.

"Luke," she gasped, stunned by his wild new kiss.

Shattered. Body, heart and soul.

Shattered, as surely as she had been the very first time they'd made love. His lips melting her skin, his tongue gently spread her tender folds. Luke's kiss deepened, capturing her in a cocoon of sweet surrender. Her entire being from head to heart, from fingers and toes revolved around the warm, slippery sensations between her thighs.

"Mmm…yes…" Genny heard herself moan.

The thrill she always felt when his manhood was inside her echoed now as his lips and tongue performed an outrageously sensual dance in the vee of her legs. Suddenly, tremors waved from her innermost core ricocheting outward to her extremities. Like liquid heat, his fiery kiss flamed into such rapturous pleasure that hot, pounding ecstasy burst and rippled within her. She gasped his name, her fingers burying themselves in his thick, brown hair as she trembled against his lips. Gradually the spasms of exotic ecstasy slowly loosened their hold on her.

"What do you call that?" she whispered in awe as Luke stood up.

"Making love," he replied meaningfully.

"I loved it."

"Me, too." Unfastening the fly of his jeans, he shoved them down and lay between her legs.

"I want to make love to you like that," she said as the tip of his velvety hard manhood touched her velvety folds.

"Next time when I can enjoy it longer."

Genny wrapped her legs around his waist and reveled in the feel of the muscular man's hard body. Sliding himself inside her, his mouth lowered, and their tongues played. She threaded her fingers through his hair again as she had when they'd begun this exhilarating new adventure. Faster and harder his body penetrated and withdrew as she matched and squeezed every rigid inch of each long thrust.

"Genny," Luke's low male groan brushed her ear as he spilled himself deep inside her. When his pulsing stopped and their heartbeats slowed, he levered himself up on his hands, hips between her thighs and loomed over her with a grin. "I have work to do and you sidetracked me."

"Did I now?" she flirted. "You're the one who came in here and *ripped* my panties off."

"That I did."

The muscles flexed in his shoulders and arms as he lowered himself just enough to kiss her. Then he stood and pulled up his jeans, never taking his eyes off her. When she held her hands out to him, he tugged her off the bed.

"I have no panties now," she said pulling the camisole over her head as he buttoned his jeans. "I'll have to improvise."

Buckling his belt, Luke nodded to the pile of new lingerie. Wanting her to feel confident and comfortable the moment they stepped off the train in New Orleans, he'd made sure she'd had plenty of opportunities to choose the latest fashions from the best shops in San Francisco. All the while he'd kept an eye out for their enemies. In Biloxi, she'd have the money, freedom and safety to shop and buy whatever, whenever she wanted whether he was with her or not.

Genny grabbed his chaps, but instead of handing them to him, she fastened them as tightly as possible around her waist. Winding her hair back into its topknot on her head she stood before him, hands on her hips. The thin camisole stretched tightly across her breasts, but the chaps drooped revealing her indented belly button. Through the opening of the chaps, he glimpsed the delicious feminine part of her that he'd just made love to. Impossibly enchanted by her, when Genny gave him a sassy nod of her head and smiled that smile Luke knew beyond a shadow of the moon he was the luckiest man alive.

"I'll bet my chaps fit you tighter in a few months," he said and cocked a brow.

"I'll bet you're right, cowboy."

Genny then twirled back to the open trunk she'd been rifling through earlier. Explaining she had to find the pocketbook that went with her new shoes, she bent over and started digging. Luke groaned at the spectacular view just as he heard Andy and one of his men returning to guard her. He patted her naked fanny before leaving the bedroom.

"Where are you going, Harper?"

"Back to the ranch before we're back in bed."

Genny watched the magnificent man swagger down the hall, her ruffles dangling from his back pocket. Remembering that the green of Luke's eyes meant energy, strength and new life, Genny stood and placed her hands to her tummy daring to hope and dream and imagine.

CHAPTER 38

"THIS HAS BEEN THE WORST WEEKS OF MY ENTIRE LIFE, Seth," Mara hissed across a table with legs so uneven half a bowl of the soup kitchen's inedible slop had just spilled in the lap of a stolen coat two sizes too big for her.

"Somehow I doubt that." Seth set his bowl down, picked up hers and slurped.

Persistent paranoia had him seeing shadows of the Monkey's Fist everywhere. Deciding Old St. Mary's church was far too close to Chinatown, he had sought out a smaller, much more obscure church in which to hide. Thus far his strategy was paying off as the Monkey's Fist had not come as dangerously close to him as they had in the Black-Eyed Susan or outside the Valencia Street Hotel. As for the police, they worried him far less than the Chinese. He hoped they all thought he had managed to flee the Bay area.

"The worst," Mara repeated, shook the slop from her lap onto the greasy floor.

"You've been in prison, Mara." Seth set the bowl down and said, "Being locked up is far worse than being on the street."

"Speaking of being on the street, you do not wear

homelessness well," she said, nose in the air. "I'm embarrassed to be seen with you."

"You think you'd win any beauty prizes, milady?" He'd burn this loathsome bitch as soon as he had Luke Harper's money.

"Normally, yes," Mara said, picking at her unkempt hair. "I can't wait for tonight."

"Once we have our new clothes, they'll never see us coming," Seth said.

"Tonight's the night," Genny fairly sang to herself as she closed the carpetbag for what she figured would be their last overnight stay at the Palace Hotel.

They would leave for town shortly. Genny smiled at the thought of Tricky being engaged before the night was over. Along with Huan and Jia, she and Luke hadn't breathed a word of Ying's secret to anyone. But when Patty and Vern, Joe and Suki, the Johnson brothers, and sweet cousins found out they would all be thrilled. Genny would certainly miss these San Francisco friends who were more like family. She and Luke had promised they would come back for a visit. Maybe with a baby in tow, Genny thought and smiled.

"Genevieve," Luke said scoldingly, as she carried her carpetbag into the front room. He took it from her and set it near the door where Roscoe was standing guard. "Please let me carry the heavier things for you."

"I'm not suddenly helpless."

"I agree." Taking her hand, he led her to the daybed where she sat down. He pulled up a chair and sliding his knees on the outside of hers, he sat facing her. "I want to talk to you."

"What about?" she asked, tucking a curl behind her ear.

"I'm looking forward to supper and the opera tonight because seeing *Carmen* means so much to you. But Evilsizer is out there insane, lurking and plotting his next move. So, tomorrow morning I'm buying tickets for the first sleeping car on the *Coast Line* to Los Angeles."

"Perfect." Genny smiled. But as Luke's tone of voice and expression soaked in, she said, "I thought we weren't leaving until Evilsizer was caught."

"I want you safe with my parents on the sugarcane plantation, not waiting around San Francisco where he can get his hands you again."

She stiffened, feeling anxious. "Are you saying you're not going with me?"

"I'm going with you as far as Los Angeles and putting you on the *Sunset Limited*. It'll take you straight to New Orleans, where Rob will pick you up and drive you on to Biloxi. But I'm coming back here from Los Angeles."

"No!" Genny snapped. "I'm not leaving you behind to face Evilsizer alone."

"I won't be alone. I'll work with Huan and the police."

"No!" Genny repeated sharply, shaking her head and clasping her hands in her lap. "You're doing this because I might be pregnant."

"Yes, but listen to me," Luke said, and took her hands in his. "I thought about sending you on ahead of me the day I proposed. I just couldn't make myself give you up. But knowing you might be pregnant is the final push I need to get you to safety."

"I'm safest with you."

"But when you're not with me you're vulnerable." Genny knew he was referring to the incidents with the poisoned meat, in the rising room and the day she'd disappeared on the trolley. Looking her in the eyes, Luke gently squeezed her hands and said, "What if Evilsizer did something to cause you to lose our baby? I couldn't forgive myself." Cocking his head to the side, he asked, "Could you?"

"No, but that won't happen, and we'll leave San Francisco together."

Luke said, "I guarantee you if they aren't caught here in

San Francisco, Evilsizer and Sinclair will follow us to Biloxi. He killed your mother and your grandfather, shanghaied the Skidmores, and set fire to Fan Zhou, Onyx and Opal in his determination to get you. Mara killed three husbands in cold blood before following me here. They are both murdering psychopaths, Genny. If I'm not with you, I can help find them. Someone has to stop them."

"That someone doesn't have to be you." Genny scooted forward and placed her hands on his knees. "If they took you from me, I wouldn't want to live."

"Is that your heart I see on your sleeve?" he asked with a soft smile and covered her hands with his. "Nothing will happen to me. But if it did, you'd go on because my gut says you're pregnant and you'd have our baby to raise."

"And if I'm not expecting, you're sending me away for nothing."

"We don't have a choice now."

"I choose not to go," Genny said, and yanked her hands from under his.

Luke stood, shoved the chair aside and strode to the open door of the house. Sunlight spilled into the room around him, but Genny felt a chill. Sticking close to Luke, Roscoe looked at Genny and tilted his head to one side.

His back to her, Luke said, "You're going, Genevieve."

Genny bristled. "Not without you."

"Dammit," Luke barked and turned to her. His stare was intense and when he spoke, his deep voice resonated with conviction. "This isn't open for discussion."

"I know I scared you in the past. I promise not to put myself at risk again under these circumstances." Genny's eyes stung with tears, but she would not cry. "Nothing will go wrong."

"It happens out of the blue." Luke shook his head and walked onto the porch as if trying to walk away from a bad memory. Genny hopped off the daybed and when she joined him, he said, "You don't see it coming."

"What do you mean, Luke?" she asked, placing a hand

on his arm. "What happened to make you so determined to send me away and to stop Evilsizer and Sinclair?"

"We'll talk about it some other time."

"Hey, boss," Andy called driving an automobile into view from the road.

"I need to give Andy some instructions while you finish packing," Luke said, making his way down the steps. "And then we'll head to the Palace."

GENNY WONDERED what it was that Luke hadn't wanted to talk about, but respecting his wishes, hadn't asked. In their hotel suite now, he'd just buttoned the back of her new green dress and the touch of his fingers on her skin never failed to thrill her.

"Is Andy escorting us to the opera?" Genny asked, and turned to him.

"Yes, along with both Rough Riders. Andy'll park the Runabout and wait near the vehicle I rented for his men to drive Patty and Vern into town and home again."

"I don't know if they are more excited about their first opera or first ride in an automobile." Genny never ceased to be amazed by his generosity. "Thank you, Luke."

When Luke shrugged, Genny took a step back and looked him up and down. Wearing his crisp white shirt and formal black suit, Luke was absolutely resplendent. His chocolate-brown hair was combed straight back and he mesmerized her now just as he had on New Year's Eve when she had mentally compared him to a Greek god. She sighed, hardly believing a man more handsome than Adonis was her fiancé.

"Now aren't you glad I borrowed your tuxedo the night we met?" she asked.

"Yes, and thanks to you, I have gold cufflinks," Luke said as he shot his sleeves.

He stayed near her in the shops, so it hadn't been easy to point out the cufflinks to the jeweler much less slip him the money, Luke always made sure she had, without being caught."When I saw those cufflinks, I knew they'd match the bands we bought today," Genny said. "I hope you'll wear them on our wedding day."

"I will, if you let me slip your wedding band next to your engagement ring that same day."

Genny smiled that spectacular smile and nodded. Her shiny black hair had been woven by the hotel hairdresser into the latest fashion of loose curls atop her head. The scooped neck of her dress teased him with a hint of alabaster cleavage especially as she straightened his forest green bow tie and smoothed the forest green initials of the monogrammed handkerchief in his jacket pocket. From here to the moon, she was the ever-enchanting elegant goddess of his heart.

"Want to know the meaning of your middle name?" she asked.

"Tell me."

"Richard means king. Powerful, strong and brave." She smiled up at him, a tear in her eye. "It describes you so well."

Luke took the love of his life in his arms and held her to his heart. As his lips touched hers, a knock sounded on the door.

Andy said, "Boss, you have guests."

Releasing Genny, Luke walked across the room. "Gentlemen," he said to Wong and Chen after opening the door. "News?"

"Yes, sir. Huan will tell," Wong said stoically.

"Has Huan arrived?"

"On way," Chen replied.

"All right," Luke said. "I have arranged for a private supper in the Tapestry Room. Andy will escort you there. I'll be down before Huan arrives."

"Yes, sir," Wong said, and with small bows, he and Chen disappeared down the hall.

Under his tuxedo Luke wore his loaded gun in a new

leather shoulder holster. Called a skeleton holster, due to securing the gun with a single, leather-covered spring-steel clip, it was made for concealment and speed. Earlier, he'd loaded Genny's gun and now he picked it up off the marble table and placed it along with her white dragon knife inside her new green purse.

"What do you think the news is, Harper?"

"That Evilsizer and Sinclair have been caught."

"By the police or the Monkey's Fist?"

"The police interrogate. The Fist cut."

Genny shivered. "Does that mean we can leave for Biloxi together?"

Picking up a green satin wrap, Luke placed it around her shoulders. "Let's go find out."

CHAPTER 39

"Welcome," Luke said, as their first guests arrived in the Tapestry Room.

"It's a pleasure to have you both with us." Genny smiled, standing beside Luke.

"We are honored." Dressed in black, Huan kept one arm around his beautiful wife as he shook Luke's hand. No doubt Huan could have had his pick of women, but feisty Jia had certainly stolen his heart.

"Hello." Jia, her black hair coiffed into a mixture of braids and small pink flowers atop her head, was absolutely stunning. Clad in a sky-blue silk, jacket-like dress Jia's arms lay clasped over her rounded stomach, her hands hidden by long sleeves embroidered with pink flowers.

"Jia, you look lovely," Genny said, standing beside Luke.

"And large," Jia said with a soft laugh. "Thank you. I return your compliment, Genevieve."

All smiles Ying, Tricky, Joe, and Suki were greeted next. Then Luke tucked Genny's arm through his and led the way further into the private dining room. There, a long table was set for fourteen with crystal, china and silver. Three waiters in tuxedos poured water into goblets and placed baskets of plump croissants alongside silver plates of sliced butter.

"Have you seen my chickens?" Tricky asked and wiggled the fingers of her left hand against her cheek. A gold ring set with a small diamond glittered in the light of the chandeliers.

"Tricky, Ying, I'm so thrilled for you," Genny said and with a smile at Ying, took Tricky's hand in hers. "Your ring is absolutely beautiful." Both she and Tricky flicked away happy tears on their cheeks and hugged.

"Congratulations," Luke said, and shook Ying's hand.

"I guess you know about Huan's wedding present to Tricky and me," Ying asked Luke as Huan and Jia talked with Joe and Suki.

"Yes, you have the ranch you wanted, Ying," Luke said with a smile.

"And two American Quarter horses to go with it." There was a catch in Ying's voice, but he swallowed and pressed on. "Huan says you are a king to rival the Monkey King. That is high praise, especially from Huan, and I agree. Thank you for everything, Luke."

"The least I could do in return for you taking me to the Cat's Eye Ranch three months ago." Luke winked at Genny. Ying's expression spoke volumes of gratitude, respect and friendship. Tricky hugged Luke and he heard a sniffle from Genny. "You're both welcome," he said, moved as well. When Tricky stood back, Luke clapped Ying on the shoulder and with a glance at Huan and Jia, said, "Huan, you'll be at one end of the table, and I'll be at the other. Let's accompany Jia to her seat."

Luke's men and Huan's bodyguards stood like sentries at the only doorway in or out of the fancy dining room. Shortly, when dinner was served, Luke would sit with Genny on his right and Huan would be seated with Jia to his right. For the moment, the ladies visited at Jia's end of the table, while Luke, Huan, Joe, and Ying were served drinks by Cocktail Boothby. Patty and Vern arrived just before Mike and Jimmy escorted Ruth and Grace into the dining room. Luke and Genny made an excellent host and hostess, introducing everyone to those whom they didn't know. After that was accomplished, Luke and Huan moved aside to talk privately.

"Do you know what Huan's news is?" Genny asked Tricky as their friends mingled.

"No," Tricky replied quietly. "Huan said it was for Luke's ears first."

The waiters returned, one with appetizers of cheeses, sweetbreads, nuts and berries. Another served up bowls of avocado dip and clam dip circled with a variety of crackers. Not to be outdone, the third waiter offered trays filled with sliced apples, plums, apricots, and pears.

As Luke and Huan made their way back across the room, Genny held her breath.

"Luke," she said, meeting up with him at the head of the table. "Please tell me the news before we're seated."

"Huan has them."

"How?" Genny could hardly believe her ears. "Where?"

"To say it as Huan did; the Monkey's Fist stopped the scarecrow and the spider from stealing the clothes off a man and woman whom they had beaten unconscious after dragging them into an alley near the Grand Opera House, South of the Slot."

"Streaks," Genny choked out under her breath.

"One of the Fist leaders and his men took the injured couple to St. Mary's Hospital."

"What about the scarecrow and the spider?" she asked, thinking how apt the descriptions were. "Are they dead or alive?"

"Alive. I'm going to see them before they're dead."

"Huan will have them killed after you see them?" Genny asked.

"While I'm there."

"No," Genny gasped softly.

"Oh. Hell. Yes."

This was the man who crossed all borders of tame and vanished into the wild.

Luke pulled out Genny's chair as did the other men for the women they were escorting. Huan made sure Jia was comfortable before sitting down. The waiters poured wine as soon as everyone was seated. Luke lifted his glass, gave a nod directly to Huan and smiled at Genny.

"From the dark side of the moon to enlightenment of the soul's deepest journey, I wish bright travels for us all," Luke said. Everyone drank to his toast and then he glanced at the opposite end of the table. "Huan?"

With a nod of acknowledgement to Luke, Huan said what he believed, "When life and work are threatened, he is immortal who wages righteous war against those bringing the evil."

Everyone drank to Huan's toast although Genny, like Jia, only took small sips. Appetizers and conversations were enjoyed as Luke and Genny's guests began giving the waiters their selections for supper. Filet, steak and prime rib were on the menu along with a variety of wild fish known to swim in the Bay, such as halibut, sablefish, sole, rockfish, spot prawns, sand dabs, and squid. Among the farmed seafood choices were trout, mussels, clams, and oysters. It was a feast among friends and family never to be forgotten.

"Oysters are an aphrodisiac, loverboy," Genny whispered after Luke swallowed one.

Luke grinned. "Are you gonna waltz with me in bed tonight, babydoll?"

Genny swallowed an oyster and replied, "I can't wait for you to fill my dance card."

"I CAN'T GET my hands loose." Seth twisted his wrists raw as blood oozed on the left side of his head, down his neck and into his coat. He had run when ordered to stop and he'd paid for that when the Monkey's Fist closed in on them from both ends of the alley. He'd thrown up his hands in surrender, claiming he hadn't heard them shout at

328 | LYNN ELDRIDGE

him. The leader of the group suggested maybe he would
hear better with one ear than two and Seth had quickly lost
his left ear to a sharp blade. "My whole head feels like it's
on fire."

"Good! You deserve it," Mara hissed, her hands also
tightly tied. "You pushed me toward those bastard
Chinamen to shield yourself and I fell into a pile of
garbage, *scarecrow*."

"Isn't pushing and falling the web spun by the black
widow, *spider*?"

"Harper will fall just like the other three." Mara
suddenly gasped and started kicking her feet. "I think a rat
crawled over my foot. Probably infected with the Black
Death."

"How long have we been trapped in this hole in the
ground? Being imprisoned is bringing on my melancholy,
Selma," Seth whined. "I can't hold on much longer. Selma!
Selma!"

"Oh, shut up, you idiot. When do you think we'll get
something to eat?"

In a falsetto voice, the answer came, "The question is;
when will we kill you."

"Seth!" Mara gulped. "Who was that?"

"Selma," the falsetto voice replied. "Seth plans to burn
you alive just like he did me, bitch."

"I'M at the opera with the most beautiful woman in the
world," Luke said, helping Genny out of the Runabout in
front of the Grand Opera House.

"You've gone mad," Genny said modestly. "Harriett Peak
said in her column the other day that San Franciscans have
gone mad about the opera."

"I'm not a San Franciscan but you'll always be the most
beautiful woman anywhere," Luke said with a grin as Andy
nodded in agreement and took his place behind the wheel

of the Runabout. "We'll meet you and your men back here after the performance, Andy."

"Yes, sir," Andy said, and drove away from the corner of Mission Street.

The spring breeze was a welcome change from the winter wind that had chilled Luke and Genny on the night they'd first met. How long ago that night seemed to Genny now.

Luke took her hand and with everyone but the brothers and cousins, who were on their way to *Babes in Toyland*, began cutting their way through the crowd. Right behind them, Wong and Chen made a careful path for Huan and Jia. Genny enjoyed every nuance of her first venture to the opera house which had boasted its opening opera twenty years prior in 1886. She and Luke were immersed among ladies in all manner of fancy, floor length gowns on the arms of gentlemen in tuxedos or black suits. After all, this was San Francisco's highbrow entertainment and according to Harriett Peak's latest column, the Metropolitan Opera Company's production of Georges Bizet's *Carmen* was *the* social event of the season.

"I can't believe we're about to see and hear Enrico Caruso sing Don José along with soprano Olive Fremstad singing the title role," Genny said to Luke as they nestled into their front row, center seats.

"Me neither," Luke said with a teasing grumble.

The others in their party filed in and Huan seated Jia next to Genny. Next to Huan was Tricky, along with Ying, Joe, and Suki. On the other side of Luke were Patty and Vern.

The thrill of the opera was upon them all.

Lights dimmed and the murmuring crowd hushed as the orchestra swelled the air with music. The curtains opened on Act One and Genny took Luke's hand losing herself in Bizet's masterpiece. Enrico Caruso's brilliant tenor performance of Don José slightly overshadowed Madame Fremstad's portrayal of Carmen. But that was not entirely unexpected as it was her debut performance in the title role of this truly fabulous and famous opera. During Acts Two and Three, Genny snuggled closer to Luke, and he placed his arm around her shoulders. When she sniffled during the final scene, Luke handed over his monogrammed handkerchief so that she could swipe at the tear on her cheek. And moments later, the curtains closed on Act Four and final scene of *Carmen*.

The standing ovation was an immediate, roaring one as Caruso, Fremstad and cast reveled in their bows and curtsies. Then chandeliers glimmered once again to light the way as opera goers filed out of the theater. Huan and his entourage said their good nights as Vern and Patty waved from the automobile chauffeured by the Rough Riders.

April seventeenth was a Tuesday night and by the time Andy returned Luke and Genny to the Palace Hotel, the city streets were quieting. Most of the three thousand people who had attended the performance would probably be in bed by midnight.

Luke and Genny certainly were and her dance card was filled.

THE SEAGULLS HAD YET to screech when Genny reached for Luke. Usually, he was rolled against her back spoon fashion, his arm around her waist and hand flattened to her tummy. Some nights she'd curl against his broad back and when he'd pat her hip, she felt protected by his warmth and muscle. Other times, like her first nap with him, her head lay on his shoulder with her leg snuggled between his, her hand over his heart. But now his side of the bed was cold.

"Luke?" she called into the dark room.

"Right here," he replied, buttoning his coat as he walked into the moonlight trickling through the bay window.

"Why are you awake and dressed?" she asked, sitting up. "What time is it?"

"It's four-thirty in the morning," he said with a glance at

his pocketwatch and then sat down on the edge of her side of the bed. "I'm going to meet Huan."

"No, Luke." Genny clutched his hand. "I wish you wouldn't. The ordeal of seeing those two put to death sounds horrific to me."

"That's why you're not going," Luke said.

"Just ask Huan to turn them over to the police."

"That hasn't been an option since Evilsizer and the Skidmores killed Fan Zhou. I'm going to make sure they're not tortured before they're put out of their misery. In an hour, it will all be over. Since you're awake why don't you get dressed and pack for us?"

"All right," Genny said. Luke stood and she crawled out of bed, following him to the door. "Tell me you're not going alone."

"I told Andy that he and his men could stay in the country with Patty and Vern. But Andy asked to see this through to the end."

A soft knock on the door sounded and Andy could be heard to say that Wong and Chen had arrived. Luke hugged Genny and kissed her.

"I know I can't talk you out of this, so please be careful, Harper."

"When I get back, I'll take you to breakfast because you have to eat," he said, his right hand flattening to her tummy. "Then we'll go get our train tickets home."

With that, Luke opened the door and was gone.

CHAPTER 40

AMIDST THE MAJESTY THAT WAS SAN FRANCISCO, THE BELL tower of Old St. Mary's Church on California Street in Chinatown, tolled the hour with five chimes. The early morning air hinted of another spectacular day. Except for the faint drifting of music from Pacific Street's dance halls and boisterous voices in the beer joints of the Barbary Coast, most of the city by the Bay was still asleep.

"Two of my men are bringing them up now," Huan said to Luke outside the inconspicuous shed. Andy joined Wong and Chen near the door. "The leaders of all five fingers of the Fist worked to make this capture. They have split the reward you, Joe and I offered."

"Good. You are a force to be reckoned with, Huan," Luke said with respect and nodded. "I can take Genny home without looking over my shoulder. I'm in your debt."

"No, Luke, I am in yours," Huan replied. "With a horse ranch in the country as home my wife and children will be safe, and you have broadened my horizons."

On that, the friends shook hands.

Huan led the way into the hut. Mara Sinclair stood blindfolded against the back wall as Seth Evilsizer, also blindfolded, hoisted himself out of a dank hole in the dirt floor. One of the Fist leaders referred to him as *Scarecrow* telling a soldier to put him next to *Spider*.

The two captives looked oddly surreal. Hell, the whole ordeal involving them had been oddly surreal. The first thing Luke noticed was their stench. The second observation was Seth Evilsizer's missing ear. He was bald and bloody, his clothes filthy and his boots worn and dirty. Around the blindfold, Mara Sinclair's face was blighted by bitterness. The ends of her hair stuck out from underneath a tattered black hat, her dress sagging and her shoes missing.

In addition to the blindfolds, their hands and wrists were bound. The blood on the ropes said they'd been struggling to free themselves for quite a while prior to climbing a ladder out of the long-deserted opium den. Two of Huan's leaders removed the blindfolds.

Monsters unmasked.

"The scarecrow and the spider," Huan said, his tone and face grim with abhorrence.

"Luke Harper," came a strange, almost womanish voice from the murderer who had plagued Luke and Genny for months. "We finally meet."

"On the day you die," Luke said, standing on the opposite side of the hole from them.

"But I'm leaving with you, Luke," Mara said. "Right, darling?"

"Wrong," Luke replied coldly. "You're as greedy, selfish and insane as Evilsizer."

"I'm not insane." Evilsizer's voice dropped, and his thin lips pulled back over crooked yellow teeth. "You said you wanted to kill him, Mara. Do it!"

Streetlights suddenly dimmed and went out.

Horses on the street whinnied.

Rats in the underground den scurried.

"Fall and die!" Mara shrilled.

Screaming oaths of hatred, tied hands drawn up in front of her like a witch's talons, she was a nightmarish vision. Lunging at Luke, Mara's claws raked his jaw and throat, but she failed to make him fall into the deep pit. Luke merely stepped back, letting her fall face first across the opening of the underground den. When her chin caught on the edge of the hole nearest his and Huan's boots Mara's jaw slammed shut, her teeth cutting off her acid tongue. Her knees hit the opposite edge with such force that her torso bent backward like a tree twig into the gaping hole.

The sound of Mara Sinclair's neck breaking was deafening. Dead on impact, her unseeing eyes bulged nearly out of her head as blood oozed from her nose, mouth and ears.

"I hated her and tripped her for you, Harper." Evilsizer's smile was sinister, his laugh maniacal. "I saved the Chinaman the trouble of killing her. You both owe me."

"That bitch tripped herself and suffered the same death as the husbands she murdered," Luke snarled, swiping the blood off his jaw with the back of his hand.

Two of Huan's soldiers rolled the lifeless killer over. One man held on to her while the other one sliced Mara's throat from ear-to-ear. Repositioning and releasing her, the guards allowed her body to bend and fall to the hell below.

"You are owed death," Huan said to Evilsizer and nodded at his men.

"No. No. Wait!" Evilsizer's horrific grin faded into a grimace. "If you take me to the Barbary Coast, I'll lead you to where I buried the watch, pearls and a cat charm I took off the bodies of the Morgans and the Chinese housekeeper. What do you say, Harper?"

Recalling Genny telling him of her grandfather's missing watch and Garnet's pearls, Luke grabbed Evilsizer by the lapels on his coat and nearly lifted him off his feet.

"I say that if you're lying, I'll cut your throat myself," Luke snarled.

"I'm telling the truth," Evilsizer said, his chewed fingernails scratching at his scrawny, dirty neck. "The valuables are hidden in Dead Man's Alley, not far from the Black-Eyed Susan. If I'm telling the truth you have to let me live. If I'm lying, you can kill me."

"You do not dictate to us what we will or won't do," Luke said, and released Evilsizer with a shove that sent him stumbling backward toward Huan's men who knocked him forward again.

"Shanghai him like the soaplocks?" Huan asked Luke, the real question was in seeking Luke's agreement that Evilsizer was to die whether there were valuables found or not.

"Yes! Yes!" Evilsizer said, bobbing his head up and down. "Shanghai me."

"Yeah." Luke looked at Huan. "Like the Skidmores."

"Meet us in Dead Man's Alley," Huan told the soldiers of the Monkey's Fist who immediately gagged Evilsizer and yanked a hood over his head. Grabbing his arms, they shoved him out a back door to an orange wagon in the alley and were gone.

When Luke emerged from the front of the shed with Huan and the others, he glanced at his pocketwatch. It was ten after five. The men spoke for a moment under a sun rising in the east that had brightened the sky to a pale blue. In the distance, trolleys could be heard leaving the car barns as surely as sacks of potatoes, onions and turnips were being unloaded in the produce district. With no sign of a storm on the horizon the abrupt and terrible roar didn't make sense.

Suddenly, Luke felt the earthquake.

His first and only thought was of Genny.

The horses and rats had sensed it first when the streetlamps went out. Now, the quake struck San Francisco with the full force of a tidal wave. The rumbling of the earthquake, like that of a thousand freight trains, devoured all normal sounds. With the fury of an erupting volcano, the quake's violent shaking demolished and devastated. Like never before, the city by the Bay was suffering a blow of immense, unimaginable and deadly magnitude.

For about forty seconds the earthquake intensified.

Heaving and surging, the bricks in the street parted like the Red Sea tearing open long trenches. The sky fell as shops and houses splintered and collapsed crushing men, women and children, horses, dogs and cats. Shifting its jagged path, the quake barreled toward Luke and Huan forcing them onto opposite sides of the deeply fracturing street with nowhere safe to run.

Somehow Luke had to get through this cataclysmic horror and find Genny.

Church bells clanging, chimneys crashing, people screaming, cornices breaking, buildings crumbling, animals running, the earthquake maimed and killed and destroyed.

Suddenly the erratic shaking ceased.

"I'm going back for Genny!" Luke yelled to Huan.

"Yes! Family!" Huan shouted.

Luke and Andy raced toward the Runabout as Huan and his men took off in the direction of Li's.

The earthquake gave them ten seconds.

Just as Luke reached his vehicle, the violent jarring struck a second time. Countless tons of earth moved, dropping the rear of the Runabout into a sinkhole. Luke jumped to avoid being sucked into the hole as the quake waved a seven-hundred-pound telegraph pole like a toothpick.

"Andy! Run!" Luke shouted, seeing that Andy was in line with the pole.

Before Andy could move, the telegraph pole crashed down on him and the Runabout. Avoiding cracks opening in the rippling street, Luke ran to him. Reaching between metal and wood tore open the back of Luke's left hand from index finger to wrist. Pressing bloody fingertips to Andy's neck, there was no pulse. Andy had been instantly crushed to death.

"Dammit!" Luke yelled in utter disbelief to no one. To everyone.

Almost unconsciously, he wrapped his monogrammed handkerchief around his bleeding left hand, hardly noticing how quickly the white turned to red. Had Huan or his men been killed, too? There was no sign of them. The wooden shed, where Mara Sinclair had fallen to her death, had been reduced to a pile of splinters. Was Evilsizer alive or dead? Or free?

Without warning, the quake threw Luke backward, landing him several feet away on the rolling street where the rapidly breaking bricks resembled a gruesome sneer of cracked teeth. Like a Great White in the ocean, the earthquake opened its jaws and swallowed Luke. In the next second, the collapsing of the brick trench swam his way.

CHAPTER 41

"DEAR GOD, PLEASE LET LUKE BE ALIVE," GENNY PRAYED ON her knees beside the bed.

She judged the second phase of the earthquake to have lasted almost thirty seconds. The overpowering fear of having nowhere safe to run, nowhere safe to hide had rooted her to the floor. Utterly at the mercy of the quake, she clutched the quilt on the bed and pulled herself to stand on unsteady feet. An eerie stillness reigned for a moment before deafening explosions split the silence. Stumbling around shifted furniture she made it to the bay window.

Everywhere towering flames burst blood red against the blue sky.

Her foremost prayer was to find Luke.

Thanks to Luke, she was dressed and ready to leave. Grabbing her purse, she remembered him telling her not to carry her carpetbag. Leaving their bags behind, she hurried out of the suite and into the wide-open corridor.

Where had Luke and Andy gone with Wong and Chen?

Other hotel guests, still in their nightclothes and rubbing their eyes, stumbled out of their rooms. Smelling smoke, Genny also recalled Luke telling her to take the stairs in case of fire. On New Year's Eve, she'd told Luke she'd pretend there was a fire and take the stairs only to pull him into the rising room with her. How she wished she could grab him right this minute. With that thought she flew down the staircase. He might be hurt and unable to come to her.

Near the bottom of the stairs, she paused to catch her breath. Sheer bedlam of panicking people replaced the routine order of the hotel. No sign of her fiancé. Harper would be cutting a calm and controlled swath though this pandemonium like no one else could...if only he would.

"Give me Vesuvius!" Enrico Caruso bellowed in the lobby.

Not far from her the famous tenor, clad in his night-shirt and covered with bits of plaster, carried an auto-graphed photograph of Teddy Roosevelt.

"San Francisco is one 'ell of a place!" Caruso boomed at no one in particular as he headed toward the Palm Court.

Straining her eyes and wishing with every fiber in her body to see Luke, he just wasn't there to see. Crossing the familiar lobby without Luke added excruciating loneliness to Genny's all-out terror. Maneuvering her way through the Palm Court, when she exited the hotel and stepped onto Market Street, she stopped with a gasp.

Mass chaos reigned in the once magnificent city by the Bay.

Dead lay in the street. Throngs of half-asleep folks wandered aimlessly, others ran in petrified terror, some attempted to help injured people and animals. Bewildered children cried, clinging to confused parents. A man across the street screamed that City Hall was in shambles. A trolley car driver yelled that at least a dozen fires were burning out of control.

"Two fires here on Market Street alone!" a policeman shouted in return.

Above countless rooftops black smoke billowed from

the fires. Drawn by four large horses and manned by four firemen, a steam powered fire engine clanged furiously.

Stunned, Genny stood unmoving. Saddened, tears rolled down her cheeks.

The three-lamp streetlight, under which Luke had first kissed her, leaned precariously. A horse pulling an orange wagon, without a driver, careened into an automobile. The teetering streetlight caught her attention again as it crashed taking a fleeing man and woman down with it. The shake of a policeman's head said the couple hadn't survived. A tragic loss amidst what had to be incalculable heartbreak unfolding across the city.

It hadn't been fifteen minutes since the earthquake had jackslapped the city when a series of jolting aftershocks hit. Genny stumbled sideways as marble, brick and concrete smashed into the street and onto the sidewalk around her.

An earthquake left one with a numbed awareness of complete vulnerability.

"Miss Morgan, please come back inside," Patrick pleaded, holding the door open for her. Smudges and concern equally covering his freckled face, the bellboy repeated, "Please."

"Patrick," she began as she reentered the Palm Court, "have you seen Mr. Harper?"

"No, ma'am," he replied, just as Harrison Jeffrey shouted his name. Hurrying toward the manager, Patrick called over his shoulder, "Please stay inside until Mr. Harper comes for you."

Genny whispered, "Luke, I need you."

"The ball, the rising room and together again." Seth Evilsizer slithered from behind a large palm tree, a maniacal gleam in his faded brown eyes. "Surely this third time will be the charm."

"One step closer and I'll scream," she warned, wondering if the earthquake or the Monkey's Fist had taken his left ear. "There's a policeman directly across the street."

"I have the man you need, but he's all tied up," Evilsizer snickered, his face a mask of evil. "If we don't reach Mara in the next ten minutes, she has orders to cut Harper's throat."

"I don't believe you."

"Scream then. On a delightful day like today, no one will care or come to your aid," he said with a surly tone and pursed lips. "By the by, Mara will push your fiancé off my favorite fishing pier to the sharks. You won't even have his body to bury or grave to visit."

Evilsizer turned and slunk away from her. Genny racked her brain as to what Evilsizer had said about his favorite pier that day in the rising room. She whirled around and raced to Patrick.

"Patrick, which fishing pier is just over a half mile from here?"

"Uh...Pier Seven," he replied. "Why?"

"Thank you for everything, Patrick." Giving him a quick hug, she took her gun and knife out of her crocheted green purse. "If by some miracle Mr. Harper comes looking for me, I'll be at Pier Seven."

"Patrick, did she take her purse with her?" Luke asked, running back across the Palm Court toward the street with the bellboy on his heels.

"No, sir, but she took her weapons," Patrick said, wide-eyed as he pulled her purse out of his pocket. At the door, he pointed a shaking finger. "Head straight down Market Street toward those columns of smoke. At the waterfront turn left and Pier Seven will be dead ahead."

After climbing out of the hole he'd been dropped in seconds before the jagged jaw of bricks could crush him Luke had swiped blood out of his eye, from a gash at his temple, and glanced right and left. He'd spied a terrified horse with reins tangled in the hands of its owner who'd been decapitated by a pile of steel and cement. Luke started toward the animal as an onslaught of rock and mortar slammed to the ground covering what remained of the owner's corpse. Luke freed and mounted the horse. Never had he ridden more dangerously than he did on his way to the Palace Hotel.

"Keep your eyes peeled for her, Patrick!" Luke yelled now, jumping back onto the horse.

"Absolutely, sir! Godspeed!" Patrick placed his hands to his head. "God help us all."

Luke rode toward the waterfront, dodging scurrying people, cracks in the street, wandering animals, dangerous sinkholes, and mounds of debris, wondering how it had all come down to this moment. People trapped in wreckage screamed for help as others tried to dig them out. Teetering towers toppled from buildings, chimneys crumbled, houses creaked and leaned precariously. One after another, explosions thundered each bringing new eruptions of shooting flames.

A conflagration. Because these fires would not...could not be stopped.

As the horse galloped toward Pier Seven, Luke recalled once thinking that all of his friends were in Biloxi, and he was on his own here in San Francisco. But he'd made great friends here, too, and now he didn't know if they were alive or dead. He didn't spot the Johnson brothers fighting any of the fires he passed, and he hadn't seen Joe Sanchez since the opera ended. Saddened by Andy's death, Luke prayed his friends in Chinatown and in the country were safe. Whatever the circumstances, for now anyway, he was on his own again.

He had to find his best friend or life wouldn't be worth living. Genny had to be alive. The love of his life just had to be alive.

On Steuart Street, a block from the waterfront, a place with a sign in the yard stating *Lodging House* was engulfed in flames. It was just part of the smoke Patrick had pointed out to him from the Palace Hotel. Firemen were on the steadily worsening scene frantically hooking their hose up to a hydrant across the street from the lodging house. They turned on the valve and braced themselves for the rush of water. A muddy drip trickled out of the hose.

And yet, the ocean was literally at their fingertips.

"Turn the valve off," a fireman yelled. "It's no use."

In a blazing path of destruction, flames had spread from the lodging house to the ships and piers. Luke nudged the horse from a gallop into an all-out run. Hearing the lapping waters of the Bay on his right and feeling the fires of hell on his left, Pier Seven indeed loomed dead ahead.

"WHERE IS LUKE?" Genny asked.

"I told you the plan is to meet up with him and Mara at my pier," Evilsizer said.

From a fire near the fallen three-lamp streetlight, Evilsizer had snatched up a torch-like piece of wood. Making her drive the orange wagon, they had careened through the annihilation of the financial district to the burning waterfront. Holding the horse's reins stretched Genny's arms forward and Evilsizer had touched the flame to her left side several times, gaffawing when she cried out in pain.

Getting to Pier Seven within ten minutes was all that mattered. Genny forced her mind away from the torture along her ribcage and recalled Luke stepping on the hem of her gown the night of the ball near this same pier. Her gown had ripped along the right side that night and Luke had teased her about the sideshow.

She strained her eyes trying to locate the man she loved with all her heart.

When Evilsizer grabbed the reins and jerked the horse to a stop, Genny deftly slipped her hands into the side pockets of her dress to check on her weapons. Luke had taught her a little trick of shooting through the crocheted material of her purse if necessary. The gun would shoot just as well through her pocket.

"Get out," Evilsizer said at Pier Seven, bringing the torch against her wrist this time.

Genny hated giving him the satisfaction of hearing her cry out. But when he burned her wrist a second time a muffled scream escaped her. Evilsizer laughed maniacally.

Grasping a rope and her right arm Evilsizer yanked her out of the wagon, forcing her across the sandy beach to the water's edge. She couldn't shoot him until she found out where Mara was holding Luke. As Evilsizer dragged her under a pier engulfed in flames overhead, chilly water soaked Genny's shoes, ankles and hem of her dress. She was torn between fighting harder and fearing he might deliver a blow to her stomach if she did.

"If you were smart enough to figure out my favorite fishing pier and confided such in that bellboy and if Harper isn't dead, he might be smart enough to find you and pay me a ransom. My sweet Mara and I were going for a million until the earthquake hit. But no matter, Mara said Harper always has plenty of money on him," Evilsizer said, hauling her further into the Bay. "Dead or alive, I'll take that diamond, the crown jewel of all, that he gave you."

"What do you mean Harper might find me?" Genny asked, now knee deep into the cold ocean water. If the gun got wet, would it still shoot? She dragged her feet. "You said Luke was tied up and Mara Sinclair would kill him if we didn't get here in ten minutes."

"That murdering bitch is dead," Evilsizer said in falsetto. Then almost in the same breath using his normal voice he said, "Stop calling Mara a bitch and shut up, Selma, or I'll burn you alive."

Genny's thoughts whirled with relief that Luke was not in their clutches.

But as surely as the earthquake had erupted, Seth Evilsizer was erupting with full blown pyromaniac, psychopath insanity. Throwing his torch onto a pile of floating, burning debris he jerked Genny against a piling. The salt-water lapped around her mid-thighs just below her pocket. Bringing his face inches from Genny's and both his skeletal hands gripping her, this monster was horrifying.

Turning the bloody left side of his head toward her, he said, "The Monkey's Fist captured Mara and me due to mistaken identity. I bravely convinced the Chinese to admit their error and they agreed to let us go. But Harper sliced off my ear and cut Mara's throat. I'll tie you to this piling and we'll see what Harper thinks about that."

"You know what Harper will think about it," Genny said.

The second Evilsizer released her and snapped the rope taut in front of her face, she backed away from him.

"Since your dearly departed grandfather couldn't swim, I doubt you can. But I can't drown you until I ransom you." There was that skin crawling laugh again as she continued retreating.

Aim dead center, squeeze the trigger and always shoot to kill.

The gunshot reverberated, knocking Evilsizer sideways. Genny's dress pocket caught fire as Luke had warned that her purse might. Nerves jangling, heart thudding, Genny had the presence of mind to dip down in the water and douse the flame.

With blood spreading across the right shoulder, a crazed look of astonishment shone in Evilsizer's eyes. He sloshed toward her, teeth bared in a yellow snarl.

Genny pulled the trigger again but when the wet gun didn't fire, she instantly turned toward the shore. However, her dress tangled around her legs slowing her escape. Then just as it had once before, seaweed stole her feet out from under her. A wave shoved her face down into the water then sucked her further into the Bay. With strength she didn't know she had, Genny swam with all her might. A brief image of swimming to Luke in the pond floated across her mind, but it was Evilsizer who caught her this time.

"So Harper taught you to swim and to...to...shoot," Evilsizer sputtered, shoving her against another piling, this one, too, in flames overhead where it supported the pier.

She punched him hard where his ear had been with her right fist and plowed her left fist into his gunshot shoulder. Shrieking in agony he seized her right wrist. Cinching the rope just above her right elbow, then her left and around her waist he effectively trapped her to the piling.

Genny concentrated on the white dragon knife that brought strength and good luck to those who were worthy. Sliding her left hand into her pocket and back out, she gripped the knife handle. Praying she was worthy she stabbed Evilsizer in his paunchy stomach. He doubled over, spat blood and in a sickening move slowly pulled the knife out. Trying to turn the knife toward Genny's stomach, the blade sliced deeply into Evilsizer's palm. With a scream as bloody as his head and stomach, shoulder and hand he aimlessly hurled the knife toward the shore.

Tied to the pier and out of weapons, Genny feared she was about to burn to death like Garnet if not drown like Grandpa. In the graying sky, black smoke billowed from ships ablaze and buildings in flames. With the conflagration of the city, the inferno on this pier was the least of anyone's concerns.

"Blast you and Harper to hell." Evilsizer grimaced, bleeding profusely.

Blood in the water, reminded her of Luke teasing her about sharks. No fins were splitting the surface...yet. But leopard sharks in particular were plentiful in the Bay. Splintering wood fell in flames from above and smacked the water next to them. Breathing heavily, Evilsizer snatched up a piece of the fiery debris.

Blood coating his teeth and dribbling down his chin, he said, "Looks like your fiancé won't be rescuing you or paying me a ransom, so you'll give me that diamond now or I'll burn your hand off to get it."

Genny turned her diamond to the inside of her palm a split second before Evilsizer dragged her left hand up through the ropes, raking off skin but leaving the ring.

Loving Luke with all her heart and certain never to see him again, Genny clenched her fist around her diamond and cried out in soul deep sorrow and pain, "Luke!"

"Turn around," came a deadly calm voice.

Evilsizer swiveled, torch arm swinging wide as he faced the beach and unblocked Genny's view. At the water's edge, gun drawn, murderous rage glinted in Luke's cold green eyes.

"Watch her burn, Harper," Evilsizer choked out bringing the torch back toward Genny.

"Bullshit," Luke replied.

The second gunshot to reverberate the pier that day drilled a hole in the middle of Seth Evilsizer's forehead. The impact slammed Evilsizer and his torch into the floating debris of fire. Burning wood caught him under the arms, supporting him in a scarecrow-like stance with wounds eerily similar to the straw man they'd used for target practice. Lapping waves closed the blazing, crackling wood around Evilsizer from all sides catching his dead body on fire.

Luke had already holstered his gun, pulled his Bowie knife out of his boot and was wading into the water. The collapsing pilings swayed precariously as Genny valiantly struggled with cold, wet fingers to untie the ropes. Reaching her, Luke sliced through the ropes.

"Good job, little *wolf*," Luke whispered.

Genny's arms circled his neck as he swept her up in his arms. As he carried her out of the Bay, she kissed the cheek where he'd been clawed and rested her head on his shoulder. A single ray of sunlight glinted off the white dragon knife lying next to her crocheted green purse on the sandy shore. Holding the woman who meant more to him than life itself, Luke kissed Genny's forehead. Her scraped left hand lay over his heart, her diamond ring glittering, as the monogrammed handkerchief on his injured left hand gently protected the burns along her ribs. Genny's lilac cat eyes shut as Luke watched Pier Seven collapse in flames.

Seth Evilsizer burned in a funeral pyre before the Bay fed him to the arriving sharks.

CHAPTER 42

July twentieth, the day of the wedding dawned without a cloud in the light blue sky. All morning and throughout the afternoon it had been a whirlwind of activities with Phoebe, Mattie, Chloe, Megan, and Audrey.

Genny now knew why Luke had been so determined in his precautions to protect her. Once they were safe in Biloxi, he'd confided that Audrey had had a twin sister, Alice. The girls had been kidnapped at the age of three by a radical political foe of Steven's.

It happens out of the blue. You don't see it coming.

The D.C. police had caught the kidnapper within twenty-four hours but returned only Audrey alive. All Audrey could tell anyone was that the scary man made Alice stop crying. The family had grieved and pressed on but would never forget the loss of that precious little girl.

Genny sat before an oval looking glass on the riverboat called *Moonstone*, docked in the Mississippi Sound. Momentarily by herself, she let her mind drift. Rob and Chloe had been at the New Orleans train station when the *Sunset Limited* chugged to a stop. Thus, Luke's brother and his wife had been the first to hear of their engagement. Genny was charmed by their drawls, so similar to Luke's. Rob, tall with a warm smile, had the Harper confidence about him. Handsome, though not as dashingly gorgeous or as muscular as Luke, the family resemblance was strong. With a look of profound relief and love, Rob had hugged his younger brother as Chloe, in all her Southern genteel charm, embraced Genny. Chloe had asked to sit in the back seat of the shiny new Cadillac with Genny so they could visit on the way home. Roscoe, who had proved to be an excellent traveling companion in their sleeping cars on the trains, rode up front curled at Luke's feet.

The foursome briefly discussed the earthquake. But the somber mood gave way to laughter when the brothers reminisced about adventures from their past. Luke smiled over his shoulder at Genny as they talked of the future that included her. This was a new family side of Luke that made Genny's heart sing with happiness. Rob was funny and friendly and Chloe, blonde and exquisite, had a catchy laugh. Thoroughly enjoying the ninety-mile trip, Genny felt as if she'd known Rob and Chloe forever by the time they arrived in Biloxi.

Rob had driven straight to Luke's French provincial mansion on the Sound. With the ocean just beyond one side of the road, black wrought iron fencing surrounded the palatial estate on the other side. Two huge white pillars securing wrought iron gates, opened to a wide circular drive. Coming into view stood a fabulous white house. Four chimneys rose from the towering black tile roof. Along the second story, was the Creole inspired wrap-around balcony along with several sets of French doors and tall windows framed by green shutters. On the ground level, matching green shutters decorated six, ten-foot-tall windows on either side of massive double front doors.

Cruising around a three-tiered flowing water fountain in the center of the drive, Rob stopped the Cadillac at the stone porch. There, black porch lamps framed the green double doors which were adorned by tall side windows and an overhead large, half moon panel of thick cut glass.

Through those glass panes, twinkling chandeliers beckoned one to enter this indescribably beautiful home.

Rob advised Luke his automobiles were ready for use and that he and Chloe would meet them later for supper at the sugarcane plantation. Luke let Roscoe jump out of the Cadillac and then helped Genny from the back seat. Luke told Genny that Jasper and Justine, a Negro couple who'd worked in one capacity or another for the Harper family for years, had said they would be honored to come from the Harper House Resort to work for Luke and Genny in their new home. No sooner had Luke smiled at an astonished Genny than the couple rushed out of the house to meet her. Jasper ruffled Roscoe's fur as Justine waved Rob and Chloe on, assuring them that they'd take excellent care of Luke and Genny and Roscoe.

"Jasper and Justine were Mattie's idea," Luke said as the loving black couple, whose big brown eyes were as welcoming as their smiles, entered the house ahead of them with a couple of bags and Roscoe. "Mattie always looked out for me and now she's looking out for you, too."

"If Mattie's anything like Rob and Chloe, I'll love her."

"She's a redheaded spitfire. Kinda reminds me of a mischief maker I know. Ready to go inside and see the place that Mattie says I need a woman's touch?"

"Luke," Genny said with an emotional gulp, pausing between the fountain and the porch somehow trying to take it all in. "With or without a woman's touch you've built a breathtakingly beautiful house. Truly, it's nothing short of a palace. But instead of cold and daunting like those on Nob Hill, it's warm and inviting. It's perfect and I love the forest green shutters."

"The shutters are a coincidence. It'll be perfect when you make it into our home." He took her hand and giving her a gentle tug he chuckled. "We're gonna need a lot of furniture."

Inside the two-story entrance hall, the chandeliers glittered. Rising from the marble floor to the towering ceiling, two massive marble pillars flanked a glorious staircase centered in the enormous foyer. A large, empty parlor was on the right and to their left was a paneled study that Luke said he planned to make into his office. Luke led the way through the open entry hall past an elegant dining room that could seat twenty, to the single largest kitchen Genny had ever seen.

"It's designed after the Harper House Restaurant's kitchen," Justine said, standing at a long marble topped, island-like table, preparing a midday snack to tide them over until supper.

Taking in the windows, counters, cupboards, huge stove, and a large sink with running water, Genny managed to say, "It's a magnificent kitchen."

"Roscoe here, looks like a magnificent dog if ever there was one," Jasper said as he set a bowl of food down next to a bowl of water and watched with delight as Roscoe ate.

"Thanks, Jasper, for seeing to him," Luke said and turned to Genny. "There are six or seven bedrooms upstairs. Want to see ours?"

"Yes," Genny whispered, overwhelmed as she followed him out of the kitchen.

"Come back when you've had a look around and eat," Justine called.

"We sure will, Justine. Thank you," Luke replied.

Luke pointed out a wing off the kitchen where Jasper and Justine had just recently taken up residence. Then instead of returning to the open foyer and grand staircase, Luke led the way down another wide hallway to a mahogany paneled room with a decorative wrought iron door.

"A rising room?" Genny asked, eyes wide. "Why am I not surprised?"

Luke opened the gate-like door, and they kissed all the way to the second floor. Leaving the rising room, Luke escorted Genny down a wide hallway past three of the six guest bedrooms and all of which had their own private baths.

Stepping into what would be her master bedroom suite with Luke, Genny gazed across a shining hardwood floor to French doors overlooking the sparkling blue Mississippi Sound. Luke pointed out his and her closets and opened the door to her closet. Since the four trunks had already arrived, Genny found her beautiful gowns, skirts, blouses, capes, and jackets all carefully pressed and hanging in her closet. Her delicate lingerie, colorful hats, matching purses, slippers, and shoes shared the space with a pair of newly polished, old red cowboy boots. With a lump in her throat and tears in her eyes, Genny smiled up at Luke. He winked and showed her their spacious bathroom with a clawfoot tub big enough for two.

Across the hall, where the grand staircase met the second floor, a sunny sitting room and a library full of books were separated by decorative white pillars. Genny immediately noticed that the sitting room was painted lilac and Luke admitted that was not a coincidence. Genny then recognized her few books had been given a shelf of their own amongst books about Mississippi, business, riverboats, horses, automobiles, and classics including *Moby-Dick*. French doors opened onto the black wrought iron balcony overlooking meticulously manicured grounds. In the distance, horses grazed in acres of green pasture surrounded by a white fence.

"Is that Etalon and Esprit I see among the other horses?" Genny asked.

"Yes." Luke moved behind her, wrapped his arms around her and flattened his hands to her tummy. "But you can't ride Esprit until after our baby comes."

"I know." With that, Genny turned in his arms and wept with unbridled joy.

"Aww come on," Luke said with a chuckle. "You'll be riding again before you know it."

"Harper," she said with a choke in her voice. "This…

this...all of this—" She waved her hand with the large diamond on it while clutching the front of his jacket with her other hand. "It's...beyond a dream come true. It's far more than I could have ever imagined." Tears rolled down her cheeks as she said, "Being pregnant with your baby is the very essence of new hope."

"That lifetime of happiness you said you saw in my eyes is there because I found you." With a gentle finger he tipped up her chin and gazed into her lilac eyes. "With all the strength and energy in my body I will keep you happy forever in our new life."

"I promise you'll never regret inviting me to come home with you." Genny's chin quivered on his finger. "I will spend the rest of my life making you happy."

"Let's pick out a bedroom for the nursery."

A soft sigh escaped Genny now as she fondly remembered choosing the baby's room. When Luke had suggested having a door cut between the master bedroom and nursery, Genny nodded and hugged him. She'd freshened up in their master bathroom and then ridden next to Luke for the first time in the Rolls Royce, known as the Silver Ghost. He'd driven her along the picturesque Sound and turned down a road canopied by oak trees dripping with moss. As the sprawling manor home on the sugarcane plantation had come into view, she saw the children first. Before Luke called out their names, Genny knew exactly who Charles and Megan and little Audrey were as they came running and waving. Then Luke's parents; John and Phoebe, as well as Rob and Chloe, Mattie and Steven, spilled onto a wide veranda to welcome them home.

After being called into the house by a butler to enjoy a sumptuous supper, a silver-haired John had stood tall and dignified at one end of the long dining room table. Phoebe, whose eyes and coloring matched Luke's, stood at the other end. Luke took his place on his father's right, with Genny standing beside him. After John made a toast to their engagement Luke announced, as planned with

Genny, there would be an addition to the Harper family around Christmas time.

Spirited congratulations with cheers and clapping ensued around the long supper table.

John shook his son's hand then embraced Genny. Phoebe came to them, hugging Luke and whispering thank you in Genny's ear when they embraced. Everyone was seated, supper was served by the Harper's long-time staff and immediately the conversation was all about a wedding; when and where? Between bites of prime rib, catfish, collard greens, fried potatoes, and buttery biscuits, Luke grinned at Genny, and she was sure her heart would burst with love and happiness. One day, if she were ever so lucky, she just might be considered part of the inner circle of this once-in-a-lifetime family.

The *Moonstone's* horn blew signaling the arrival of more guests. It brought Genny back from recalling her first wonderful day in Biloxi to this sensational day of her wedding. Audrey entered the room and handed Genny a letter Luke had asked her to deliver from Joe Sanchez.

Dear Luke and Genevieve, All of your San Francisco friends send their best wishes and we are with you in spirit as you celebrate your wedding in Biloxi. For remaining here an extra week to see us all safely settled and for your generous contribution to the fund for earthquake survivors, I am awed and grateful. It's been almost three months since bidding you farewell and the city has been slowly on the mend. But it's a sad fact that the Palace Hotel and Grand Opera House are gone forever along with most of the financial, mission, market, and retail districts. Hard to believe the bells of Old St. Mary's Church will never chime again. The fires that took the mansions of the Big Four and devastated Nob Hill spared Harriett Peak's home. I will not miss the Barbary Coast, but grieve the loss of Chinatown. I predict the hardworking Chinese will rebuild better than ever. I saw Huan yesterday. He and Jia and their twins are adapting nicely to life on a ranch. They named the boy Sun and the girl Song. Ying and Tricky got married, have a dog and are thriving in the country as well. Happy to have so many new neighbors, Patty and Vern continue to dote on Bruno and the little mare they named Lucky. Back to the city; what's being called the Ham-and-Eggs Fire was started by a woman cooking breakfast who didn't know she had a toppled chimney and a flue broken by the quake. It eventually burned an area larger than any of the other fifty conflagrations in San Francisco. All-in-all, we've heard the earthquake and fires claimed as many as 3,000 lives and destroyed at least 28,000 buildings. With our antiquated cisterns and mains broken by the quake, our firemen were nothing short of heroic in stopping as many fires as they did. Speaking of firemen, after the earthquake, the Johnson brothers were awarded the abandoned ten-acre Skidmore farm by authorities grateful not to have had a burned countryside in addition to their city. Mike and Jimmy purchased additional land and their property now borders that of Grace and Ruth whom they are still courting. Last, but I hope not least, since my house suffered little damage Suki and I are there and engaged. But as many as 225,000 folks were left homeless, so we volunteer twice a week at one of the numerous refugee camps. Your bellboy friend, Patrick, was hired to help oversee that massive operation and says hello to his favorite hotel guests. At the Jefferson Square refugee camp yesterday we heard someone singing, 'There'll be a Hot Time in the Old Town Tonight'. Thus, life goes on in the city by the Bay. Your friend, Joe Sanchez.

Genny wiped away the tear on her cheek and placed the letter on the dressing table.

"Aunt Genny?" Audrey closed a new edition of *Heidi*, which Genny had given her as a thank you for being in the wedding. Coming to Genny's side, she asked, "Are you all right?"

"Yes," Genny said to the sweet seven-year-old dressed in lilac and ready to be one of her two flower girls. "I'm just so happy to be marrying your Uncle Luke today."

"I'm really happy, too. Will you move out of Grandpa and Grandma's house into Uncle Luke's house now?" Audrey's blue eyes sparkled, and red ringlets bounced as she twined a slender arm around Genny's neck.

"Yes, I'll be moving in with your Uncle Luke," Genny said.

With a nod to tradition, but mostly out of respect for his parents, she had been staying with John and Phoebe. Luke had often whisked Genny away to the magnificent mansion for 'decorating and furnishing' purposes. Occasionally, they had a dance lesson in preparation for their wedding waltz. Each time they were alone they'd made love but had not yet spent the night together there. Luke assured her that he would lose his mind if he didn't have her for the whole night and *damn soon.* He'd even tried to talk her out of the wedding reception, but Genny had laughed, kissed him and said there had to be a reception.

"When I'm not in Washington, D.C., Mama or Papa can walk me to your and Uncle Luke's house here on the Sound," Audrey said. "I only live ten houses and a resort away you know."

"Yes, and I can come get you and walk with you, too," Genny said, loving the little girl so much and hugging her. The Winsteds lived five houses to the west of Harper House Resort. Her sprawling new home with Luke was five houses to the east, nearer the Biloxi Lighthouse. "I will look forward to every one of your visits, Audrey."

"The two of you are going to ruin Aunt Genny's beautiful wedding dress and veil," Mattie said to Genny and Audrey upon entering the cozy room.

"I don't think they care," Chloe said, her tinkling, catchy laugh making Genny smile as she and Megan followed Mattie into the room.

Standing, Genny held out her other arm to Megan and the pretty blonde flower girl rushed to her. Genny hugged her soon-to-be nieces as Mattie and Chloe swiped at their tears and smiled. Then they, too, joined in the hugging.

"Well, land's sake," Phoebe drawled, chic in purple lace as she stood in the doorway. "Steven says it's time for Charles to escort the mother of the groom to her seat and here I find all of you laughing or sobbing or mercy me, I don't know what you're doing."

"Come join us, Mama," Mattie said with a teary-eyed smile and holding out her arm.

It took Charles knocking and finally Steven cracking open the door to get Phoebe away from the other females and out to the parlor where two hundred guests anxiously awaited the entrance of the bride. As a ten-piece stringed ensemble played, Mattie maneuvered one of Genny's Gibson girl locks back into place while Chloe fluffed her delicate white veil. Megan straightened the long train of Genny's fabulous white lace gown and Audrey stood at-the-ready with two lilac baskets of white rose petals: one for her and one for her cousin, Megan.

John, the undisputed patriarch of the Harper clan, entered then. Clad in a black tuxedo, he gently shooed the matrons of honor and flower girls on their way and closed the door.

"All right now," John said when he and Genny were alone in the room. "My son-in-law has ushered in the last of the guests, a Harriett Peak, to her seat."

"Harriett made it." Genny clasped her hands under her chin in delight.

"Oh yes, indeed. Miss Peak informed me this is *the* wedding of the year," John replied as the gentle rocking under their feet indicated the riverboat was pulling away from the dock to cruise the Sound. Genny smiled at Luke's father, and he continued, "My grandson has seated my lovely wife. Your groom and my older son, as his best man, are about to take their places. Before we take ours," he paused and cleared his throat, "I'm here to tell you how it's going to be."

CHAPTER 43

"Please tell me," Genny said softly and took John's large, rough hands in hers.

"Miss Morgan, you are the most beautiful lady, inside and out, that Phoebe and I could have ever imagined for our youngest child," John said, and swallowed a catch in his deep voice. "We are honored to have you as our daughter. As part of the Harper family, you will always be cherished and protected. You will be loved by all of us until death do us part and that's exactly how it's going to be, Genny, my girl."

"Yes, sir," Genny whispered. Giving his hands a gentle squeeze, she said with conviction, "I will love all of you as long as I live. I will forever love and remain devoted to your son who gave me back the parts of my soul that I had lost."

They hugged each other deeply treasuring this moment and both loving Luke with all their hearts. Then from a marble table John picked up the bridal bouquet of lilac roses surrounding a single red rose blooming in the heart of this sentimental arrangement. Handing the fragrant spray of flowers to Genny, he opened the door, and she took his arm. The matrons of honor were waiting near the doors to the parlor which had been transformed into a glorious garden of white roses among rows of chairs adorned with lilac satin bows. The wedding march began and the guests, filling both sides of the aisle rose to their feet. The flower girls sprinkled white petals with the matrons of honor following behind them.

Straight ahead stood the most commandingly handsome Adonis to be found anywhere on Earth. Clad in black tuxedos, Rob, Steven and Charles stood with Luke to the right of the minister. Mattie, Chloe, Megan, and Audrey would soon stand on the left as they'd rehearsed.

"Best bet you've ever won, little brother," Rob said and nudged Luke.

"Goddess of the heart and moon, big brother," Luke said.

An ethereal vision in white glided toward Luke on the arm of his father who was beaming just as he had when walking Mattie down the aisle to Steven. Beneath the gossamer veil over her face, Genny's lilac eyes glistened, melting his heart. In the vee of her lace décolletage, the moonstone pendant sparkled against a hint of alabaster cleavage. So taken with the beautiful woman who was about to become his wife, Luke placed his right hand over his heart. At that gesture of his love, Genny's pink lips parted in the radiant smile which had captured him from the very beginning. The flower girls and their mothers took their places and then John brought Genny forward giving her to Luke.

Luke nodded at his father and mother, smiled at Genny and tucked her hand in his arm. She patted his arm and smiled up at him. The guests were seated, and the minister began speaking. When he asked Luke and Genny to face each other their eyes locked. Then he inquired if Luke would accept the vow to love Genevieve, comfort her, honor and keep her in sickness and in health and forsaking all others as long as they both should live.

"I do," Luke said with conviction. Rob handed Luke the wedding band and Luke took Genny's hand in his. Her hand, scraped raw under the burning pier, had healed as had her scorched wrist and ribcage. He silently pledged she would never be hurt like that again. Slipping the band next to the diamond ring on Genny's finger, Luke added for her ears alone, "As the bringer of light, I will always protect you from darkness."

At that precise moment, a yellow glow from the lighthouse shone in the windows. Genny gazed at Luke, amazement reflected in her eyes at his perfect timing. The minister turned to Genny then and she handed her bouquet to Mattie who in turn gave her Luke's wedding band. Mattie choked back a happy sob and Luke cocked a playful brow at his sister. Genny heard Chloe's catchy laugh and smiled up at Luke again who grinned. The minister cleared his throat and repeated the vows for Genny as to Lucas.

"I do," Genny said, and winked at him as he had at her so many times. She took Luke's left hand and meaningfully traced her thumb over the fading scar. The wounds to his jaw, neck and temple, like her injuries had long since healed. As she slipped the ring on Luke's finger she whispered her promise, "As the moonstone, I will always protect you on water and on land."

"By the power vested in me, I pronounce you husband and wife," the minister said.

Luke lifted Genny's veil to reveal the love of his life. He gently placed his hands to her petal soft cheeks and as the minister began saying he could kiss the bride, Luke was already doing so. Everyone cheered and clapped and dabbed at happy tears.

With a big smile, the minister said, "I present to you, Mr. and Mrs. Harper."

As Luke once again tucked her arm through his, Genny didn't think her feet were touching the white runner as her husband escorted her as Genevieve Moonstone Harper down the center aisle. The wedding party formed a receiving line outside the parlor where well wishes to the newlyweds and family were hearty and heartfelt.

The two hundred guests then filed into the riverboat's dining room. All meals prepared by the Harper House Restaurant were fit for royalty and the wedding supper was truly sumptuous. Everything from fresh seafood to filet mignon, from potato pancakes to candied yams, from fried green tomatoes to sweet corn on the cob, melted in the mouths of family and friends.

The three-tiered wedding cake was cut, and the groom and his bride politely fed each other a bite. Champagne flowed as music from the orchestra signaled it was time for the bride and groom's first dance. Doors to the parlor of roses, now cleared of the chairs, were thrown wide open and guests thronged around all four sides of the room. Luke escorted Genny to the parlor and the newlyweds took center stage for their first dance as a married couple.

"How lucky I am you waltzed into my life," Luke said.

"How lucky I am you didn't mind me stomping your feet."

How different this waltz was from their first one. And through all that had happened between the two dances, they had survived…revived…and thrived.

Luke led with gentle command and Genny followed with flawless grace. During the dance, Luke placed her arms around his neck and hugged her to the length of his body. Genny tilted up her chin and when his mouth lowered to hers, she felt the butterfly-like movement.

"Was that your stomach growling after our wedding supper?" Luke teased softly.

"That was your baby kicking for the first time," Genny said, smiling up at him. When he eased her back there was wetness at the corner of his eye. "Lucas Richard Harper, that's the very first tear you've had since I've known you."

"No, ma'am. It's just the first one I've let you see."
Holding her to his heart he said, "I love you, Mrs. Harper."

"I love you, Mr. Harper."

As planned, John cut in after the first dance and Luke danced with a beaming Phoebe. Then Rob and Steven danced with Genny as Luke did with Mattie and Chloe. Charles, a handsome heartbreaker in the making and always a good sport, danced with Megan. When Luke claimed his bride again, they noticed Audrey standing alone on the sideline. Luke motioned to Audrey and Genny held out an arm. Audrey hurried to the newlyweds who took her little hands and the three of them danced together. When the song ended, Audrey's small arms wrapped around the bride and groom as she hugged them with all her might. Through her own tears, Genny did not see a dry eye anywhere.

The next number was a fast one that Luke had requested just that day. He snared Genny's hand and recognizing the tune she picked up the train of her wedding gown.

"*It'll be a Hot Time in the ol' Town Tonight?*" she asked with a smile, ready for the lively jig.

"It will be when I get you alone," he said, taking her hand and twirling her around with just their fingertips touching. Bringing her back into his arms, he asked, "Ready to go home with me, babydoll?"

"Yes, you can carry your baby and me over the threshold, loverboy."

"Well, I'll sure try," he teased.

"Harper!" She laughed, the thickening of her waist barely discernible. She stopped dancing and placed her hands on her hips. "You'll try?"

The groom swept his bride up in his arms and carried her across the dancefloor. Women sighed and men cheered. At the doors, Mattie called to them, and Luke stopped long enough for his sister to hand Genny the bouquet. Still in Luke's arms, Genny plucked out the single red rose, closed her eyes and tossed the bouquet into the crowd. Luke turned around just as a smiling Harriett Peak caught the flowers.

"Goodnight, everybody," Luke called over his shoulder as Genny blew a kiss to family and friends.

EPILOGUE

Washington, DC
July 20, 1908

"ONE MORE KISS MRS. HARPER, AND THEN WE HAVE TO GO or we'll be late," Luke said, holding their beloved nineteen month old son.

They stood in the foyer of a stately, red brick rowhouse the Winsteds had purchased new in 1905. Located in the northwest quadrant of Washington, D.C., this fashionable, up and coming neighborhood, known as Bloomington, was less than two miles from the United States Capitol. The two-story home, with the classic spires along the vaulted roof, was well suited for a senator and his family.

"Samuel Lucas Harper, with your green eyes, you look more like your papa every day," Genny said, tucking a lock of the baby's chocolate brown hair behind his little ear.

"He does favor Luke," John Harper agreed. "And he has your winning smile, Genny."

"Yeah, that smile is their secret weapon to get me to do whatever they want," Luke said with a chuckle. "Give Mama a big grin Sam, so I can convince her to come with me."

Genny and the little boy smiled at each other. Luke

wrapped an arm around Genny as she kissed their son's cheek. The baby clapped his chubby hands and then pressed his mouth to her cheek. Sam happily clung to both parents at once as Luke kissed his forehead. Phoebe held out her arms and Sam went to his grandmother just as the others in the household gathered in the foyer. John hugged Charles and Megan to him as Audrey skipped to her grandmother and took hold of Sam's chubby little hand.

"Let's go," Steven said, ushering Mattie out the front door.

"Luke, I don't know if I can leave Samuel," Genny said with a catch in her voice.

"Yes, you can. I'd never hear the end of it if I let you miss out on tonight," Luke said. This was difficult for him, too, as it would be their first full night away from their son. "Come on."

"Bye-bye, little lamb. Mama and Papa love you," Genny said, and blew the baby a kiss.

"Bye-bye," Sam said with a big smile.

When Audrey waved goodbye, Sam did, too. Luke looped Genny's arm through his and led her out the door. Then along with the Winsteds, Rob and Chloe, they were on their way.

"THE WHITE HOUSE was restored in nineteen and two. Since then, it has become the perfect and proper setting for official entertaining," Genny said to Luke, feeling nervous and excited.

In the East Wing, they were standing in the receiving line to meet the President and First Lady of the United States of America. White House state dinners, such as this one, were held for members of Congress, the president's cabinet and other dignitaries. Washington society included senators and representatives along with their families, small circles of friends and select residents of the Capitol. Tonight's gathering was a representation of exactly that.

Steven, like Roosevelt, was a Republican and an anecdote Steven had shared with them was that no matter what the rest of the country called the president, Mr. Roosevelt disliked being referred to as Teddy.

Before arriving in D. C., Luke had confided that his first meeting with the president was during Audrey and Alice's kidnapping which had taken place a year or so after Roosevelt had assumed office, due to President William McKinley's assassination. Steven had been a newly elected senator in 1902, and the president's heart along with his wife, Edith's, had gone out to young Steven and Mattie. The fact that little Alice didn't survive the ordeal was painful for the president. Having two daughters and four sons, he empathized, perhaps particularly so, as the eldest of his children was also named Alice.

Luke had told Genny that President Roosevelt was instrumental in the quick capture of the kidnapper. Like Leon Czolgosz, the man who assassinated President McKinley, the kidnapper had also been found guilty and within five weeks of the verdict was executed by electric chair. It was after McKinley's assassination that Congress passed legislation to officially place the Secret Service in charge of protecting the president.

"When I was here for the president's inauguration in nineteen and five, I met him upstairs in his book-lined study," Luke said. "But this state dinner is a first. I'm glad you're here with me, Mrs. Harper."

"Me, too, Genny," Mattie said, turning around as she stood in line ahead of them. "I'm so glad you're both here. The White House state rooms, where we've been invited to spend the night, are a neoclassical design. I'm anxious to see them."

"That's because the guest rooms are typically used for heads of state and other foreign diplomats," Steven said. "The president wants them to reflect America's influence and power."

Steven was the first of their family group to be received

by the president. Mr. Roosevelt, with his dark, short hair parted on the side, pale blue eyes, and friendly smile under his bushy mustache, was a robust and popular commander-in-chief. The president enthusiastically congratulated Steven at being elected to his second term in the United States Senate. The two men shook hands as Mrs. Roosevelt embraced Mattie. A trim and attractive brunette, Edith Roosevelt had recently been described by a White House aide as, 'always the gentle, high-bred hostess'. Genny overheard the First Lady say the names Alice and Audrey, remembering the lost child as well as acknowledging her surviving twin. Mrs. Roosevelt and Mattie exchanged a few softly spoken private words before the First Lady briefly embraced her and then Steven.

"Mr. President, you know my brother-in-law, Luke Harper," Steven said.

"Yes, Senator Winsted, I certainly do," President Roosevelt replied and turned to Luke. "Nice to see you again, Luke."

"Mr. President, it is an honor to be here, sir," Luke said as they shook hands.

"Luke, my boy, Biloxi has become known as the playground of the South. You and your family have built yourselves quite the empire. When my term as president is over, I'm coming to Biloxi for a cruise on one of your riverboats. Sightseeing, games of chance and romance, I hear they are all booked months in advance. So please consider this my request for a reservation for Mrs. Roosevelt and me."

"Yes, sir. I will make the riverboat of your choice available to you whenever you want it and I hope you'll stay at the Harper House Resort as our guests," Luke said, and the president nodded eagerly. "I'd like you to meet my wife, Genevieve, or Genny as we call her."

"It's an honor to meet you, Mr. President," Genny said, knowing she would not be meeting this twenty-sixth leader of the American people if not for Luke.

"Mrs. Harper, the pleasure is mine." Theodore

Roosevelt took her hand in his and she sensed his cowboy-style persona as he said, "No matter what my Secret Service said, I would have been proud to have such a beautiful woman as one of my Rough Riders."

"Thank you, sir," Genny said with a soft laugh, catching the conspiratorial look the president gave to Luke and Steven. "Not realizing your Volunteer Cavalry had been disbanded when you came through San Franciso in nineteen and three, I was ready to ride out with your Rough Riders that very day."

"So I've heard," the president said with a friendly chuckle and patted her hand. "Genny, I hope a stay in one of our White House state bedrooms will make up for that missed opportunity."

"It most certainly will, Mr. President," Genny said. "Thank you for your gracious hospitality."

"She's one of a kind, Luke. Don't ever let her get away," Roosevelt said and clapped Luke on the back. "That's a presidential order."

"Yes, sir." Luke smiled at Genny and then acknowledged the president's wife.

"Luke, it's nice to see you again," Mrs. Roosevelt said. "Mattie tells me that her little brother finally met his match and got married a couple of years ago."

"Yes, ma'am, two years ago today. Mrs. Roosevelt, I'd like you to meet my wife, Genny."

"I'm so pleased to meet you, Mrs. Roosevelt."

"I'm pleased to meet you as well and happy anniversary," Mrs. Roosevelt said. "Steven told me you two were lucky to survive the earthquake and that you've since had a son."

"Yes," Luke replied. "His name is Samuel Lucas and he's a handful."

"Indeed, he is," Genny said and smiled up at Luke. "Sam takes after his father."

"My step-daughter, Alice, is a handful, too. She smokes, chews gum and plays with guns. When she's not dabbling with voodoo or maybe even when she is, Alice can be seen about the Capitol with her pet snake." Rolling her eyes, Mrs. Roosevelt waved that away and said, "I'm glad to hear that little Audrey Winsted is doing so well."

"Yes, very well," Luke said with lingering smile at all the First Lady had said about the president's daughter from his late, first wife. "Audrey loves her Aunt Genny and cousin, Sam."

"Good. Please tell Sam and Audrey I said hello and bring the children with you next time," Mrs. Roosevelt said. "We'll talk more at dinner. And Genny, I hope you'll sign a copy of your weekly syndicated newspaper column for me. I never miss *Genny's Friends and Fashion*."

"I would be honored to do so, Mrs. Roosevelt."

Genny heard Rob and Chloe, who'd been in line behind them, speaking with the president and his wife as she and Luke were escorted to a fancy table and seated beside Steven and Mattie. Senator Winsted and his wife were on President Roosevelt's right and Luke sat next to Mattie with Genny next to him. Rob and Chloe took seats next to Genny.

During the president's favorite meal of fried chicken with white gravy, the Harpers were privy to his presidential hopes and dreams for the country. When the Square Deal was mentioned, Luke grinned at Genny who raised a brow that said he'd better be quiet as she rubbed her toe against his leg. She was enjoying every exciting minute and each delicious mouthful of this exclusive dinner. But it was the night in the state bedroom with her husband that she most anticipated.

"Fat Rascals for dessert," President Roosevelt said as they were served with coffee and tea.

Fat Rascals were a cross between a scone and a bun and packed full of nuts, typically almonds, with glazed cherries on top. Rob stretched his arm along the back of Genny's chair and tapped Luke on the shoulder. Then he and Luke leaned back in order to see each other.

"Gonna use the fat rascal tonight," Rob said barely loud enough for his brother to hear.

"Yeah," Luke said with a chuckle and sat forward again.

After the dinner, goodbyes were said to the president and his wife who were the first to leave. Other dinner guests mingled for just a moment and then departed for their homes in the city. The three couples from Biloxi were escorted to their state rooms. Before they parted ways into their separate bedrooms, Steven chuckled and then so did Luke and Rob.

"Don't waste your fat rascals tonight," Steven said and was shushed by a blushing Mattie who pulled him toward their room.

Genny had figured out what a fat rascal meant to these three very distinguished and successful businessmen and polititian. How wonderful that they could let down their guards and enjoy a private joke. Luke winked at her, and it was at that very moment Genny realized she was a true member of the Harper family's inner circle.

After they had all disappeared into their respective rooms, Luke shut and locked their door. He turned to Genny with a cocked brow and a grin so sexy, her heart raced. Shrugging off his jacket, he tossed it on a nearby chair and swaggered to her. Taking her into his arms, he kissed her as she wrapped her arms around his neck. Running her fingers through his hair, she felt him unfastening the buttons down the back of her gown. As always, this man caused her to tremble with wanton desire. She trailed her fingers around his collar to his tie, loosened it and gave it a toss. Stepping out of her dress, she slipped off her petticoat and stockings as he shrugged out of his shirt and britches. Pulling the camisole over her head, and clad only in her panties, she backed away to the bed that had already been turned down for them. Holding out her arms to Luke, she wiggled the fingers on both hands in a come to me motion.

"Wanna make our next baby here in the White House?" Luke asked.

"Yes. On this second anniversary and all the ones to come, I want everything with you."

Luke tenderly eased down her panties, then sweeping her up in his arms he kissed her again before laying her in the middle of the bed. Naked, he stretched out on top of her and nibbled her ear and neck. She arched her back and his heart pounded as her breasts cushioned his chest. Kissing his way down her throat he took one and then the other nipple into his mouth. She moaned feeling his tongue play with her belly button and spread her legs for his most intimate kiss. Luke felt her building response and held her when she climaxed with his name escaping her is a sensuous whisper. Genny pulled him to her, and he grinned as she rolled him to his back.

"My turn to show my husband what all I've learned," she flirted and smiled that smile.

Luke knew that with every lesson he had given her, she had wooed him, won him and turned his heart inside out. Blushing the first few times, this sea nymph no longer hesitated to kiss him so boldly. The tongue of this mischief maker, who once labeled him a city slicker, now slid down the length of him. As her warm mouth closed tightly around the tip of him and began a slow sensuous ride, he remembered pulling a babydoll off her galloping horse and through his window to the bed where she'd called him loverboy.

When he whispered her name, she kissed the velvety hard tip of him. Then gentle hands of the tomboy he'd taught to fight, grasped the hard length of him as she repositioned herself to straddle his hips. The sea siren guided him to her silky folds of irresistible delight, sinking onto him as she had once sunk in the pond. He placed his hands to her waist encouraging her tonight just as he had the day he taught her to swim. A little lamb had shot a gun and used a knife to keep herself and their unborn baby alive.

This little wolf had become an expert driver who had indeed driven Sam to the doctor for his most recent checkup in her shiny red Runabout.

"Goddess of the moon and every star in the sky."

"Adonis whose light led us to our destinies."

Luke rolled the gorgeous woman off him and lay between her slender legs. Entering her, he pressed all the way in and pulled almost out. Her arms and legs wrapped around him, and they moved together faster and harder. Genny's moan of ecstasy was his undoing. Luke spilled himself inside her with the satisfied groan of a man deeply in love with his wife.

"Promise me all of your kisses will always be wilder than the west, Harper."

"Promise you'll never be too tame to let me kiss you from head to toe, Genevieve."

"We'll never tame the wild."

A LOOK AT: REMEMBER THE PASSION

BY LYNN ELDRIDGE

Blaze Bowie and his brother Shade are not only on the verge of losing their Louisiana plantation and timberland, but are accused of causing a local woman's death. Refusing to give up their birthright without a fight, Blaze hopes to find cousin Jim Bowie in Texas along with a long lost, secret key to saving the land. With foreclosure threatened and bullets flying, the brothers ride out with Davy Crockett and his Tennessee Mounted Volunteers to the Alamo.

Noelle Charbonnez, barely surviving in a tiny hut near the Alamo, promises her dying mother she will return to her estranged grandmother in Natchez. If the rumor is true that old friend Jim Bowie, who once lived across the Mississippi River from them, is now in Texas, Mama wants Noelle to ask him to take her home. Noelle mistrusts all Bowies and vows never to befriend much less travel anywhere with anyone named Bowie.

When handsome Blaze meets beautiful Noelle, worlds collide and clash. Bodies soon sizzle while hearts begin to dream. They must not only conquer old grudges and face new fears, but battle the siege of the Alamo, confront the Napoleon of the West, meet up with the Commander-in-Chief of the Texas Army, search for the Pirate of the Gulf, and find the long lost, secret key if they are to always love and laugh.

AVAILABLE JANUARY 2022

ABOUT THE AUTHOR

Lynn Eldridge is a former president of the West Virginia Chapter of Romance Writers of America and earned an honorable mention in their Golden Heart Contest. Lynn is the author of several historical and contemporary romance novels including, Desire in Deadwood, Remember the Passion, and Tame the Wild. Her next book, soon to be released, is Skyrocket to Surrender, and she is currently working on another historical romance titled Hearts and Mountains. In addition to her writing career, Lynn is a licensed clinical therapist and dedicates one day a week in an outpatient behavioral health facility in Charleston, West Virginia. Visit her online at:

www.lynneldridgeauthor.com

Made in the USA
Middletown, DE
09 October 2023

40200875R00229